PRAISE FOR

# MIDNIGHT BAYOU

"Roberts is in peak form with this combination of historical romantic suspense and contemporary ghost story. . . . Roberts has cleverly crafted an enticing tangle of times and relationships. . . . To add to the pleasure, tastefully choreographed, highly erotic scenes are seamlessly woven into a novel that exemplifies storytelling at it's finest."  —*Booklist*

"This amazingly talented and prolific author has cooked up an entertaining and engrossing story from the mix. . . . As always, her dialogue sparkled, her love scenes steamed up my glasses, and her secondary characters added humor and interest."  —The Romance Reader

"Quick wit and snappy conversation . . . steamy."
—*The Lexington Herald-Leader* (KY)

*Turn the page for a complete list of titles by*
*Nora Roberts and J. D. Robb from Berkley. . . .*

## *Nora Roberts*

HOT ICE
SACRED SINS
BRAZEN VIRTUE
SWEET REVENGE
PUBLIC SECRETS
GENUINE LIES
CARNAL INNOCENCE
HONEST ILLUSIONS
DIVINE EVIL
PRIVATE SCANDALS
HIDDEN RICHES
TRUE BETRAYALS
MONTANA SKY
SANCTUARY
HOMEPORT
THE REEF
RIVER'S END
CAROLINA MOON
THE VILLA
MIDNIGHT BAYOU
THREE FATES
BIRTHRIGHT
NORTHERN LIGHTS
BLUE SMOKE
ANGELS FALL
HIGH NOON
TRIBUTE
BLACK HILLS
THE SEARCH
CHASING FIRE
THE WITNESS
WHISKEY BEACH
TONIGHT AND ALWAYS
THE COLLECTOR
THE LIAR
THE OBSESSION

# Series

**Irish Born Trilogy**

BORN IN FIRE
BORN IN ICE
BORN IN SHAME

**Dream Trilogy**

DARING TO DREAM
HOLDING THE DREAM
FINDING THE DREAM

**Chesapeake Bay Saga**

SEA SWEPT
RISING TIDES
INNER HARBOR
CHESAPEAKE BLUE

**Gallaghers of Ardmore Trilogy**

JEWELS OF THE SUN
TEARS OF THE MOON
HEART OF THE SEA

**Three Sisters Island Trilogy**

DANCE UPON THE AIR
HEAVEN AND EARTH
FACE THE FIRE

**Key Trilogy**

KEY OF LIGHT
KEY OF KNOWLEDGE
KEY OF VALOR

**In the Garden Trilogy**

BLUE DAHLIA
BLACK ROSE
RED LILY

**Circle Trilogy**

MORRIGAN'S CROSS
DANCE OF THE GODS
VALLEY OF SILENCE

**Sign of Seven Trilogy**

BLOOD BROTHERS
THE HOLLOW
THE PAGAN STONE

**Bride Quartet**

VISION IN WHITE
BED OF ROSES
SAVOR THE MOMENT
HAPPY EVER AFTER

**The Inn BoonsBoro Trilogy**

THE NEXT ALWAYS
THE LAST BOYFRIEND
THE PERFECT HOPE

**The Cousins O'Dwyer Trilogy**

DARK WITCH
SHADOW SPELL
BLOOD MAGICK

**The Guardians Trilogy**

STARS OF FORTUNE
BAY OF SIGHS
ISLAND OF GLASS

### Ebooks by Nora Roberts

#### Cordina's Royal Family

AFFAIRE ROYALE
COMMAND PERFORMANCE
THE PLAYBOY PRINCE
CORDINA'S CROWN JEWEL

#### The Donovan Legacy

CAPTIVATED
ENTRANCED
CHARMED
ENCHANTED

#### The O'Hurleys

THE LAST HONEST WOMAN
DANCE TO THE PIPER
SKIN DEEP
WITHOUT A TRACE

#### Night Tales

NIGHT SHIFT
NIGHT SHADOW
NIGHTSHADE
NIGHT SMOKE
NIGHT SHIELD

#### The MacGregors

PLAYING THE ODDS
TEMPTING FATE
ALL THE POSSIBILITIES
ONE MAN'S ART
FOR NOW, FOREVER
REBELLION/IN FROM THE COLD
THE MACGREGOR BRIDES
THE WINNING HAND
THE MACGREGOR GROOMS
THE PERFECT NEIGHBOR

#### The Calhouns

COURTING CATHERINE
A MAN FOR AMANDA
FOR THE LOVE OF LILAH
SUZANNA'S SURRENDER
MEGAN'S MATE

#### Irish Legacy

IRISH THOROUGHBRED
IRISH ROSE
IRISH REBEL

LOVING JACK
BEST LAID PLANS
LAWLESS

BLITHE IMAGES
SONG OF THE WEST
SEARCH FOR LOVE
ISLAND OF FLOWERS
THE HEART'S VICTORY
FROM THIS DAY
HER MOTHER'S KEEPER
ONCE MORE WITH FEELING
REFLECTIONS
DANCE OF DREAMS
UNTAMED
THIS MAGIC MOMENT
ENDINGS AND BEGINNINGS
STORM WARNING
SULLIVAN'S WOMAN
FIRST IMPRESSIONS
A MATTER OF CHOICE

LESS OF A STRANGER
THE LAW IS A LADY
RULES OF THE GAME
OPPOSITES ATTRACT
THE RIGHT PATH
PARTNERS
BOUNDARY LINES
DUAL IMAGE
TEMPTATION
LOCAL HERO
THE NAME OF THE GAME
GABRIEL'S ANGEL
THE WELCOMING
TIME WAS
TIMES CHANGE
SUMMER LOVE
HOLIDAY WISHES

## Nora Roberts & J. D. Robb

REMEMBER WHEN

## J. D. Robb

NAKED IN DEATH
GLORY IN DEATH
IMMORTAL IN DEATH
RAPTURE IN DEATH
CEREMONY IN DEATH
VENGEANCE IN DEATH
HOLIDAY IN DEATH
CONSPIRACY IN DEATH
LOYALTY IN DEATH
WITNESS IN DEATH
JUDGMENT IN DEATH
BETRAYAL IN DEATH
SEDUCTION IN DEATH
REUNION IN DEATH
PURITY IN DEATH
PORTRAIT IN DEATH
IMITATION IN DEATH
DIVIDED IN DEATH
VISIONS IN DEATH
SURVIVOR IN DEATH
ORIGIN IN DEATH
MEMORY IN DEATH
BORN IN DEATH
INNOCENT IN DEATH
CREATION IN DEATH
STRANGERS IN DEATH
SALVATION IN DEATH
PROMISES IN DEATH
KINDRED IN DEATH
FANTASY IN DEATH
INDULGENCE IN DEATH
TREACHERY IN DEATH
NEW YORK TO DALLAS
CELEBRITY IN DEATH
DELUSION IN DEATH
CALCULATED IN DEATH
THANKLESS IN DEATH
CONCEALED IN DEATH
FESTIVE IN DEATH
OBSESSION IN DEATH
DEVOTED IN DEATH
BROTHERHOOD IN DEATH
APPRENTICE IN DEATH

## Anthologies

FROM THE HEART
A LITTLE MAGIC
A LITTLE FATE

MOON SHADOWS
(with Jill Gregory, Ruth Ryan Langan, and Marianne Willman)

## The Once Upon Series

(with Jill Gregory, Ruth Ryan Langan, and Marianne Willman)

ONCE UPON A CASTLE
ONCE UPON A STAR
ONCE UPON A DREAM

ONCE UPON A ROSE
ONCE UPON A KISS
ONCE UPON A MIDNIGHT

SILENT NIGHT
(with Susan Plunkett, Dee Holmes, and Claire Cross)

OUT OF THIS WORLD
(with Laurell K. Hamilton, Susan Krinard, and Maggie Shayne)

BUMP IN THE NIGHT
(with Mary Blayney, Ruth Ryan Langan, and Mary Kay McComas)

DEAD OF NIGHT
(with Mary Blayney, Ruth Ryan Langan, and Mary Kay McComas)

THREE IN DEATH

SUITE 606
(with Mary Blayney, Ruth Ryan Langan, and Mary Kay McComas)

IN DEATH

THE LOST
(with Patricia Gaffney, Mary Blayney, and Ruth Ryan Langan)

THE OTHER SIDE
(with Mary Blayney, Patricia Gaffney, Ruth Ryan Langan, and Mary Kay McComas)

TIME OF DEATH

THE UNQUIET
(with Mary Blayney, Patricia Gaffney, Ruth Ryan Langan, and Mary Kay McComas)

MIRROR, MIRROR
(with Mary Blayney, Elaine Fox, Mary Kay McComas, and R. C. Ryan)

DOWN THE RABBIT HOLE
(with Mary Blayney, Elaine Fox, Mary Kay McComas, and R. C. Ryan)

## Also available...

THE OFFICIAL NORA ROBERTS COMPANION
(edited by Denise Little and Laura Hayden)

# MIDNIGHT
# BAYOU

## NORA ROBERTS

BERKLEY
NEW YORK

BERKLEY
An imprint of Penguin Random House LLC
penguinrandomhouse.com

ISBN: 9780593198803

The Library of Congress has catalogued the G. P. Putnam's Sons hardcover edition of this book as follows:

Roberts, Nora.
Midnight Bayou / Nora Roberts.
p. cm.
ISBN 0-399-14824-8
1. Home ownership—Fiction.   2.  New Orleans (La.)—Fiction.
PS3568.O243 M536   2000       2001041643
813'.54—dc21

G. P. Putnam's Sons hardcover edition / October 2001
Jove international edition / November 2001
Jove mass-market edition / December 2002
Berkley trade paperback edition / June 2020

Printed in the United States of America
5th Printing

Cover design and photocomposition by Rita Frangie
Book design by Kristin del Rosario
Interior art: foggy swamp by lukaszsokol / Shutterstock

*For Leslie Gelbman,*
*a woman who understands*
*the value of time*

God stands winding His lonely horn,
And time and the world are ever in flight;
And love is less kind than the gray twilight,
And hope is less dear than the dew of the morn.

—WILLIAM BUTLER YEATS

# PROLOGUE

Death, with all its cruel beauty, lived in the bayou. Its shadows ran deep. Cloaked by them, a whisper in the marsh grass or rushes, in the tangled trap of the kudzu, meant life, or fresh death. Its breath was thick and green, and its eyes gleamed yellow in the dark.

Silent as a snake, its river swam a sinuous line—black water under a fat white moon where the cypress knees broke the surface like bones piercing skin.

Through the dark, moon-dappled water, the long, knobby length of an alligator carved with barely a ripple. Like a secret, its threat was silent. When it struck, its tail whipping a triumphant slice through the water, when it clamped the unwary muskrat in its killing jaws, the bayou echoed with a single short scream.

And the gator sank deep to the muddy bottom with its prey.

Others had known the cruel, silent depths of that river. Knew, even in the vicious summer heat, it was cold, cold.

Vast with secrets, the bayou was never quite still. In the night, under a high hunter's moon, death was busy. Mosquitoes, voracious vampires of the swamp, whined in a jubilant cloud of greed. Players of the marsh music, they blended with the buzzes, hums and drips that were punctuated by the shocked squeals of the hunted.

In the high limbs of a live oak, shadowed by moss and leaves, an owl hooted its two mournful notes. Alerted, a marsh rabbit ran for his life.

A breeze stirred the air, then was gone, like the single sigh of a ghost.

The owl swooped from its perch with a swift spread of wings.

Near the river, while the owl dived and the rabbit died, an old gray house with a swaying dock slept in shadows. Beyond, rising over a long, lush spread of grass, a great white manor stood watchful in the moonlight.

Between them, teeming with life, vigorous with death, the bayou laid its line.

# ONE

MANET HALL, LOUISIANA
DECEMBER 30, 1899

The baby was crying. Abigail heard it in dreams, the soft, unsettled whimper, the stirring of tiny limbs under soft blankets. She felt the first pangs of hunger, a yearning in the belly, almost as if the child were still inside her. Her milk came down before she was fully awake.

She rose quickly and without fuss. It gave her such pleasure—that overfull sensation in her breasts, the tenderness of them. The purpose of them. Her baby needed and she would provide.

She crossed to the *recamier*, lifted the white robe draped over its back. She drew in the scent of the hothouse lilies—her favorite—spearing out of a crystal vase that had been a wedding present.

Before Lucian, she'd been content to tuck wildflowers into bottles.

If Lucian had been home, he would have woken as well. Though she would have smiled, have stroked a hand over his silky blond hair as she told him to stay, to sleep, he would have wandered up to the nursery before she'd finished Marie Rose's midnight feeding.

She missed him—another ache in the belly. But as she slipped into her night wrapper, she remembered he would be back the next day. She would start watching for him in the morning, waiting to see him come galloping down the *allée* of oaks.

No matter what anyone thought or said, she would run out to meet him. Her heart would leap, oh, it always leaped, when he sprang down from his horse and lifted her off her feet into his arms.

And at the New Year's ball, they would dance.

She hummed to herself as she lit a candle, shielding it with her hand as she moved to the bedroom door, out into the corridor of the great house where she had once been servant and was now, well, if not daughter of the house at least the wife of its son.

The nursery was on the third floor of the family wing. That was a battle she'd fought with Lucian's mother, and lost. Josephine Manet had definite rules about behavior, domestic arrangements, traditions. Madame Josephine, Abigail thought as she moved quickly and quietly past the other bedroom doors, had definite ideas on everything. Certainly that a three-month-old baby belonged in the nursery, under the care of a nursemaid, and not in a cradle tucked into the corner of her parents' bedroom.

Candlelight flickered and flew against the walls as Abigail climbed the narrowing stairs. At least she'd managed to keep Marie Rose with her for six weeks. And had used the cradle that was part of her own family's traditions. It had been carved by her *grand-père*. Her own mother had slept in it, then had tucked Abigail in it seventeen years later.

Marie Rose had spent her first nights in that old cradle, a tiny angel with her doting and nervous parents close at hand.

Her daughter would respect her father's family and their ways. But Abigail was determined that her child would also respect her mother's family, and learn their ways.

Josephine had complained about the baby, about the homemade cradle, so constantly that she and Lucian had given in. It was, Lucian said, the way water wears at rock. It never ceases, so the rock gives way or wears down.

The baby spent her nights in the nursery now, in the crib made in France, where Manet babies had slept for a century.

It was a proper if not cozy arrangement, Abby comforted herself. Her *petite* Rose was a Manet. She would be a lady.

And as Madame Josephine had pointed out, again and again, other members of the household were not to have their sleep disturbed by fretful cries. However such matters were done in the bayou, here in Manet Hall, children were tended in the nursery.

How her lips curled when she said it. *Bayou*—as if it were a word to be spoken only in brothels and bars.

It didn't matter that Madame Josephine hated her, that Monsieur Henri ignored her. It didn't matter that Julian looked at her the way no man should look at his brother's wife.

Lucian loved her.

Nor did it matter that Marie Rose slept in the nursery. Whether they were separated by a floor or a continent, she felt Marie Rose's needs as she felt her own. The bond was so strong, so true, it could never be broken.

Madame Josephine may win battles, but Abigail knew she herself had won the war. She had Lucian and Marie Rose.

There were candles glowing in the nursery. Claudine, the nursemaid, didn't trust the gaslight. She already held Marie Rose and was trying to quiet her with a sugar tit, but the baby's fists were shaking, little balls of rage.

"Such a temper she has." Abigail set the candle down and was laughing as she crossed the room, her arms already outstretched.

"Knows what she wants, and when she wants it." Claudine, a pretty Cajun with sleepy dark eyes, gave the baby a quick cuddle, then passed her off. "She hardly made a fuss yet. Don't know how you hear her way off downstairs."

"I hear her in my heart. There now, *bébé. Maman*'s here."

"Diaper's wet."

"I'll change her." Abigail rubbed her cheek on the baby's and smiled. Claudine was a friend—a battle won. Having her established in the nursery, in the household, gave Abigail comfort and the companionship none of Lucian's family would offer her.

"Go on back to bed. Once she's nursed, she'll sleep till morning."

"Good as gold, she is." Claudine brushed fingertips over Marie Rose's curly hair. "If you don't need me, maybe I'll take a walk down to the river. Jasper, he's gonna be there." Her dark eyes lit. "I told him maybe, if I can get away, I come down around midnight."

"You oughta make that boy marry you, chère."

"Oh, I'm gonna. Maybe I run down for an hour or two, if you don't mind, Abby."

"I don't mind, but you be careful you don't catch nothing more than some crawfish. Anything more," she corrected as she prepared to change Marie Rose's soiled linen.

"Don't you worry. I'll be back before two." She started out through the connecting door and glanced back. "Abby? You ever think, when we were kids, that you'd be mistress of this house one day?"

"I'm not mistress here." She tickled the baby's toes and had Marie Rose gurgling. "And the one who is'll probably live to a hundred and ten off of spite just to make sure I never am."

"If anybody could, it'd be that one. But you will be, one day. You fell into the luck, Abby, and it looks real fine on you."

Alone with the baby, Abby tickled and cooed. She powdered and smoothed, then tidily fastened the fresh diaper. When Marie Rose was tucked into a fresh gown and swaddled, Abby settled in the rocker, bared her breast for that tiny, hungry mouth. Those first greedy tugs, the answering pull in her womb, made her sigh. Yes, she'd fallen into the luck. Because Lucian Manet, the heir of Manet Hall, the shining knight of every fairy tale, had looked at her. And loved.

She bent her head to watch the baby nurse. Marie Rose's eyes were wide open, fixed on her mother's face. A tiny crease of concentration formed between her eyebrows.

Oh, she had such hope those eyes would stay blue, like Lucian's. The baby's hair was dark like her own. Dark and curling, but her skin was milk white—again like her papa's rather than the deeper tone, the dusky gold of her Cajun mama's.

She would have the best of both of them, Abby thought. She would have the best of everything.

It wasn't only the money, the grand house, the social position, though she wanted that for her children now that she had tasted it herself. It was the acceptance, the learning, the *knowing* you belonged in such a place. Her daughter, and all the children who came after, would read and write, would speak proper English, proper French, in fine voices.

No one would ever look down on them.

"You'll be a lady," Abigail murmured, stroking the baby's cheek as Marie Rose's hand kneaded her breast as if to hurry the milk along. "An *educated* lady with your papa's sweet heart and your mama's good sense. Papa'll be home tomorrow. It's the very last day of a whole century, and you have your whole life to live in it."

Her voice was quiet, a singsong rhythm to lull both of them.

"It's so exciting, Rosie, my Rosie. We're going to have a grand ball tomorrow night. I have a new gown. It's blue, like your eyes. Like your papa's eyes. Did I tell you I fell in love with his eyes first? So beautiful. So kind. When he came back to Manet Hall from the university, he looked like a prince coming home to his castle. Oh, my heart just pounded so."

She leaned back, rocking in the fluttering light of the candles.

She thought of the New Year's celebration the next evening, and how she would dance with Lucian, how her gown would sweep and swirl as they waltzed.

How she would make him proud.

And she remembered the first time they had waltzed.

In the spring, with the air heavy with perfume from the flowers, and the house alight like a palace. She'd sneaked into the garden, away from her duties, because she'd wanted to see it so much. The way the gleaming white hall with its balusters like black lace stood against the starry sky, the way the windows flamed. Music had spilled out of those windows, out of the gallery doors where guests had stepped out for air.

She'd imagined herself inside the ballroom, whirling, whirling, to the music. And so had whirled in the shadows of the garden. And, whirling, had seen Lucian watching her on the path.

Her own fairy tale, Abby thought. The prince taking Cinderella's hand and drawing her into a dance moments before midnight struck. She'd had no glass slipper, no pumpkin coach, but the night had turned into magic.

She could still hear the way the music had floated out through the balcony doors, over the air, into the garden.

*"After the ball is over, after the break of morn . . ."*

She sang the refrain quietly, shifting the baby to her other breast.

*"After the dancers leaving, after the stars are gone . . ."*

They had danced to that lovely, sad song in the moonlit garden with the house a regal white and gold shadow behind them. Her in her simple cotton dress, and Lucian in his handsome evening clothes. And as such things were possible in fairy tales, they fell in love during that lovely, sad song.

Oh, she knew it had started before that night. For her it had begun with her first glimpse of him, astride the chestnut mare he'd ridden from New Orleans to the plantation. The way the sun had beamed through the leaves and the moss on the live oaks along the *allée*, surrounding him like angel wings. His twin had ridden beside him—Julian—but she'd seen only Lucian.

She'd been in the house only a few weeks then, taken on as an under-maid and doing her best to please Monsieur and Madame Manet so she might keep her position and the wages earned.

He'd spoken to her—kindly, correctly—if they passed each other in the house. But she'd sensed him watching her. Not the way Julian watched, not with hot eyes and a smirk twisting his lips. But, she liked to think now, with a kind of longing.

In the weeks that went by she would come upon him often. He'd sought her out. She knew that now, prized that now, as he'd confessed it to her on their wedding night.

But it had really begun the evening of the ball. After the song had ended, he'd held her, just a moment longer. Then he bowed, as a gentleman bows to a lady. He kissed her hand.

Then, just as she thought it was over, that the magic would dim, he tucked the hand he'd kissed into the crook of his arm. Began to walk with her, to talk with her. The weather, the flowers, the gossip of the household.

As if they were friends, Abby thought now with a smile. As if it were the most natural thing in the world for Lucian Manet to take a turn in the garden with Abigail Rouse.

They'd walked in the garden many nights after that. Inside the house, where others could see, they remained master and servant. But all through that heady spring they walked the garden paths as young lovers, telling each other of hopes, of dreams, of sorrows and joys.

On her seventeenth birthday he brought her a gift, wrapped in silver paper with a bright blue bow. The enameled watch was a pretty circle dangling from the golden wings of a brooch. Time flew, he told her as he pinned the watch to the faded cotton of her dress, when they were together. And he would rather have his life wing by than spend it apart from her.

He'd gotten down on one knee and asked her to be his wife.

It could never be. Oh, she'd tried to tell him through the tears. He was beyond her reach, and he could have anyone.

She remembered now how he'd laughed, how the joy had burst over his beautiful face. How could he be beyond her reach when she had his hand in hers even now? And if he could have anyone, then he would have her.

"So now we have each other, and you," Abby whispered and shifted the drowsing baby to her shoulder. "And if his family hates me for it, what does it matter? I make him happy."

She turned her face into the soft curve of the baby's neck. "I'm learning to speak as they speak, to dress as they dress. I will never think as they think, but for Lucian, I behave as they behave, at least when it shows."

Content, she rubbed the baby's back and continued to rock. But when she heard the heavy footsteps on the stairs, the stumbling climb, she rose quickly. Her arms tightened in a circle of protection around the baby as she turned toward the crib.

She heard Julian come through the door and knew without seeing he would be drunk. He was nearly always drunk or on his way to becoming so.

Abby didn't speak. She lay the baby in the crib, and when Marie Rose whimpered restlessly, stroked her quiet again.

"Where's the nursemaid?" he demanded.

Still, Abby didn't turn. "I don't want you in here when you've been drinking."

"Giving orders now?" His voice was slurred, his balance impaired. But he was thinking clearly enough. Liquor, he'd always believed, helped clarify the mind.

And his was clarified when it came to his brother's wife. If Lucian had a thing—and what was a woman but a thing?—Julian wanted it.

She was small, almost delicate of build. But she had good strong legs. He could see the shape of them where the firelight in the nursery grate shimmered through her thin nightclothes. Those legs would wrap around him as easily as they did his brother.

Her breasts were high and full, fuller now since she'd had the whelp. He'd gotten his hands on them once, and she'd slapped him for it. As if she had a say in who touched her.

He closed the door at his back. The whore he'd bought that night had only whetted his appetite. It was time to sate it.

"Where's the other bayou slut?"

Abby's hand fisted at her side. She turned now, guarding the crib with her body. He looked so like Lucian, but there was a hardness in him Lucian lacked. A darkness.

She wondered if it was true, what her *grand-mère* said. That with twins, sometimes traits get divvied up in the womb. One gets the good, the other the bad.

She didn't know if Julian had come into the world already spoiled. But she knew he was dangerous when drunk. It was time he learned she was dangerous as well.

"Claudine is my friend, and you have no right to speak of her that way. Get out. You have no right to come in here and insult me. This time Lucian will hear of it."

She saw his gaze slide down from her face, watched lust come into his eyes. Quickly, she tugged her wrapper over the breast still partially exposed from nursing. "You're disgusting. *Cochon!* To come in a child's room with your wicked thoughts for your brother's wife."

"Brother's whore." He thought he could smell her anger and her fear now. A heady perfume. "You'd have spread your legs for me if I'd been born fifteen minutes sooner. But you wouldn't have stolen my name the way you stole his."

Her chin came up. "I don't even see you. No one does. You're nothing beside him. A shadow, and one that stinks of whiskey and the brothel."

She wanted to run. He frightened her, had always frightened her on a deep, primal level. But she wouldn't risk leaving him with the baby. "When I tell Lucian of this, he'll send you away."

"He has no power here, and we all know it." He came closer, easing his way like a hunter through the woods. "My mother holds the power in this house. I'm her favorite. Timing at birth doesn't change that."

"He *will* send you away." Tears stung the back of her throat because she knew Julian was right. It was Josephine who reigned in Manet Hall.

"Lucian did me a favor marrying you." His voice was a lazy drawl now, almost conversational. He knew she had nowhere to run. "She's already cut him out of her will. Oh, he'll get the house, she can't change that, but I'll get her money. And it's her money that runs this place."

"Take the money, take the house." She flung out her hands, dismissing them, and him. "Take it all. And go to hell with it."

"He's weak. My sainted brother. Saints always are, under all the piety."

"He's a man, so much more a man than you."

She'd hoped to make him angry, angry enough to strike her and storm out. Instead he laughed, low and quiet, and edged closer.

When she saw the intent in his eyes, she opened her mouth to scream. His hand whipped out, gripped a hank of the dark hair that curled to her waist. And yanking had her scream gurgling into a gasp. His free hand circled her throat, squeezed.

"I always take what's Lucian's. Even his whores."

She beat at him, slapped, bit. And when she could draw in air, screamed. He tore at her wrapper, pawed at her breasts. In the crib, the baby began to wail.

Fueled by the sound of her child's distress, Abby clawed her way free. She spun, stumbled over the torn hem of her nightgown. Her hand closed over the fireplace poker. She swung wildly, ramming it hard against Julian's shoulder.

Howling in pain, he fell back against the hearth, and she flew toward the crib.

She had to get the baby. To get the baby and run.

He caught her sleeve, and she screamed again as the material ripped.

Even as she reached down to snatch her daughter from the crib, he dragged her back. He struck her, slicing the back of his hand over her cheek and knocking her back into a table. A candle fell to the floor and guttered out in its own wax.

"Bitch! Whore!"

He was mad. She could see it now in the feral gleam in his eyes, the drunken flush on his cheeks. In that instant fear turned to terror.

"He'll kill you for this. My Lucian will kill you." She tried to gain her feet, but he hit her again, using his fist this time so the pain radiated from her face, through her body. Dazed, she began to crawl toward the crib. There was blood in her mouth, sweet and warm.

*My baby. Sweet God, don't let him hurt my baby.*

His weight was on her—and the stench of him. She bucked, called for help. The sound of the baby's furious screams merged with hers.

"Don't! Don't! You damn yourself."

But as he yanked up the skirt of her nightgown, she knew no amount of pleading, no amount of struggle, would stop him. He would debase her, soil her, because of who she was. Because she was Lucian's.

"This is what you want." He drove himself into her, and the thrill of power spurted through him like black wine. Her face was white with fear and shock, and raw from the blows of his hands. Helpless, he thought, as he pounded out his raging envy. "This is what all of you want. Cajun whores."

Thrust after violent thrust, he raped her. The thrill of forcing himself into her spumed through him until his breathing turned to short bursts grunted between clenched teeth.

She was weeping now, huge choking sobs. But screaming, too. Somehow screaming as he hammered his fury, his jealousy, his disgust into her.

As the great clock began to chime midnight, he closed his hands around her throat. "Shut up. Damn you." He rammed her head against the floor, squeezed harder. And still the screaming pierced his brain.

Abby heard it, too. Dimly. The baby's frantic cries pealed through her head along with the slow, formal bongs of the midnight hour. She slapped, weak protests against the hands that cut off her air, tried to shut her body off from the unspeakable invasion.

*Help me. Mother of Jesus. Help me. Help my baby.*

Her vision dimmed. Her heels drummed wildly on the floor as she convulsed.

The last thing she heard was her crying daughter. The last thing she thought was, *Lucian.*

The door of the nursery burst open. Josephine Manet stood just inside the nursery. She summed up the scene quickly. Coldly.

"Julian."

His hands still vised around Abby's throat, he looked up. If his mother saw madness in his eyes, she chose to ignore it. With her gilt hair neatly braided for the night, her robe sternly buttoned to the neck, she stepped over, stared down.

Abby's eyes were wide and staring. There was a trickle of blood at the corner of her mouth, and bruises blooming along her cheeks.

Dispassionately, she leaned down, laid her fingers against Abby's throat.

"She's dead," Josephine announced and moved quickly to the connecting door. She opened it, glanced into the maid's room. Then closed it, locked it.

She stood for a moment, her back against it, her hand at her own throat as she thought of what could come. Disgrace, ruin, scandal.

"It was . . . an accident." His hands began to shake as they slid away from Abby's throat. The whiskey was whirling in his head now, clouding it. It churned in his belly, sickening it.

He could see the marks on her skin, dark and deep and damning. "She . . . tried to seduce me, then, she attacked . . ."

She crossed the room again, her slippers clicking on wood. Crouching down, Josephine slapped him, one hard crack of flesh on flesh. "Quiet. Be quiet and do exactly as I say. I won't lose another son to this creature. Take her down to her bedroom. Go out through the gallery and stay there until I come."

"It was her fault."

"Yes. Now she's paid for it. Take her down, Julian. And be quick."

"They'll . . ." A single tear gathered in the corner of his eye and spilled over. "They'll hang me. I have to get away."

"No. No, they won't hang you." She brought his head to her shoulder, stroking his hair over the body of her daughter-in-law. "No, my sweet, they won't hang you. Do what Mama says now. Carry her to the bedroom and wait for me. Everything's going to be all right. Everything's going to be as it should be. I promise."

"I don't want to touch her."

"Julian!" The crooning tone snapped into icy command. "Do as I say. Immediately."

She rose, walked over to the crib, where the baby's wails had turned to miserable whimpers. In the heat of the moment, she considered simply laying her hand over the child's mouth and nose. Hardly different than drowning a bag of kittens.

And yet . . .

The child had her son's blood in her, and therefore her own. She could despise it, but she couldn't destroy it. "Go to sleep," she said. "We'll decide what to do about you later."

As her son carried the girl he'd raped and murdered from the room, Josephine began to set the nursery to rights again. She picked up the candle, scrubbed at the cooling wax until she could see no trace.

She replaced the fireplace poker and, using the ruin of Abby's robe, wiped up the splatters of blood. She did it all efficiently, turning her mind away from what had caused the damage to the room, keeping it firmly fixed on what needed to be done to save her son.

When she was certain all was as it should be, she unlocked the door again, left her now-sleeping grandchild alone.

In the morning, she would fire the nursemaid for dereliction of duty.

She would have her out of Manet Hall before Lucian returned to find his wife missing.

The girl had brought it on herself, Josephine thought. No good ever came from trying to rise above your station in life. There was an order to things, and a reason for that order. If the girl hadn't bewitched Lucian—for surely there was some local witchery involved—she would still be alive.

The family had suffered enough scandal. The elopement. Oh, the embarrassment of it! Of having to hold your head high when your first-born son ran off with a penniless, barefoot female who'd grown up in a shack in the swamp.

Then the sour taste of the pretense that followed. It was essential to save face, even after such a blow. And hadn't she done all that could be done to see that creature was dressed as befitted the family Manet?

Silk purses, sow's ears, she thought. What good were Paris fashions when the girl had only to open her mouth and sound of the swamp? For pity's sake, she'd been a servant.

Josephine stepped into the bedroom, shut the door at her back, and stared at the bed where her son's dead wife lay staring up at the blue silk canopy.

Now, she thought, Abigail Rouse was simply a problem to be solved.

Julian huddled in a chair, his head in his hands. "Stop screaming," he muttered. "Stop the screaming."

Josephine marched to him, clamped her hands on his shoulders. "Do you want them to come for you?" she demanded. "Do you want to drag the family through disgrace? To be hanged like a common thief?"

"It wasn't my fault. She enticed me. Then she attacked me. Look. Look." He turned his head. "See how she clawed my face?"

"Yes." For a moment, just for a moment, Josephine wavered. The heart inside the symbol she'd become reared up in protest against the horror of the act all women fear.

Whatever she was, she'd loved Lucian. Whatever she was, she'd been raped and murdered within feet of her own child's crib.

Julian forced her, struck her, defiled her. Killed her.

Drunk and mad, he'd killed his brother's wife. God's pity.

Then she shoved it viciously aside.

The girl was dead. Her son was not.

"You bought a prostitute tonight. Don't turn away from me," she snapped. "I'm not ignorant of the things men do. Did you buy a woman?"

"Yes, Mama."

She nodded briskly. "Then it was the whore who scratched you, should anyone have the temerity to ask. You were never in the nursery tonight." She cupped his face in her hands to keep his eyes level with hers. And her fingers dug into his cheeks as she spoke in low, clear tones. "What reason would you have to go there? You went out, for drink and women and, having your fill of both, came home and went to bed. Is that clear?"

"But, how will we explain—"

"We'll have nothing to explain. I've told you what you did tonight. Repeat it."

"I—I went into town." He licked his lips. Swallowed. "I drank, then I went to a brothel. I came home and went to bed."

"That's right. That's right." She stroked his scored cheek. "Now we're going to pack some of her things—some clothes, some jewelry. We'll do it quickly, as she did it quickly when she decided to run off with a man she'd been seeing in secret. A man who might very well be the father of that child upstairs."

"What man?"

Josephine let out a long sigh. He was the child of her heart, but she often despaired of his brain. "Never mind, Julian. You know nothing of it. Here." She went to the chifforobe, chose a long black velvet cloak. "Wrap her in this. Hurry. Do it!" she said in a tone that had him getting to his feet.

His stomach pitched, and his hands trembled, but he wrapped the body in velvet as best he could while his mother stuffed things in a hatbox and a train case.

In her rush she dropped a brooch of gold wings with a small enameled watch dangling from it. The toe of her slipper struck it so that it skittered into a corner.

"We'll take her into the swamp. We'll have to go on foot, and quickly. There are some old paving bricks in the garden shed. We can weigh her down with them."

And the gators, she thought, the gators and fish would do the rest.

"Even if she's found, it's away from here. The man she ran away with killed her." She dabbed her face with the handkerchief in the pocket of her robe, smoothed a hand over her long, gilded braid. "That's what people will believe if she's found. We need to get her away from here, away from Manet Hall. Quickly."

She was beginning to feel a little mad herself.

There was moonlight. She told herself there was moonlight because fate understood what she was doing, and why. She could hear her son's rapid breathing, and the sounds of the night. The frogs, the insects, the night birds all merging together into one thick note.

It was the end of a century, the beginning of the new. She would rid herself of this aberration to her world and start this new century, this new era, clean and strong.

There was a chill in the air, made raw with wet. But she felt hot, almost burning hot as she trudged away from the house, laden with the bags she'd packed and weighed down. The muscles of her arms, of her legs, protested, but she marched like a soldier.

Once, just once, she thought she felt a brush against her cheek, like the breath of a ghost. The spirit of a dead girl who trailed beside her, accusing, damning, cursing her for eternity.

Fear only made her stronger.

"Here." She stopped and peered out over the water. "Lay her down."

Julian obeyed, then rose quickly, turned his back, covered his face with his hands. "I can't do this. Mama, I can't. I'm sick. Sick."

He tumbled toward the water, retching, weeping.

Useless boy, she thought, mildly annoyed. Men could never handle a crisis. It took a woman, the cold blood and clear mind of a female.

Josephine opened the cloak, laid bricks over the body. Sweat began to pour down her face, but she approached the grisly task as she would any other. With ruthless efficiency. She took the rope out of the hatbox, carefully tied hanks around the cloaked body, top, bottom, middle. Using another, she looped the line through the handles of the luggage, knotted it tight.

She glanced over now to see Julian watching her, his face white as bone. "You'll have to help. I can't get her into the water alone. She's too heavy now."

"I was drunk."

"That's correct, Julian. You were drunk. Now you're sober enough to deal with the consequences. Help me get her into the water."

He felt his legs buckle and give with each step, like a puppet's. The body slid into the water almost soundlessly. There was a quiet plop, a kind of gurgle, then it was gone. Ripples spread on the surface, shimmered in the moonlight, then smoothed away again.

"She's out of our lives," Josephine stated calmly. "Soon, she'll be like those ripples. Like she never was. See that you clean your boots thoroughly, Julian. Don't give them to a servant."

She slid her arm through his, smiled, though her smile was just a little wild. "We need to get back, get some rest. Tomorrow's a very busy day."

# TWO

MANET HALL, LOUISIANA
JANUARY 2002

His mother was right—as always. Declan Fitzgerald stared through the mud-splattered windshield into the driving winter rain and was glad she wasn't there to gloat.

Not that Colleen Sullivan Fitzgerald ever stooped to a gloat. She merely raised one perfect eyebrow into one perfect arch and let her silence do the gloating for her.

She'd told him, very succinctly, when he'd stopped by before driving out of Boston, that he'd lost his mind. And would rue the day. Yes, he was pretty sure she'd said "rue the day."

He hadn't sunk as low as ruing—yet—but studying the jungle of weeds, the sagging galleries, the peeling paint and broken gutters of the old plantation house, he was no longer confident of his mental health.

What had made him think he could restore this rambling old derelict into its former splendor? Or, more to the point, that he should? For God's sake, he was a lawyer, a Fitzgerald of the Boston Fitzgeralds, and more tuned to swinging a nine-iron than a hammer.

Rehabbing a town house in his spare time over a two-year period was

a far cry from relocating to New Orleans and pretending he was a contractor.

Had the place looked this bad the last time he'd been down here?
Could it have? Of course that was five, no, six years before. Certainly it
couldn't have looked this bad the first time he'd seen it. He'd been
twenty and spending a crazed Mardi Gras interlude with his college
roommate. Eleven years, he thought, dragging his fingers through his
dark blond hair.

The old Manet Hall had been a niggling germ in his brain for eleven
years. As obsessions went, it was longer than most relationships. Certainly longer than any of his own.

Now the house was his, for better or for worse. He already had a
feeling there was going to be plenty of worse.

His eyes, as gray, and at the moment as bleak, as the rain, scanned
the structure. The graceful twin arches of the double stairs leading to the
second-floor gallery had charmed him on that long-ago February. And
all those tall arched windows, the whimsy of the belvedere on the roof,
the elegance of the white columns and strangely ornate iron balusters.
The fanciful mix of Italianate and Greek Revival had all seemed so in-
credibly lush and Old World and *southern*.

Even then he'd felt displaced, in a way he'd never been able to explain, in New England.

The house had pulled him, in some deep chamber. Like a hook
through memory, he thought now. He'd been able to visualize the interior even before he and Remy had broken in to ramble through it.

Or the gallon or two of beer they'd sucked down had caused him to
think he could.

A drunk boy barely out of his teens couldn't be trusted. And neither,
Declan admitted ruefully, could a stone-sober thirty-one-year-old man.

The minute Remy had mentioned that Manet Hall was on the block
again, he'd put in a bid. Sight unseen, or unseen for more than half a

decade. He'd *had* to have it. As if he'd been waiting all his life to call it his own.

He could deem the price reasonable if he didn't consider what he'd have to pour into it to make it habitable. So he wouldn't consider it—just now.

It was his, whether he was crazy or whether he was right. No matter what, he'd turned in his briefcase for a tool belt. That alone lightened his mood.

He pulled out his cell phone—you could take the lawyer out of Boston, but . . . Still studying the house, he put in a call to Remy Payne.

He went through a secretary, and imagined Remy sitting at a desk cluttered with files and briefs. It made him smile, a quick, crooked grin that shifted the planes and angles of his face, hollowed the cheeks, softened the sometimes-grim line of his mouth.

Yes, he thought, life could be worse. He could be the one at the desk.

"Well, hey, Dec." Remy's lazy drawl streamed into the packed Mercedes SUV like a mist over a slow-moving river. "Where are you, boy?"

"I'm sitting in my car looking at this white elephant I was crazy enough to buy. Why the hell didn't you talk me out of it or have me committed?"

"You're here? Son of a bitch! I didn't think you'd make it until tomorrow."

"Got antsy." He rubbed his chin, heard the scratch of stubble. "Drove through most of last night and got an early start again this morning. Remy? What was I thinking?"

"Damned if I know. Listen, you give me a couple hours to clear some business, and I'll drive out. Bring us some libation. We'll toast that rat-trap and catch up."

"Good. That'd be good."

"You been inside yet?"

"No. I'm working up to it."

"Jesus, Dec, go on in out of the rain."

"Yeah, all right." Declan passed a hand over his face. "See you in a couple hours."

"I'll bring food. For Christ's sake, don't try to cook anything. No point burning the place down before you've spent a night in it."

"Fuck you." He heard Remy laugh before he hung up.

He started the engine again, drove all the way to the base of what was left of those double stairs that framed the entranceway. He popped the glove compartment, took out the keys that had been mailed to him after settlement.

He climbed out and was immediately drenched. Deciding he'd leave the boxes for later, he jogged to the shelter of the entrance gallery, felt a few of the bricks that formed the floor give ominously under his weight, and shook himself like a dog.

There should be vines climbing up the corner columns, he thought. Something with cool blue blossoms. He could see it if he concentrated hard enough. Something open, almost like a cup, with leaves shaped like hearts.

Must've seen that somewhere, he mused, and turned to the door. It was a double, with carvings and long arched panels of glass on either side and a half-moon glass topper. And tracing his fingers over the doors, he felt some of the thrill sneak into him.

"Welcome home, Dec," he said aloud and unlocked the door.

The foyer was as he remembered it. The wide loblolly pine floor, the soaring ceiling. The plaster medallion overhead was a double ring of some sort of flowers. It had probably boasted a fabulous crystal chandelier in its heyday. The best it could offer now was a single bare bulb dangling from a long wire. But when he hit the wall switch, it blinked on. That was something.

In any event, the staircase was the focal point. It rose up, wide and straight to the second level, where it curved right and left to lead to each wing.

What a single man with no current prospects or intentions of being otherwise needed with two wings was a question he didn't want to ask himself at the moment.

The banister was coated with gray dust, but when he rubbed a finger over it, he felt the smooth wood beneath. *How many hands had gripped there? How many fingers had trailed along it?* he wondered. These were the sort of questions that fascinated him, that drew him in.

The kind of questions that had him climbing the stairs with the door open to the rain behind him, and his possessions still waiting in the car.

The stairs might have been carpeted once. There probably had been runners in the long center hallway. Some rich pattern on deep red. Floors, woodwork, tabletops would have been polished religiously with beeswax until they gleamed like the crystal in the chandeliers.

At parties, women in spectacular dresses would glide up and down the stairs—confident, stylish. Some of the men would gather in the billiard room, using the game as an excuse to puff on cigars and pontificate about politics and finance.

And servants would scurry along, efficiently invisible, stoking fires, clearing glasses, answering demands.

On the landing, he opened a panel. The hidden door was skillfully worked into the wall, the faded wallpaper, the dulled wainscoting. He wasn't certain how he'd known it was there. Someone must have mentioned it.

He peered into the dim, dank corridor. Part of the rabbit warren of servants' quarters and accesses, he believed. Family and guests didn't care to have underfoot those who served. A good servant left no trace of his work, but saw to his duties discreetly, silently and well.

Frowning, Declan strained his eyes to see. Where had that come from? His mother? As tight-assed as she could be from time to time, she'd never say something that pompous.

With a shrug, he closed the door again. He'd explore that area another time, when he had a flashlight and a bag of bread crumbs.

He walked along the corridor, glancing in doorways. Empty rooms, full of dust and the smell of damp, gray light from the rain. Some walls were papered, some were down to the skeletal studs.

Sitting room, study, bath and surely the billiard room he'd imagined, as its old mahogany bar was still in place.

He walked in to circle around it, to touch the wood, to crouch down and examine the workmanship.

He'd started a love affair with wood in high school. To date, it was his most lasting relationship. He'd taken a summer job as a laborer even though his family had objected. *He'd* objected to the idea of spending those long summer days cooped up in a law office as a clerk, and had wanted to work outdoors. To polish his tan and his build.

It had been one of the rare times his father had overruled his mother and sided with him.

He'd gotten sunburns, splinters, blisters, calluses, an aching back. And had fallen in love with building.

Not building so much, Declan thought now. Rebuilding. The taking of something already formed and enhancing, repairing, restoring.

Nothing had given him as big a kick, or half as much satisfaction.

He'd had a knack for it. A natural, the Irish pug of a foreman had told him. Good hands, good eyes, good brain. Declan had never forgotten that summer high. And had never matched it since.

Maybe now, he thought. Maybe he would now. There had to be more for him than just getting from one day to the next doing what was expected and acceptable.

With pleasure and anticipation growing, he went back to exploring his house.

At the door to the ballroom he stopped, and grinned. "Wow. Cool!"

His voice echoed and all but bounced back to slap him in the face. Delighted, he walked in. The floors were scarred and stained and spotted. There were sections damaged where it appeared someone had put up partitions to bisect the room, then someone else had knocked them out again.

But he could fix that. Some moron had thrown up drywall and yellow paint over the original plaster walls. He'd fix that, too.

At least they'd left the ceiling alone. The plasterwork was gorgeous, complicated wreaths of flowers and fruit. It would need repairing, and a master to do it. He'd find one.

He threw open the gallery doors to the rain. The neglected, tumbled jungle of gardens spread out, snaked through with overgrown and broken bricked paths. There was likely a treasure of plantings out there. He'd need a landscaper, but he hoped to do some of it himself.

Most of the outbuildings were only ruins now. He could see a portion of a chimney stack, part of a vine-smothered wall of a derelict worker's cabin, the pocked bricks and rusted roof of an old *pigeonnier*—Creole planters had often raised pigeons.

He'd only gotten three acres with the house, so it was likely other structures that had belonged to the plantation were now tumbling down on someone else's land.

But he had trees, he thought. Amazing trees. The ancient live oaks that formed the *allée* dripped with water and moss, and the thick limbs of a sycamore spread and twisted like some prehistoric beast.

A wash of color caught his attention, had him stepping out into the rain. Something was blooming, a tall, fat bush with dark red flowers. What the hell bloomed in January? he wondered, and made a mental note to ask Remy.

Closing his eyes a moment, he listened. He could hear nothing but rain, the whoosh and splash of it on roof, on ground, on tree.

He'd done the right thing, he told himself. He wasn't crazy after all. He'd found his place. It *felt* like his, and if it wasn't, what did it matter? He'd find another. At least, finally, he'd stirred up the energy to look.

He stepped back in and, humming, walked back across the ballroom toward the family wing, to check out each of the five bedrooms.

He caught himself singing under his breath as he wandered through the first of them.

*"After the ball is over, after the break of morn; After the dancers leaving, after the stars are gone . . ."*

He stopped examining baseboard and looked over his shoulder as if expecting to see someone standing behind him. Where had that come from? he wondered. The tune, the lyrics. With a shake of his head, he straightened.

"From the ballroom, idiot," he mumbled. "Ballroom on the mind, so you start singing about a ball. Weird, but not crazy. Talking to yourself isn't crazy, either. Lots of people do it."

The door to the room across the hall was closed. Though he expected the creak of hinges, the sound still danced a chill up his spine.

That sensation was immediately followed by bafflement. He could have sworn he smelled perfume. Flowers. Lilies. Weddings and funerals. And for an instant he imagined them, pure and white and somehow feral in a tall crystal vase.

His next feeling was irritation. He'd only sent a few pieces ahead, including his bedroom furniture. The movers had dumped it in the wrong room, and he'd been very specific. His room would be the master at the corner, overlooking the garden and pond at the rear, and the avenue of oaks from the side.

Now he'd have to settle for this room, or haul the damn stuff himself.

The scent of lilies was overpowering when he shoved the door all the way open. Almost dizzying. Confused, he realized it wasn't even *his* furniture. The bed was a full tester draped in deep blue silk. There was a carved chifforobe, a tall chest of drawers, all gleaming. He caught the scent of beeswax under the floral. Saw the lilies in that tall, crystal vase on a woman's vanity table, its legs curved like the necks of swans. The chair was delicate, its seat an intricate needlepoint pattern of blue and rose.

Silver-backed brushes, a brooch of gold wings with an enameled watch. Long blue draperies, ornate gaslight sconces set on a low, shimmering light. A woman's white robe tossed over the back of a blue chaise.

Candlesticks on the mantel, and a picture in a silver frame.

He saw it all, snapshot clear. Before his brain could process the how of it, he was staring into an empty room where rain streamed outside uncurtained windows.

"Jesus Christ." He gripped the doorjamb for balance. "What the hell?"

He drew in a breath. There was nothing in the air but must and dust.

Projecting, he told himself. Just projecting what the room might have looked like. He hadn't seen anything, or smelled anything. He'd just gotten caught up in the charm of the place, in the spirit of it.

But he couldn't make himself step over the threshold.

He closed the door again, walked directly down to the corner room. His furniture was there, as ordered, and the sight of it both relieved and steadied him.

The good, solid Chippendale bed with its headboard and footboard unadorned. The one point of agreement he'd had, always, with his mother was a love of antiques, the respect for the workmanship, the history.

He'd bought the bed after he and Jessica had called off the wedding. Okay, after he'd called it off, he admitted with the usual tug of guilt. He'd wanted to start fresh, and had searched out and purchased the pieces for his bedroom.

He'd chosen the bachelor's chest not only because it appeared he was going to remain one, but also because he'd liked the style of it, the double herringbone inlay, the secret compartments, the short, turned legs.

He'd selected the armoire to conceal his television and stereo, and the sleek Deco lamps because he'd liked the mix of styles.

Seeing his things here in the spacious room with its handsome granite fireplace in dark green, the arched gallery doors, the gently faded wallpaper, the pitifully scarred floors, clicked him back into place again.

The adjoining dressing area made him smile. All he needed was a valet, and white tie and tails. The connecting bath, modernized from the look of it sometime in the woeful seventies, had him wincing at the avocado-green decor and yearning for a hot shower.

He'd take a quick walk through the third floor, he decided, do the same on the main level, then take the ugly green tub for a spin.

He headed up. The tune was playing in his head again. Around and around, like a waltz. He let it come. It was company of sorts until Remy showed up.

*Many the hopes that have vanished, after the ball.*

The staircase was narrower here. This level was for children and staff, neither of whom required fancy touches.

He'd save the servants' wing for later, he decided, and circled around toward what he assumed were nursery, storage, attics.

He reached for a doorknob, the brass dull with time and neglect. A draft, cold enough to pierce bone, swept down the corridor. He saw his breath puff out in surprise, watched it condense into a thin cloud.

As his hand closed over the knob, nausea rose up so fast, so sharp, it stole his breath again. Cold sweat pearled on his brow. His head spun.

In an instant he knew a fear so huge, so great, he wanted to run screaming. Instead he stumbled back, braced himself against the wall while terror and dread choked him like murderous hands.

*Don't go in there. Don't go in.*

Wherever the voice in his head came from, he was inclined to listen to it. He knew the house was rumored to be haunted. He didn't mind such things.

Or thought he didn't mind them.

But the idea of opening that door to whatever was behind it, to whatever waited on the other side, was more than he cared to face alone. On an empty stomach. After a ten-hour drive.

"Just wasting time anyway," he said for the comfort of his own voice. "I should be unloading the car. So, I'm going to unload the car."

"Who you talking to, *cher*?"

Declan jumped like a basketball center at the tip-off, and barely managed to turn a scream into a more acceptable masculine yelp. "God *damn* it, Remy. You scared the shit out of me."

"You're the one up here talking to a door. I gave a few shouts on my way up. Guess you didn't hear."

"Guess I didn't."

Declan leaned back against the wall, sucked in air and studied his friend.

Remy Payne had the cocky good looks of a con artist. He was tailor-made for the law, Declan thought. Slick, sharp, with cheerful blue eyes and a wide mouth that could, as it was now, stretch like rubber into a disarming smile that made you want to believe everything he said, even as you caught the distinctive whiff of bullshit.

He was on the skinny side, never had been able to bulk up despite owning the appetite of an elephant. In college he'd worn his deep-brown hair in a sleek mane over his collar. He'd shortened it now so it was almost Caesarean in style.

"I thought you said a couple hours."

"Been that. Damn near two and a half. You okay there, Dec? Look a little peaky."

"Long drive, I guess. God, it's good to see you."

"'Bout time you mentioned that." With a laugh, he caught Declan in a bear hug. "Whoo, boy. You been working out. Turn around, lemme see your ass."

"You idiot." They slapped backs. "Tell me one thing," Declan remarked as he took a step back. "Am I out of my fucking mind?"

"'Course you are. Always have been. Let's go on down and have our-selves a drink."

They settled in what had once been the gentlemen's parlor, on the floor with a pepperoni pizza and a bottle of Jim Beam.

The first shot of bourbon went down like liquid silk and untied all the knots in Declan's belly. The pizza was good and greasy, and made him decide the strangeness he'd experienced had been a result of fatigue and hunger.

"You planning on living like this for long, or buying yourself a chair or two?"

"Don't need a chair or two." Declan took the bottle back from Remy, swigged down bourbon. "Not for now anyway. I wanted to cut things down to the bone for a while. I got the bedroom stuff. Might toss a table up in the kitchen. I start buying furniture, it'll just be in the way while I'm working on this place."

Remy looked around the room. "Shape this place is in, you'll need a fucking wheelchair before you're finished."

"It's mostly cosmetic. People who bought it last got a good start on the big work, from what I hear. Seems they had an idea about turning it into a fancy hotel or some such thing. Gave it nearly six months before they turned tail. Probably they ran out of money."

Lifting his eyebrows, Remy ran a finger over the floor, studied the layer of dust he picked up. "Too bad you can't sell this dirt. You'd be filthy rich. Ha. Oh yeah, I forgot. You already are filthy rich. How's your family?"

"About the same as always."

"And they think, our boy Dec, *il est fou*." Remy circled a finger by his ear. "He's gone round the bend."

"Oh yeah. Maybe they're right, but at least it's finally *my* damn bend. If I'd gone to one more deposition, faced one more meeting, handled one more pretrial negotiation, I'd have drowned myself in the Charles."

"Corporate law's what stifled you, *cher*." Remy licked sauce from his fingers. "You should've tried criminal, like me. Keeps the blood moving. You say the word, we'll hang out a shingle together tomorrow."

"Thanks for the thought. You still love it."

"I do. I love the slippery, sneaking angles of it, the pomp and ceremony, the sweaty wrestling, the fancy words. Every damn thing." Remy shook his head, tipped back the bottle. "You never did."

"No, I never did."

"All those years busting ass through Harvard, tossed aside. That what they're saying to you?"

"Among other things."

"They're wrong. You know that, Dec. You're not tossing anything aside. You're just picking up something different. Relax and enjoy it. You're in New Orleans now, or close enough. We take things easy here. We'll wear some of that Yankee off you soon enough. Have you doing the Cajun two-step and stirring up some red beans and rice on wash day."

"Yeah, that'll happen."

"You come on into town once you're settled in, Effie and I'll take you out to dinner. I want you to meet her."

Remy had pulled off his tie, shucked his suit jacket, rolled up the sleeves of his lawyerly blue shirt. Except for the hair, Declan thought, he didn't look that different than he did when they'd been at Harvard sucking down pizza and bourbon.

"You're really doing it? Getting married."

Remy let out a sigh. "Twelfth of May, come hell or high water. I'm settling my bad ass down, Dec. She's just what I want."

"A librarian." It was a wonder to Declan. "You and a librarian."

"Research specialist," Remy corrected and hooted out a laugh. "Damn prettiest bookworm I ever did see. She's a smart one, too. I'm crazy in love with her, Dec. Out of my mind crazy for her."

"I'm happy for you."

"You still got the guilts over . . . what was her name? Jennifer?"

"Jessica." Wincing, Declan took another swig to cut the taste her name brought to his tongue. "Calling off a wedding three weeks before you're due to walk down the aisle ought to give you the guilts."

Remy acknowledged this with a quick shrug. "Maybe so. Feel worse if you'd gone through with it."

"Tell me." Still, his gray eyes remained broody as he stared at the bottle. "But I think she'd have handled it better if we'd done the thing, then gone for a divorce the next day." It still gave him a twinge. "Couldn't have handled it any worse, anyway. She's seeing my cousin James now."

"James . . . James . . . That the one who squeals like a girl or the one with the Dracula hair?"

"Neither." Declan's lips twitched. Jesus, he'd missed this. "James is the perfect one. Plastic surgeon, polo player, collects stamps."

"Short guy, receding chin, broad Yankee accent."

"That's him, but the chin doesn't recede anymore. Implant. According to my sister, it's starting to look serious between them, which just serves me right, I'm told."

"Well, hell, let your sister marry Jennifer."

"Jessica, and that's what I told her," he said, gesturing with the bottle for emphasis. "She didn't speak to me for two weeks. Which was a relief. I'm not very popular with the Fitzgeralds right now."

"Well, you know, Dec, I'd have to say, given the circumstances and such . . . screw 'em."

With a laugh, Declan handed Remy the bottle. "Let's drink to it."

He took another slice of pizza from the box. "Let me ask you something else, about this place. I've researched the history, did a chunk of it way back after we came here the first time."

"Stumbling around like drunken fools."

"Yeah, which we may do again if we keep hitting this bourbon. Anyway, I know it was built in 1879—after the original structure burned down in an unexplained fire, which was very likely set due to politics, Reconstruction and other post–Civil War messiness."

"That's the War of Northern Aggression, son." Remy pointed a warning finger. "Remember which side of the Mason-Dixon Line you're plopping your Yankee ass down on now."

"Right. Sorry. Anyway. The Manets scooped up the land, cheap, according to the old records, and built the current structure. They farmed sugar and cotton primarily and divvied off plots to sharecroppers. Lived well for about twenty years. There were two sons, both died young. Then the old man died and the wife held on until she apparently stroked out in her sleep. No heirs. There was a granddaughter on record, but she was cut out of the will. Place went to auction and has passed from hand to hand ever since. Sitting empty more than not."

"And?"

Declan leaned forward. "Do you believe it's haunted?"

Remy pursed his lips, copped the last piece of pizza. "That whole history lesson was your way of working around to asking that one question? Boy, you got the makings for a fine southern lawyer. Sure it's haunted." His eyes danced as he bit into the pizza. "House been here this long and isn't, it'd have no self-respect whatsoever. The granddaughter you mentioned. She was a Rouse on her mama's side. I know that, as I'm fourth or fifth cousins with the Simones, and the Simones come down from that line. Girl was raised, I believe, by her maternal grandparents after her mama took off with some man—so it's said. Don't know if I recollect what happened to her daddy, but others will if you want to know. I do know that Henri Manet, his wife, Josephine, and the one son—damned if I know what his name was—all died in this house. One of them doesn't have the gumption to haunt it, that's a crying shame."

"Natural causes? The people who died here?"

Curious, Remy frowned. "Far as I know. Why?"

"I don't know." Declan had to fight off a shudder. "Vibes."

"You want someone to come through here? Little gris-gris, little voodoo, chase off your ghost, or maybe summon the spirit for a little conversation? You can find yourself a witch or psychic every second corner in town."

"No, thanks."

"You let me know if you decide different." Remy winked. "I'll put you onto somebody who'll give you a fine show."

He didn't want a show, Declan decided later. But he did want that shower, and bed. With Jim Beam buzzing pleasantly in his blood, he hauled in boxes, pawed through them to find sheets and towels. He carted what he figured he'd need for the night upstairs.

It was good old Catholic guilt rather than any need for order that had him making the bed. He treated himself to a ten-minute shower, then climbed into the fresh sheets to the sound of the incessant rain.

He was asleep in thirty seconds.

There was a baby crying. It didn't strike him as odd at all. Babies tended to cry in the middle of the night, or whenever they damn well pleased. It sounded fretful and annoyed more than alarmed.

Someone ought to go pick it up . . . do whatever people did with crying babies. Feed it. Change it. Rock it.

When he'd waked from nightmares as a child, his mother or his nanny, sometimes his father, had come in to stroke his head and sit with him until the fear faded away again.

The baby wasn't frightened. The baby was hungry.

It didn't strike him as odd that he thought that. That he knew that.

But it did strike him as odd, very odd, to wake, bathed in sweat, and find himself standing outside the door with the dull brass knob on the third floor.

# THREE

S leepwalking. That was something he hadn't done since childhood. But in the watery light of day it was simple enough to see how it had happened. Jim Beam, pepperoni pizza and talk of ghosts.

A little harder to accept was the gut-clenching terror he'd felt when he'd surfaced and found himself outside that third-level door. He'd snapped out of the fugue and into a nightmare of panic—one where he'd been certain he'd heard the fading echoes of a baby's restless crying.

He'd run. He couldn't have opened that door if he'd had a gun to his head. So he'd run, with his own bright fear chasing him, to lock himself back in the bedroom. Like a mental patient, he thought now over a lukewarm cup of instant coffee.

At least there'd been no one around to see it.

But if you thought about it, it was a rather auspicious first night. Cold spots, baby ghosts, fugues. It sure beat sitting in his empty town house in Boston, sucking on a beer and watching ESPN.

Maybe he would spend some time digging deeper into the history of the house. His house, he corrected, and with his coffee, he leaned on the damp iron rail of the gallery outside his bedroom.

His view. And it was a beaut once you skimmed over the wreck of the gardens.

Leaves dripped from the rain in steady, musical plops, and the air shimmered with the weight the storm had left behind. Mists crawled over the ground, smoky fingers that trailed and curled around the trees to turn them into romantic and mysterious silhouettes.

If the sun broke through, the glittery light would be spectacular, but it was nothing to sneeze at now.

There was a pond, a small one, choked with lily pads, and fields— some fallow, some already planted for a spring that came so much sooner here. He could see the thin curve of the river that ribboned its way through the deep shadows of the bayou.

A rickety little bridge crossed the water in a hump, then a dirt road pushed into the trees toward a house mostly hidden by them. He could just make out a puff of smoke that rose up to mix with the hazy air.

He'd already been up on the belvedere that morning, and had been relieved to find it, the roof, the chimneys, all in good repair. The last owners had seen to that and this second-floor gallery before they'd thrown in the towel.

It looked as if they'd started on the rear gallery as well, had started preliminary work on closing it into a screened porch.

Which might not be a bad idea. He'd think about it.

Declan wasn't certain if they'd run out of money or energy, or both, but he considered it his good fortune.

He had plenty of money, and just now, watching the steam rising over the weeds and water, plenty of energy.

He lifted the cup to his lips, then lowered it again as he saw a woman—a girl?—slip through the trees toward the curve of the river. A huge black dog lumbered along beside her.

She was too far away from him to make out features. He saw she wore a red checked shirt and jeans, that her hair was long and dark and madly curling. Was she old? he wondered. Young? Pretty or plain?

He decided on young and pretty. It was, after all, his option.

She tossed a ball in the air, fielded it smartly when the dog gave a leap. She tossed it twice more while the dog jumped and ran in circles. Then she reared back like a pitcher in the stretch and bulleted it through the air. The dog gave chase and didn't hesitate, but leaped toward the pond, shagging the ball with a snap of teeth an instant before he hit the water.

Hell of a trick, Declan thought and, grinning, watched the girl applaud.

He wished he could hear her. He was sure she was laughing, a low, throaty laugh. When the dog swam to the edge, scrambled out, he spit the ball at her feet, then shook himself.

It had to have drenched her, but she didn't dance away or brush fussily at her jeans.

They repeated the routine, with Declan a captive audience.

He imagined her walking with the dog closer to the Hall. Close enough that he could wave from the gallery, invite her in for a cup of bad coffee. His first shot at southern hospitality.

Or better yet, he could wander down. And she'd be wrestling with the dog. She'd slip on the wet grass, tumble into the pond. He'd be right at hand to pull her out. No, to dive in after her and save her because she couldn't swim.

Then one thing would lead to another, and they'd have sex on that damp grass, in the watery sunlight. Her body, wet and sleek, would rise over his. He'd fill his hands with her breasts, and . . .

"Jeez." He blinked, saw her disappearing into the trees again.

He wasn't sure if he was embarrassed or relieved to find himself hard. He'd had sex only once in the six months since he'd broken things off with Jessica. And that had been more a reflex than real desire.

So if he could find himself fully aroused over some ridiculous fantasy of a woman whose face he hadn't seen, that area was coming back to normal.

He could check worry over his manhood off his list of concerns.

He tossed the last swallows of cold coffee away. He didn't mind starting the day with a stray erotic fantasy, but he did mind starting it with bad coffee. It was time to get down to practicalities.

He went back in, grabbed his wallet and keys and headed into town for supplies.

It took him most of the day. Not just to get the supplies, but to reacquaint himself with the city he was going to call his own.

If Boston was a respectable wife, with a few seamy secrets, New Orleans was a sensual mistress who celebrated her darker sides.

He treated himself to an enormous breakfast, so loaded with cholesterol he imagined his heart simply keeling over from the shock.

He bought coffee beans and a grinder. Bagels and beignets. He loaded up on the single-male cuisine of packaged dinners, frozen pizza, dry cereal. Hit the liquor store for beer, bourbon and some good wine.

He loaded it into his car, then struck out again, as much for the joy of wandering the streets as the recollection he needed something to eat on and with. He settled for paper plates and plastic ware, and stopped to watch a street musician set out his trumpet case, prime it with a few coins, then fill the air with a stream of magic.

Declan gave him his first dollar of the day.

He avoided the temptation of the antique shops and the lure of the Quarter. Lunchtime music was already pumping out of clubs and exotic scents wafted from restaurants. He bought himself a muffuletta—that marvel of meat and cheese and oil on Italian bread—to take back home for later.

As he walked to his car again, he noted the tourists with their bags from Café du Monde or the Riverwalk shops, the card readers sitting at folding tables around the perimeter of Jackson Square who would tell your fortune for ten dollars a pop. He caught the faint drift of marijuana under the ripening stench of garbage as he walked by an alleyway.

And saw an enormous black woman, smoking in indolent puffs, on the plant-jammed gallery above a shop that advertised erotic candles.

He bought one for Remy of a naked woman with breasts like torpedoes, and grinned over it all the way back to his car.

He drove home energized. He hauled in supplies, stuffed them wherever seemed logical at the time, then began a serious room-by-room inspection of the main level. He made notes on problems, on potentials, on plans and on priorities.

The kitchen was a definite first. He had experience there from his own house in Boston, and from two remodels where he'd assisted friends.

He couldn't claim to cook more than the occasional omelette or toasted sandwich, but he thought of the kitchen as the heart of any home. The latest transition of the Manet Hall kitchen was early eighties—stark white and chrome with a slablike island work counter and blinding white flooring.

The good points were the generous windows, the old and serviceable brick hearth and the pretty coffered ceiling. He liked the enormous pantry, but thought it would serve better as a mudroom. He'd hack down to the original wood flooring, strip off the overly sweet teapot-themed wallpaper, yank out the island in favor of an antique baker's table or some such thing.

Decorating wasn't his strong point. He'd left that to Jessica, who'd favored pale colors and classic lines.

And now that he thought about it, he preferred stronger colors and the charm of the fanciful. He *liked* details and fuss. It was his house, damn it, and he'd do it his way. Top to bottom.

He'd put in some old glass-fronted cabinets where he could display antique kitchen appliances. Cracked, mismatched dishes, bottles and Mason jars. Cluttered.

Good solid surface countertops. Copper faucets. He didn't care if they tarnished. They'd just look more real.

Big-ass refrigerator. State-of-the-art dishwasher and range. All fronted with distressed wood.

Now, we're cooking.

He took reams of notes, measured, remeasured. He dragged out his research books and pored over them on the floor of the empty library while he ate half his sandwich and drank enough coffee to make his ears ring.

He could see it, so perfectly. The floor-to-ceiling shelves jammed with books, the deep green walls and the soft cream of the plaster ceiling and trim. Thick silver candlesticks on the mantel. He'd have to have all the chimneys checked professionally so he could start building fires, knock the chill out of the air.

The trim would be restored where it needed it, sanded smooth as satin. The pocket doors here, and the massive ones separating the gentlemen's and ladies' parlors, were in excellent shape.

Someone along the way had refinished the library flooring.

He crawled around, running his hands over the wood. Sand it down lightly, slap on a couple coats of clear varnish, and they'd be set. The area rugs had protected it well—the good, thick Aubussons Josephine had ordered from Paris.

He smelled brandy, leather, beeswax and roses, but thought nothing of it. His eyes were cloudy and distant when he stopped at the tiled hearth, flicked his thumb over the chip at the corner. That section would have to be replaced, or if it couldn't be matched, rounded off. They'd been hand painted and glazed in Italy, at considerable expense.

Julian had knocked the candlestick off the mantel, and it had chipped the tile. Drunk again. Raging again.

The cell phone in his pocket rang and had Declan sitting back on his heels. Blinking, displaced, he gazed around the empty room. What had he been doing? Thinking? He glanced down at his thumb and saw he'd rubbed it raw on the jagged tile. Disoriented, he dragged out his phone.

"Yeah. Hello?"

"There he is. I was about to give you up." Remy's cheerful voice jangled in his head as Declan stared at the tile. He'd been thinking about the tile. Something . . .

"I'm, ah, doing a room by room. Measuring. Stuff."

"How about you get yourself out of there for a while? I got me a late meeting, thought you could meet me for a drink after. Effie, too, if I can drag her out."

"What time is it?" Declan turned his wrist to check his watch. "Midnight? It's midnight?"

"Not yet it's not. You been drinking already?"

"Just coffee." He frowned at his watch, tapped the face. "Battery must've gone."

"It's just after six. I should be able to wiggle loose by nine. Why don't you come on in? I'll meet you at Et Trois, in the Quarter, on Dauphine about a block off Bourbon."

"Yeah." Absently, he shoved at his hair, found his forehead was lightly beaded with sweat. "Yeah, that sounds fine."

"You need directions, Yankee boy?"

"I'll find it." He rubbed his throbbing thumb. "Remy?"

"That's my name."

Declan shook his head, laughed at himself. "Nothing. See you later."

He drove in early. He wasn't particularly interested in drinking, but wanted to see the metamorphosis of New Orleans from day to night. The streets gleamed under the carnival of lights, teemed with the crowds who streamed along, looking for entertainment.

It was neither the tourists nor the merchants who ran the show, in Declan's opinion. It was the city itself. And its wheels turned on music.

It pumped from doorways, cool jazz, hot rock, melting blues. Overhead, restaurant galleries were thick with diners who warded off the January chill with spicy sauce and alcohol. The strip club hawkers promised all manner of visual delights, and in the shops cash registers rang as tourists gorged on T-shirts and Mardi Gras masks. The bars served hurricanes to the Yankees, and beer and liquor to those who knew better.

But it was the music that kept the parade marching.

He soaked it in as he strolled down Bourbon, past doorways, bright lights and sudden, unexpected courtyards. He skirted around a group of women who clutched together on the sidewalk chattering like magpies.

He caught the scent of them—flowers and candy—and felt the typical male reaction of pleasure and panic when they burst into giggles.

"Nice ass," one of them commented, and Declan kept on walking.

Women in packs were dangerous and mysterious entities.

It occurred to him that if he were going to meet Effie, he should take her a token. Some sort of engagement gift. He didn't know what she liked, or what she *was* like, come to think of it. But if there was one thing he was good at, it was buying gifts.

Wishing he'd thought of it earlier, he poked through a couple of shops without much hope. Nearly everything in this section was geared for the tourist trade, and he didn't think a wind-up, plastic penis was quite the thing for a first introduction. A gift could wait, he reflected, or he could just fall back on the basket of girl lotions and potions.

Then he saw it. The silver frog squatted on all fours as if it was about to take a good, springy hop. It had a cheerfully wicked face and a big, smart-ass grin. And reminded Declan instantly of Remy.

If this Effie had fallen for his old college pal, she had to appreciate whimsy. He had it wrapped in fancy paper with a big red bow.

It was still shy of nine when he turned onto Dauphine.

He was ready to sit in a bar, away from the center ring of the circus. Maybe listen to some music and work on a beer. For the next several weeks, he was going to have to toe the line. Spend his days tearing into the kitchen, his evenings planning his next point of attack. He had to track down specific craftsmen. Get bids. Get started.

For tonight, he'd spend some time with friends, then go home and get a solid eight hours' sleep.

He spotted the sign for Et Trois. It was hard to miss as it danced cheerfully in cool blue over the scarred wooden door of a building barely two good strides from the street.

The second floor boasted the typical gallery and lacy iron baluster. Someone had decked it out with fat clay pots of hot pink geraniums and strung little white fairy lights along the eaves. It made a pretty, feminine picture. The kind of spot where you might sit, drink a glass of wine and contemplate the people strolling by below.

He opened the door to a blast of jumpy zydeco, the scent of garlic and whiskey.

On the small stage was a five-piece band—washboard, fiddle, drums, guitar, accordion. The little dance floor was already packed with people executing the quick, fancy two-step the music cried for.

Through the dim light he could see that none of the round wooden tables scooted to the side were free. He turned toward the bar. The wood was nearly black with age, but it gleamed. A dozen backless stools were jammed together. Declan copped the single one left before someone beat him to it.

Bottles lined the mirror behind the bar, and interspersed with them were salt and pepper shakers in a variety of themes. An elegant couple in evening dress, dogs, Rocky and Bullwinkle, Porky and Petunia, the round, naked breasts of a reclining woman, carnival masks and winged fairies.

He contemplated them, considered the sort of person who would collect and display fairies and body parts, and decided it was someone who understood New Orleans.

Onstage, the fiddle player began to sing in Cajun. She had a voice like a rusty saw that was inexplicably appealing. Tapping his foot, Declan glanced down to the end of the bar. The man tending had dreadlocks down to his waist, a face that might have been carved by a very skilled hand out of a polished coffee bean and hands that moved with balletic grace as he worked taps and poured shots.

He started to lift his hand to get the bartender's attention. And then she walked out of the door behind the bar.

Later, when he could think clearly, he would decide it had been like having a sledgehammer plowed into his chest. Not stopping his heart, but jump-starting it. His heart, his blood, his loins, his brain. Everything went from holding pattern to quick march in an instant.

*There you are!* something in his mind shouted. *Finally.*

He could hear the race of his body like a hard hum that drowned out the music, the voices. His vision focused in on her so completely it was as if she were spotlighted on a black stage.

She wasn't beautiful, not in any classic sense. What she was, was spectacular.

Her hair was midnight black, a gypsy mane that spilled wild curls over her shoulders. Her face was fox-sharp—the narrow, somewhat aristocratic nose, the high, planed cheeks, the tapered chin. Her eyes were long and heavy-lidded, her mouth wide, full and painted blood-lust red.

It didn't quite go together, he thought as his brain jumbled. The elements in the face shouldn't work as a whole. But they were perfect. Striking, sexy, superb.

She was small, almost delicately built, and wore a tight scooped-neck shirt the color of poppies that showed off the lean muscles of her arms, the firm curve of her breasts. Tucked into the valley of those breasts was a silver chain with a tiny silver key.

Her skin was dusky, her eyes, when they flicked to his, the deep, rich brown of bitter chocolate.

Those red lips curved—a slow, knowing smile as she strolled over, leaned on the bar so their faces were close enough for him to see the tiny beauty mark just above the right curve of her top lip. Close enough for him to catch the scent of night-blooming jasmine, and start to drown in it.

"Can I do something for you, *cher*?"

*Oh yeah*, he thought. *Please.*

But all that came out was: "Um . . ." She gave her head a little toss, then angled it as she sized him up. She spoke again, in that easy Cajun rhythm. "You thirsty? Or just . . . hungry tonight?"

"Ah . . ." He wanted to lap his tongue over those red lips, that tiny mole, and slurp her right up. "Corona."

He watched her as she got the bottle, snagged a lime. She had a walk like a dancer, somewhere between ballet and exotic. He could literally feel his tongue tangling into knots.

"You want to run a tab, handsome?"

"Ah." *God, Fitzgerald, pull yourself together.* "Yeah, thanks. What's it unlock?" When she lifted her eyebrows, he picked up the bottle. "Your key?"

"This?" She reached down, trailed a finger over the little key and sent his blood pressure through the roof. "Why, my heart, *cher.* What'd you think?"

He reached out a hand for hers. If he didn't touch her, he was afraid he might break down and sob. "I'm Declan."

"Is that right?" She left her hand in his. "Nice name. Not usual."

"It's . . . Irish."

"Uh-huh." She turned his hand over, leaned down as if reading the palm. "What do I see here? You haven't been in New Orleans long, but you hope to be. Got yourself out of the cold, cold North, did you, Declan?"

"Yeah. Guess that's not hard to figure."

She looked up again, and this time his heart did stop. "I can figure more. Rich Yankee lawyer down from Boston. You bought Manet Hall."

"Do I know you?" He felt something—like a link forged onto a chain—when his hand gripped hers. "Have we met before?"

"Not in this life, darling." She gave his hand a little pat, then moved down the bar filling more orders.

But she kept an eye on him. He wasn't what she'd expected from Remy's description. Though she was damned if she knew what she'd expected. Still, she was a woman who liked surprises. The man sitting at her bar, watching her out of storm-gray eyes, looked to be full of them.

She liked his eyes. She was used to men looking at her with desire, but there'd been more in his. A kind of breathless shock that was both flattering and sweet.

And it was appealing to have a man who looked like he could handle anything you tossed at him fumble when you smiled at him.

Though he'd barely touched his beer, she worked her way back to him, tapped a finger to the bottle. "Ready for another?"

"No, thanks. Can you take a break? Can I buy you a drink, coffee, a car, a dog?"

"What's in there?"

He glanced at the little gift bag he'd set on the bar. "It's just a present for someone I'm meeting."

"You buy gifts for lots of women, Declan?"

"She's not a woman. I mean, not my woman. I don't actually have one—it's just . . . I used to be better at this."

"Better at what?"

"At hitting on women."

She laughed—the low, throaty sound of his fantasies.

"Can you take a break? We'll kick somebody away from a table and you can give me another chance."

"You're not doing so bad with the first one. I own the place, so I don't get breaks."

"This is your place?"

"That's right." She turned as one of the waitresses came to the bar with a tray.

"Wait. Wait." He reached for her hand again. "I don't know your name. What's your name?"

"Angelina," she said softly. "But they call me Lena, 'cause I ain't no angel. *Cher.*" She trailed a finger down his cheek, then stepped away to fill orders.

Declan took a deep, long swallow of beer to wash back the saliva that had pooled in his mouth.

He was trying to work out another approach when Remy slapped him on the back. "We're going to need us a table, son."

"View's better from here."

Remy followed the direction of Declan's gaze. "One of the best the city offers. You meet my cousin Lena?"

"Cousin?"

"Fourth cousins, I'm thinking. Might be fifth. Angelina Simone, one of New Orleans's jewels. And here's another. Effie Renault. Effie darling, this is my good friend Declan Fitzgerald."

"Hello, Declan." She wiggled between him and Remy and kissed Declan's cheek. "I'm so happy to meet you."

She had a cloud of blond hair around a pretty, heart-shaped face, and eyes of clear summer blue. Her lips had a deep, Kewpie doll curve and were a rosy pink.

She looked like she should be leading cheers at the local high school.

"You're too pretty to waste yourself on this guy," Declan told her. "Why don't you run away with me instead?"

"When do we leave?"

With a chuckle, Declan slid off the stool and returned her kiss. "Nice job, Remy."

"Best work I ever did." Remy pressed his lips to Effie's hair. "Sit on down there, darling. Place is packed. Bar might be the best we do. You want wine?"

"The house white'll be fine."

"Get you a refill there, Declan?"

"I'll get it. I'm buying."

"If that's the case, get my girl here the good chardonnay. I'll have what you're having."

"Look what the cat dragged." Lena sent Remy a grin. "Hey, Effie. What's everybody drinking tonight?"

"A glass of chardonnay for the lady. And two more Coronas," Declan told her. "Then maybe you can call nine-one-one. My heart stops every time I look at you."

"Your friend's got himself a smooth way once he gets rolling, Remy." Lena took a bottle of wine from the cooler.

"Those Harvard girls were putty in his hands."

"We southern girls are too used to the heat to melt easy." She poured wine, topped the beers with lime wedges.

"I do know you." It bounced back in his memory. "I saw you, this morning, playing with your dog. Big black dog, near the pond."

"Rufus." It gave her a little jolt to realize he'd watched her. "He's my grandmama's dog. That's her house back the bayou. I go out sometimes and stay with her if she's feeling poorly. Or just lonely."

"Come by the Hall next time you're out. I'll give you the tour."

"Just might. I've never been inside." She set a fresh bowl of pretzels on the bar. "Y'all want something from the kitchen?"

"We'll think about that," Remy said.

"Just let us know." She swung around and through the back door.

"You gonna want to mop that drool off your chin, Dec." Remy squeezed Declan's shoulder. "It's embarrassing."

"Don't tease him, Remy. A man doesn't get a little worked up around Lena, he's got some essential parts missing."

"You definitely should run away with me," Declan decided. "But meanwhile. Best wishes." He nudged the gift bag in front of her.

"You bought me a present? Aren't you the sweetest thing!" She tore into it with an enthusiasm that made Declan grin. And when she held up the frog, she stopped, stared. Then threw back her head and let out a hooting laugh. "It looks like Remy. Look here, honey, he's got your smile."

"I don't see it."

"I do. Dec did." She swiveled on the stool and beamed up into Declan's face. "I like you. I'm so glad I like you. I love this moron here so much I can hardly stand it, so I'd've pretended I liked you even if I didn't. But I don't have to pretend."

"Oh now, don't start watering up, Effie." Remy dug out a handkerchief as she sniffled. "She does that when she's happy. Night I asked her to marry me, she cried so much it took her ten minutes to say yes."

He pulled her off the stool. "Come on, *chère,* you dance with me till you dry up again."

Declan got back on the stool, picked up his beer and watched them circle the floor.

"They look good together," Lena commented from behind him.

"Yeah. Yeah, they do. Interested in seeing how we look together?"

"You are persistent." She let out a breath. "What kind of car you going to buy me?"

"Car?"

"You offered to buy me a drink, coffee, a car or a dog. I can buy my own drinks, and I like my own coffee. I got a dog, more or less. A car, too. But I don't see why I shouldn't have two cars. What car are you buying me?"

"Your choice."

"I'll let you know," she replied, then moved down the bar once more.

# FOUR

He worked solidly for three days. There was little, in Declan's opinion, more satisfying than tearing something apart. Even putting it back together again didn't reach into the gut with that same primal zing.

He gutted the kitchen, ripping out the center island, the counters and cabinets. He steamed off wallpaper and yanked up linoleum.

He was left with a shell of plaster and wood, and endless possibilities.

In the evenings he nursed his blisters and strained muscles, and pored through design books.

Every morning, before he started the day, he took his first cup of coffee out on the gallery and hoped for a glimpse of Lena and the big black dog she'd called Rufus.

He contacted workmen and craftsmen, ordered materials, and in a frenzy of enthusiasm, bought a full-sized pickup truck straight off the lot.

The first night he was able to build a fire in the downriver parlor, he toasted the occasion, and himself, with a solitary glass of Merlot.

There'd been no more sleepwalking, but there had been dreams. He could remember only snatches of them upon waking. Music—often the tune had seemed to be lodged in his brain like a tumor. Or raised voices.

Once he'd dreamed of sex, of soft sighs in the dark, of the lazy glide of flesh over flesh, and the need rising up like a warm wave.

He'd woken with his muscles quivering and the scent of lilies just fading from his senses.

Since dreaming about sex seemed to be the best he could manage, he put his energies into the work.

When he did take a break, it was to pay a call, and he went armed with a bouquet of white daisies and a rawhide bone.

The bayou house was a single-story cypress, shotgun style. Tobacco-colored water snaked around it on three sides. A small white boat swayed gently at a sagging dock.

Trees hemmed it in where the water didn't. The cypress and live oak and pecan. From the limbs hung clear bottles half-filled with water. And nestled into the gnarled roots of a live oak stood a painted statue of the Blessed Virgin.

There were purple pansies at her feet.

A little porch faced the dirt drive, and there were more potted flowers on it along with a rocking chair. The shutters were painted a mossy green. The screen door was patched in two places, and through the checkerboard net came the strong, bluesy voice of Ethel Waters.

He heard the deep, warning barks of the dog. Still, Declan wasn't prepared for the size and speed as Rufus burst out of the door and charged.

"Oh, Jesus," was all he managed. He had an instant to wonder if he should dive through the window of the pickup or freeze when the black mass the size of a pony skidded to a halt at his feet.

Rufus punctuated those ear-splitting barks with rumbling growls, liquid snarls and a very impressive show of teeth. Since he doubted he could beat the dog off with a bunch of daisies, Declan opted for the friendly approach.

"Hey, really, really big Rufus. How's it going?"

Rufus sniffed at his boots, up his leg and dead into the crotch.

"Oh man, let's not get that personal right off." Thinking of those teeth, Declan decided he'd rather risk his hand than his dick, and reached out slowly to give the massive head a little shove and pat.

Rufus looked up with a pair of sparkling brown eyes, and in one fast, fluid move, reared up on his hind legs and planted his enormous paws on Declan's shoulders.

He swiped a tongue about the size of the Mississippi over Declan's face. Braced against the side of the truck, Declan hoped the long, sloppy licks were a greeting and not some sort of tenderizing.

"Nice to meet you, too."

"Get on down now, Rufus."

At the mild order from the front doorway, the dog dropped down, sat, thumped his tail.

The woman standing on the porch was younger than Declan had expected. She couldn't have been far into her sixties. She had the same small build as her granddaughter, the same sharp planes to her face. Her hair was black, liberally streaked with white, and worn in a mass of curls.

She wore a cotton dress that hit her mid-calf with a baggy red sweater over it. Stout brown boots covered her feet with thick red socks drooping over them. He heard the jangle of her bracelets as she fisted her hands on her narrow hips.

"He liked the smell of you, and the sound of you, so he gave you a welcome kiss."

"If he didn't like me?"

She smiled, a quick flash that deepened the lines time had etched on her face. "What you think?"

"I think I'm glad I smell friendly. I'm Declan Fitzgerald, Mrs. Simone. I bought Manet Hall."

"I know who you are. Come on inside and sit for a spell." She stepped back, opened the rickety screen door.

With the dog plodding along beside him, Declan walked to the porch. "It's nice to meet you, Mrs. Simone."

She studied him, a frank and cagey stare out of dark eyes. "You sure are a pretty one, aren't you?"

"Thanks." He held out the flowers. "You, too."

She took the flowers, pursed her lips. "You come courting me, Declan Fitzgerald?"

"Can you cook?"

She laughed, a thick foggy sound, and he fell a little in love. "I got some fresh corn bread, so you can see for yourself."

She led the way in, down the wire-straight center hall. He caught glimpses of the parlor, of bedrooms—one with an iron crucifix over a simple iron bed—a sewing room, that all managed to be cozily cluttered and pin-neat.

He smelled furniture polish and lavender, then a few steps from the kitchen, caught the country scent of baking.

"Ma'am? I'm thirty-one, financially solvent, and I got a clean bill of health my last physical. I don't smoke, I usually drink in moderation and I'm reasonably neat. If you marry me, I'll treat you like a queen."

She chuckled and shook her head, then waved to the kitchen table. "Sit yourself down there and stretch those long legs under the table so they don't trip me up. And since you're sparking me, you can call me Miss Odette."

She uncovered a dish on the counter, got plates out of a cupboard. While she cut squares of corn bread, Declan looked out her kitchen door.

The bayou spread, a dream of dark water and cypress knees with the shadowy reflection of trees shimmering on the surface. He saw a bird with bright red wings spear through the air and vanish.

"Wow. How do you get anything done when you could just sit here and look all day?"

"It's a good spot." She took a pitcher of dark tea from an old refrigerator that was barely taller than she was. "My family's been here more'n a hundred-fifty years. My grandpapa, he had him a good still out back that stand of oaks. Revenuers never did find it."

She set the glass, the plate in front of him. "*Manger.* Eat. What your grandpapa do?"

"He was a lawyer. Actually, both of them were."

"Dead now, are they?"

"Retired."

"You, too, huh?" She got out a fat, pale blue bottle as he took the first bite of corn bread.

"Sort of, from the law anyway. This is wonderful, Miss Odette."

"I got a hand with baking. I like daisies," she added as she put them in the bottle she'd filled with water. "They got a cheerful face. You gonna give Rufus that bone you brought along, or make him beg for it?"

As Rufus was currently sitting at his feet with one weighty paw on his thigh, Declan decided he'd begged enough. He pulled the bone out of its bag. The dog took it with a surprisingly delicate bite, wagged his tail from side to side twice, like a whip, then plopped down and began to gnaw.

Odette put the flowers in the center of the table, then sat in the chair next to Declan's. "What're you going to do with that big old place, Declan Fitzgerald?"

"All kinds of things. Put it back the way it used to be, as much as I can."

"Then what?"

"I don't know. Live there."

She broke off a corner of her corn bread. She'd already decided she liked the look of him—the untidy hair, the stone-gray eyes in a lean face. And the sound of him—Yankee, but not prim. And his manners were polished but natural and friendly.

Now she wanted to see what he was made of.

"Why?"

"I don't know that, either, except I've wanted to since the first time I saw it."

"And how's the Hall feel about you?"

"I don't think it's made up its mind. Have you ever been inside?"

"Hmm." She nodded. "Been some time ago. Lotta house for one young man. You got you a girl back up there in Boston?"

"No, ma'am."

"Handsome boy like you, past thirty. Not gay, are you?"

"No, ma'am." He grinned as he lifted his glass of tea. "I like girls. Just haven't found the right fit yet."

"Let me see your hands." She took one in hers, turned it over. "Still got city on them, but you're taking care of that right quick." Her thumb passed over healing blisters, scrapes, the ridge of forming callus. "I got some balm I'll give you before you go, keep these blisters from troubling you. You got a strong hand, Declan. Strong enough that you changed your fate. Took yourself a new road. You didn't love her."

"I'm sorry?"

"This woman." Odette smoothed her fingernail over the side of his palm. "The one you stepped back from. She wasn't for you."

Frowning, he leaned closer, stared down at his own hand. "You see Jessica on there?" Fascinating. "Does she end up with James?"

"What do you care? She didn't love you, either."

"Well, ouch," he said and laughed a little.

"You've got love coming, the kind that'll knock you flat on your behind. It'll be good for you."

Though she continued to stroke her thumb over his palm, her gaze lifted to his face. Her eyes seemed to deepen. It seemed he could see worlds in them.

"You've got strong ties to Manet Hall. Strong, old ties. Life and death. Blood and tears. Joy, if you're strong enough, smart enough. You're a clever man, Declan. Be clever enough to look front and back to find yourself. You're not alone in that house."

His throat went dry, but he didn't reach for his tea. He didn't move a muscle. "It's haunted."

"What's there's kept others from settling in. They'd say it was the money, the time or some such, but what's in that house frightened them away. It's been waiting for you."

The chill shot up his spine in a single, icy arrow. "Why?"

"That's for you to find out." She gave his hand a squeeze, then released it, picked up her tea.

He curled his fingers into his tingling palm. "So you're, like, a psychic?"

Amused, she rose to bring the pitcher of tea to the table. "I see what I see from time to time. A little kitchen magic," she said as she refilled the glasses. "It doesn't make me a witch, just a woman." She noted his glance at the silver cross she wore, tangled with colored beads around her neck. "You think that's a contradiction? Where do you think power comes from, *cher*?"

"I guess I never thought about it."

"We don't use what the good Lord gave us, whatever talent that might be, we're wasting his gift." She angled her head, and he saw she wore earrings as well. Fat blue stones dangling from tiny lobes. "I hear you called Jack Tripadoe about maybe doing some plumbing work in that place of yours."

"Ah . . ." He struggled to shift his brain from the fantastic to the practical, while his palm continued to vibrate from the skim of her fingers. "Yes. My friend Remy Payne recommended him."

"That Remy." Her face lit, and any mystery that had been in it vanished. "He's a caution. Jack, he's a cousin of my sister's husband's brother's wife. He'll do good work for you, and if he doesn't give you a fair price, you tell him Miss Odette's gonna want to know why."

"I appreciate that. You wouldn't happen to know a plasterer? Somebody who can handle fancy work?"

"I'll get you a name. It'll cost you a pretty bag of pennies to put that place back to what it was and keep it that way."

"I've got a lot of pennies. I hope you'll come by sometime so I can show you around. I can't make corn bread, but I can manage the tea."

"You got a nice manner, *cher*. Your mama, she raised you right."

"Would you mind writing that down, signing it? I can mail it to her."

"I'm going to like having you around," she declared. "You come back to visit anytime."

"Thank you, Miss Odette." Reading his cue, he got to his feet. "I'm going to like having you around, too."

The sun beamed across her face as she looked up at him. The angle of it, the amusement in her dark eyes, the teasing curve of lips, shot him back to the dim bar in the Quarter. "She looks so much like you."

"She does. You got your eye on my Lena already?"

He was a little flustered to realize he'd spoken out loud, so he tried a grin. "Well, we established I like girls, right?"

She gave the table a little slap to punctuate the laugh as she rose. "I like you just fine, Declan."

He liked her, too. Enough that he decided to buy a couple of chairs after all, so she'd have somewhere to sit when she came by. He'd find something on Saturday, he thought as he went back to prepping the kitchen walls. He could hunt some down in the afternoon, before he was due to have dinner with Remy and Effie.

Then, he'd cap off the evening with a drink at Et Trois.

And if Lena wasn't working that night, he'd just walk back out and throw himself in front of a speeding car.

———————

He worked until well after dark, then treated himself to a beer along with his Hungry-Man chicken dinner. He ate sitting on a sawhorse and admiring the progress of the kitchen.

The walls were stripped, repaired and prepped for paint. His pencil marks on them indicated the measurements of the cabinets he would start to build the next day. He'd even tried his hand at pointing up the bricks in the hearth, and didn't think he'd done a half-bad job of it. The old pine flooring was exposed and protected now with drop cloths. He'd finally settled on the traffic pattern, and had earmarked the spots for the range and the refrigerator.

If he couldn't find the right china cabinet for the long wall, he'd damn well build that, too. He was on a roll.

He carried a bottle of water upstairs, took his now-traditional nine-minute shower, then stretched out on the bed with his notes, drawings and books. Halfway through adjusting his plans for the front parlor, he conked out.

And woke, shivering with cold, in full dark. The baby had wakened him. The thin cries were still in his ears as he sat straight up with his heart banging like a hammer against his ribs.

He didn't know where he was, only that he was on the floor instead of in bed. And it was cold enough that he could see the white mist of his own breath pluming into the inky dark.

He rolled over, gained his feet. Reaching out like a blind man, he felt at the air as he took a cautious step forward.

Lilies. His body shuddered as he registered the scent. He knew where he was now—in the room down the hall from his own. The room, like the one on the third floor, he'd so carefully avoided over the last several days.

He was in it now, he thought as he took another shuffling step. And though it was insane, he knew he wasn't alone.

"You can scare me. But you won't scare me away."

His fingers brushed something solid. He yelped, snatched them back an instant before he realized it was a wall. Taking several steadying breaths, he felt his way along it, bumped over trim, tapped over glass. Fumbling, he found the knob for the gallery doors and flung them open.

The January air felt warm and heavy against his chilled skin. He stumbled forward, gripped the rail. The night was like the inside of a cave. The old adage was true, he decided. There was no dark like country dark.

When his eyes adjusted to it, he turned back, pulled the door to the room firmly closed.

"This is my house now." He said it quietly, then walked down the gallery, opened the door of his bedroom and went back inside.

S leepwalking?" Remy scooped up another forkful of rice.

"Yeah. I went through it for about six months when I was around eleven." Declan shrugged, but couldn't quite dismiss the weight of it.

He hadn't meant to bring it up, at least no more than in passing. The dinner Effie had fixed in Remy's Garden District apartment was welcome, as was the company. But somehow he'd gone from telling them about the progress of the rehab to his nighttime adventures.

"It must be terrifying," Effie said, "to wake up and find yourself somewhere else."

"Spooky anyway. It's funny I'd end up in the two rooms that make me the most uneasy. Or, I guess it's logical. Some subconscious deal."

"As long as you stay inside the house," Remy put in. "I don't want to hear you've sleepwalked your way into the swamp."

"That's a nice thought. Thanks."

"Remy." Effie slapped his hand. "I think you should see a doctor," she told Declan. "You could take something to help you sleep better."

"Maybe. Been there a week, and it's only happened twice. Anyway, taking a couple of tranqs isn't going to do anything about the ghost."

"It's just drafts and old wood settling."

Remy grinned. "Effie doesn't believe in ghosts."

"Or in tarot cards or reading tea leaves or any such nonsense." Her voice was prim, and just a little defensive.

"My girl, she's very grounded in the here and the now."

"Your girl just has good sense," she shot back. "Dec, it just stands to reason you'd have some strange feelings, staying way out there in that big old house all alone. And I bet you're not eating right, either. You ought to live here with Remy for a while, until you get used to things."

"She won't." Remy jerked his head in Effie's direction.

"I'll live with you when we're married, and not before."

"Oh, but, *chère*. May's so far away. I miss you when you're not here." He took her hand, kissing it lavishly as he spoke.

"Tell you what, Effie, you come out and stay with me for a few nights. Strictly platonic," he said with a grin as Remy narrowed his eyes. "I bet you shift your stand on ghosts after one or two nights."

"Sorry. I'm a city girl. What do you do out there all by yourself, Declan, when you're not working?"

"Read. And speaking of that, I need to come by the library, see if you can help me dig up more about Manet Hall. I've been taking a few whacks at the garden, too. Take walks. Drove over to visit Miss Odette."

"You met Miss Odette?" Remy asked as he polished off his dinner. "Something, isn't she?"

"I really liked her. Truth is, the house is keeping me so busy I usually drop off by ten at night. I finally got a TV hooked up, and I never think to turn it on. But I did buy a table and chairs this afternoon, and some other things."

It was always a mistake, he chided himself, to let him through the door of an antique shop.

"We're not going to have you locking yourself out there and working yourself to the bone," Effie decided. "I expect you to come into town and see us at least once a week from now on. And, Remy, you should start going out there on Saturdays and giving Dec a hand. Spending too much time alone," she declared as she pushed back from the table. "That's what's wrong with you. Now, y'all ready for pie?"

M aybe she was right, Declan thought as he hunted up a place to park. If she wasn't right, Effie was certainly definite. He'd try mixing it up a little more. He could drive into town once or twice a week for a real meal. Maybe have Remy and Effie out for one—a very informal one.

He could spend an evening reading something other than research.

More, he thought. He was going to gear himself up soon and push himself through the mental block he'd erected about the third-floor room.

He had to park a block and a half from Et Trois, but when he stepped in, saw Lena at the bar, he thought the walk had been worth it.

He couldn't even snag a stool tonight, but he did manage to squeeze between customers and claim a corner of the bar. The music was loud and lively, and so was the crowd.

There was a blond behind the bar tonight in addition to its owner and Dreadlock Guy. Each of them was hopping.

Lena flicked him a glance as she served two drafts and a gin fizz.

"Corona?"

"Better make it a Coke."

She looked just as good as he remembered. Just exactly as good. She wore blue tonight—a shirt that was unbuttoned low and rolled to the elbows. Her lips were still red, but she'd scooped her hair back on the sides with silver combs. He could see the glint of hoops at her ears.

She set a tall glass in front of him. "Where y'at?"

"Ah, I think I'm right here."

"No." She gave him that quick, smoky laugh. "Don't you speak New Orleans, *cher*? When I say 'where y'at,' I'm asking how you're doing."

"Oh. Fine, thanks. Where you at?"

"There you go. Me, I'm fine, too. Busy. Let me know if you want anything else."

He had to content himself with watching her. She worked her third of the bar, filling orders, having a quick word, slipping into the kitchen and out again without ever seeming to rush.

He never considered going home. When a stool freed up, he climbed on, settled in.

It was like being studied by a big, handsome cat, Lena thought. Steady and patient and just a little dangerous. He nursed his Coke, took a refill, and was still sitting when the place began to thin out.

She swung by again. "You waiting for something, handsome?"

"Yeah." He kept his eyes on hers. "I'm waiting."

She wiped up a spill with her bar rag. "I heard you went by to see my grandmama."

"A couple of days ago. You look like her."

"They say." Lena tucked the end of the rag in her back pocket. "You go over there so you could lay on your Yankee charm and she'd put in a good word for you with me?"

"I was hoping that'd be a side benefit, but no. I went over because she's a neighbor. I expected she was an *old* neighbor—elderly woman, living alone—and thought she'd like to know someone was around who could give her a hand with things. Then I met her and realized she doesn't need me to give her a hand with anything."

"That's nice." Lena let out a breath. "That was nice. Fact is, she could do with a strong back now and again. Dupris, honey?" she called out with her gaze locked on Declan's. "You close up for me, okay? I'm going on home."

She pulled a small purse from behind the bar, slung its long strap over her shoulder.

"Can I walk you home, Lena?"

"Yeah, you can do that."

She came out from behind the bar, smiled when he opened the door for her.

"So, I hear you're working hard on that house of yours."

"Night and day," he agreed. "I started on the kitchen. I've made serious progress. Haven't seen you near the pond in the mornings."

"Not lately." The truth was she'd stayed away deliberately. She'd been curious to see if he'd come back. She strolled down the sidewalk.

"I met Rufus. He likes me."

"So does my grandmama."

"What about you?"

"Oh, they like me fine."

She turned toward the opening of a tall iron gate when he laughed. They moved into a tiny, paved courtyard with a single iron table and two chairs.

"Lena." He took her hand.

"This is where I live." She gestured back toward the steps leading to the second-floor gallery he'd admired the first night.

"Oh. Well, so much for seducing you with my wit and charm on the long walk home. Why don't we—"

"No." She tapped a finger on his chest. "You're not coming up, not tonight. But I think we'll get this out of the way and see what's what."

She rose on her toes, swayed in. Her hand slipped around to the back of his neck as she brought his mouth down to hers.

He felt himself sink. As if he'd been walking on solid ground that had suddenly turned to water. It was a long, steep drop that had a thousand impressions rushing by his senses.

The silky slide of her lips and tongue, the warm brush of her skin, the drugging scent of her perfume.

By the time he'd begun to separate them, she eased back.

"You're good at that," she murmured, and laid a fingertip on his lips. "I had a feeling. 'Night, *cher.*"

"Wait a minute." He wasn't so shell-shocked he couldn't function.

He grabbed her hand. "That was practice," he told her, and spun her stylishly into his arms.

He felt the amused curve of her lips against his and, running his hands up her back, into her hair, let himself drown.

Whoops! That single thought bounced into her head as she felt herself slip. His mouth was patient, but she felt the quick flashes of hunger. His hands were gentle, but held her firmly against him.

The taste of him, like something half remembered, began to seep into her blood.

Someone opened the door of the bar. Music jumped out, then shut off again. A car gunned by on the street behind her, another blast of music through the open windows.

Heat shimmered over her skin, under it, so that the hands she rested on his shoulders trailed around, linked behind his neck.

"Very good at it," she repeated, and turned her head so her cheek rubbed his. Once, then twice. "But you're not coming up tonight. I have to think about you."

"Okay. I'll keep coming back."

"They always come back for Lena." *For a while*, she thought as she eased away. "Go on home now, Declan."

"I'll just wait until you get inside."

Her brows lifted. "Aren't you the one." Because it was sweet, she kissed his cheek before she walked to the steps and headed up.

When she unlocked her door and glanced back, he was still there. "You have sweet dreams now, *cher*."

"That'd be a nice change," he muttered when she closed the door behind her.

# FIVE

MANET HALL

JANUARY 2, 1900

I t was lies. It had to be lies, of the cruelest, coldest nature. He would not believe, *never* believe that his sweet Abby had run away from him. Had left him, left their child.

Lucian sat on the corner of the bed, trapped in the daze that had gripped him since he'd returned home two days before. Returned home to find the Hall in an uproar, and his wife missing.

Another man. That's what they were saying. An old love she'd met in secret whenever Lucian had gone into New Orleans on business.

Lies.

He had been the only man. He had taken an angel to wife, a virgin to their wedding bed.

Something had happened to her. He opened and closed his hand over the watch pin he'd given her when he'd asked her to marry him. Something terrible.

But what? What could have pushed her to leave the house in the night?

A sick relation, he thought as he rose to pace and pace and pace.

But he knew that wasn't the case. Hadn't he ridden like a wild man into the marsh, to ask, to demand, to beg her family, her friends, if they knew what had become of her?

Even now people were searching for her, on the road, in the swamp, in the fields.

But the rumors, the gossip, were already rushing along the river.

Lucian Manet's young wife had run off with another man.

And he could hear the whispers behind the whispers. *What did he expect? Cajun trash. Likely that girl-child got started in the bayou and she passed it off as his.*

Horrible, vicious lies.

The door opened. Josephine hadn't bothered with even a cursory knock. Manet Hall was hers, now and always. She entered any room at her whim.

"Lucian."

He spun around. "They've found her?" He'd yet to change the clothes soiled from his last search, and hope shone through the dirt on his face.

"They have not." She closed the door at her back with a testy snap. "Nor will they. She is gone, and is probably at this moment laughing at you with her lover."

She could almost believe it. Soon, she thought, it would be the truth.

"She did not run away."

"You're a fool. You were a fool to marry her, and you remain a fool." She strode to the armoire, threw it open. "Can't you see some of her clothes are missing? Hasn't her maid reported as much?"

All he could see was the blue ball gown with the flounces and rosettes she'd been so proud of.

"The maid is mistaken." But his voice shook.

"You're mistaken. What of her jewelry?" Josephine pulled the leather box from the shelf, tossed the lid up. "Where are the pearls you gave her for Christmas? The diamond bracelet you bought her when she had the child?"

"Someone stole them."

On a sound of disgust, Josephine upended the jewelry on the bed. "She took whatever sparkled the most. A girl of her type knows nothing but glitter. She bewitched you, caused you to embarrass your family, your name, now she has disgraced us all."

"No." He squeezed his eyes shut as his heart ripped to pieces. "She wouldn't leave me. She would never leave Marie Rose."

"However much affection she might have had for the child, I doubt either she or her lover wanted to be saddled with a baby. How do you know, Lucian, that the child is yours?"

The red rage of fury stained his cheeks. "How can you ask such a question? How could you have lived in the same house with her for a year, and say such a thing about her?"

The doubt, Josephine thought coldly, had been planted. She would help it bloom. "Because I did live in the same house with her, but I wasn't blinded by lust or bewitched by whatever spell she put on you. This is your fault as much as hers. If you had satisfied your appetites as other men, paid her, given her a few trinkets, we would not have this new scandal on our hands."

"Paid her. Like a whore. Like Julian pays his women." Lucian stepped forward, so angry his hands trembled. "My wife is not a whore."

"She used you," Josephine said in a vicious whisper. "She took your dignity, and smeared ours. She came into this house a servant, and left it with the spoils of her deception. Like a thief in the night, with her child crying behind her."

She gripped his arms and shook. "You tried to change what cannot be changed. You expected too much of her. She could never have been mistress of Manet Hall." *I am.* "At least she had the sense to know it. Now, she's gone. We will hold our heads up until the gossip dies down. We are Manets, and we will survive this."

She turned away, walked to the door. "I expect you to make yourself presentable and join the family for dinner. Our lives have been disrupted long enough."

Alone, Lucian sat on the bed and, with the watch pin in his hand, fell to weeping.


I gotta hand it to you, boy." With his hands on his hips, Remy turned a circle in the kitchen. "You made a hell of a mess here."

"Come back in a couple weeks," Declan called out from the adjacent dining room, where he'd set up what he thought of as his carpentry shop.

Effie lifted a corner of the drop cloth. "The floor's going to be beautiful. It's a blank canvas," she said as she looked around the gutted kitchen. "He had to wipe it clean so he could paint the right picture."

"Effie, ditch that moron and come live here with me."

"You stop trying to make time with my girl." Remy walked to the doorway. Declan stood at a power saw, a tool belt slung at his hips and a carpenter's pencil behind his ear. It looked to Remy as if his friend hadn't used a razor in a good three days.

And damned if the scruffy, handyman look didn't suit him.

"You got something you want me to do around here, or should we just stand around admiring how manly you look?"

"I could sure use one or two laborers." He ran the saw through wood with a satisfying buzz and a shower of sawdust, switched it off before he glanced over. "You really up for it?"

"Sure." Remy slung an arm around Effie's shoulder. "We'll work for beer."


Four hours later, they sat on the gallery outside the freshly painted kitchen. Effie, dwarfed in the old denim shirt Declan had given her for a smock, had freckles of paint on her nose. The beer was cold and crisp, and on Declan's countertop stereo, Foghat was taking a slow ride.

As he worked his latest splinter out of his thumb, Declan decided it didn't get much better.

"What's that bush blooming out there?" He gestured toward the wreck of gardens.

"Camellia," Effie told him. "These gardens are a sin, Dec."

"I know. I've got to get to them."

"You can't get to everything. You ought to get someone out here to clean it up."

"Big Frank and Little Frankie." Remy took a long swallow of beer. "They'd do the job for you. Do good work."

"Family business?" He always trusted family businesses. "Father and son?"

"Brother and sister."

"A brother and sister, both named Frank?"

"Yeah. Frank X.—that's for Xavier—he's got him some ego. Named both his kids after him. I'll give you the number. You tell them Remy told you to call."

"I'm going to go clean up." Effie looked down at her paint-speckled hands. "Is it all right if I wander around the house some?"

"Sweetheart." Declan took her hand, kissed it. "You can do anything you want."

"Good thing I saw her first," Remy commented as Effie went inside.

"Damn right."

"Seems to me you got your mind on another woman, the way you keep looking toward the bayou."

"I can't have Effie unless I kill you, so I'm courting Miss Odette as a testament to our friendship."

"Yeah, you are." With a laugh, Remy leaned back on his elbows. "That Lena, she tends to stir a man up, get him thinking all kinds of interesting things."

"You got a girl."

"Don't mean my brain stopped working. Don't you worry, though, Effie's all I want." He let out a long sigh of a contented man. "Besides, Lena and me, we did our round some time back."

"What do you mean?" Declan set his beer back down and stared at his friend. "You and Lena. You . . . and Lena?"

Remy winked. "One hot, sweaty summer. Must've been close to fifteen years ago. Ouch." He leaned up to rub his heart. "That hurts. I was about . . . yeah, I was seventeen, just graduated high school. That'd make her fifteen, seems to me. We spent some memorable evenings in the backseat of my old Chevy Camaro."

He noted Declan's brooding look. "Hey, I saw her first, too. I was in a hot trance over that girl, a good six months. Thought I'd die if I didn't have her. You know how it is at seventeen."

"Yeah. I know how it is at thirty-one, too."

Remy chuckled. "Well, I mooned over her, danced around her, sniffed at her heels. Took her to the movies, for long drives. To my senior prom. God, what a picture she was. Then one moonstruck June night, I finally got her clothes off in the back of that Camaro. It was her first time." He shot Declan a look. "You know, they say a woman never forgets her first. You got your work cut out for you, *cher.*"

"I think I can do better than a randy teenager." Despite, he admitted, the fact that she made him feel like one. "What happened between you?"

"Drifted is all. I went up North to school, she stayed here. Fever burned itself out, and we slid into being friends. We are friends, Dec. She's one of my favorite people."

"I know a warning when I hear one. You want all the girls, Remy?"

"Just thinking to myself that I'd hate to see two of my friends hurt each other. The two of you, boy, you come with a lot of baggage."

"I know how to store mine."

"Maybe. God knows she's worked hard to keep hers locked in the attic. Her mother—" He broke off when Effie screamed.

Beer spewed over the floor when Remy kicked the bottle over as he leaped up. He was through the kitchen door one stride ahead of Declan and shouting Effie's name.

"Upstairs." Declan veered left and charged up the kitchen stairway. "She's upstairs."

"Remy! Remy, come quick!"

She sat on the floor, hugging her arms, and threw herself into Remy's the instant he crouched beside her. "Baby, what happened? Are you hurt?"

"No. No. I saw . . ." She turned her face into his shoulder. "In there. On the bed in there."

Declan looked at the open door. The only bed in there was the one he'd imagined. Slowly, he pushed the door open the rest of the way. He could see the layer of dust on the floor, where it had been disturbed when Effie had started to go in. The sun beamed through the windows onto nothing but wood and faded wallpaper.

"What did you see, Effie?" Declan asked.

"On the bed. A woman—her face. She was dead."

"Baby." Staring into the room, Remy stroked her hair. "There's nothing in there. Look now. There's nothing there."

"But I saw . . ."

"Tell me what you saw." Declan knelt down beside her. "What did you see in there?"

"I saw . . ." She shuddered, then pressed her lips into a firm line. "Help me up, Remy."

Though her face was stark white, she got to her feet and stepped to the doorway.

"Effie darling, you're shaking. Let's get you downstairs."

"No. No, wait." Her eyes were wide, and her heart continued to beat wildly as she scanned the room. "I couldn't have seen anything. It's an empty room. Just an empty room. I must've imagined . . ."

"A tester bed? Blue drapes? A chest of drawers and mirrored bureau. A woman's vanity and a blue chaise. Gaslight sconces, candles on the mantel and a framed picture."

"How do you know what I saw?"

"Because I saw it, too. The first day I was here. I smelled lilies."

"White lilies in a tall vase," Effie continued, and a tear trickled down her cheek. "I thought it was odd, and sort of sweet, that you'd have flowers in there. Then I thought, for just a minute, well, how did he fix this room up so beautifully, why didn't he mention it? And I stepped in and saw her on the bed. I'm sorry. I really need some air."

Without a word, Remy scooped her off her feet.

"My hero," she murmured as he carried her toward the stairs.

"You gave me a hell of a fright, *chère*. Declan, you get my girl some water."

For a long moment, Declan stared into the room. Then he followed them down.

He fetched a glass of water, took it out to the gallery where Remy sat with Effie cradled in his lap.

"How do you feel about ghosts now?"

She took the water, sipped while she studied Declan over the rim. "I imagined it."

"A white robe over the chaise. A silver brush set, some sort of gold and enamel pin."

"Watch pin," she said quietly. She let out a shuddering breath. "I can't explain it."

"Can you tell me about the woman?"

"Her face was all bruised and bloody. Oh, Remy."

"Ssh now." He stroked her hair, gathered her closer. "You don't have to think about it. Let her be, Declan."

"No, it's all right." Taking slow breaths, Effie laid her head on Remy's shoulder. Her eyes met Declan's and held. "It's just so strange, so awful and strange. I think she was young, but it was hard to tell. Dark hair, a lot of dark, curling hair. Her clothes—nightgown—it was torn. There were terrible bruises on her neck—like . . . God, like she'd been strangled. I knew she was dead. I screamed and stumbled back. My legs just gave out from under me."

"I need to find out who she was," Declan declared. "There's got to be a way to find out who she was. Family member, servant, guest. If a young woman died violently in there, there's a record somewhere."

"I can do some research." Effie lowered the water and managed a smile. "That's my job, after all."

"If there was a murder, it seems we'd have heard stories over the years." Remy shook his head. "I never have. Honey, I'm going to take you home."

"I'm going to let you." Effie reached out, touched Declan's arm. "Come on with us. I don't know if you should be staying here."

"I've got to stay. I want to stay."

Needed to stay, he thought when he was alone and the whooshing sound of his nail gun echoed through the dining room. He wasn't just restoring the house, he was making it his own. If a murdered girl was part of it, then she was his, too.

He wanted to know her name, to know her story. Where had she come from? Why had she died? Maybe he'd been meant to come here, to find those things out.

If those images, those feelings, had driven others away, they were only locking him in.

He could live with ghosts, Declan thought as he ran his hand over the side of his first completed cabinet. But he wouldn't rest until he knew them.

But when he finally called it a day and went to bed, he left the lights on.

For the next few days, he was too busy to think about ghosts or sleepwalking, or even those nights out he'd promised himself. The electrician and plumber he'd hired were hard at work with their crews. The house was too full of noise and people for ghosts.

Frank and Frankie, who were as alike as their names, with beefy shoulders and mud-colored hair, trudged around his gardens, made mouth noises that may have been approval or disgust. Little Frankie seemed to be the brains of the operation, and after an hour's survey gave Declan a bid for clearing out underbrush and weeds. Though he wondered if they intended to retire on the profit from the job, Declan trusted Remy and hired them.

They came armed with shovels, pickaxes and mile-long clippers. From the dining room where he worked on cabinets, Declan could hear the lazy rise and fall of their voices, the occasional thump and tumble.

When he glanced out, he noticed that the tangle was disappearing.

The plasterer Miss Odette sent him was a rail-thin black man whose name was Tibald, and his great-grandpappy, so Declan was told, once worked as a field hand for the Manets.

They toured the house with Tibald scribbling in a tiny, dog-eared notepad. When they reached the ballroom, Tibald looked up at the ceiling with a dreamy expression.

"I always think I've put a picture in my head that isn't there," he said. "Don't think I'd ever get used to seeing this kind of work."

"You've been in here before."

"Have. The Rudickers took a bid for me on plasterwork. They'd be the people you bought the Hall from. They had big, fine ideas, the Rudickers. But they never did much about them. Anyhow, they were going to hire someone from Savannah. So I heard."

"Why?"

Tibald just kept smiling at the ceiling. "They had those big, fine ideas, and didn't see how locals could put a polish on them. Seems to me they figured the more money they spent, the higher the gloss. If you know what I mean."

"Yeah, I get it. The way I look at it, you hire local, you're liable to get people who're more invested in the job. Can you repair and duplicate this kind of work?"

"I did the plasterwork in the Harvest House down on the River Road. I got pictures out in my truck, like a reference. You maybe want to take a look at them, maybe go on down to Harvest House and take a study. They give public tours and hold fancy events there now. Do some work in New Orleans, in Baton Rouge and Metairie. Can give you names."

"Let's take a look at the pictures."

One look at the before and after shots of various cornices, walls, medallions, showed Declan his man was an artist. For form, he asked for a bid, and after promising to have one written up by the end of the week, Tibald offered his hand.

"I admit, I'd love to get my hands on that ballroom." Tibald glanced back over at the house. "You doing any work on the third floor?"

"Eventually."

"Maybe you want to talk to my sister, Lucy. She cleans houses."

"I'm a long way from needing a housekeeper."

Tibald laughed, took out a pack of Big Red chewing gum. "No, sir, I don't mean that kind of clean." He offered Declan a stick before taking one himself, folding it in half, and sliding it into his mouth. "Spirit clean. You got some strong spirits in that place." He chewed contemplatively. "'Specially on the third floor."

"How do you know?"

"Feel it breathing on my neck. Can't you? When the Rudickers were working on the place, they lost two laborers. Those men just hightailed it out and kept on going. Never went back. Could be one of the reasons they looked farther afield for workers here."

Tibald shrugged, chewed his Big Red. "Could be the reason they never finished up those big, fine ideas."

"Do you know what happened on the third floor?"

"Nope. Don't know of anyone who does. Just know a few who wouldn't go up there, no matter what you paid them. Any plasterwork needs doing on the third floor, you give my sister, Lucy, a call first."

They both turned at the sound of a car coming down the drive. "That's Miss Lena's car, and Miss Odette with her." Tibald's grin spread as the ancient MG stopped beside his truck.

"Afternoon, ladies." Tibald walked to the passenger's side to open the door for Odette. "Where y'at?"

"Oh, fine and well, Tibald. How's that family of yours?"

"Nothing to complain about."

Lena climbed out as Declan opened the door. Her jeans were intriguingly snug, worn with a shirt the color of polished turquoise. "My grandmama thought it was time to pay a call." She scanned the drive, noted the number of pickups. "What did you do, *cher*? Hire yourself an army?"

"Just a battalion." She smelled of jasmine, he thought. She smelled of night. He had to concentrate on basic manners or swallow his gum. "Can I give you a tour?"

"Mmm. We'll get to it. Tibald, you say hey to Mazie for me, won't you?"

"I will. Gotta be on my way. I'll get that bid to you, Mr. Fitzgerald."

"Declan. I'll be looking for it. Miss Odette." Declan took her hand as Tibald climbed into his truck. She wore a cotton dress the color of ripe squash, and a dark green sweater against the mid-winter chill. Today's socks matched it.

She smelled of lavender and jingled with her chains and bracelets. Everything about her relaxed him. "Welcome to Manet Hall. Such as it is."

Odette winked at Lena when Declan kissed her hand. "We'll take a look at it when we've finished out here. Heard you hired Big Frank and Little Frankie," she said, nodding toward their pickup. "How're they working out for you?"

"They seem to be doing the job. I don't know how." He studied the patchy front gardens with his thumbs hooked through his belt loops. "I can't catch them actually doing anything, but I blink and a couple truckloads of underbrush are gone. Would you like to walk around the grounds?"

"I would. Lena honey, get those spirit bottles out of the trunk. We'll hang them on these live oaks to start."

"Spirit bottles?"

"To keep the evil spirits away." Lena began lifting bottles half filled with water from her trunk.

"Should I be worried about evil spirits?" Declan asked.

"An ounce of prevention." And taking two, Odette moved off toward the trees.

"Spirit bottles," Declan reported, lifting one. He'd seen them hanging outside the shotgun house. "Just how do they work?"

"It's an old voodoo trick," Lena told him. "The clanking sound they make scares the evil spirits away."

Testing, he bumped two together. It sounded pleasant enough, he thought, and not particularly scary. "You believe in voodoo?"

"I believe in that ounce of prevention." She strolled off, small and curvy, to join her grandmother.

Voodoo or old glass bottles, he liked the way they looked hanging from his trees. And when he tapped two together again, he liked the sound they made.

It took nearly an hour to wind their way around the house and into it as there had to be conversations with the landscapers, inquiries about their family, speculation on the weather, discussion of the garden.

When he finally got them into the kitchen, Odette fisted her hands on her hips and nodded. "That's a good color, like a nicely baked pastry crust. Most men, they don't know anything but white. Brings out these good pine floors."

"I should have the cabinets ready to install next week." He gestured toward the dining room. "I'm using pine there, too. With glass fronts."

Lips pursed, Odette walked in, ran her hand over a cabinet. "This is nice work, Declan. You got a talent."

"Thanks."

"And it makes you happy."

"It sure does. Would you like to go into the parlor? I've got a table in there. We'll have some tea." He glanced up as something heavy hit the floor above. "Sorry about the noise."

"Work's rarely a quiet activity. Lena and I will just wander along, if you don't mind. We'll find the parlor."

"You can't miss it. It's the only room with a table."

"He's a very nice young man," Odette commented as she and Lena walked out of the dining room.

"He is."

"Good-looking, too."

"Very."

"Got a hot eye for you, *chère*."

Now Lena laughed. "He does."

"What're you going to do about it?"

"I'm still thinking. Lord, what a place." Lena trailed her hands over a wall. "Doorways wide enough to drive a car through. It makes you cry to see how it's been let go."

"Let go? I don't know. Seems to me it's just been waiting. Isn't this just like a man," she said when they stepped into the parlor. "Living with one table and two chairs. Bet he hasn't fixed a decent meal for himself since he got here."

Lena cocked an eyebrow. "Grandmama, you're not going to make me feel sorry enough for him to cook his dinner." Amused, Lena wandered to the window. "It's beautiful, what you see from here. Imagine what it would've been like to stand here when the house was in its glory. Horses coming through the *allée*, those funny old cars rumbling up the drive."

"It'll be beautiful again. But it needs a woman—just like that boy needs one."

Lena toyed with the little key that hung around her neck. "I said I'm still thinking. Chilly in here yet," she added. "Needs a fire going."

"I'll build one," Declan told her as he came in with a pitcher of over-steeped tea and plastic cups.

I t was a good hour, Declan thought. And not counting Remy and Effie, his first real company.

He liked having them there, the female presence in his parlor with the fire he'd built crackling cheerfully and the late afternoon sun fighting through the dust on the windows.

"I'm going to come back," Odette told him, "to see your kitchen when it's finished."

"I hope you'll come back often. I'd be glad to show you the rest of the house."

"You go on and show Lena. Me, I'm going to walk on home."

"I'll take you home, Grandmama."

"No, you stay awhile." However casual her tone, there was a sly look in her eye. "I want to walk, then it'll be time for my nap." As she started to rise, Declan got up, offered his hand. And made her smile. "You got a pretty manner about you. You come back and see me when you're not busy. I'll make you some *sauce patate*—potato stew—before you get so skinny your clothes fall off your bones."

"I got the phones hooked up." He dug in his pocket for a scrap of paper, found a pencil in his shirt pocket and wrote down the number. "If you need anything, just call."

"Yes, indeed, a very pretty way." She turned her cheek up, inviting his kiss. When he walked her to the door, she gestured for him to lean down again. "I approve of you sparking my Lena. You'll have a care with her, and most don't."

"Is that your way of telling me I don't have a chance with you, Miss Odette?"

She laughed and patted his cheek. "Oh. If I was thirty years younger, she'd have a run for her money. Go on now, and show her your house."

He watched her walk by the trees with the spirit bottles dangling.

"You like my grandmama," Lena said from the parlor doorway.

"I'm love-struck. She's wonderful. Listen, it's a long walk to her place. You ought to—"

"If she wants to walk, she walks. There's no stopping her from doing anything." She wandered to the front door to stand beside him. "Look there, it's Rufus come to walk her home. I swear, that dog has radar when it comes to her."

"I kept hoping he'd come around." He turned to Lena. "Bring you with him. I started out two nights this week to go to your place, and talked myself out of it."

"Why's that?"

"There's persistence, and there's stalking." He reached up to twirl her hair around his finger. "I figured if I could hold out until you came by here, you wouldn't consider getting a restraining order."

"If I want a man to go away, I tell him to go away."

"Do men always do what you tell them?"

Her lips curved into that cat smile that made him want to lick at the little black mole. "Mostly. You going to show me this big house of yours, *cher*?"

"Yeah." He caught her chin in his hand, kissed her. "Sure. By the way." Now he took her hand as he led her toward the staircase. "I have Miss Odette's permission to spark you."

"Seems you need my permission, not hers."

"I intend to charm you so completely, we'll slip right by that step. Fabulous staircase, isn't it?"

"It is." She trailed a red-tipped finger along the banister. "Very grand, this place of yours, Declan. And from what I've seen of it, I realize you're not a rich lawyer after all."

"Ex-lawyer. And I don't follow you."

"You got enough to put this place back, to keep it—you do mean to keep it?"

"Yeah, I do."

"Then you're not rich. Step up from rich. You're wealthy. Is that the case?"

"Well, money's not a problem. It doesn't buy happiness, either."

She stopped on the landing and laughed. "Oh, *cher*, you think that, you just don't know where to shop."

"Anytime you want to help me spend some of it."

"Maybe." She looked down over the banister toward the grand foyer. "You'll be needing furniture eventually. There's some places I know."

"You have a cousin?"

"One or two." She lifted her eyebrows at the noise and cursing from the end of the long hall.

"Plumber," Declan explained. "I had him start on the master bath. It was . . . well, it was an embarrassment of avocado. If you know anyone who wants some really ugly bathroom fixtures, let me know."

He started to steer her away from the door of what he now thought of as his ghost room. But she turned the knob, opened it. Declan found himself holding his breath as she stepped inside.

"Cold in here." She hugged her arms, but couldn't stop the shiver. "You ought to try to save the wallpaper. It's a pretty pattern. Violets and rosebuds."

She was halfway to the gallery doors when she stopped, and the shiver became a shudder. The feeling that poured into her was grief. "It's a sad room, isn't it? It needs light. And life."

"There's a ghost. A woman. I think she was killed here."

"Do you?" She turned back to him. Her face was a little pale, her eyes a little wide. "It doesn't feel . . . violent. Just sad. Empty and sad."

Her voice had thickened. Without thinking, he went in, went to her. "Are you all right?"

"Just cold."

He reached down to rub her arms, and at the contact, felt a quick shock.

With a half-laugh, she stepped back. "I don't think that's what Grandmama meant by you sparking me, *cher*."

"It's this room. There's something strange in this room."

"Ghosts don't worry me. Shouldn't worry you. They can't hurt you." But she walked to the door, had to fight a need to rush her steps.

She wandered through the other bedrooms, but experienced none of that grief, the dread, the dragging loneliness that had driven her out of the first.

At the door to Declan's room, she smiled. "Well, not so rough in here. You got taste, *cher*." She poked her head in the bathroom, where workmen clanged and cursed. "Which is more than I can say for whoever did this bathroom. That you there, Tripadoe? Your mama know you eat with that mouth?"

She leaned on the doorjamb, spent a few minutes chatting with his plumbers. And Declan could stand back and just look at her.

It was pathetic, he told himself, this puppy-dog crush he'd developed.

And when she glanced at him over her shoulder, he felt the jolt right down to the soles of his feet.

"Why don't I show you the ballroom. It's going to be the showcase."

"Sure, I'd like to see that." But when they started out, she gestured toward the stairs. "What's up there?"

"More empty rooms. Storage, some of the servants' quarters."

"Let's have a look."

"It's nothing special." He made a grab for her hand, but she was already going up.

"Can you get to the belvedere from here?" she asked. "I used to look over at that and imagine standing up there."

"It's easier from the—don't!"

His sharp order had her hand freezing on the dull brass knob of the nursery. "What's wrong? You got a woman chained in here? All your secrets locked inside here, *cher*?"

"No, it's just . . ." He could feel the panic rising, burning the base of his throat. "There's something wrong with that room."

"Something wrong with most of them," she tossed back, and opened the door.

He was right. It hit her immediately, that same throbbing sense of grief and loss and loneliness. She saw walls and floor and windows, dust and neglect. And felt as if her heart were breaking.

Even as she started to speak, the cold swept in. She felt it blow over her skin like breath, pass through her hair like fingers.

"It's the center," she declared, though she was far from sure what she meant, or how she knew. "Can you feel it? Can you?"

He swayed in the doorway. Bearing down, he dug his fingers into the jamb. His fear was unreasonable, spearing like knives into bones. It was his house, he reminded himself grimly. His goddamn house. He took a step inside, then a second.

The room spun. He heard a scream, saw Lena's face, the alarm that leaped over it. He thought he saw her mouth move, form his name. Then his vision grayed, white spots dancing through the mist.

"Declan. Here now, *cher*. Here, darling."

Someone was stroking his hair, his face. He felt lips brush over his. He opened his eyes to a blur, so simply closed them again.

"No, you don't." She tapped his cheeks now with fingers that trembled lightly. He'd gone down like a tree under the ax, right after his face had drained of color and his eyes had rolled back white. "Open your eyes."

"What the hell happened?"

"You fainted."

His eyes opened now, focused on her face. Mortification warred with a vague nausea. "Excuse me, men don't faint. We do, on occasion, pass out or lose consciousness. But we do not faint."

The breath she let out was a shudder of relief. He may have cracked his head, she thought, but he'd come to with his wits about him. "I beg your pardon. You passed out. Cold. Hit the floor hard enough to bounce your head off it." She leaned down again, brushed her lips over the raw scrape on his forehead. "You're going to have a bruise, *bébé*. I couldn't catch you. I guess if I had, you'd've taken us both down."

She had managed to roll him over, and now stroked her fingers over his pale cheeks. "You do a lot of passing out?"

"Usually I have to drink myself into oblivion first, which I haven't done since college. Look, at the risk of embarrassing myself twice in a matter of minutes, I really have to get the hell out of this room."

"Okay. All right. Can you stand? I don't think I can haul you up, *cher*. You're a pretty big guy."

"Yeah." He got to his knees, tried to catch his breath, but it was clogging again. It felt like a semi had parked on his chest, and his heart was tripping to try to find a beat. He staggered up, stumbled.

Lena wrapped an arm around his waist, took as much of his weight as she could manage. "One step, two steps. We'll just get you downstairs so you can lie down."

"It's okay. I'll be okay." His ears were ringing. The minute he got out of the room, he headed for the steps, then just sank down and put his head between his knees. "Jesus."

"There now, sweetheart." She stroked his hair.

"Close that door, would you? Just close it."

She hurried back, slammed it shut. "You get your breath back, then we'll get you down and into bed."

"I've been wanting to hear you say that since the first time I laid eyes on you."

The clutching in her belly eased a bit. "You're coming back, aren't you?"

"Better." He could breathe again, and the nausea was fading. "I'll just have to go beat someone up, or shoot some small mammal so I can regain my manhood."

"Let me see your face." She tipped his head back, studied him. "Still a little pale, but you got some color again. I bet Grandmama's right. You don't eat. What'd you eat today, *cher*?"

"Wheaties. Breakfast of champions." He managed a wan smile. "Doesn't seem to have worked."

"I'm going to fix you a sandwich."

"Really?" The simple pleasure of the idea trickled through him. "You're going to cook for me?"

"A sandwich isn't cooking."

"In my world it is. Lena, that room . . ."

"We'll talk about that—after you get something in your stomach."

The pickings were sparse. One look in the secondhand refrigerator currently gracing the dining room had Lena sending Declan one long, pitying look. "How old are you? Twelve?"

"I'm a guy," he replied with a shrug. "Guys' grocery habits never age. I've got peanut butter to go with that jelly." He glanced around the room. "Somewhere."

He also had one lonely slice of deli ham, two eggs, some anemic-looking cheese and a half bag of pre-cut salad. "Looks like I'm going to cook for you after all. Where's the stove?"

"Right here." He tapped the top of a microwave.

"Well, we'll make do. Bowl? Knife? Fork?"

"Ah . . ." He rooted through the box of his current kitchen supplies and came up with the plastic ware.

"Honey, this is just sad. Sit yourself down, and Lena'll take care of you. This one time," she added.

He hitched onto a sawhorse and watched her beat some eggs, shred in the ham, the cheese, sprinkle in some of the contents of the salad bag.

"You got any herbs, *cher*? Any spices?"

"I got salt and pepper. That counts," he muttered when she sighed. "Explorers discovered whole continents for salt."

"Grew up with a cook, didn't you?"

"Yeah. So?"

"What did you do when you moved out on your own?"

"Takeout, delivery and the microwave. With those three things, no man need starve."

She set the bowl in the microwave, programmed it, then turned back to him. "Living out here, you'd best hire yourself another cook."

"Name your price."

"You're a funny man, Declan." His color was good now, his eyes clear. The knot that had been in her belly since he'd pitched over loosened. "How come you don't have a woman?"

"I had one, but it turned out I didn't really want her."

"That so?" She opened the oven when it beeped, whisked the egg mixture around, then programmed it again. "What happened?"

"Remy didn't tell you?"

"He doesn't tell me everything."

"I was engaged. I called it off three weeks before the wedding, which makes me, you know, a cad. A lot of people in Boston are still cursing my name."

He was trying to make it a joke, she thought, but wasn't quite pulling it off. "Is that why you left?"

"No, it's why I realized I could leave."

"You didn't love her."

"No, I didn't love her."

"It makes you sad to say that." She drew out the bowl, got a fresh plastic fork, then handed it to him. His eyes were stormy again, she noted. With regret. "She love you?"

"No. We looked good together. We were used to each other. She thought we wanted the same things."

"But you didn't."

"We never did. And the closer it got to D Day, the more I saw my life just . . . narrowing down until I was squeezed into this tiny slot. No room, no air. No light. I realized I felt the same way about marrying Jessica as I did about practicing corporate law, and if that was going to be the rest of my life, I could jump off a bridge or get out of the slot while I had the chance."

She brushed the hair from his forehead. "It was braver to get out than to jump."

"Maybe. This is good," he said as he scooped up more egg. "Why don't you have a man?"

She cocked her head. "Who says I don't?"

He grabbed her hand before she could turn away. "I need to know if you do."

She looked down at his hand, back to his face. "Why is that?"

"Because I can't stop thinking about you. I can't get you out of my head, from under my skin. Because every time I see you, my heart kicks in my chest."

"You're good at that, too. At saying things that stir a woman up." If it had just been that, just a matter of being stirred by him, she might have eased in between those long legs and satisfied them both. But this wasn't a simple man, she thought.

Being with him wouldn't be simple.

"Eat your eggs," she told him, and slid her hand free of his. "Why are you starting with the kitchen if you eat peanut butter and don't have a single dish to your name?"

"I've got dishes, just not the kind you wash. The kitchen's the heart of a house. The house where I grew up—this big, old wonderful house with big, wonderful rooms. We had that cook, but it was the kitchen where we ended up if there was a crisis or a celebration, or just something to talk over. I guess I want that here."

"That's nice." She leaned back on a cabinet to study him. "You want to have sex with me, *cher*?"

His pulse lurched, but he managed to hop nimbly off the sawhorse. "Sure. Just let me kick the plumber out." He loved the way she laughed. "Oh, you didn't mean right this minute. That was, what, like a true or false type of question. Let me check." He laid his fingers on his wrist. "Yeah, I'm still alive, so the answer is true."

She shook her head, took the empty bowl from him and dumped it in the box he was using for trash. "You're an interesting man, Declan. And I like you."

"Uh-oh. Hold on a minute." He glanced around, picked up the screwdriver lying on a plank. "Here you go," he said as he handed it to her.

"What's this for?"

"So you can plunge it into my heart when you tell me you just want to be friends."

"I bet Jessica's still kicking herself for letting you slip away. I do want to be friends." She turned the screwdriver in her hand, then set it down again. "I don't know yet if I just want to be friends. I have to think about it."

"Okay." He took her arms, ran his hands up to her shoulders. "Think about it."

She didn't try to pull away, but lifted her face so his lips could meet hers. She liked the easy glide from warmth to heat, the fluid ride offered by a man who took his time.

She understood desire. A man's. Her own. And she knew some of those desires could be sated only in quick, hot couplings in the dark.

From time to time, she'd sated hers in just that fashion.

There was more here, and it came like a yearning. Yearnings, even met, could cause a pain desire never could.

Still, she couldn't resist laying her hands on his face, letting the kiss spin out.

Inside her, deep inside her, something sighed.

"Angelina."

He said her name, a whisper of sound, as he changed the angle of the kiss. As he deepened it. A thousand warnings jangled in her brain and were ignored. She gave herself over for one reckless moment, to the heat, to the need. To the yearning.

Then she drew back from all of it. "That's something to think about, all right."

She pressed a hand to his chest when he would have pulled her into him again. "Settle down, *cher.*" She gave him a slow, sleepy smile. "You've got me worked up enough for one day."

"I was just getting started."

"I believe it." She let out a breath, pushed her hair back. "I've got to go. I'm working the bar tonight."

"I'll come in. Walk you home."

However calm his voice, his eyes had storms in them. The sort, she imagined, that would provide a hell of a thrill before they crashed over your head. "I don't think so."

"Lena. I want to be with you. I want to spend time with you."

"Want to spend time with me? You take me on a date."

"A date?"

"The kind where you pick me up at my door and take me out to a fancy dinner." She tapped a finger on his chest. "Take me dancing after, then walk me back to my door and kiss me good-night. Can you handle that?"

"What time do you want me to pick you up?"

She smiled, shook her head. "I'm working tonight. I got Monday night off. Place isn't so busy Monday nights. You pick me up at eight."

"Monday. Eight o'clock."

He grabbed her arms again, jerked her against him. There was no glide into heat this time, but a headlong dive into it.

Oh yeah, she thought, it would be quite a thrill before the crash.

"Just a reminder," he told her.

A warning, more like, she thought. He wasn't nearly as tame as he pretended to be. "I won't forget. See you later, *cher*."

"Lena. We didn't talk about what happened upstairs."

"We will," she called back, and kept going.

She didn't breathe easy until she was out of the house. He wasn't going to be as simple to handle as she'd assumed. The good manners weren't a veneer, they went straight through him. But so did the heat, and the determination.

It was a package she admired, and respected.

Not that she couldn't handle him, she told herself as she got into her car. Handling men was one of her best skills.

But this man was a great deal more complicated than he seemed on the surface. And a great deal more intriguing than any she'd met before.

She knew what men saw when they looked at her. And she didn't mind it because there was more to her than what they saw. Or wanted to see.

She had a good brain, a strong back and a willingness to use both to get what she wanted. She ran her life the same way she ran her bar. With an appreciation for color and a foundation of order beneath the chaos.

She glanced in her rearview mirror at Manet Hall as she drove away. It worried her that Declan Fitzgerald could shake that foundation the way no one had before.

It worried her that she might not find it so easy to shore up the cracks when he walked away.

They always walked away. Unless you walked first.

He fell asleep thinking of Lena, and drifted into dreams of her. Strong, full-bodied dreams where she lay beneath him, moved under him with hard, quick jerks of her hips. Damp skin, like liquid gold. Dark chocolate eyes, and red, wet lips.

He could hear the sound of her breath, the catch and release, little gulps of pleasure. He smelled her, that siren's dance of jasmine that made him think of harems and forbidden shadows.

He dropped deeper into sleep, aching for her.

And saw her hurrying along a corridor, her arms full of linens. Her hair, all that gorgeous hair, was ruthlessly pinned back, and that tempting body covered from neck to ankle in a baggy dress covered with tiny, faded flowers.

Her lips were unpainted and pressed tightly together. And in the dream, he could hear her thoughts as if they were his own.

She had to hurry, to get the linens put away. Madame Manet was already up and about, and she didn't care to see any of the undermaids scurrying in the hallways. If she wasn't quick, she could be noticed.

She didn't want Madame to notice her. Servants stayed employed longer when they were invisible. That's what Mademoiselle LaRue, the housekeeper, said, and she was never wrong.

She needed the work. Her family needed the money she could bring in, and oh, but she loved working in the Hall. It was the most beautiful house she'd ever seen. She was so happy and proud to have some part of tending to it.

How many times had she stared at it from the shadows of the bayou? Admiring it, longing for a chance to peek in the windows at all the beauty inside.

And now she *was* inside, responsible in some small way for the tending of that beauty.

She loved to polish the wood, to sweep the floors. To see the way the glass sparkled after she'd scrubbed it.

In his dream, she came out of the corridor through one of the hidden doors on the second level. Her eyes tracked everywhere as she hurried along—the wallpaper, the rugs, the wood and glass. She slipped into a dressing room, put the linens away in a cupboard.

But as she turned back toward the door, something caught her attention, and she tiptoed to the window.

He saw, as she saw, the riders approaching through the grand oaks of the *allée*. He felt, as she felt, a stumble of heart as her gaze locked on the man who rode a glossy chestnut. His hair was gold, and streamed as he galloped. Straight as a soldier in the saddle, with a gray coat over his broad shoulders and his black boots shining.

Her hand went to her throat, and she thought, quite clearly, *Here is the prince come home to his castle.*

She sighed, as girls sigh when they fall foolishly in love. He smiled, as if smiling at her, but she knew it was the house that caused that joy to fill his handsome face.

With her heart pounding, she hurried out of the room, back to the servants' door and into the maze.

The young master was home, she thought. And wondered what would happen next.

D eclan woke with a jolt, in the dark, in the cold. He smelled damp and dust and felt the hard wood of the floor under him.

"What the hell?" Groggy, disgusted, he stretched out a hand and hit wall. Using it for reference, he got to his feet. He felt along, waiting to come to a corner, to a door. It took a moment to register that the wall wasn't papered.

He wasn't in his ghost room this time. He was in one of the servants' passageways, as the girl in his dream had been.

Somehow, he thought, he'd walked as she had walked.

The idea of stumbling around in the dark until he found a way out had little appeal, but slightly more than the idea of spending the next few hours in there, waiting for dawn.

He inched along. By the time he felt the seam of a door, he was drenched in sweat.

He shoved his way out, offered up a prayer of thanksgiving when he gulped in fresher air, saw in the faint light the shape of the second-level corridor.

There were cobwebs in his hair; his hands and feet were filthy.

If this kept up, he told himself, he was going to see a doctor and get some sleeping pills. Hoping the night's adventures were over, he went to wash, to chug down water for his burning throat. And to lock himself in the bedroom.

# SEVEN

D eclan took the load of books out of Effie's arms, then kissed her cheek. "You didn't have to come all this way to bring me these. I'd've come to you."

"I didn't mind. I had a meeting cancel, and some time to spare. And the fact is . . ." Breathing slowly, she turned a circle. "I had to prove to myself I wouldn't just turn tail and run when I started to come in this place."

"Doing okay?"

"Yeah." She let out one of those slow breaths, then nodded briskly. "Doing just fine." Then she frowned at the shadows dogging his eyes. "Now, you, on the other hand, look worn out."

"Not sleeping so well." But he didn't want to talk about the dreams, the sleepwalking. The sounds that so often wakened him in the dead of night. "Come on back to the kitchen so I can show off. I've got some lemonade—not from actual lemons, but it's wet and it's cold."

"All right." She touched his arm in a kind of silent acknowledgment and, because she understood, lightened her tone. "I've only got about half an hour, but I've got some information for you. Information and speculation. What's going on in here?"

She glanced into the front parlor. There were papers stacked on the floor, books spread open, a pile of paint and fabric samples.

"My next project. I thought I'd start on a room where people could actually sit down when it was finished. What kind of information?"

"On the Manets. Facts were easy enough," she said as they continued through the house. "Henri Manet married Josephine Delacroix. They both came from wealthy and prominent Creole families. Henri was active politically. It's rumored his father profited handsomely by running supplies during the War Between the States. The family became staunch Republicans during Reconstruction, and again it's rumored they used their power and influence to buy votes and politicians. Oh my goodness, Dec, just look at this!"

She stepped into the kitchen and beamed at the base cabinets he'd installed. "Why, they're beautiful."

He hooked his thumbs in his back pockets, and his grin was crooked. "You sound surprised."

"Well, I am, but in a very complimentary sort of way. Remy can barely hammer a nail in the wall to hang a picture." She ran her hand over the wood, opened and closed a door. "These are really fine. You must be so proud."

"I'm feeling pretty pleased with myself. Counter guys just left. I'm going with solid surface. It'll look like slate. Ordered this giant Sub-Zero refrigerator—for reasons I've yet to explain to myself—and a range, a dishwasher. I'm going to make panels so all you'll see is wood."

He set the books down on a sheet of plywood he had over the top of the base cabinets. "Want that lemonade?"

"That'd be nice." She wandered into the dining room behind him. He had two of the top cupboards finished, and a third started. "My, aren't they going to be pretty. You must be working night and day."

*Losing weight,* she thought. *Getting a gaunt look in your face.*

"Better than sleepwalking." He was jittery, and found himself dipping hands into his pockets again to keep them still. "Tell me more, Effie."

"All right." She suppressed the urge to fuss over him and went back to the facts. "The original owners had lost most of their money during the war. They hung on, selling off parcels of land, or renting it out to sharecroppers. Their politics and the Manets' were in opposition. There was a fire, burned the house down to the ground. Wiped them out. The Manets bought the land, and had this place built. They had two sons, twins. Lucian and Julian. Both went to Tulane, where Lucian did very well and Julian majored, you could say, in drinking and gambling. Lucian was the heir, and was meant to run the family businesses. Most of the Manet money had dwindled, but Josephine had a considerable inheritance. Both sons died before their twenty-third birthday."

Declan handed her a glass. "How?"

"Here we have rumors and speculation." She sipped. "The strongest speculation is they killed each other. No one seems to know why, family argument gone violent. It's said Lucian went into New Orleans, on his mother's orders, to fetch his brother back out of one of the brothels he frequented. Julian didn't want to be fetched, they argued, and one of them—odds are on Julian here—pulled a knife. They fought, struggled for the knife, were both wounded. Julian died on the spot. Lucian lingered about another week, then somehow got out of bed, wandered outside, and fell into the pond, where he drowned."

The pond, he thought, choked with lily pads, steaming with mists at dawn. "That had to be rough on the parents."

"The father's heart gave out a few years later. Josephine lived several years more, but had a reversal of financial fortune. She had the house, some land, but had all but run out of money. Again, speculation is Julian had gambled a large part of it away, and it was never fully recouped."

"Remy said there was a granddaughter. Lucian's or Julian's?"

"There's speculation there, too. Though the records show that Lucian married an Abigail Rouse in 1898, and that a daughter was born the next year, there's no record of Abigail's death. After Lucian was killed, the Manets declaimed the child, legally. Had her written out of the will. She was, apparently, raised by the Rouses. I can't find anything on Abigail Rouse beyond the legal records of her birth and her marriage."

"Maybe they kicked her out when Lucian died."

"Maybe. I talked to Remy about it." She wandered toward the windows, stared out at the messy gardens. "He's a little vague, but seems to recall hearing stories about how she ran off with another man."

She turned back. "Stories from the Rouse side differ sharply. They lean toward foul play. You'd get a fuller picture of her, and what might've happened, if you talk to someone from the Rouse or Simone families."

"A clear picture about a girl who ran off or died a hundred years ago."

"Honey, this is the South. A hundred years ago was yesterday. She was seventeen when she married Lucian. She was from the bayou. His family could not have approved of such a match. I doubt her life in this house was rosy. Running off might've been just what she did. On the other hand . . . I saw something, someone, in that room upstairs. I don't believe in that sort of thing. Didn't." Effie fought back a shiver. "I don't know what I think about it now, but I sure would like to find out."

"I'll ask Miss Odette. And Lena. I've got a date with her Monday."

"Is that so?" The idea brightened her mood. "Looks like we'll have more rumor and speculation." She handed him back the glass. "I have to get on. I'm sending Remy out here tomorrow to give you a hand and keep him out of my hair. I've got a fitting for my wedding gown and other bridal things to take care of."

"I'll keep him busy."

"Why don't you come back into town with him?" she said as she headed out. She wanted to lock her arm around his and tug him through the door and away. "We'll have some dinner, go out to the movies."

"Stop worrying about me."

"I can't help it. I think about you way out here, alone in this house, with that room up there." She glanced uneasily up the staircase. "It gives me the shivers."

"Ghosts never hurt anybody." He kissed her forehead. "They're dead."

B ut in the night, with the sound of the wind and rain, and the bang of spirit bottles, they didn't seem dead.

H e gave himself Sunday. He slept late, woke to a sky fighting to clear, and spent another hour in bed with the books Effie had brought him.

She'd marked pages she felt would have the most interest for him. He scanned and studied old photographs of the great plantation houses. And felt a thrill race through him as he looked at the old black-and-white picture of Manet Hall in its turn-of-the-century splendor.

Formal photographs of Henri and Josephine Manet didn't bring the same thrill. With those there was curiosity. The woman had been undeniably beautiful, very much in the style of her day with the deep square bodice of her ball gown edged with roses, and the high, feathered comb adorning her upswept hair.

The gown, tucked into an impossibly small waist, gave her a delicacy accented by the sweep of the brocade skirts, the generously poofed sleeves that met the long white gloves.

But there was a coldness to her face, one Declan didn't think was a result of the rigidity of the pose or the quality of the print. It overwhelmed that delicacy of build and made her formidable.

But it was the photograph of Lucian Manet that stopped him in his tracks.

He'd seen that face, in his dream. The handsome young man with streaming gold hair, riding a chestnut horse at a gallop through the moss-laced oaks.

The power of suggestion? Had he simply expected the face in the dream to be real, and was he projecting it now onto the doomed Lucian?

Either way, it gave him the creeps.

He decided he'd drive into New Orleans and treat himself to a few hours' haunting the antique shops.

Instead, less than an hour later, he found himself walking into Et Trois.

It did a strong Sunday-afternoon business, he noted. A mix of tourists and locals. He was pleased he was learning to distinguish one from the other. The jukebox carried the music now, a jumpy number by Beau-Soleil that do-si-doed around the chatter from tables and bar.

The scent of food, deeply fried, reminded his stomach he'd skipped breakfast. Recognizing the blond tending bar from his second visit, Declan walked up, tried a smile on her. "Hi. Lena around?"

"Back in the office. Door to the right of the stage."

"Thanks."

"Anytime, cutie."

He gave the door marked PRIVATE a quick knock, then poked his head in. She was sitting at a desk, working at a computer. Her hair was clipped back and made him want to nibble his way up the nape of her neck.

"Hi. Where y'at?"

She sat back, gave a lazy stretch of her shoulders. "You're learning. What're you doing at my door, *cher*?"

"I was in the neighborhood and thought I'd see if you'd let me buy you lunch. Like a prelude to tomorrow night."

She'd been thinking about him, more than was comfortable. Now here he was, all tall and rangy and male. "I'm doing my books."

"And I've interrupted you. Don't you hate that?" He came in anyway, sat on the edge of the desk. "Bought you a present."

It was then that she noticed the little gift bag he carried. "I don't see how you could've fit a new car in there."

"We're working up to the car."

She kept her eyes on his a moment longer as she took the bag from him. Then she dipped in for the box. It was wrapped in gold paper, with a formal white bow. She took her time with it; she'd always believed the anticipation was as important as the gift.

The bow and ribbon she tucked neatly back into the bag, and after she'd picked at the top, slid the box out, folded the paper precisely.

"How long does it take you to open your presents Christmas morning?" he asked.

"I like taking my time." She opened the box, felt her lips twitch, but kept her expression sober as she took out the grinning crawfish salt and pepper shakers. "Well now, aren't they a handsome pair?"

"I thought so. They had alligators, too, but these guys seemed friendlier."

"Are these part of your charm campaign, *cher*?"

"You bet. How'd they work?"

"Not bad." She traced a finger over one of the ugly grins. "Not bad at all."

"Good. Since I've interrupted you, and charmed you, why don't you let me feed you? Pay you back for the eggs."

She eased back in her chair, swiveled it as she considered. "Why do I get the feeling, every time I see you, I should start walking fast in the opposite direction?"

"Search me. Anyway, my legs are longer, so I'd just catch up with you." He leaned over the desk, lifted his brows. She was wearing a skirt, a short one. His legs might've been longer, but they wouldn't look half as good in sheer stockings. "But you could eat up some ground with those. How come you're dressed up?"

"I'm not dressed up. Church clothes. I've been to Mass." Now she smiled. "Name like yours, I figure you for a Catholic boy."

"Guilty."

"You been to Mass today, Declan?"

He could never explain why a question like that made him want to squirm. "I'm about half-lapsed."

"Oh." She pursed her lips. "My grandmama's going to be disappointed in you."

"I was an altar boy for three years. That ought to count."

"What's your confirmation name?"

"I'll tell you if you come to lunch." He reached over for the crawfish, made them dance over her desk. "Come on, Lena, come out and play with me. It's turned into a nice day."

"All right." Mistake, her practical mind said, but she got to her feet, picked up her purse. "You can buy me lunch. But a quick one." She leaned over, saved her file, and closed down her computer.

"It's Michael," he said, holding out a hand. "Declan Sullivan Michael Fitzgerald. If I was any more Irish, I'd bleed green."

"It's Louisa. Angelina Marie Louisa Simone."

"Very French."

"*Bien sûr.* And I want Italian." She put her hand in his. "Buy me some pasta."


From his previous visits Declan knew you had to work very hard to find a bad meal in New Orleans. When Lena led the way to a small, unpretentious restaurant, he didn't worry. All he had to do was take one sniff of the air to know they were going to eat very well.

She waved a hand at someone, pointed to an empty table, and apparently got the go-ahead.

"This isn't a date," she said to him when he held her chair.

He did his best to look absolutely innocent, and nearly succeeded. "It's not?"

"No." She eased back, crossed her legs. "A date is when we have a time arranged and you pick me up at my house. This is a drop-on-by. So tomorrow, that's our first date. Just in case you're thinking of that three-date rule."

"We guys don't like to think you women know about that."

Her lips curved. "There's a lot y'all don't like to think we know about." She kept her eyes on his, but lifted up a hand to the dark-haired man who stopped at the table. "Hey there, Marco."

"Lena." He kissed her fingers, then handed her a menu. "Good to see you."

"This is Remy's college friend from Boston. Declan. I brought him by so he can see how we do Italian food here in the Vieux Carre."

"You won't do better." He shook Declan's hand, gave him a menu. "My mama's in the kitchen today."

"Then we're in for a treat," Lena said. "How's your family, Marco?"

Declan saw how it happened then. When she shifted in her chair, lifted her face, looked at Marco, it was as if the two of them were alone on a little island of intimacy. It was sexual, there was no question about it, but it was also . . . attentive, he decided.

"Good as gold. My Sophie won a spelling bee on Friday."

"That's some bright child you got."

They chatted for a few moments, but Declan entertained himself by watching her face. The way her eyebrows lifted, fell, drew together according to the sentiment. How her lips moved, punctuated by that tiny mole.

When she turned her head, he shook his. "Sorry, did you say something to me? I was looking at you. I get lost."

"They got some smooth talkers up North," Marco said.

"Pretty, too, isn't he?" Lena asked.

"Very nice. Our Lena here's having the seafood linguini. You know what you want, or you need some time to decide?"

"You don't get the same." Lena tapped a finger on the menu Declan had yet to read. "Else it's no fun for me picking off your plate. You try the stuffed shells, maybe. Mama makes them good."

"Stuffed shells, then." He had a feeling he'd have tried crushed cardboard if she'd requested it. "Do you want wine?"

"No, because you're driving and I'm working."

"Strict. San Pellegrino?" He glanced at Marco.

"I'll bring you out a bottle."

"So . . ." She tucked her hair behind her ear as Marco left them. "What're you up to today, *cher*?"

"I thought I'd hit some of the antique stores. I'm looking for a display cabinet for the kitchen, and stuff to stick in it. I thought I might go by and see Miss Odette on the way back. What does she like? I want to take her something."

"You don't have to take her anything."

"I'd like to."

Lena hooked an arm over the back of her chair, drummed her fingers on the table as she studied him. "You get her a bottle of wine, then. A good red. Tell me something, *cher*, you wouldn't be using my grandmama to get to me, would you?"

She saw the temper flash into his eyes—darker, hotter than she'd expected from him. Should've known, she thought, that all that easy manner covered something sharp, something jagged. It was impressive, but more impressive was the lightning snap from mild to fury, and back to mild again.

A man who could rein himself in like that, she decided, had a will of iron. That was something else to consider.

"You've got it backwards," he told her. "I'm using you to get to Miss Odette. She's the girl of my dreams."

"I'm sorry."

"Good, you should be."

Lena waited until their water and bread were served. His tone had raised her hackles. Mostly, she could admit, because she'd deserved the quick slap. Folding her arms on the table, she leaned toward him.

"I am sorry, because that was nasty. I'm going to tell you something, Declan, nasty words have a habit of popping right out of my mouth. I don't always regret saying them. I'm not a sweet-mannered, even-tempered sort of woman. I don't have a trusting nature. I've got good points, but I've got just as many bad. I like it that way."

He mimicked her posture. "I'm single-minded, competitive and moody. I've got a mean temper. It takes a lot to get it going, which is a fortunate thing for the general population. I don't have to have my way in the little things, but when I decide I want something, really want it, I find a way to get it. I want you. So I'll have you."

She'd been wrong. He hadn't snapped back to mild. Anger was still simmering behind his eyes. As the one person she tried to be honest with at all times was herself, she didn't bother to pretend it didn't excite her.

"You're saying that to make me mad."

"No, that's just a side benefit." He eased back, picked up the basket of bread and offered it. "You want to fight?"

Feeling sulky, she picked out a piece. "Maybe later. Getting riled up spoils my appetite. Anyway." She shrugged, bit into the bread. "You don't want to go by Grandmama's today. She's over visiting her sister this afternoon."

"I'll stop in later this week. I got the kitchen counters installed. Remy gave me a hand, so to speak, with the wall units yesterday. It should be finished in a couple of weeks."

"Good for you." She wanted to brood, and could see by his amused expression that he knew it. "You been back up on the third floor?"

"Yeah." He'd had to prime himself with a good shot of Jim Beam first, but he'd gone back. "Didn't fall on my face this time, but I had a major panic attack. I'm not prone to panic attacks. I found out more about the Manet family history, but there are pieces missing. Maybe you've got them."

"You want to know about Abigail Rouse."

"That's right. How much do—" He broke off because she'd turned her attention away from him and back to Marco, who brought out their pasta. He reminded himself as they fell into a lazy discussion about the food, that the wheel turned more slowly in the South.

"How much do you know about her?" he asked when they were alone again.

Lena rolled up a forkful of pasta, slid it between her lips. She sighed deep, swallowed. "Mama Realdo. She's a goddess in the kitchen. Try yours," she ordered, and leaned over to sample from his plate.

"It's great. Best meal I've had since a microwave omelette."

She smiled at him, one long, slow smile that lodged in his belly. Then went back to eating. "I know the stories that came down in my family. Nobody can say for sure. Abigail, she was a maid in the big house. Some of the rich families, they hired Cajun girls to clean for them, to fetch and carry. Story is that Lucian Manet came home from Tulane and fell in love with her. They ran off and got married. Had to run off, because nobody's going to approve of this. His family, hers."

She broke off a chunk of bread, nibbled on it as she studied him. "Mixing classes is an uneasy business. He moved her into the Hall after, and that was an uneasy business, too. People say Josephine Manet was a hard woman, proud and cold. People started counting on their fingers, but the baby, she don't come for ten months."

"That room upstairs. It must've been the nursery. They'd have kept the baby there."

"Most like. There was a nursemaid. She married one of Abigail's brothers later. Most of the stories about the Hall come from her. It seems a couple days before the end of the year, Lucian was off in New Orleans on business. When he came back, Abigail was gone. They said she'd run off with some bayou boy she'd been seeing on the side. But that doesn't ring true. The nursemaid, her name was . . . Claudine, she said Abigail never would've left Lucian and the baby. She said something bad had to have happened, something terrible, and she blamed herself because she was off meeting her young man down by the river the night Abigail disappeared."

A dead girl on the tester bed in a cold room, Declan thought, and the pasta lodged in his throat like glue. He picked up the fizzy water, drank deep. "Did they look for her?"

"Her family looked everywhere. It's said Lucian haunted the bayou until the day he died. When he wasn't looking there, he was in town trying to find a trace of her. He never did, and didn't live long himself. With him gone, and the twin his mother favored by all accounts, dead as well, Miss Josephine had the baby taken to Abigail's parents. You've gone pale, Declan."

"I feel pale. Go on."

This time, when she broke off a hunk of bread, she buttered it, handed it to him. Her grandmama was right, Lena thought, the man needed to eat.

"The baby was my grandmama's grandmama. The Manets cast her out, claiming she was a bastard and no blood of theirs. They brought her to the Rouses with the dress she had on, a small bag of crib toys. Only thing she had from the Hall was the watch pin Claudine gave to her, which had been Abigail's."

Declan's hand shot out to cover hers. "Is the pin still around?"

"We hand such things down, daughter to daughter. My grandmama gave it to me on my sixteenth birthday. Why?"

"Enameled watch, hanging from small, gold wings."

Color stained her cheeks. "How do you know?"

"I saw it." The chill danced up his spine. "Sitting on the dresser in the bedroom that must have been hers. An empty room," he continued, "with phantom furniture. The room where Effie saw a dead girl laid out on the bed. They killed her, didn't they?"

Something in the way he said it, so flat, so cold, had her stomach dropping. "That's what people think. People in my family."

"In the nursery."

"I don't know. You're spooking me some, Declan."

"You?" He passed a hand over his face. "Well, I guess I know who my ghost is. Poor Abigail, wandering the Hall and waiting for Lucian to come home."

"But if she did die in the Hall, who killed her?"

"Maybe that's what I'm supposed to find out, so she can . . . you know. Rest."

He wasn't pale now, Lena thought. His face had toughened, hardened. That core of determination again. "Why should it be you?"

"Why not? It had to be one of the Manets. The mother, the father, the brother. Then they buried her somewhere and claimed she ran away. I need to find out more about her."

"I imagine you will. You've got a mulish look about you, *cher*. Don't know why that should be so appealing to me. Talk to my grandmama. She might know more, or she'll know who does."

She nudged her empty plate back. "Now you buy us some cappuccino."

"Want dessert?"

"No room for that." She opened her purse, pulled out a pack of cigarettes.

"I didn't know you smoked."

"I get one pack a month." She tapped one out, ran her fingers up and down its length.

"One a month? What's the point?"

She put the cigarette between her lips, flicked the flame on a slim silver lighter. As she had with the first bite of pasta, she sighed over that first deep drag. "Pleasure, *cher*. There are twenty cigarettes in a pack, thirty or thirty-one days to a month. 'Cept for February. I dearly love the month of February. Now, I can smoke up the whole pack in a day, and just about lose my mind for the rest of the month. Or I can dole them out, slow and careful, and make them last. Because there's no buying another pack before the first of the month."

"How many do you bum from other people during the month?"

Her eyes glittered through the haze of smoke. "That would be cheating. I don't cheat. Pleasure's nothing, sugar, unless you got the willpower to hold off until you really appreciate it."

She trailed a fingertip over the back of his hand, and for the hell of it, rubbed the side of her foot against his leg under the table. "How are you on willpower?" she asked.

"We're going to find out."


It was dusk when he got back to the house. The back of his four-wheel was loaded with treasures he'd hunted up in antique shops. But the best was the kitchen cabinet he'd found, and had begged and bribed to have delivered the next day.

He carried what he could on the first trip and, when he stepped inside, set everything down in the foyer. He closed the door behind him, then stood very still.

"Abigail." He said the name, listened to it echo through the house. And waited.

But he felt no rush of cold air, no sudden shift in the silence.

And standing at the base of the grand staircase, he couldn't explain how he knew he wasn't alone.

# EIGHT

H e woke to a crashing thunderstorm, but at least he woke in his own bed. Lightning slashed outside the windows and burst a nova of light through the room.

A glance at the bedside clock showed him a minute to midnight. But that had to be wrong, Declan thought. He hadn't gone to bed until after one. Wondering if the storm had knocked out his power, he turned the switch on the bedside lamp.

Light speared out, half blinding him.

"Damn it." He rubbed his shocked eyes, then grabbed the bottle of water he'd set on the table next to the bed. And rising, went out on the gallery to watch the show.

It was worth the price of a ticket, he decided. Lashing rain, pitchfork lightning, and a wind that was whipping through the trees in moans and howls. He could hear the excited clanging of the spirit bottles and the fierce jungle war of thunder.

And the baby crying.

The water bottle slid out of his fingers, bounced at his feet and soaked them.

He wasn't dreaming, he told himself, and reached out to grip the wet baluster. He wasn't sleepwalking. He was awake, fully aware of his surroundings. And he heard the baby crying.

He had to order himself to move, but he walked back into the bedroom, dragged on sweats, checked his flashlight. Barefoot, shirtless, he left the security of his room and started toward the third floor.

He waited for the panic to come—that clutching in the belly, the sudden shortness of breath, the pounding of his heart.

But it didn't come this time. The steps were just steps now, the door just a door with a brass knob that needed polishing.

And the baby wasn't crying any longer.

"Come this far," he grumbled.

His palms were sweaty, but it was nerves instead of fear. He reached out, turned the knob. The door opened with a whine of hinges.

There was a low fire in the hearth. Its light, and the light of candles, danced in pretty patterns over walls of pale, pale peach. At the windows were deep blue drapes with lacy under-curtains. The floor was polished like a mirror with two area rugs in a pattern of peaches and blues.

There was a crib with turned rails, a small iron cot made up with white linen.

She sat in a rocking chair, a baby at her breast. He could see the baby's hand on it, white against gold. Her hair was down, spilling over her shoulders, over the arms of the rocker.

Her lips moved, in song or story he didn't know. He couldn't hear. But she stared down at the child as she nursed, and her face was lit with love.

"You never left her," Declan said quietly. "You couldn't have."

She looked up, toward the doorway where he stood so that for one heart-stopping second, he thought she'd heard him. Would speak to him. When she smiled, when she held out a hand, he took a step toward her.

Then his knees went loose as he saw the man cross the room—pass through him like air—and walk to her.

His hair was golden blond. He was tall and slim of build. He wore some sort of robe in a deep burgundy. When he knelt by the rocker, he stroked a fingertip over the baby's cheek, then over the tiny fingers that kneaded at the woman's breast.

The woman, Abigail, lifted her hand, pressed it over his. And there, surrounded by that soft light, the three of them linked while the baby's milky mouth suckled and the woman gently rocked.

"No. You never left them. I'll find out what they did to you. To all of you."

As he spoke, the door slammed shut behind him. He jolted, spun and found himself plunged back into the dark, with only the lightning blasts and the beam of his flashlight. The weight fell into his chest like a rock, cutting off his air. The room was empty, freezing, and the panic leaped at his throat.

He dragged at the doorknob, his sweat-slicked hands sliding off the icy brass. He could feel his choked gasps wanting to rise into shouts and screams, pleas and prayers. Dizziness drove him down to his knees, where he fumbled frantically with the knob, wrenched and tugged at the door.

When he managed to pull it open, he crawled out on his hands and knees, then lay facedown on the floor with his heart thundering in his chest as the storm thundered over the house.

"Okay, I'm okay. I'm okay, goddamn it, and I'm getting up off the floor and going back to bed."

He might be losing sleep, Declan thought as he got shakily to his feet, but he'd learned a couple of things.

If what he'd seen inside the nursery was truth and not some self-generated fantasy, Abigail Rouse Manet hadn't left Manet Hall of her own free will.

And he had more than one ghost on his hands.

She was probably making a mistake, Lena thought as she slicked a little black dress down her body. She'd already made several small mistakes where Declan Fitzgerald was concerned. It irritated her, as she rarely made mistakes when it came to men.

If there was one thing she'd learned from her mother, it was how to handle the male species. It was a reverse tutelage. She made a habit of doing exactly the opposite of what Lilibeth did and had done when it came to relationships.

The process had kept Lena heart-whole for nearly thirty years. She had no desire, and no intention, of putting herself into a man's hands. Metaphorically speaking, she thought with a smirk as she painted her lips.

She liked being in the right man's hands well enough, when she was in the mood to be handled.

A woman who didn't enjoy sex, in her opinion, just didn't know how to pick her partners cannily enough. A smart woman culled out men who were willing and able to be shown how that woman wanted to be pleasured. And a woman pleasured tended to give a man a good, strong ride.

Everybody ended up winning.

The problem was, Declan had the talent for putting her in the mood for sex all the damn time. She was *not* in the habit of being guided by her hormones.

The wisest, safest thing for a woman to do about sex was to be in control of it. To decide the when, the where, the who and how. Men, well, they were just randy by nature. She couldn't blame them for it.

And women who claimed not to try to stir men up were either cold-blooded or liars.

If she'd believed she and Declan were headed toward a simple affair that began and ended with a mutual buzz, she wouldn't have been concerned. But there was more to him than that. Too many layers to him, she thought, and she couldn't seem to get through them all and figure him out.

More, and much more worrying, there was another layer to her reaction to him besides simple lust. That, too, was complicated and mysterious.

She liked the look of him, and the Yankee bedrock sound of his voice. And then he'd gone and hit her soft spot with his obvious affection for her grandmama.

Got her blood heated up, too, she admitted. The man had a very skilled pair of lips.

And when he wasn't paying attention, a wounded look in his eyes. She was a sucker for hurting hearts.

Best to take it slow. She arched her neck and ran the crystal wand of her perfume bottle over her skin. Slow and easy. No point in getting to the end of the road unless you'd enjoyed the journey.

She trailed the wand over the tops of her breasts and imagined his fingers there. His mouth.

It had been a long time since she'd wanted a man quite this . . . clearly, she realized. And since it was too late for a quick, anonymous roll in the sheets, it would be wise to get to know him a little better before she let him think he'd talked her into bed.

"Right on time, aren't you, *cher*?" she commented aloud at the knock on her door. She gave her reflection a last check, blew herself a kiss, and walked to the front door.

He looked good in a suit. Very classy and *GQ*, she decided. She reached out, ran the stone-gray lapel between her thumb and fingers. "Mmm. Don't you clean up nice, *cher*."

"Sorry, all the blood just drained out of my head so the best I can come up with is, wow."

She sent him that sassy, under-the-lashes look and turned a slow circle on stiletto heels. "This work okay for you, then?"

The dress clung, dipped and shimmied. His glands were doing a joyful jig. "Oh yeah. It's working just fine."

She crooked her finger. "Come here a minute."

She stepped back, then slid a hand through his arm and turned toward an old silver-framed mirror. "Don't we look fine?" she said, and her reflection laughed at his. "Where you taking me, *cher*?"

"Let's find out." He picked up a wide, red silk scarf, draped it over her shoulders. "Are you going to be warm enough?"

"If I'm not, then this dress isn't working after all." With this she strode out on her little gallery. She started to hold out a hand for his, then just stared down at the white stretch limo at the curb.

She was rarely speechless, but it took her a good ten seconds to find her voice, and her wits. "You buy yourself a new car, darling?"

"It's a rental. This way, I figure we can both have all the champagne we want."

As first dates went, she thought as he led her down, this one had potential. It only got better when the uniformed driver opened the door and bowed her inside.

There were two silver buckets. One held a bottle of champagne and the other a forest of purple tulips.

"Roses are obvious," he said and pulled a single flower out to offer her. "And you're not."

She twirled the tulip under her nose. "Is this how you charm the girls in Boston?"

He poured a flute of champagne, held it out to her. "There are no other girls."

Off balance, she took a sip. "You're dazzling me, Declan."

"That's the plan." He tapped his glass to hers. "I'm really good at seeing a plan through."

She leaned back, crossed her legs in a slow, deliberate motion she knew would draw his gaze down to them. "You're a dangerous man. You know what makes you really dangerous? It doesn't show unless you take a good look under all the polish."

"I won't hurt you, Lena."

"Oh, hell you won't." But she let out a low, delightful laugh. "That's just part of the trip, sugar. Just part of the trip. And so far, I'm enjoying it."

He went for elegant, Old-World French where the waiters wore black tie, the lighting was muted, and the corner table was designed for intimacy.

Another bottle of champagne arrived seconds after they were seated, telling her he'd prearranged it. And possibly a great deal more.

"I'm told the food is memorable here. The house is early twentieth century," he continued. "Georgian Colonial Revival, and belonged to an artist. A private home until about thirty years ago."

"Do you always research your restaurant's history?"

"Ambience matters. Especially in New Orleans. So does cuisine. They tell me the *caneton a l'Orange* is a house specialty."

"Then one of us should have it." Intrigued, she set her menu aside. He wasn't just fun, she thought. He wasn't just sexy and smart. He was *interesting.* "You choose. This time."

He ordered straight through from appetizers to chocolate soufflé with the ease of a man accustomed to fine dining in exclusive restaurants.

"You have good French, at least for ordering food. Do you speak it otherwise?"

"Yes, but Cajun French can still throw me."

"Have you been to Paris?"

"Yes."

She leaned forward in that way she had, her arms folded on the edge of the table, her gaze fastened to his. "Is it wonderful?"

"It is."

"One day I'd like to go. To Paris and Florence, to Barcelona and Athens." They were hot, colorful dreams of hers, and the anticipation of them as exciting as the wish. "You've been to those places."

"Not Athens. Yet. My mother liked to travel, so we went to Europe every year when I was growing up. Every other to Ireland. We still have family there."

"And what's your favorite?" She rested her elbows on the table and her chin in her laced fingers. "Of all the places you've been."

"Hard to say. The west coast of Ireland, the hills in Tuscany, a sidewalk café in Paris. But at the moment, right here is my favorite place."

"There's that silky tongue again. All right then, tell me about Boston."

"It's a New England harbor city of great historical importance." When she laughed, he sat back and soaked it in. "Oh, that's not what you meant."

"Tell me about your family. You have brothers, sisters?"

"Two brothers, one sister."

"Big family."

"Are you kidding? My parents were pikers in the go-forth-and-multiply area. Mom has six brothers and sisters, my father comes from a family of eight. None of their siblings had less than five kids. We are legion."

"You miss them."

"I do? Okay, I do," he admitted reluctantly. "From this nice, safe distance, I've realized I actually like my family."

"They'll come visit you?"

"Eventually. Everyone will wait for my mother to start actually speaking to me again. In our house if it's not one thing, it's your mother."

She sampled the appetizer he'd ordered for her. She wore no rings, and he wondered why. She had lovely hands, slim, elegant, delicate. The silver key rested against that smooth, dusky skin, and there was a glint of silver at her ears. But her fingers, her wrists were bare. Beautifully bare, he realized, and wondered if the lack of ornamentation was some sort of female ploy to make a man notice every line, every curve, every sweep of her.

It was sure as hell working that way on him.

"You think she's mad at you? Your mama?"

He had to blink himself back to the threads of conversation. "Not mad. Irritated, annoyed, baffled. If she was really angry, she'd be down here in my face, chipping away until I crumbled to her terrifying will."

"Does she want you to be happy?"

"Yes. We love each other like idiots. She'd just be more satisfied if my happiness aligned with her point of view."

Her head angled, and again he caught that wink of silver through the thick, dark curls of her hair. "Why don't you let her know she hurts your feelings?"

"What?"

"If you don't let her know she hurts them, how is she going to stop?"

"I let them down."

"Oh, you did not," she replied, with a kind of impatient sympathy. "You think your family wants you to be miserable and unfulfilled? Married to a woman you don't love, working at a career that you don't want?"

"Yes. No," he answered. "I don't honestly know."

"Then it seems to me you ought to ask them."

"Do you have any siblings?"

"No. And tonight we're going to talk about you. We'll save me for another time. Did you find what you wanted at your antique shops?"

"And then some." More comfortable talking about acquisitions than family, he gave her a blow-by-blow that took them into the main course.

"How do you know what you want before you have the room done?"

"I just do." He moved his shoulders. "I can't explain it. I've got this great davenport on hold for the upriver parlor. That's where I'm starting next, and it's not nearly as big a job as the kitchen. Walls and floors mostly. I want to get a good start on the interiors so I can concentrate on the galleries, the double stairs, have the place painted starting in April, if I'm lucky. That way, we should be able to shift back inside before the summer heat."

"Why are you pushing so hard? The house isn't going anywhere."

"Remember the single-minded, competitive nature I told you about?"

"Doesn't mean you can't relax a bit. How many hours are you putting in in a week?"

"I don't know. Ten, twelve a day generally." Then he grinned and reached for her hand. "You worried about me? I'll take more time off if you'll spend it with me."

"I'm not that worried about you." But she left her hand in his, let it be held against that hard, calloused palm. "Still, Mardi Gras's coming. If you don't take some time to enjoy that, you might as well be in Boston." She looked at the double soufflé their waiter set in the middle of the table. "Oh my. My, my." She leaned forward, closed her eyes, and sniffed. And was laughing when she opened them again. "Where's yours?"


He took her dancing. He'd found a club that played the slow foxtrots and jazzy swings of the thirties, and surprised her by whirling her around the floor until her legs were weak.

"You're full of surprises."

"Bet your ass." He swung her into his arms, had her blood pressure spiking when he ran his hands down her body and gripped her hips. Her body rolled against his, a wave sliding under a wave while a tenor sax wailed.

He dipped her, had her laughing even as her pulse went thick. She let her head fall back, her hair stream down as he lowered his face toward hers. His lips skimmed over her chin, just a hint of teeth, then he swept her up again, circled her, seduced her.

The lights were a warm, smoky blue, and his movements fluid so it was like moving underwater. The yearning she wasn't ready for crawled into her belly. With her eyes half closed, she skimmed a hand into his hair, brought his face closer, that last inch closer so his mouth met hers.

"You fit, Lena. We fit."

She shook her head, turned it so her cheek rested against his. "You make love half as well as you dance, you must have a trail of female smiles in your wake."

"Let me show you." He nipped at her earlobe, and felt her quick shiver. "I want to touch you. I know how your skin will feel under my hands. I dreamed about it."

She kept her eyes closed, tried to lock away the yearning. "Just dance with me. It's getting late, and I want one more dance."


She rested her head on his shoulder in the limo. The music, the wine, the soft lights were all still playing in her head. She felt drenched in romance, and knowing that had been his intention didn't diminish the effect. It only enhanced it.

He was a man who would trouble himself with the details. The large and the small. With the house he'd chosen, with the woman he wanted.

She admired that. Admired him.

"You show a girl a good time, *cher*."

"Let me show you one tomorrow night."

"I work tomorrow night."

"Your next night off, then."

"I'm going to think about that. I'm not being coy, Declan." She sat up so she could look at him. "I don't like coy. I'm being cautious. I can't say I care much for that, either, but where you're concerned I think it's the smart thing to be. And I do like being smart."

As the limo glided to the curb in front of her home, she trailed a finger down his cheek. "Now you walk me to my door, and kiss me good-night."

He carried the silver bucket with the purple tulips. He set them down in front of her door, then framed her face in his hands.

The kiss was sweeter than she'd expected. She'd been prepared for heat, the persuasive, pervasive heat that might melt her resistance. Instead he gave her the sweet, and the gentle, ending the evening as he'd begun it. With romance.

"How about before you go to work?" He lifted her hand to his lips now. "I'll take you on a picnic."

Undone, she stared at him. "A picnic?"

"It should be warm enough. We can spread a blanket by the pond. You can bring Rufus along as chaperone. I like watching him jump in."

"Damn it." She caught his face in her hands now. "Damn it. I want you to go on down to that big white limo."

"Okay." He touched her hair. "I'll just wait until you're inside."

"Go down to the limo," she repeated. "And pay that driver, and tell him to go on home. Then you come back up."

He closed his hands over her wrists, felt the trip of her pulse. "Five minutes. Don't change your mind. Two minutes," he amended. "Time me."

As he bolted down the stairs, she picked up her flowers, let herself inside. If it was a mistake, she thought, it wouldn't be her first. Or her last.

She lit the candles, put on some Billie Holiday. Sex should be easy, she reminded herself. When it was between two unattached adults with, well, at least some affection along with the lust, it should be a celebration.

Whether or not she'd been persuaded, the decision was hers. There was no point in regretting it before it had even begun.

He knocked. The idea that he would, rather than just walking in, made her smile. Good manners and hot blood. It was an interesting combination. Irresistible.

She opened the door, and Billie Holiday's heartbreak streamed out. Declan slid his hands into his pockets and smiled at her.

"Hi."

"Hi back, handsome." Lena reached out and grabbed his tie. "Come on in here." She tugged, and pulled him in the door. And, walking backward, would have pulled him straight into the bedroom.

But he laid his hands on her hips, drew her to him. "I like your music." He eased her into a dance. "When I can see something besides you, I'll tell you if I like your place."

"Did you take lessons on what to say to have women falling for you?"

"Natural gift." He brushed his lips at each corner of her mouth. Over that sexy little mole. "The streets of Boston are littered with my conquests. It was playing hell with traffic, so the city council asked me to leave." He skimmed his cheek over hers. "I smell you in my sleep. And wake up wanting you."

Her heart began to shiver, like something feeling warmth after a long freeze. "I knew you were trouble, the minute you stepped up to my bar." She stretched under the hand that ran down her back. "I just didn't know how much trouble."

"Plenty." He scooped her off her feet, crushed his mouth to hers until they both moaned. "Which way?"

"Mmm. I've got a number of ways in mind."

What blood was left in his head shot straight down to his loins. "Ha. I meant which way is your bedroom."

With a low laugh, she chewed on his bottom lip. "Door on the left."

He had a number of impressions as he carried her across the room, through the doorway. Vibrant colors, old wood. But most of his senses were wrapped around the woman in his arms. The weight of her, the shape and scent. The surprise that flickered over her face when he set her on her feet beside the bed instead of on it.

"I'd like to take my time with this, if it's all the same to you." He trailed a fingertip down her collarbone, over the lovely curve of breast the dress displayed. "You know, like unwrapping a present."

"I can't say I mind that."

She'd expected a rush—fast hands, hungry mouth—to match the reckless lust she'd seen in his gaze. When his hands took hers, linked fingers, and his lips lay silky on her lips, she remembered how ruthlessly he'd controlled his temper the day before.

It seemed his control reached to other passions as well.

She wasn't prepared for romance. He'd realized it when she'd seen the tulips. More than surprise, there'd been suspicion in her eyes. Just as there was now as he slowed the pace, lingered over the quiet pleasure of a kiss.

Seducing her into bed was no longer enough. He wanted to seduce that suspicion into helpless pleasure.

Her lips were warm and willing. It was no hardship to mate his with them, to float on that lazy slide of tongues while their bodies swayed together as if they were still dancing.

He knew when her fingers went limp in his that she floated with him.

He lowered the zipper of her dress in one slow glide and traced his fingers over the newly exposed flesh. She arched her back, and all but purred.

"You've got good hands, *cher*, and very sexy lips." Watching him now, as he watched her, she loosened the knot of his tie. "Let's see about the rest of you."

There was something about undressing a man in a suit, she thought. The time it took to remove all the layers to get to skin, built anticipation, honed curiosity. He touched her as she unbuttoned his shirt, easing the dress off her shoulders so that it clung, erotically, to the curve of her breasts. He nibbled at her mouth, never hurrying, never groping.

And when she opened his shirt, ran her hands over his chest with a little hum of approval, she felt the heavy beat of his heart under her palms.

"Some build you've got for a lawyer."

"Ex-lawyer." It was like dying, he thought, dying by inches to have those long, slender fingers with those hot red nails running over him. She pinched lightly at his biceps, licked her lips.

"Yes indeed, you're just full of surprises. I like a strong man."

She tapped her nails on his belt buckle, and her smile was female. Feline. "Let's see what other surprises you've got for me."

They were dancing again, the oldest dance, and somehow she'd taken the lead. His stomach muscles quivered when she whipped the belt off, tossed it over her shoulder.

In his mind he saw himself throwing her down on the bed, pounding himself and this outrageous need into her. She'd accept it.

She'd expect it.

Instead, he took both her hands before she could unhook his trousers and lifted them to his lips. Watching her over them, he saw the surprise—and again the suspicion.

"I seem to be falling behind," he said playfully. "And since I've been wondering what you've got on under that dress, I'd like to find out how close my speculations were to reality."

He laid his lips on her bare shoulder, used them to nudge the material down her arm. And blessed the laws of gravity when it slid down and puddled at her feet.

She wore black lace.

She was every man's fantasy. Dusky skin, tumbled hair, full, high breasts barely restrained in that fancy of lace. The slim torso, the gently rounded hips with more midnight lace riding low. Shapely legs in sheer black stockings and man-killer heels.

"Close." The breath was already burning in his lungs. "Very close. What's this?" He traced a fingertip over the tattoo on her inner thigh, just above the lacy edge of her stocking.

"That's my dragon. He guards the gates." She was trembling, and wasn't ready to tremble. "A lot of men think they can get past him. A lot of men get burned."

He stroked his finger up, along that sensitive valley between lace and thigh. "Let's play with fire."

He yanked her against him, devoured her mouth. And when that wasn't enough, whirled her around to scrape his teeth along her shoulder, the side of her neck. With his face buried in her hair he ran his hands up her body, filled them with her lace-covered breasts.

She arched back to him, hooked her arms around his neck and offered. The spin from patient to urgent left her dizzy, brutally aroused and ready to be taken. She felt the greed from him now, and felt her own rise to match it.

His hand slid down, cupped between her legs, pressed, and brought her to the jagged edge of release. Before she could fall, he trailed his fingers down her thigh and with one fast flick, unhooked a garter.

Her breath caught. Her body strained. *"Mon Dieu."*

"When I'm inside you, you won't be able to think about anything else." He unhooked a second garter. "But first, I need to touch you, the way I've been dreaming of touching you." He rubbed his lips over her shoulder, nudged the strap of her bra aside. "Angelina."

He turned her to face him, let his fingers dive into her hair, draw her head back. "You're mine tonight."

Denial, defiance, fought their way through seduction. "I belong to myself."

He scooped her up, laid her back on the bed. "Tonight, we're going to belong to each other."

He closed his mouth over hers, stopping her words, drugging her brain. She turned her head to take a breath, to try to steady herself again. But his lips trailed down to her breast, over flesh, over lace, under it. The long, liquid tugs in her belly loosened her muscles, melted her will.

She yielded, telling herself she was surrendering to her own needs, and not to him.

He felt her give, the softening of her. Heard it in the low, throaty moan that was pleasure and acceptance.

So he took what he'd been aching for since the first moment he'd seen her in the morning mist.

Her body was a treasure, scented skin, female curves. He fed himself on the taste of it in slow sips and long gulps. Then freed her breasts to his hands, his mouth. His blood raged like a firestorm, but he let himself burn and tortured them both.

When he rolled the lace down her hips, she arched. Opened. He traced his fingers over her, watching her face in the candlelight as her eyes closed, her lips trembled on a groan. And when he slid them into her, into the hot wet velvet of her, she bowed up, cried out. Drove him mad.

Pressing his face to her belly, he sent her flying.

Her body was a mass of aches, of joys, with the sharp edge of sensation slicing through like a bolt of light. It burst in her, sent her helplessly hurtling.

She reached for him, closed her hand around him. He was hard as stone. She wanted him inside her as much as she wanted her next breath.

"Now. I want you." She felt him quiver, even as she quivered. Saw herself in his eyes as he rose over her. "I want you to fill me. Fill me up."

He clung to that slippery line of control, and as her legs wrapped around him, slid slowly, very slowly into her. Slid deep when she rose to meet him. Held there with his breath caught in his throat and everything he was lost in her.

Sighs now, and a quick, rushing gasp. They kept their eyes on each other and moved, an almost lazy pace that spread pleasure like a warm pool. Their lips met, and he felt hers curve against his before he lifted his head to see her smile.

Flesh glided over flesh, silky friction. Music, the tragic sob of it from her living room, a sudden celebratory burst of it from the street below, merged together in his head with her quickening breaths.

She tensed beneath him, her head going back to bare the line of her throat for his lips. She tightened around him, shuddered, shuddered.

Once again he buried his face in her hair, and this time, let himself fly with her.

Later, he lay watching the light play on the ceiling, stroking his hand along her back. Drenched in her. "Are you going to let me stay?" he asked. "Or do I catch a cab?"

She stared into the shadows. "Stay."

# NINE

He woke just after daybreak. She'd curved into him in sleep, but he saw that she had her arm between them and a fist curled over her heart. As if she were guarding it, he thought. The little silver key lay against the side of her hand.

He wanted to lift that hand, gently uncurl the fingers. Bare her heart to him, he realized. He'd already lost his to her. Had lost it, he decided, the moment he'd seen her.

It was a jolt, and a shock for a man who'd come to believe he simply wasn't capable of love. Unless it was family or friendship. His personal crisis over Jessica, who everyone—including Jessica—had claimed was perfect for him, had convinced him he'd blown his one chance at a lasting, content relationship with a woman.

It had been tough to swallow for a man who, at the core, believed strongly in family, in home, in marriage. And swallowing it, he realized, had been largely responsible for the restless unhappiness that had trailed after him like a faithful dog for months.

Now he was looking at the woman who was the answer. And he didn't think she was going to be willing to listen to the question.

So, he'd have to persuade her. One way or the other, and sooner or later. Because he'd meant what he'd said the night before. They were going to belong to each other.

He considered waking her up and reminding her how good they were together in bed. He couldn't think of a better way to start the day, especially since she was warm and soft and draped around him.

But it didn't seem quite fair to wake her when they'd barely slept. Her workday started a great deal later than his.

He slid away from her, with no little regret, and eased out of bed. She stirred, sighing in sleep, and rolled into the warmth he'd left behind.

He grabbed his trousers and headed into the shower.

In his opinion, you could tell a lot about a person by their bathroom. Hers was both rigorously clean and indulgent. Thick towels of forest green offset the white fixtures and picked up the small diamond chip pattern scattered through the floor tile.

Lush green plants lined the windowsill, and a trio of daffodils speared out of a slim bottle of pale green.

There were other bottles, jewel colors, and covered boxes that held fragrant oils and lotions, bath salts. She liked fancy soaps, he noted, and kept them in a pretty bowl.

He also discovered her hot water lasted longer than his. He smiled through the bliss of a fifteen-minute shower that steamed up the room like a Turkish bath.

She was still sleeping when he stepped out. Sprawled now over the sheets with the morning sun slanted over the lean length of her naked back. He turned his mind firmly from sliding back into bed with her and focused it on finding coffee.

Her living area had lofty ceilings and dark wood floors. She'd sponged the walls with a bluish paint that made them look like faded denim. Against one stood a fireplace framed in that same dark wood with a sunburst mantelpiece he immediately coveted. Its woodwork was distressed, its cream-colored paint peeling.

He understood why she'd left it that way. Its history and character came through.

To complement the faded walls, she'd hung colorful framed posters. Advertising posters, he noted. Elegant women selling champagne, sleek-looking men toting cigars.

A high-backed sofa in royal blue sat in the center of the room covered, as women mysteriously cover sofas and beds, with pillows.

He admired the style she'd formed here. Old, subtly battered tables and slashing colors. And he liked seeing his tulips on her coffee table.

He wandered through to the kitchen and found himself grinning. It wasn't often you found black-and-white photos of nudes—male and female—on kitchen walls.

But he was happier yet to find coffee.

He closed the pocket door so the sound of grinding beans wouldn't carry to the bedroom. And while the coffee brewed, he stood at her kitchen window, looking out at her section of New Orleans.

He heard the slide of the kitchen door.

She wore a short red robe, and her eyes were heavy with sleep, her smile lazy with it.

"Sorry, I thought I'd muffled the coffee grinder."

"I didn't hear it." She drew a deep breath. "But I smelled the results. You making breakfast, *cher*?"

"Want toast? It's my best thing."

"Oh, I think I had a taste of your best thing last night." Still smiling, she sauntered toward him, slid her hands around his neck. "Gimme another," she said and lifted her mouth to his.

She'd woken lonely, sure he'd gone. She never let men stay the night in her bed. It was too easy for them to slip out the door. Better to send them along, to sleep alone, than to wake lonely.

Then she'd seen his shirt, his jacket, his shoes, and had been delighted. Too delighted. When a man had that much power, it was time to take some back. The surefire way was to cloud his mind with sex.

"Why didn't you just roll over and wake me up, sugar?"

"Thought about it." Was still thinking about it. "I figured since you're working tonight, you need more than ten minutes' sleep. But since you're awake . . ."

She laughed and slipped away. "Since I'm awake I want coffee." She opened a cupboard door, sent him that knowing glance over her shoulder. "Maybe if you ask nice, I'll fix you some breakfast."

"Do you want me to beg standing up, on my knees or completely supine?"

"You tickle me, Declan. I'll make you some toast. *Le pain perdu*," she added when his face fell. "French toast. I got me most of a nice baguette." She handed him a thick white mug filled with black coffee.

"Thanks. Since you're good in the kitchen, we won't have to hire a cook when we get married and raise our six kids."

"Six?"

"I feel obligated to uphold the Sullivan-Fitzgerald tradition. I really like your kitchen art. Not the usual spot for nudes."

"Why?" She got out a black iron skillet. "Cooking's an art, and it's sexy if you do it right."

She got out a blue bowl. He watched her crack an egg on its side, slide white and yolk in, one-handed.

"I see what you mean. Do it again."

She chuckled and cracked a second egg. "Why don't you go on out and put some music on? This won't take long."

They ate at a little gateleg table she had tucked under one of the living room windows.

"Where'd you learn to cook?" he asked her.

"My grandmama. She tried to teach me to sew, too, but that didn't stick so well."

"I'm surprised you didn't open a restaurant instead of a bar."

"I like to cook when I like to cook. Do it for a living, do it all the time."

"There's that. How did you end up running a bar?"

"I wanted my own business. You work for somebody else, they say do this, don't do that, come here, go there. That doesn't set with me. So I went to business school, and I think, what business do I want to have? I don't want to sell souvenirs, don't want a gift shop, don't want to sell dresses. I think, all those things sell in New Orleans, but what sells even more? Pleasure sells. A little harmless sin and a good time, that's what people come to the Big Easy for. So . . . Et Trois."

"How long have you had it?"

"Let's see now." She'd already eaten her toast, so speared a slice from the four she'd piled on his plate. "Going on six years now."

"You opened a bar when you were twenty-three?"

"Hey, how do you know how old I am?"

"Remy."

She looked up at the ceiling. "*Et là!* Gonna have to take a strip off his ass for that. Man oughta know better than flapping about a woman's age. What else he flap about?"

Declan gave his breakfast his undivided attention. "This is really great. What do you put in this stuff?"

She said nothing for a full ten seconds. "I see. Men just can't stop themselves from crowing about their sexual exploits."

Uneasy, for himself and his friend, Declan replied, "It wasn't like that. It was nostalgic. And it was sweet. You meant something to him. You still do."

"It's a good thing for him I know that. And that I feel the same. Do you remember the first girl you got into the backseat, Declan? Do you remember her fondly?"

"Sherry Bingham. A pretty little blond. I loved her desperately through most of my junior year in high school."

She liked him for coming out with a name, instantly. Even if he'd made it up. "What happened?"

"She dumped me for a football player. Left tackle. Jesus, a football player with no neck and the IQ of a pencil. I'm still pissed off at her. But to get back to you—and by the way, you're really good at deflecting personal questions, but I was a lawyer. Anyway, how did you manage to pull it off? Twenty-three's pretty young to establish a business, one that's proven itself out when most go under within three years."

She leaned back. "What difference does it make? Counselor."

"Okay." He shrugged and kept eating. "I'll just assume you robbed a bank, paid off the mob, seduced then murdered the previous owner—after he left you the building in his will. And continue to run illegal gambling and prostitutes out of the back room."

"Why I've been so busy. But I like your version better. Mine's very dull in comparison. I worked after school and summers, saved my pennies. I'm very good at saving pennies if I need to. Then I worked, tending bar, serving drinks, and went to business school part-time. Just before I turned twenty-two, my grandpapa died. Fell off a ladder, broke his damn fool neck."

Her eyes filled as she said it. "Guess I'm still pissed off at him."

"I'm sorry." He covered her hand with his. "You were close."

"I loved him more than any man in the world. Pete Simone, with his big laugh and his big hands. He played the fiddle and always carried a red bandanna. Always. Well . . ." She blinked away the tears. "He had an insurance policy, bigger than it ought to have been considering. Half for me, half for Grandmama. In the end she made me take all of it. Nothing you can do to change her mind when she digs her heels in. So I invested the money, and a year later I opened my place."

"There's nothing dull about that. You run a good bar, Lena."

"Yes, I do." She rose, picked up the plates. "You'd best get yourself dressed, *cher*, if you want a ride home."

———

H e couldn't talk her into coming inside. He had to settle for a mind-numbing kiss before she pushed him out of her car and drove away.

Arriving home at nine in the morning in a wrinkled suit gained him a grin and a wink from Big Frank as the man carted dead tree limbs to a burn pile.

"You fell into some luck last night, Mister Dec."

Into something, Declan thought and, rubbing his heart, went into the house to get to work.

She wouldn't see him that night, or the next. He had to content himself with phone calls that made him feel like a teenager as he wandered the house with his portable phone and rattled his brains for any conversational ploy that would keep her on the line.

Mardi Gras celebrations, and business, were under way, she told him. While they were, she didn't have time to come out and play.

He knew when he was being tested and stalled and tangled. And decided he'd let her string out his line. Until he reeled her in.

Remy dropped by one afternoon wearing Hugo Boss and gold beads. He took the beads off, tossed them over Declan's head. "When you coming into town?"

"I thought I might join the insanity over the weekend."

"*Cher*, it's Mardi Gras. Every night's the weekend."

"Not out here. Come take a look." He led the way into the parlor, where Tibald was high on a ladder patiently detailing the ceiling plasterwork.

"Hey, Tibald." Remy hooked his thumbs into his pockets and craned his neck back. "That's some job."

"It surely is. How's Effie doing these days?"

"Driving me to drink with wedding plans. Picked out the cake yesterday, and you'd think it was a matter of life and death whether it has yellow rosebuds or full-blown roses around the edges."

"Best thing a man can do in these situations is nod at whatever she likes best, and just show up on the day."

"You might've said something of that nature before I told her I liked the big, fat roses when it turned out she had her mind set on the buds." He pulled a small bottle of Tylenol out of his pocket. "You got something I can down this with, Dec? That woman's given me the mother of all headaches."

Declan picked up a half-empty bottle of water. "Did you come out here to hide?"

"Till she cools off." Gulping down the pills and water, Remy wandered over the drop cloth. "You do these walls in here, Dec, or you hire them out?"

"I did them." Pleased, Declan ran his fingers over the smooth surface of the Paris green walls. "Spent the last three days on this room." And nights, he thought. "I think this color will make the room seem cooler than a patterned paper, and I like the way it looks with the trim."

"You're a regular Bob Vila and Martha Stewart combined. What do you tackle next?"

"The library. Still some details to deal with in here, and the kitchen, but the library's on the slate for next week. After that, I'm hoping to move outside for a while. Give me a couple of those aspirin."

"Sure." Remy handed over the pills and the water. "You got work problems or female problems?"

"A little of both. Come out on the back gallery, take a look at what the Franks have done with the rear gardens."

"Heard you escorted our Lena around in a big, white limo a few nights ago," Remy said as they walked toward the back of the house. "Classy stuff."

"I'm a classy guy." He handed the water back to Remy and opened the French doors of the dining room.

"You got romancing her in mind, that's a good start."

"I've got more than that in mind," Declan said as Remy tipped back the bottle. "I'm going to marry her."

Water spewed out as Remy choked.

"Pretty good spit take," Declan commented. "Keep the bottle."

"Jesus, Dec. Jesus Christ, you and Lena are getting married?"

"I'd like to have the wedding here, in the fall. September maybe." He scanned his gallery, his gardens. He wondered what kind of bird it was that was currently singing its lungs out. "The place won't be finished, but that'd be part of the charm. Of course, if it takes me longer to pin her down, we could do it next spring."

"That's some fast work."

"Not really. It's just a matter of keeping at it." He smiled now as he studied Remy's baffled face. "Oh, you don't mean the house. Lena. I haven't asked her yet. She'd just say no. Look out there, bulbs coming up. Daffodils, tulips, calla lilies, the Franks tell me. Buried under all those weeds and vines, maybe blooming under it for years. That's something."

"Dec, I think you need something stronger than Tylenol."

"I'm not crazy. I'm in love with her. I'm starting to think I was in love with her before I even met her. That's why there was never anyone else who really mattered. Not like this. Because she was here, and I just hadn't found her yet."

"Maybe I need something stronger."

"Bourbon's in the kitchen. Ice is in the cooler. New fridge is due to come in tomorrow."

"I'm fixing us both a drink."

"Make mine short and weak," Dec told him absently. "I've got work to do yet today."

Remy brought back two glasses and took a long sip of his as he studied Declan's face. "Declan, I love you like a brother."

"I know you do."

"So, I'm going to talk to you like I would a brother—if I had one instead of being plagued with sisters."

"You think I've lost my mind."

"No. In some situations, hell, in most situations, a man thinks with his dick. By the time that thought process works all the way to his head, he usually sees that situation more clearly."

"I appreciate you explaining that to me, Dad."

Remy only shook his head and paced up and down the gallery. "Lena's a very sexy woman."

"No argument there."

"She just sort of exudes those pheromones or whatever the hell they are the way other women do the perfume they splash on to get a man stirred up. She stirs you up just by breathing."

"You're trying to tell me I'm infatuated, or in the heavy wave of first lust."

"Exactly." Remy laid a supportive hand on Declan's shoulder. "Not a man alive would blame you for it. Add to that, son, you've had a rough few months on the relationship train, and knowing the way you cart guilt around like it was your personal treasure chest, I don't imagine you've been clearing your pipes regular since you broke it off with Jennifer."

"Jessica, you asshole." Amused, touched, Declan leaned back on the baluster. "It's not infatuation. I thought it was, with a good dose of that lust tossed in. But that's not it. It's not a matter of clogged pipes, and I'm not thinking with my dick. It's my heart."

"Oh, brother." Remy took another good gulp of whiskey. "Dec, you haven't been down here a full month yet."

"People are always saying something like that, as if time is a factor." And because the critical part of his brain had said the same thing, he was irritated to hear the sentiment from his closest friend. "What, is there a law somewhere that states you can't fall in love until a reasonable, rational period of time has passed during which the parties will socialize, communicate and, if possible, engage in sexual intercourse in order to assure compatibility? If there is, and it worked, explain the divorce rate."

"A couple of lawyers stand here debating the subject, we'll be here till next Tuesday."

"Then let me say this. I've never felt like this before, never in my life. I didn't think I could. I figured something inside me just didn't work the way it was supposed to."

"Well, for Christ's sake, Dec."

"I couldn't love Jessica." The guilt slid back into his voice. "I just couldn't, and I tried to. I damn near settled for affection, respect and mutual backgrounds because I thought it was all I'd get, or be able to give. But it's not. I've never felt like this, Remy," he said again. "And I like it."

"If you want Lena, then I want her for you. The thing is, Dec, no matter how you feel, it doesn't guarantee she's going to feel the same."

"Maybe she'll break my heart, but feeling too much is a hell of a lot better than feeling nothing." He'd been telling himself that, repeatedly, since he'd realized he was in love with her. "One way or the other, I've got to try."

He swirled the whiskey he'd yet to drink. "She doesn't know what to make of me," Declan murmured. "It's going to be fun letting her find out."


That night, he heard weeping. A man's raw and broken sobs. Declan tossed in sleep, weighed down with the grief, unable to stop it, unable to give or seek comfort.

Even when silence came, the sorrow stayed.

# TEN

BAYOU ROUSE
MARCH 1900

He didn't know why he came here, to stare at the water while thick green shadows spread around him, as night gathered to eat away at the day.

But he came, time and again, to wander through the marsh as if he would somehow come upon her, strolling along the curve of the river where the swamp flowers blossomed.

She would smile at him, hold out her hand.

And everything would be right again.

Nothing would ever be right again.

He was afraid he was going mad, that grief was darkening his mind as night darkened the day. How else could he explain how he could hear her whispering to him in the night? What could he do but shut off the sound of her, the pain of her?

He watched a blue heron rise from the reeds like a ghost, beautiful, pure, perfect, to skim over the tea-colored water and glide into the trees. Away from him. Always away from him.

She was gone. His Abby had winged away from him, like the ghost bird. Everyone said it. His family, his friends. He'd heard the servants whispering about it. How Abigail Rouse had run off with some no-account and left her husband and bastard baby daughter behind.

Though he continued to look in New Orleans, in Baton Rouge, in Lafayette, though he continued to haunt the bayou like a ghost himself, in the loneliest hours of the night, he believed it.

She'd left him and the child.

Now he was leaving, in all but body. He walked through each day like a man in a trance. And God help him, he could not be a father to the child, that image of Abigail he secretly, shamefully doubted carried his blood. Just looking at her brought him unspeakable sorrow.

He no longer went up to the nursery. He hated himself for it, but even the act of climbing the stairs to the third floor was like drowning in a sea of despair.

They said the child wasn't his.

No. In the dimming light of dusk, with the night coming alive around him, Lucian covered his face with his hands. No, he could not, would not believe that of her. They had made the child together, in love, in trust, in desire.

If even that was a lie . . .

He lowered his hands, stepped toward the water. It would be warm, as her smile had been warm. Soft, as her skin had been soft. Even now the color was deepening and was almost the color of her eyes.

"Lucian!"

He froze, on the slippery edge.

*Abby*. She was rushing toward him, pushing through the fronds of a willow, with her hair spilling over her shoulders in midnight curls. His heart, deadened with grief, woke in one wild leap.

Then the last shimmer of sunlight fell over her face, and he died again.

Claudine gripped his hands. Fear made her fingers cold. She'd seen what had been in his eyes, and it had been his death.

"She would never want this. She would never want you to damn your soul by taking your life."

"She left me."

"No. No, that isn't true. They lie to you. They lie, Lucian. She loved you. She loved you and Marie Rose above all things."

"Then where is she?" The rage that lived under the numbness of his grief leaped out. He gripped Claudine's arms, hauled her to her toes. Part of him, some dark, secret part, wanted to pound his fists into her face. Erase it for its connection to Abigail, and his own drowning despair. "Where is she?"

"Dead!" She shouted it, and her voice rang in the warm, sticky air. "They killed her. Death is the only way she would leave you and Rosie."

He shoved her aside, staggered away to lean against the trunk of a live oak. "That's just another madness."

"I tell you I know it. I *feel* it. I've had dreams."

"So did I." Tears stung his eyes, turned the light watery. "So did I have dreams."

"Lucian, you must listen. I was there that night. She came to the nursery to tend the baby. I've known Abby since we were babies ourselves. There was nothing in her but love for you and Marie Rose. I should never have left the Hall that night." Claudine crossed her hands over her breast, as if to hold together the two halves of her broken heart. "The rest of my life I'll beg her forgiveness for not being there."

"She took clothes, jewelry. My mother is right." He firmed his lips on what he believed was an act of strength, but was only his weakened faith. "I have to accept."

"Your mama hated Abby. She kicked me out the next day. She's afraid to keep me in the house, afraid I might find out—"

He whirled around, his face so contorted with fury, Claudine stepped away. "You want me to believe my mother somehow killed my wife, then disguised the crime, the sin, the horror, by making it appear Abby ran away?"

"I don't know what happened. But I know Abby didn't leave. Mama Rouse, she went to Evangeline."

Lucian waved a hand, turned away again. "Voodoo nonsense."

"Evangeline's got power. She said there was blood, and pain, and fear. And a dark, dark sin. Death, she said, and a watery grave. She said you got two halves, and one is black as a cave in hell."

"I killed her then? I came home in the night and murdered my wife?"

"Two halves, Lucian, that shared one womb. Look to your brother."

The chill stabbed through him, bringing a raw sickness to the belly, a vile roaring in his head. "I won't listen to any more of this. Go home, Claudine. Keep away from the Hall."

He dug into his pocket, took out the watch pin, pressed it into Claudine's hand. "Take this, keep it for the child." He could no longer call her by name. "She should have something that was her mother's."

He stared down, grieving, at the symbol in her hand. Time had stopped for Abigail.

"You kill her again by not believing in her."

"Stay away from me." He staggered away, toward Manet Hall, toward his chosen hell. "Stay away."

"You know!" Claudine shouted after him. "You know she was true."

Clutching the watch to her breast, Claudine vowed to pass it, and the truth, along to Abigail's daughter.


MANET HALL

FEBRUARY 2002


From his gallery, Declan watched the day come to life. Dawn was a rosy blush on the eastern sky, with hints of mauve, like sleepy bruises, just beneath. The air was warming. He could feel the rise of it almost every day. It wasn't yet March, but winter was bowing out.

The gardens that a month before had been a sorrowful wreck showed hints of their former grandeur. Strangling vines, invasive weeds, deadwood and broken bricks had been hauled away, revealing foot by foot the wandering paths, the shrubs, even the bulbs and plants that had been too stubborn to die away.

An old iron arbor was wild with what the Franks told him was wisteria, and there was an island of massive azaleas that showed the beginning of hopeful buds.

He had magnolia, crape myrtle, camellia, jasmine. He'd written down everything he could remember the Franks reeled off in their lazy voices. When he'd described the vine he imagined on the corner columns, they'd told him what he wanted was morning glory.

He liked the sound of it. Mornings here were full of glory.

He thought his body was adjusting to the five or six hours of disturbed sleep a night he was able to snatch. Or maybe it was just nervous energy that was fueling him.

Something was pushing him, driving him step by step through the transformation of the house that was his. Yet somehow, not only his.

If it was Abigail hovering, she was a damn fickle female. There were times he felt utterly comfortable, totally at peace. And others when cold fear prickled the back of his neck. Times when he felt in his gut he was being watched.

Stalked.

Well, that was a woman for you, he thought as he sipped his morning coffee. All smiles one minute, and slaps the next.

Even as he thought it, he saw Lena and the big black dog step out of the trees.

He didn't think twice, but set his coffee aside and started for the gallery steps.

She'd seen him long before he'd seen her. From the shelter of the trees and morning mists, she'd stood, idly rubbing Rufus's head, and had studied the house. Studied him.

What was it about the place and the man that pulled at her so? she wondered. There were any number of great old houses here, along the River Road, on toward Baton Rouge.

God knew there were any number of good-looking men, if a woman was in the market for one.

But it was this house that had always snagged her interest and imagination. Now it seemed it was this man, jogging down the thick stone stairs in a ratty shirt, rattier jeans, his face rough with the night's beard, who had managed to do the same.

She didn't like to want. It got in the way of things. And when that want involved a man, well, it was just bound to mess up your life.

She'd built her life brick by goddamn brick. And she liked it, just as it was. A man, no matter how amiable he was, would, at best, alter the design. At worst, he'd send those bricks tumbling down to ruin.

She'd kept away from him since the night she'd taken him into her bed. Just to prove she could.

But she had a smile ready for him now, a slow, cat-at-the-mouse-hole smile, and stood her ground as the dog raced over, tearing through the ground fog, to meet him.

Rufus leaped, slopped his tongue over Declan's face, then collapsed, belly up, for a rub.

It was, Lena knew, Rufus's way of showing unconditional love.

Charms dogs, too, she thought as Declan crouched down to rub and wrestle. The man had entirely too much appeal for anybody's good. Especially hers.

"Rufus!" she called out, bringing the dog to his feet in a flurry of muscle and limbs that nearly put Declan on his ass. And laughing, she tossed the ball she carried high in the air, nipped it handily on its fall. Rufus charged her, a blur of black fur and enthusiasm. She hurled the ball over the pond. Rufus sailed up, over the water, and nabbed the ball with his teeth seconds before his massive splash.

"The Bo Sox could use you two." As the dog paddled his way to shore, Declan strode up, cupped his hands under Lena's elbows, and lifted her off her feet. He had an instant to see her blink in surprise before he covered her mouth with his, and took her under.

She gripped his shirt, not for balance, though her feet were dangling several inches off the ground. But because he was under it, all that muscle and heat and man.

She heard the dog bark, three deep throaty rumbles, then the water he shook off himself drenched her. She wouldn't have been surprised if it had steamed off her skin.

"Morning," Declan said and dropped her back on her feet. "Where y'at?"

"Woo." She had to give him credit for both greetings, and pushed a hand through her hair. "Where y'at?" she responded, then reached up and rubbed a hand over his rough cheek. "Need a shave, *cher.*"

"If I'd known you'd come walking my way this morning, I'd have taken care of that."

"I wasn't walking your way." She picked up the ball Rufus had dropped at her feet and sent it, and the dog, flying again. "Just playing with my grandmama's dog."

"Is she all right? You said you stayed over with her when she wasn't feeling well."

"She gets the blues sometimes, is all." And damn it, *damn* it, his instant and genuine concern touched her. "Missing her Pete. She was seventeen when they got married, and fifty-eight when he died. More'n forty years is a long time to mesh lives."

"Would she like it if I went by later?"

"She likes your company." Because Rufus was thumping his tail impatiently, she winged the ball again.

"You said she has a sister. Any other family?"

"Two sisters, a brother, all still living."

"Children?"

Her face shut down. "I'm all she's got there. You been into town for any of the partying?"

Off limits, he decided. He let it go, for the moment. "Not yet. I figured I'd go in tonight. Are you working?"

"Nothing but work till Ash Wednesday. People do like to drink before Lent comes."

"Late hours for you. You look a little tired."

"I don't much care for being up this early, but Grandmama, she's an early bird. She's up, everybody's up." She lifted her arms high, stretched. "You're an early bird yourself, aren't you, *cher*?"

"These days. Why don't you come back to the house with me, have some coffee, see what I've been doing with my time since I haven't been able to spend any with you."

"I've been busy."

"So you said."

Her brows knit, forming a long, shallow line of annoyance between them. "I say what I mean."

"I didn't say different. But I'm making you edgy. I don't mind that, Lena." He reached out to tug on her hair, amused and delighted to see temper darken her face. "But I would mind if you think I'd settle for one night with you."

"I sleep with you if I want, when I want."

"And I'd mind," he continued mildly, though the hand that gripped her arm before she could spin away was very firm. "I'd mind a great deal if you think all I want is to get you in the sheets."

"Men don't touch me unless I tell them they can touch me." She shoved at his hand.

"You've never dealt with me before, have you?" There was steel in his fingers, in his tone. "Just simmer down. Picking a fight isn't going to shake me loose, either. You wanted to keep your distance this week, okay. I'm a patient man, Lena, but I'm not a doormat. Don't think you're going to walk over me on your way out the door."

Anger, she realized, wasn't the way to handle him. She had no doubt she could scrape away at that control and stir him up into a good shouting match of a fight. It would be interesting, even entertaining. But she had a fifty-fifty chance of losing it.

She didn't care for the odds.

Instead, she stroked a hand over his cheek. "Aw now, *cher*." Her voice was liquid silk. "What you getting so het up about? You got me irritable, that's all. I'm not at my best so early in the day, and here you being all tough and surly. I don't mean to hurt your feelings."

She rose on her toes and kissed his cheek.

"What *do* you mean to do, Angelina?"

There was something about the way he used her whole name that put her back up. A kind of warning. "Now, Declan honey, I like you. I truly do. And the other night, why, you just about swept me off my feet. We had ourselves a real good time, too, didn't we? But you don't want to be making more out of it than it was."

"What was it?"

She lifted her shoulders. "A very satisfying interlude, for both of us. Why don't we leave it at that and be friends again?"

"We could. Or, we could try it this way."

He yanked her to him, dragged her up to her toes. And plundered her mouth. No patience this time, no reason, no dreamy mating of lips. It was a branding, and they both knew it.

Rufus gave a warning growl as she struggled. Even when the growl turned to a snarl, Declan ignored it. He fisted a hand in her hair, pulled her head back, and took them both deeper. Temper, hurt and hunger all stormed inside him and flavored the kiss.

She couldn't resist it. Not when the punch of emotions slammed into her system, liberating needs she'd hoped to lock down. On a muffled oath, she wrapped her arms around his neck and met the ferocity of the kiss.

With a whine, Rufus settled down to chew at the ball.

"We're not done with each other." Declan ran proprietary hands down her arms.

"Maybe not."

"I'll come in tonight, take you home after you close. Wednesday, after things quiet down, I'd like you to come out here. We'll have dinner."

She managed to smile. "You cooking?"

He grinned, touched his lips to her brow. "I'll surprise you."

"You usually do," she retorted when he walked away.

S he was irritated with herself. Not just for losing a battle, but for cowardice. It was cowardice that had pushed her to start the fight in the first place.

She trudged through the marsh while Rufus raced into the trees, through the thick green undergrowth in hopes of scaring up a rabbit or a squirrel.

She stopped at the curve of what had been known as far back as memory stretched as Bayou Rouse. This mysterious place with its slow-moving, shadowy water, its cypress bones and thick scents, was as much her world as the crooked streets and lively pace of the Quarter.

She'd run in this world as a child, learned the difference between a wren and a sparrow, how to avoid a copperhead nest by its cucumber whiff, how to drop a line and pull up a catfish for supper.

It was the home of her blood, as the Quarter had become the home of her ambition. She didn't come back to it only when her grandmother was feeling blue, but when she herself was.

She caught a glimpse of the knobby snout of an alligator sliding by. It was, she thought, what was under the surface that could take you down, one quick, ugly snap, if you weren't alert and didn't keep your wits about you.

There was a great deal under the surface of Declan Fitzgerald. She'd have preferred if he'd been some spoiled, rich trust-fund baby out on a lark. She could've enjoyed him, and dismissed him when they were both bored.

It was a great deal more difficult to dismiss what you respected. She admired his strength, his purpose, his humor. As a friend, he would give her a great deal of pleasure.

As a lover, he worried the hell out of her.

He wanted too much. She could already feel him sucking her in. And it scared her, scared her that she didn't seem able to stop the process.

Toying with the key around her neck, she started back toward the bayou house. It would run its course, she told herself. Things always did.

She pasted on a smile as she neared the house and saw her grandmother, shaded by an old straw hat, fussing in her kitchen garden.

"I smell bread baking," Lena called out.

"Brown bread. Got a loaf in there you can take home with you."

Odette straightened, pressed a hand lightly to the small of her back. "Got an extra you could take on by the Hall for that boy. He doesn't eat right."

"He's healthy enough."

"Healthy enough to want a bite outta you." She bent back to her work, her sturdy work boots planted firm. "He try to take one this morning? You've got that look about you."

Lena walked over, dropped down on the step beside the garden patch. "What look is that?"

"The look a woman gets when a man's had his hands on her and didn't finish the job."

"I know how to finish the job myself, if that's the only problem."

With a snorting laugh, Odette broke off a sprig of rosemary. She pinched at its needle leaves, waved it under her nose for the simple pleasure of its scent. "Why scratch an itch if someone'll scratch it for you? I may be close to looking seventy in the eye, but I know when I see a man who's willing and able."

"Sex doesn't run my life, Grandmama."

"No, but it sure would make it more enjoyable." She straightened again. "You're not Lilibeth, 't poulette."

The use of the childhood endearment—little chicken—made Lena smile. "I know it."

"Not being her doesn't mean you have to be alone if you find somebody who lights the right spark in you."

She took the rosemary Odette offered, brushed it against her cheek. "I don't think he's looking for a spark. I think he's looking for a whole damn bonfire." She leaned back on her elbows, shook back her hair. "I've lived this long without getting burned, and I'm going to keep right on."

"It always was right or left for you. Couldn't drive you to middle ground with a whip. You're my baby, even if you are a grown woman, so I'll say this: Nothing wrong with a woman walking alone, as long as it's for the right reasons. Being afraid she might trip, that's a wrong one."

"What happens if I let myself fall for him?" Lena demanded. "Then he has enough of swamp water and trots on back to Boston? Or he just has his fill of dancing with me and finds himself another partner?"

Odette pushed her hat back on the crown of her head, and her face was alive with exasperation. "What happens if it rains a flood and washes us into the Mississippi? Pity sakes, Lena, you can't think that way. It'll dry you up."

"I was doing fine before he came along, and I'll do fine after he goes." Feeling sulky, she reached down to pet Rufus when he butted his head against her knee. "That house over there, Grandmama, that house he's so set on bringing back, it's a symbol of what happens when two people don't belong in the same place. I'm her blood, and I know."

"You don't know." Odette tipped back Lena's chin. "If they hadn't loved, if Abby Rouse and Lucian Manet hadn't loved and made a child together, you and I wouldn't be here."

"If they'd been meant, she wouldn't have died the way she did. She wouldn't be a ghost in that house."

"Oh *chère*." Both the exasperation and all the affection colored Odette's voice. "It isn't Abby Rouse who haunts that place."

"Who, then?"

"I expect that's what that boy's there to find out. Might be you're here to help him."

She gave a sniff of the air. "Bread's done," she said an instant before the oven buzzer sounded. "You want to take a loaf over to the Hall?"

Lena set her jaw. "No."

"All right, then." Odette walked up the steps, opened the back door. "Maybe I'll take him one myself." Her eyes were dancing when she glanced over her shoulder. "And could be I'll steal him right out from under your nose."

Declan had every door and window on the first level open. Ry Cooder blasted out of his stereo with his lunging rhythm and blues. Working to the beat, Declan spread the first thin coat of varnish on the newly sanded floor of the parlor.

Everything ached. Every muscle and bone in his body sang with the same ferocity as Ry Cooder. He'd thought the sheer physical strain of the sanding would have worked off his temper. Now he was hoping the necessary focus and strain of the varnishing would do the job.

The rosy dawn hadn't lived up to its promise.

The woman pushed his buttons, he thought. And she knew it. One night she'd wrapped herself all over him in bed, and the next she won't give him more than some conversation on the phone.

Snaps out in temper one minute, melts down to sexy teasing the next. Trying to turn the night they'd spent together into the classic one-night stand.

Fuck that.

"Aw, *cher*, what you wanna get all het up about?" he muttered. "You haven't seen het up, baby. But you're going to before this is done."

"You look to be in the middle of a mad."

He spun around, slopping varnish. Then nearly went down to his knees when he saw Odette smiling at him from the doorway.

"I didn't hear you come in."

"Not surprising." With the privilege of age, she leaned down and turned down the volume on his portable stereo as Cooder switched pace, lamenting falling teardrops. "Like Cooder myself, but not that loud. Brought you by a loaf of the brown bread I baked this morning. You go on and finish what you're doing. I'll put it back in the kitchen for you."

"Just give me a minute."

"You don't have to stop on my account, *cher*."

"No. Please. Five minutes. There's . . . something, I forget what, to drink in the fridge. Why don't you go on back, help yourself?"

"I believe I will. It's a bit close out already, and not even March. You take your time."

When he'd finished up enough to join her, Odette was standing in front of his kitchen display cabinet, studying the contents.

"My mama had an old waffle iron just like this. And I still got a cherry seeder like the one you got in here. What do they call these dishes here? I can't remember."

"Fiestaware."

"That's it. Always sounds like a party. You pay money for these old Mason jars, *cher*?"

"I'm afraid so."

She clucked her tongue at the wonder of it. "There's no accounting for things. Damn if they don't look pretty, though. You come look through my shed sometime, see if there's anything in there you want." She turned now, nodded at the room. "This is fine, Declan. You did fine."

"It'll come together when the counters are in and I finish the panels for the appliances."

"It's fine," she said again. "And the parlor where you're working, it's as lovely as it can be."

"I've already bought some of the furniture for it. A little ahead of myself. Would you like to sit down, Miss Odette?"

"For a minute or two. I've got something from the house you might like to have, maybe put on the mantel in the parlor or one of the other rooms."

She took a seat at the table he'd moved in, and pulled an old brown leather frame from a bag. "It's a photograph, a portrait, of Abigail Rouse."

Declan took it and gazed down on the woman who haunted his dreams. It might have been Lena, he thought, but there was too much softness, too much yet unformed in this face. Her cheeks were rounder, her long-lidded eyes too gullible, and far too shy.

So young, he mused. And innocent despite the grown-up walking dress with its high, fur-trimmed collar, despite the jaunty angle of the velvet toque with its saucy feathers.

This was a girl, he reflected, where Lena was a woman.

"She was lovely," Declan said. "Lovely and young. It breaks your heart."

"My grandmama thought she was 'round about eighteen when this was taken. Couldn't've been more, as she never saw her nineteenth birthday."

As she spoke, a door slammed upstairs, as if in temper. Odette merely glanced toward the ceiling. "Sounds like your ghost's got mad on, too."

"That just started happening today. Plumber's kid shot out of here like a bullet a couple hours ago."

"You don't look like you're going anywhere."

"No." He sat across from her as another door slammed, and looked back down at Abigail Rouse Manet's shy, hopeful smile. "I'm not going anywhere."

# ELEVEN

There was a madness about Mardi Gras. The music, the masks, the mayhem all crashing together into a desperate sort of cele-bration managed to create a tone that was both gleefully inno-cent and rawly sexual. He doubted the majority of the tourists who flocked here for the event understood or cared about the purpose of it. That rush to gorge on pleasures before the forty days of fasting.

Wanting a taste of it himself, Declan opted to wander through the crowds, even snagged some beads when they were tossed in a glitter of cheap gold from one of the galleries. His ears rang with the blare of brass, the wild laughter.

He decided the sight of naked breasts, which a couple of coeds flashed as they followed tradition and jerked up their shirts, would be less alarming after a couple of drinks.

As would being grabbed by a total stranger and being treated to a tonsil-diving kiss. The tongue currently invading his mouth trans-ferred the silly sweetness of many hurricanes and happily drunken lust onto his.

"Thanks," he managed when he freed himself.

"Come on back here," the masked female shouted. *"Laizzez les bon temps rouler!"*

He didn't want to let the good times roll when it involved strange tongues plunged into his mouth, and escaped into the teeming crowds.

Maybe he was getting old, he thought—or maybe it was just the Boston bedrock—but he wanted to get someplace where he could sit back and observe the party rather than being mobbed by it.

The doors to Et Trois were flung open, so the noise from within poured out and tangled with the noise of the streets. He had to weave his way through the revelers on the sidewalk, those packed inside, and squeeze his way to a standing spot at the bar.

The place was full of smoke, music and the slap of feet on wood as dancers shoehorned together on the dance floor. Onstage, a fiddler streamed out such hot licks, Declan wouldn't have been surprised to see the bow burst into flame.

Lena was pulling a draft with one hand, pouring a shot of bourbon with the other. The two other bartenders were equally busy, and from what he could see, she had four waitresses working the tables.

He spotted his crawfish grinning from their spot on the shelf behind the bar and was ridiculously pleased.

"Beer and a bump," she said and slid the glasses into waiting hands. When she spotted Declan, she held up a finger, then served three more customers as she worked her way down to him.

"What's your pleasure, handsome?"

"You are. You're packed," he added. "In here and out on the side-walk."

"Banquette," she corrected. "We call them banquettes 'round here." She'd pulled her hair back, wound purple and gold beads through it. The little silver key dangled against skin dewed with perspiration. "I can give you a drink, *cher*, but I don't have time to talk right now."

"Can I give you a hand?"

She pushed at her hair. "With what?"

"Whatever."

Someone elbowed in, shouted out a request for a tequila sunrise and a Dixie draft.

Lena reached back for the bottle, shifted to pull the draft. "You know how to bus tables, college boy?"

"I can figure it out."

"Redheaded waitress? She's Marcella." She nodded in the general direction of mayhem. "Tell her you're hired. She'll show you what to do."

By midnight, he figured he'd carted about a half a ton of empties into the kitchen, and dumped the equivalent of Mount Rainier in cigarette butts.

He'd had his ass pinched, rubbed, ogled. What *was* it with women and the male behind? Someone ought to do a study on it.

He'd lost track of the propositions, and didn't care to think about the enormous woman who'd hauled him into her lap.

It had been like being smothered by a three-hundred-pound pillow soaked in whiskey.

By two, he was beyond amazement at the human body's capacity for vice, and had revised any previous perception of the skill and endurance required in food-service occupations.

He made sixty-three dollars and eighty-five cents in tips, and vowed to burn his clothes at the first opportunity.

The place was still rolling at three, and he decided Lena hadn't been avoiding him. Or if she had, she'd had a reasonable excuse for it.

"What time do you close?" he asked when he carted another load toward the kitchen.

"When people go away." She poured bottled beer into the plastic to-go cups, handed them off.

"Do they ever?"

She smiled, but it was quick and distracted as she scanned the crowd. "Not so much during Mardi Gras. Why don't you go on home, *cher*? We're going to be another hour or more in here."

"I stick."

He carried the empties into the kitchen and came back in time to see a trio of very drunk men—boys really, he noted—hitting on Lena and hitting hard.

She was handling them, but they weren't taking the hint.

"If y'all want to last till Fat Tuesday, you gotta pace yourself a bit." She set to-go cups under the taps. "Y'all aren't driving now, are you?"

"Hell no." One, wearing a University of Michigan T-shirt under an avalanche of beads, leaned in. Way in. "We've got a place right over on Royal. Why don't you come back there with me, baby? Get naked, take a spin in the Jacuzzi."

"Now, that's real tempting, *cher*, but I've got my hands full."

"I'll give you a handful," he said and, grabbing his own crotch, had his two companions howling and hooting.

Declan stepped forward, ran a proprietary hand over Lena's shoulder. "You're hitting on my woman." He felt her stiffen under his hand, saw the surly challenge in the Michigan boy's eyes.

Under other circumstances, Declan thought as he sized the kid up—six-one, a toned one-ninety—he might be the type to make his bed every morning, he might visit old ladies in nursing homes. He might rescue small puppies. But right now, the boy was drunk, horny and stupid.

To prove it, Michigan bared his teeth. "Why don't you just fuck off? Or maybe you want to take it outside, where I can kick your ass."

Declan's voice dripped with bonhomie. "Now, why would I want to go outside and fight about it, when all you're doing here is admiring my taste? Spectacular, isn't she? You didn't try to hit on her, I'd have to figure you're too drunk to see."

"I see just fine, fuckface."

"Exactly. Why don't I buy you and your pals a drink? Honey, put those drafts on my tab."

Declan leaned conversationally on the bar, nodded toward the T-shirt. "Spring break? What's your major?"

Baffled and boozy, Michigan blinked at him. "Whatzit to ya?"

"Just curious." Declan slid a bowl of pretzels closer, took one. "I've got a cousin teaching there, English department. Eileen Brennan. Maybe you know her."

"Professor Brennan's your cousin?" The surly tone had turned to surprised fellowship. "She damn near flunked me last semester."

"She's tough, always scares the hell out of me. If you run into her, tell her Dec said hi. Here's your beer."


It was past four when Lena let them into her apartment over the bar. "Pretty smooth with those college jerks, *cher*. Smooth enough I won't give you grief for the 'my woman' comment."

"You are my woman, you just haven't figured it out yet. Besides, they were easy. My cousin Eileen has a rep at the U of M. Odds were pretty good he'd heard of her."

"Some men would've flexed their muscles." She set her keys aside. "Gone on outside and rolled around in the street to prove who had the biggest dick." Weary, she reached up to tug the beads loose as she studied him. "I guess it's the lawyer in you, so you just talk yourself out of a confrontation."

"Kid was maybe twenty-two."

"Twenty-one last January. I carded them."

"I don't fight with kids. Plus, I really hate having bare knuckles rammed into my face. It seriously hurts." He tipped her chin up. She looked exhausted. "Had a long one, didn't you?"

"Going to be a long time till Wednesday. I appreciate the help, sugar. You pulled your weight."

More than, she thought. The man had slid right into the rhythm of her place and *worked*. Charmed her customers, tolerated the grab-hands and avoided a potentially ugly situation by using his wit instead of his ego.

The longer she knew him, she reflected, the more there was to know.

She tugged an envelope out of her back pocket.

"What's this?"

"Your pay."

"Jesus, Lena, I don't want your money."

"You work, I pay. I don't take free rides." She pushed the envelope into his hands. "Off the books, though. I don't want to do the paperwork."

"Okay, fine." He stuffed it into his own pocket. He'd just buy her something with it.

"Now, I guess I'd better give you a really good tip." She wound her arms around his neck, slithered her body up his. Eyes open, she nibbled on his lip, inching her way into a kiss.

His hands ran down her sides, hooked under her hips, then hitched them up until her legs wrapped around his waist. "You need to get off your feet."

"Mmm. God, yes."

He nuzzled her neck, her ear, worked his way back to her mouth as he carried her into the bedroom. "Know what I'm going to do?"

Lust was a low simmer under the bright glory of being off her aching feet. "I think I have a pretty good notion."

He laid her on the bed, could almost feel her sigh of relief at being horizontal. He pried off one of her shoes. "I'm going to give you something women long for." He tossed the shoe aside, then climbing onto the bed, removed the other.

Weary or not, her face went wicked. "A sale at Saks?"

"Better." He skimmed a finger over her arch. "A foot rub."

"A what?"

Smiling, he flexed her foot, rubbed her toes and saw her eyes go blurrier yet with pleasure.

"Mmmm. Declan, you do have a good pair of hands."

"Relax and enjoy. The Fitzgerald Reflexology Treatment is world famous. We also offer the full-body massage."

"I bet you do."

The worst of the aches began to evaporate. When he worked his way up to her calves, overworked muscles quivered with the combination of pain and pleasure.

"Do you take any time off after Mardi Gras?"

She'd been drifting, and struggled to focus at the sound of his voice. "I take Ash Wednesday off."

"Boy, what a slacker." He tapped a careless kiss to her knee. "Here, let's get your clothes off."

He unbuttoned her jeans. She lifted her hips, gave a lazy stretch. He doubted she realized her voice was husky, her words slurring. "What else you got in mind to rub, *cher*?"

He indulged himself by cupping her breasts, enjoyed her easy response, the way she combed her fingers through his hair, met his lips. He tugged her shirt up and away, snapped open the front catch of her bra. Kissed his way down to her breasts while she arched back to offer.

Then he flipped her onto her stomach. She jerked, groaned, then all but melted when he kneaded her neck. "Just as I thought," he announced. "Carry most of your tension here. Me, too."

"Oh. God." If she'd had a single wish at that moment, it would've been that he keep doing what he was doing for a full week. "You could make a good living out of this."

"It's always been my fall-back career. You've got yourself some serious knots here. Doctor Dec's going to fix you up."

"I just love playing doctor."

She waited for him to change the tone, for his hands to become demanding. He was a sweetheart, she thought sleepily. But he was a man.

She'd just take herself a little catnap, and let him wake her up.

T he next thing she knew, the sun was beating through her windows. A groggy glance at her bedside clock showed her it was twenty after ten. Morning? she thought blearily. How did it get to be morning?

And she was tucked into bed as tidily as if her grandmother had done the job. Tucked in alone.

She rolled over on her back, stretched, yawned. And realized with a kind of mild shock that nothing ached. Not her neck, not her feet, not her back.

Doctor Dec, she mused, had done a very thorough job. And was probably at home sulking because she hadn't paid his fee. Hard to blame him, when he'd been such a sweetie pie, and she'd done nothing but lie there like a corpse.

*Have to make it up to him,* she told herself, and crawled out of bed to put coffee on before she hit the shower.

She walked into the kitchen, stared at the full coffeepot on her counter, and the note propped in front of it. Frowning, she picked up the note, switched the pot back to warm as she read.

*Had to go. Counter guys coming this morning. Didn't know when you'd surface, so I was afraid to leave the pot on. But it's fresh as of seven-ten A.M., that is, if you end up sleeping 'round the clock. By the way, you look pretty when you sleep.*

*I'll give you a call later.*

*Declan*

"Aren't you the strangest thing," she muttered as she tapped the note against her palm. "Aren't you just a puzzlement."

She needed to stop into the bar to check on her lunch shift, to check on supplies. Then, needing her curiosity satisfied, she drove out to Manet Hall.

The door was open. She imagined he was one of the few who'd lived here who would leave that impressive front door open to whoever might wander in. Country living or no, someone should put a bug in his ear about a security system.

She could hear the racket of workmen from the back of the house, but took her time getting there.

The parlor grabbed her attention. She crouched down, touched her fingers to the glossy floors, and found them hard and dry, and, stepping in, just looked.

He took care, was all she could think. He took care of what was his. Paid attention to details and made them matter. Color, and wood, the elegant fireplace, the gleam of the windows, which she imagined he'd washed personally.

Just as she imagined he would furnish this room personally—and with care and attention to detail.

She'd never known a man to take so much . . . bother, she supposed, with anything. Or anyone. And maybe, she was forced to admit, she'd spent too much time with the wrong kind of man.

"What do you think?"

She turned and, framed by the windows, by the light, looked at him as he stood in the doorway. "I think this house is lucky to have you. I think you see it as it should be, and you'll work to make it come to life again."

"That's nice." He crossed to her. "That's very nice. You look rested."

"A man's not supposed to tell a woman she looks rested. He's supposed to tell her she looks gorgeous."

"I've never seen you look otherwise. Today you look rested on top of it."

"You are the smoothie." She wandered away, toward the fireplace. She trailed a palm over the mantel, stopped when she came to the brown leather frame holding the photograph of a young woman. "Abigail," she whispered, and the ache went into her. Went deep.

"Miss Odette gave it to me. You look like her, a little."

"No, I never looked as innocent as this." Compelled, Lena traced a fingertip over the young, hopeful face.

She'd seen the photograph before, had even studied it, point by point, during a period in her life when she'd found the story, the mystery of it, romantic. During a period when she herself had been young enough to see romance in tragedy.

"It's odd," Lena said, "seeing her here. Seeing part of me here."

"She belongs here. So do you."

She shook that off, and the sorrow those dark, clear eyes coated over her heart. Turning, she gave Declan a long, considering look. Work clothes, she thought, tool belt, a night's stubble. It was getting harder and harder to picture him wearing a pin-striped suit and carrying a fancy leather briefcase.

It was getting harder and harder to picture her life without him in it.

"Why did you leave my place this morning?"

"Didn't you see the note? Counter guys." He jerked a thumb back toward the kitchen. "I had to beg and pay extra to get them to schedule me for a Saturday morning. I had to be here."

"That's not what I meant. You didn't come into the city, work—what was it, about six hours busing tables?—and give me a foot rub because you didn't have anything better to do on a Friday night. You came in for sex, *cher*, and you left without it. Why is that?"

He could feel his temper prick holes in his easy mood. "You're a piece of work, Lena. You've got a real talent for turning something simple into the complicated."

"That's because things are rarely as simple as they look."

"Okay, let's clear it up. I came into the city because I wanted to see you. I bused tables because I wanted to help you. I rubbed your feet because I figured you'd been on them about twelve hours straight. Then I let you sleep because you needed to sleep. Hasn't anyone ever done you a favor?"

"Men don't, as a rule, unless they're looking for one in return. What're you looking for, Declan?"

He gave himself a moment, waiting for the first lash of anger to pass. "You know, that's insulting. If you're worried about your pay-for-work ethic, I can spare about twenty minutes now. We can go up, have sex, even the score. Otherwise, I've got a lot to do."

"I didn't mean to insult you." But she saw, quite clearly, she had. "I just don't understand you. The men I've known, on an intimate level, would have been irritated by what didn't happen between us this morning. I expected you to be, and I wouldn't have blamed you. I would've understood that."

"It's harder for you to understand that I could care about you enough to put sex on the back burner so you could get a few hours' sleep?"

"Yes."

"Maybe that's not insulting. Maybe that's just sad." He saw the color deepen in her cheeks as the words hit her. Embarrassed color, he realized. "Everything doesn't boil down to sex for me. It helps things percolate, but it's not all that's in the pot."

"I like knowing where I stand. If you don't know where you stand, you can't decide if that's where you want to be, or which direction you'd like to go from there."

"And I'm fucking up your compass."

"You could say that."

"Good. I'm a pretty agreeable guy, Lena, but I'm not going to be lumped in with others you've dealt with. In fact, you won't deal with me at all. We'll deal with each other."

"Because that's the way you want it."

"Because that's the way it is." His tone was flat, final. "Nothing between us is like, or going to be like, anything either of us has had before. You may need some time to get used to that."

"Is this how you get your way?" she demanded. "By listing off the rules in that annoyingly reasonable tone?"

"Facts, not rules," he corrected in what he imagined she would consider that annoyingly reasonable tone. "And it's only annoying because you'd be more confident having a fight. We've already eaten into the twenty minutes we could've earmarked for sex. Good sex, or a good fight, take time. I'm going to have to take a rain check on both."

She stared at him, tried to formulate any number of withering remarks. Then just gave up and laughed. "Well, when you cash in your rain checks, let's do the fight first. Then we can have make-up sex. That's like a bonus."

"Works for me. Do you have to get right back, or have you got a few minutes? I could use a hand hauling in and unrolling the rug I've got for in here. I was going to snag one of the counter guys, but with what I'm paying them, I'd as soon they stick with the counters."

"Pinching pennies now? And you with all those big tubs of money."

"You don't keep big tubs of money if you let yourself get hosed. Besides, this way I'd get to keep you here and look at you a little while longer."

"That's clever." And the fact was, she wanted to stay, wanted to be with him. "All right, I'll help you with your rug before I go. Where is it?"

"Next parlor." He gestured to the connecting doors. "I've got most of what I've bought so far stuffed in here. I'm working in the library next, so I can clean out what goes in the front parlor and in there before I start on this one."

Lena moved to the pocket doors he opened, then just goggled. Aladdin's cave, she thought, outfitted by a very rich madman with very eclectic taste. Tables, sofas, carpets, lamps, and what her grandmother would call doodads were spread everywhere.

"God Almighty, Declan, when did you get all this?"

"A little here, a little there. I tell myself no, but I don't listen. Anyway"—he began to pick his way through the narrow aisles his purchases formed—"it's a big house. It needs lots of . . . stuff. I thought about sticking with the era when the house was originally built. Then I decided I'd get bored. I like to mix things up."

She spotted a brass hippo on what she tagged as a Hepplewhite side table. "Mission accomplished."

"Look at this lamp." He ran his fingers over the shade of a Tiffany that exploded with gem colors. "I've got a weakness for lamps."

"*Cher*, looking 'round here, I'd say you've got a weakness for every damn thing."

"I sure have one for you. Here's the rug." He patted the long, rolled carpet leaning against the wall. "I think we can drag it, snake it through. I should've put it closer to the door, but I wasn't sure where I was going to use it when I bought it. Now I am."

Between them, they managed to slide it to the floor, then with Declan walking bent over and backward, they wove it around the islands of furniture. He had to stop once to move a sofa, again to shove a table aside.

"You know," Lena said as they both went down on their knees, panting a little, in the parlor, "in a couple months you're going to be rolling this up again. Nobody leaves rugs down through the summer around here. Too damn hot."

"I'll worry about that in June."

She sat back on her heels, patted his cheek. "*Cher*, you're going to start thinking summer before April's over. Okay." She pushed up her sleeves, put her palms on the roll. "Ready?"

On their hands and knees, they bumped along, pushing the carpet, revealing the pattern. She could catch only glimpses of the colors and texture, but it was enough to see why he wanted it here.

The greens of leaves were soft, like the walls, and blended with faded pink cabbage roses against a deeper green background. Once it was unrolled, she got to her feet to study the effect while he fussed with squaring it up.

"You bought yourself a rose garden, Declan. I can almost smell them."

"Great, huh? Really works in here. I'm going to use the two American Empire sofas, and I think the Biedermeier table. Start with those, then see." He looked up at the ceiling medallion. "I saw this great chandelier— blown glass, very Dale Chihuly. I should've bought it."

"Why don't we see how your sofas do first?"

"Hmm? Oh, they're heavy, I'll get Remy to give me a hand with them later. He's supposed to come by."

"I'm here now."

"I don't want you to hurt yourself."

She merely shot him a look and started back into his makeshift storeroom.

They'd just set the second one in place, she'd only stepped back to ponder the arrangement, when she heard the baby crying.

She glanced over at Declan, but he seemed lost in thought.

"Did one of your counter men bring a baby with him?" she asked, and Declan closed his eyes, sank down on the sofa.

"You hear it? Nobody else hears it. The doors slamming, yeah. And water running when there's nobody in the room to turn on the taps. But nobody hears the baby."

A chill whipped up her back, had her glancing uneasily toward the hallway. "Where is it?"

"The nursery, mostly. Sometimes in the bedroom on the second floor. Abigail's room. But usually the nursery. It stops when I get to the door. Remy's been here twice when it started. He didn't hear it. But you do."

"I have to see. I can't stand hearing a baby crying that way." She walked into the foyer, started up the stairs. And it stopped.

For an instant, it seemed the whole house hushed. Then she heard the clamor from the kitchen, the stream of music from a radio, the hum of men's voices as they worked.

"That's so strange." She stood on the staircase, one hand on the banister. And her heart thumping. "I was thinking, I wanted to pick up the baby. People say you need to let babies cry, but I don't know why they should. I was thinking that, and she stopped crying."

"It's weird, isn't it, that you were thinking about picking up your great-great-grandmother? It's Marie Rose," he said when Lena turned on the stairs to look down at him. "I'm sure of it. Maybe you can hear her because you're blood. I guess I can because I own the house. I have a call in to the previous owners. I wanted to ask them, but they haven't gotten back to me."

"They may not tell you."

"Well, they can't tell me if I don't ask. Does it scare you?"

She looked up the stairs again and asked herself the same question. "I guess it should, but no, it doesn't. It's fascinating. I think—" She broke off as a door slammed upstairs. "Well, no baby did that." So saying, she ran upstairs.

"Lena." But she was already rounding the curve to the landing and gave him no choice but to bolt after her.

Marching down the hall, she flung doors open. As she reached Abigail's room, the cold swept in. The shock of it had her breath huffing out. Mesmerized by the vapor it caused, she wrapped her arms tightly over her chest.

"This isn't like the baby," she whispered.

"No. It's angry." When he laid his hands on her shoulders to warm her, to draw her away, the door slammed in their faces.

She jumped—she couldn't help it. And heard the nerves in her own strangled laugh. "Not very hospitable, this ghost of yours."

"That's the first time I've seen it." There was a hard lump at the base of his throat. His heart, Declan thought as he took two steadying breaths. "Whoever it is—was—is seriously pissed off."

"It's Abigail's room. We Cajuns can have fierce tempers if we're riled."

"It just doesn't feel like a girl's anger. Not that pretty young thing in the photograph downstairs."

"A lot you know about girls then, *cher*."

"Excuse me, I have a sister, and she can be mean as a scalded cat. I meant it feels more . . . full-blown. More vicious."

"Somebody killed me and buried my body in some unmarked grave, I'd be feeling pretty vicious." Lena made herself reach out, grip the icy knob. "It won't turn."

Declan laid his hand over hers. The cold swept out again; the knob turned easily. And when they opened the door, there was only an empty room, full of sunlight and shadows.

"It's a little scary, isn't it?" But she stepped over the threshold.

"Yeah, a little bit."

"You know what I think, *cher*?"

"What?"

"I think that anybody who stays in the house alone, night after night, who goes out and buys rugs and tables and lamps for it . . ." She turned around and slid her arms around his waist. "I think a man who does that has big steel balls."

"Yeah?" Reading invitation, he lowered his head and kissed her. "I could probably carve out another twenty minutes for that sex now."

She laughed and gave him a hard hug. "Sorry, sugar. I've got to get on back. Saturday night's coming on. But if you happened to be in the neighborhood, say, at three, four in the morning, I think I could stay awake long enough to . . ." She cupped her hand between his legs and stroked over denim. "Stay awake long enough to give those big, steel balls a workout."

He managed not to whimper, but it was a close call. "Wednesday," he told her. "When you're clear."

She still had her hand between his legs, could feel the hard line of him. "Wednesday?"

"When you're clear." But he did crush his mouth to hers to give her some taste of what he was feeling. "Come out here. We'll have dinner. And stay." He backed her against the wall. Used his teeth on her. "Stay the night. I want you in my bed. Wednesday. Tell me you'll come out and be with me."

"All right." She wiggled free. Another few minutes of that, she thought, they wouldn't wait till Wednesday and she'd have him right here on the floor. "I have to get back. I shouldn't have stayed so long."

She looked up and down the hall as she stepped out of the room. "I don't believe I've ever spent the night in a haunted house. What time should I come by?"

"Early."

"I might do that, too. You don't need to see me to the door, *cher*." She sent him a wicked grin. "Walking's got to be a little bit of a problem for you, shape you're in just now. You come on into the bar if you change your mind."

She laid a fingertip on her lips, kissed it, then pointed it at him like a gun before she walked away.

It was an apt gesture, Declan thought. There were times a look from her was as lethal as a bullet.

All he had to do was hold out until Wednesday, then he could get shot again.

# TWELVE

Rain moved in Saturday night and camped out like a squatter through the rest of the weekend. It kept Declan inside, and kept him alone. With Blind Lemon Jackson playing on his stereo, he started preliminary work on the library.

He built a fire as much for cheer as warmth, then found himself sitting on the hearth, running a finger over the chipped tile. Maybe he'd leave it as it was. Not everything should be perfect. Accidents should be accepted, and the character of them absorbed.

He wanted to bring the house to life again, but did he want to put it back exactly the way it had been? He'd already changed things, and the changes made it his.

If he had the tile replaced, was he honoring the history of the Hall, or re-creating it?

It hadn't been a happy home.

The thought ran through him like a chill, though his back was to the snapping fire.

A cold, cold house, full of secrets and anger and envy.

Death.

*She wanted a book. Reading was a delight to her—a slow and brilliant delight. The sight of the library, with row after row after row of books, made her think of the room as reverently as she did church.*

*Now, with Lucian closeted with his father in the study going over the business of land and crops, and the rain drumming against the windows, she could indulge herself in a quiet afternoon of reading.*

*She wasn't quite accustomed to the time to do as she pleased and so slipped into the room as if it were a guilty pleasure. She no longer had linens to fold, tables to dust, dishes to carry.*

*She was no longer a servant in this place, but a wife.*

Wife. *She hugged the word to her. It was still so new, so shiny. As the life growing inside her was new. So new, she had yet to tell Lucian.*

*Her curse was late, and it was never late. She'd awakened ill three days running. But she would wait, another week. To speak of it too soon might make it untrue.*

*And oh, she wanted a child. How she wanted to give Lucian a child. She laid a hand on her belly as she wandered along the shelves and imagined the beautiful son or daughter she would bring into the world.*

*And perhaps, just perhaps, a child would soften Lucian's mother. Perhaps a child would bring joy into the house as the hope for one brought joy to her heart.*

*She selected Austen's* Pride and Prejudice. *The title, she thought, spoke to her. Manet Hall had so much of both. She bit her lip as she flipped through the pages. She was a slow, painstaking reader, but Lucian said that only meant she savored the words.*

*Stumbled over them, she thought, but she was getting better. Pleased with herself, she turned and saw Julian slouched in one of the wine-colored chairs, a snifter in his hand, a bottle by his elbow.*

*Watching her.*

*He frightened her. Repulsed her. But she reminded herself she was no longer a servant. She was his brother's wife, and should try to be friends.*

"Hello, Julian. I didn't see you."

He lifted the bottle, poured more brandy into his glass. "That book," he said, then drank deep, "has words of more than one syllable."

"I can read." Her spine went arrow-straight. "I like to read."

"What else do you like, chère?"

Her fingers tightened on the book when he rose, then relaxed again when he strolled to the fireplace, rested a boot on the hearth, an elbow on the mantel.

"I'm learning to ride. Lucian's teaching me. I'm not very good yet, but I like it." Oh, she wanted to be friends with him. The house deserved warmth and laughter, and love.

He laughed, and she heard the brandy in it. "I bet you ride. I bet you ride a man into a sweat. You may work those innocent eyes on my brother— he's always been a fool. But I know what you are, and what you're after."

"I'm your brother's wife." There had to be a way to take the first step beyond this hate. For Lucian, for the child growing inside her, she took it, and walked toward Julian. "I only want him to be happy. I make him happy. You're his blood, Julian. His twin. It isn't right that we should be at odds this way. I want to try to be your sister. Your friend."

He knocked back the rest of the brandy. "Want to be my friend, do you?"

"Yes, for Lucian's sake, we should—"

"How friendly are you?" He lunged toward her, grabbed her breasts painfully.

The shock of it froze her. The insult flashed through the shock with a burning heat. Her hand cracked across his cheek with enough force to send him staggering back.

"Bastard! Animal! Put your hands on me again, I'll kill you. I'm Lucian's. I'm your brother's wife."

"My brother's whore!" he shouted as she ran for the door. "Cajun slut, I'll see you dead before you take what's mine by rights."

Raging, he shoved away from the mantel. The heavy silver candlestick tumbled off, smashed against the edge of the tile, snapped off the corner.

Declan hadn't moved. When he came back to himself he was still sitting on the hearth, his back to the snapping fire. The rain was still beating on the ground, streaming down the windows.

As it had been, he thought, during the . . . vision? Fugue? Hallucination?

He pressed the heel of his hand between his eyes, where the headache speared like a spike into his skull.

Maybe he didn't have ghosts, he thought. Maybe he had a goddamn fucking brain tumor. It would make more sense. Anything would make more sense.

Slamming doors, cold spots, even sleepwalking were by-products of the house he could live with. But he'd *seen* those people, inside his head. Heard them there—the words, the tone. More, much more disturbing, he'd felt them.

His legs were weak, nearly gave way under him as he got to his feet. He had to grip the mantel, his fingers vising on so that he wondered the marble didn't snap.

If something was wrong with him, physically, mentally, he had to deal with it. Fitzgeralds didn't bury their heads in the sand when things got tough.

Figuring he was as steady as he was going to get, he went into the kitchen to hunt up aspirin. Which, he decided as he shook out four, was going to be like trying to piss out a forest fire. But he gulped them down, then ran the cold glass over his forehead.

He'd fly up to Boston and see his uncle. His mother's baby brother was a cardiologist, but he'd know the right neurosurgeon. A couple of days, some tests, and he'd know if he was crazy, haunted or dying.

He started to reach for his phone, then stopped and shook his head. Crazy, he thought, just got one more point. If he went to Uncle Mick, word of his potential medical problems would run through the family like an airborne virus.

Besides, what was he running back to Boston for? New Orleans had doctors. He'd get the name of Remy's. He could tell his friend he just wanted to get a doctor, a dentist and so on in the area. That was logical.

He'd get himself a physical, then ask the doctor to recommend a specialist. Simple, straightforward and efficient.

If ghosts couldn't drive him out of Manet Hall, damn if a brain tumor would.

As he set the glass down, a door slammed on the second floor. He simply glanced up at the ceiling and smiled grimly.

"Yeah, well, I'm in a pretty crappy mood myself."

B y Wednesday, he had a handle on things again. Maybe it was the anticipation of seeing Lena that lifted his spirits—in combination with the work he'd managed to get done on those last days before Lent. He had an appointment with Remy's doctor the following week and, having taken that step, was able to put most of the concern about the state of his brain aside.

There had been no more fugues. At least, he thought, none he was aware of.

The rain had finally moved on to plague Florida, and had left him with the first tender trumpets of daffodils scattered along one of his garden paths.

The morning weather report had detailed a ten-inch snowfall in Boston.

He immediately called his mother to rub it in.

Sunshine and the tease of spring had him switching gears earlier than he'd intended. He postponed work on the library and set up outdoors to reinforce the second-floor gallery, to replace damaged boards.

He listened to Ray Charles, and felt healthy as a horse. He was going to have the Franks do most of the early planting, he decided. He just didn't have time. But next year, he'd do his own. Or as much as he could manage.

Next spring, he'd sit out here on the gallery on Sunday mornings, eating beignets, drinking café au lait—with Lena. Long, lazy Sundays, looking out over the lawns, the gardens. And a few years down the road, looking out at the kids in the yards, in the gardens.

He wanted a family of his own, and it was good to know it. He'd never had that need inside him before, the need to hold on to the now and look to tomorrow at the same time.

So he knew it was right, what he felt for her. What he planned for them. He'd help her in the bar if she needed it, but he'd have his own work.

He turned his hands over, studied the palms, the calluses he'd built. The little nicks and scars he looked on as personal medals of valor.

He'd use them, his back and his imagination, to transform other houses. People in the parish would think of Declan Fitzgerald when they needed a contractor.

You should've seen that old house before he got ahold of it, they'd say. You need the job done, you just call Dec. He'll fix you up.

The idea made him grin as he ripped out the next rotten board.

By four, he'd finished the long front sweep of the gallery floor and stretched out on it, belly down, to take a break. He fell asleep with B. B. King pleading with Lucille.

And was sleeping still when he rose and walked down the shaky, sagging curve of stairs to the front lawn.

The grass was thick under his feet, and the heat of the sun poured over his face, beat down on his head despite the hat he wore as protection.

The others were inside, but he'd wanted to look at the pond, at the lilies. He'd wanted to sit in the shade of the willow that danced over the water, and read.

He liked the music of the birds, and didn't mind the heat so much. The heat was honest. The air inside the Hall was cold and false.

It was heartbreaking to watch the house he loved rotting away from bitterness.

He stopped at the edge of the pond, looking down at the green plates of the pads, the creamy white lilies that graced them. He watched a dragonfly whiz by, the sun glinting off the wings so it was an iridescent blur. He heard the plop of a frog and the call of a cardinal.

When he heard his name, he turned. And smiled as his beloved crossed the velvet lawn toward him. As long as they were together, he thought, as long as they loved, the Hall would stand.

"Declan. Declan."

Alarmed, Lena gripped his arms and shook. She'd seen him coming down those treacherous stairs as she'd driven down his lane, and how he'd walked toward the pond in an awkward, hesitant gait so unlike his usual easy stride.

His eyes were open but glazed in a way that made her think he was looking through her and seeing something—someone—else.

"Declan." She kept her voice firm, and her hands, as she took his face in them. "Look at me now. Hear me? It's Lena."

"Let's sit under the willow where no one can see us."

There was no willow, only the rotted stump of one. Fear tickled the back of her throat, but she swallowed it. Going with instinct, she rose up on her toes and laid her lips warmly on his.

His response was slow, dreamy, a kind of sliding to her. Against her. Into her. So she knew the instant he snapped back by the way his body stiffened. He started to sway, but she held on.

"Steady now, *cher*. You just hang on to me till you get your legs under you."

"Sorry. Need to sit." He dropped straight down on the grass, laid his brow on his knees. "Whoa."

"You're okay now. You're fine now." She knelt beside him, brushing at his hair and murmuring in Cajun—her language of comfort. "Just get your breath back."

"What the hell's wrong with me? I was on the gallery. I was working on the gallery."

"Is that the last thing you remember?"

He looked up now, over the pond. "I don't know how I got out here."

"You walked down the stairs, the ones on the right of the house. I thought you were going to go straight through them." Her heart still hitched when she thought of how unsteady they were. "They don't look safe, Declan. You ought to block them off."

"Yeah." He scrubbed his hands over his face. "Lock myself in a padded room while I'm at it."

"You're not crazy."

"I'm sleepwalking—in the daylight now. I'm hallucinating. I'm hearing voices. That doesn't sound sane to me."

"That's just the Yankee talking. Down here that doesn't even come up to eccentric. Why, my great-aunt Sissy has whole conversations with her husband, Joe, and he's been dead for twelve years come September. Nobody thinks she's crazy."

"What do they talk about?"

"Oh, family business, current events, the weather. Politics. Great-Uncle Joe dearly loved complaining about the government. Feeling better now, *cher*?"

"I don't know. What did I do? What did you see me do?"

"You just came down the stairs and walked across the grass toward the pond. You weren't walking like you, so I knew something was wrong."

"What do you mean?"

"You've got a smooth, lanky kind of gait, and you weren't moving like that. Then you stopped at the pond."

She didn't tell him she'd had one shocked moment when she'd been sure he meant to walk straight into the water.

"I kept calling you. And finally you turned around and smiled at me." Her stomach muscles tightened as she remembered. "But not *at* me. I don't think you were seeing me. And you said you wanted to sit under the willow, where no one could see us."

"There's no willow here."

"Well." She pointed toward the stump. "There was, once. Seems like you're having dreams where maybe you can see things that happened before. That's a kind of gift, Declan."

"Where do I return it?" He shook his head. "I don't know, because I can't remember once I wake up. But I'm starting to think I should tie myself to the bedpost at night."

"I can take care of that for you tonight."

"You trying to cheer me up with bondage fantasies?"

"How'd I do?"

"Pretty good." He let out a breath, then frowned at the smudge on her forehead. "You've got some soot or something," he began, and she tipped her head back before he could rub at it.

"Those are my holy ashes."

"Oh, right." His brain had definitely gone on holiday. "Ash Wednesday. I not only don't know where I am, but when I am."

She couldn't bear to watch him sink into the dark again, and kept her voice brisk, just a little lofty. "I take it you didn't get to church today, on this holy day of obligation."

He winced. "You sound like my mother. I forgot. Sort of."

She arched an eyebrow. "Seems to me you could use all the blessings you can get." So saying, she rubbed her thumb on the print of ash on her forehead, then rubbed it on his. It made him smile.

"That's probably sacrilegious, but thanks. What time is it?" He looked at his watch and swore. "I have to get this sucker into the shop. It keeps stopping on me. I know it's past noon, and it sure isn't midnight."

"It's about five. You did say to come early."

"Yeah, I did. Why don't we go sit out back and have some wine?"

She watched him closely for the first few minutes, but he appeared to be steady again as he selected a wine. Got some lovely old stemware out of his new cupboards.

He'd frightened her, Lena could admit, and badly. She'd been certain he'd intended to walk into the water, to drown himself among the lily pads just as Lucian Manet had done.

And with the realization, a whole new realm of possibilities opened in her mind. "Declan . . ."

"I got steaks and I got a grill," he said as he poured the wine. He needed to focus on ordinary things—to steep himself in the here and now. "All real men can grill steaks. If you tell me you don't eat red meat, we're going to have to go for the frozen pizza."

"If I eat meat, why should I care what color it is? Let's go out and sit. I've got an idea I want to run by you."

They walked to the two wooden crates he was using for chairs and sat.

"What if it's not ghosts? Or not only ghosts?" she asked him.

"Oh, that's a cheering thought. What else have I got? Vampires? Werewolves? Maybe some flesh-eating zombies. I'm going to sleep much better now, thanks."

"What do you think about reincarnation?"

"Past lives? Recycling souls?" He shrugged his shoulders. "I don't know."

"It always seemed efficient to me—and fair, too. Everybody deserves more than one chance, don't you think? Maybe you're remembering things that happened here because you lived here before. Maybe you're Lucian, come back after all these years for his Abigail."

"That's a romantic notion. I'll be Lucian if you'll be Abby."

"You don't get to choose. And if you're going to make fun of the idea, I won't say another word about it."

"Okay, don't get testy." He sipped his wine, brooded into space. "So your theory is I'm here, and these things are happening because I lived a past life, as Lucian Manet."

"It's no more farfetched then the place being haunted, which you swallowed easy enough. It would explain why you bought this place, needed it. Why you're working so hard to restore its beauty. How you saw the furniture in his bedroom upstairs."

"Reincarnation," he repeated. "Sounds better than a brain tumor."

"What?"

He shook his head, drank again. "Nothing."

"You're thinking you got a tumor in your brain? That's nonsense, Declan." Her voice was sharper than she'd intended, so she continued more gently. "That's just nonsense, *cher*. There's not a thing wrong with your head or any other part of you."

"Of course not. I was just thinking out loud."

But she saw it on his face and, rising, slid onto his lap, straddling him. "You're really worried you've got something inside your head making you see things, do things?"

"I'm not worried. I'm just . . . Look, I'm going to have some tests, eliminate the possibility."

"You're not sick, *cher*." She touched her lips to his cheek, then the other. There'd never been another man who'd so consistently, so effortlessly, nudged out her tender side. "I guarantee it. But if having some fancy doctor tell you the same thing settles your mind, that's fine."

"Don't mention this to Remy." He took her hand until she eased back to meet his eyes. "He's got the wedding coming up. That's enough for him to think about right now."

"So, you're planning on going to have brain tests all by yourself? That's not the way we do things around here, *cher*. You don't want Remy to know, all right. But you tell me when this is set up for, and I'll go with you."

"Lena, I'm a big boy."

"You're not going by yourself. So I go with you, or I tell Remy and we gang up on you."

"Okay. I'll let you know when it's scheduled and you can hold my hand. In the meantime, I'm going to put my money on your reincarnation theory. It's weird, but it's a lot less messy than brain surgery."

"They say Lucian Manet was a handsome man, like a young golden god." She trailed her fingers through Declan's disordered hair. It was a dark blond, she mused, thick, lush, and she bet it would streak up sexily with the summer sun. "I think you've improved on him this time around."

"Oh yeah?" He hooked his arms around her waist. "Tell me more."

"I never much cared for the golden-god type. Usually too pretty for my taste." She cocked her head, eased forward to kiss him. "You suit my taste, *cher*."

He brought her closer and, sitting on the wooden crate, rested his chin on her shoulder as he looked out over the gallery railings. "I love you, Lena."

"If you're trying to sweet-talk me into bed before you feed me—"

He drew her back, and the grin faded from her face as she saw his. "I love you," he repeated. "I never understood what that meant before, and I didn't think I could."

He held her in place when she tried to scramble up and away. "You need to settle down now," she told him.

"Yeah, I do—but I don't think you mean it the same way. I need to settle down, right here, with you. I don't care if it's the first time or the fiftieth time we've gone around. You're what I've been waiting for."

"Declan, you're making more out of this than you should." Her voice wanted to shake. God knew, her stomach already was. "We went out to dinner. We went to bed. We've seen each other a handful of times."

"It only took one look at you."

His eyes were so deep, she thought, so clear. Like the surface of a lake at twilight. "You don't even know me."

He pulled her back a second time, reminding her that there was steel in him, and an edge to it. "You're wrong. I know you're smart, and you're strong. Enough to carve out your own place from almost nothing. I know you pay your debts. I know you're loyal and you're loving. I know somebody hurt you, and it wouldn't take much to knock the scab off. And I know I'm scaring you right now because you don't think you're ready to hear what I'm saying to you."

The beat of her heart was painful, like the strike of a fist on a raw wound. "I'm not looking for love, Declan. I'm sorry."

"Neither was I, but there you go. We don't have to rush it. I wasn't going to say anything to you yet but . . . I needed to."

"*Cher*, people, they fall in and out of love all the time. It's just a dazzle of chemicals."

"He really hurt you."

Frustrated, she pushed away, and this time he let her go. "You're wrong. There's no man, no ghost of some lover who broke my heart. I look like a cliché to you?"

"You look like everything to me."

"*Mon Dieu.*" The man made her throat fill up, then snap shut. Deliberately she fought back the sensation and spoke clearly. "I like you, Declan, and I enjoy your company. I want you in bed. If that's not enough for you, I walk now and save us both a lot of trouble and disappointment."

"Do you always get so pissed off when somebody tells you he loves you?"

No one ever had, she nearly said. No one ever had who meant it. "I don't like being pushed, and when I am, I make a point of not going in that direction."

"I have to admire that." His grin was easy as he got to his feet. "I like you, too, Lena. And I enjoy your company, want you in bed. That's enough for now. Are you hungry? I think I'll heat up the grill."

I f it was a trick, Lena thought, or some sort of strategy to keep her off balance, it was well done.

She just couldn't quite puzzle the man out, and his seamless shift of moods was a surefire way to push her to keep trying.

He cooked like a man who didn't trust himself in an actual kitchen. Jacketed potatoes on the grill, the steaks. And he sweet-talked her into making the salad.

He didn't say another word about love.

He asked her about work, how her business had done during the two days of rain. He put on music, kept it low, and talked through the kitchen door as the grill smoked and she chopped vegetables.

They might have been casual friends, or the most comfortable of lovers.

They ate in his pretty kitchen, by candlelight. Even the house behaved. Despite it—or perhaps because of it—she stayed on edge throughout the meal.

He took a bakery cake out of the fridge. Lena took one look, sighed. "I can't."

"We can save it for later."

"I can't for forty days. I gave up chocolate for Lent. I've got a powerful taste for chocolate."

"Oh." He stuck it back in. "I've probably got something else."

"What'd you give up?"

"Wearing women's underwear. It's tough, but I think I can hold out till Easter."

"You talk like that, I'm going to take my ashes back." He was making her itchy, she thought. The best way to solve that was to make him itch more. She stepped behind him as he searched his refrigerator, then wrapped her arms around his waist, pressed her body to his. "You need to give something up, *cher*, something you've got a powerful taste for."

"It sure as hell isn't going to be you."

He let her spin him around, shove him back against the refrigerator.

Oh, he knew her, he thought as she used her lips to set off explosions in his bloodstream. He knew she was using sex to keep one step ahead of him. One step back from him.

If she didn't realize he could love her as much as he wanted her, it was up to him to show her.

"In your bed, you said." Her mouth was reckless, restless as it raced over his face. "In your bed."

She pulled him toward the doorway. He nearly pulled her back, toward the kitchen stairs, but decided it might be interesting to take the long way around.

He pushed her against the wall in the hallway, assaulted her throat with his teeth. "We'll get there."

He reached down, yanked her shirt up, over her head, threw it aside. Wrapped together, they did a quick vertical roll along the wall, and finally stopped with their positions reversed. With impatient hands she pulled his shirt open so that buttons danced along the floor.

They fought with clothes on their way to the steps. Shoes landed with thumps. Her bra fluttered over the banister, his jeans plopped on the third step.

They were breathless before they reached the landing.

His hands were rough, a workingman's hands now that thrilled as they streaked over her. Her skin came alive.

"Hurry." She sank her teeth into his shoulder as need raged through her, a firestorm of violent heat that burned away all caution. "God, hurry."

He nearly took her where they stood, but he wanted her under him. Bucking, arching.

With his mouth savaging hers, he wrapped his arms around her waist, lifted her two inches off the floor. Something raw and primitive stabbed through him at the knowledge that there was no choice now. No choice for either of them but to mate.

Shadows cloaked them as they moved toward the bedroom.

Cold from doorways seeped out, made her shiver.

"Declan."

"This is us. This is ours." As he spoke, his voice a snarl, as he held her, his grip like iron, the cold curled back.

They fell on his bed, a tangle of limbs and urgency. When he plunged into her, her nails dug into his back. Pleasure, dark and desperate, drenched her, the feral glory of it drove her up so that she twined herself around him and matched the furious pace.

No control, nor the desire for it. Only the wild thirst to take and take and take. And with it, the gnawing hunger to give.

She clung to him, riding through the storm of sensation, sprinting up and up toward that jagged brink again.

Dimly, she heard a clock begin to strike in deep, heavy bongs. On the twelfth, she shattered with him.

When he started to shift away, she tightened her grip. "Mmm. Don't move yet."

"I'm too heavy for you." He rubbed his lips at the curve of her throat.

"I like it. I like this." Lazily, she angled her head so he could work his way up to her jaw. Her body felt used and bruised and wonderfully loose. "Even better than chocolate cake."

He laughed and rolled over, taking her with him so she sprawled over his chest. "There, now I don't have to worry about crushing you."

"A gentleman to the last." Content, she settled in. "I've always liked a clock that chimes the hours," she said. "But you need to set it. It's not midnight yet."

"I know."

"Sounded like a big, old grandfather clock. Where'd you put it? In the parlor."

"No." He stroked a hand over her hair, down her back. "I don't have a clock that chimes."

"*Cher*, you absolutely ring my bells, but I heard a clock chime twelve."

"Yeah, so did I. But I don't have a clock."

She lifted her head, let out a slow breath. "Oh. Well then. Does it scare you?"

"No."

"Then it doesn't scare me, either," she said, and laid her head back over his heart.

# THIRTEEN

The best way, in Declan's opinion, to break through the obstacles and opposition to any goal, was not to ram headfirst against them and risk a skull fracture, but to chip away at them. Gradually, reasonably. Relentlessly. Whether it was a lawsuit, a sporting event or a love affair, it was imperative to keep the end in sight in order to select the correct means.

He found out which Mass Lena and her grandmother attended, and at which church. Research was essential in any strategy.

When he slipped into the pew beside them on Sunday morning, he got a long speculative look from Lena, and a conspirator's wink from Odette.

He figured God would understand and appreciate the ploy, and not hold it against him for using Sunday Mass as a means to his end.

But he wouldn't mention the brainstorm to his mother. She was, in Declan's experience, a lot less flexible than the Almighty.

Aiming the leading edge of his charm toward Odette, he talked them into brunch afterward, and got another cool stare from Lena when he gave his name to the hostess. He'd already made reservations for three.

"Sure of yourself, aren't you, *cher*?"

His eyes were the innocent gray of a former altar boy. "Just prepared."

"You ain't no Boy Scout, sugar," she told him.

"Your granddaughter's very cynical," Declan responded as he offered his arm to Odette.

"What she is, is smart." Odette patted a hand on his and had her bracelets jangling. "A woman's got to be about smooth-talking, handsome men. Man who comes into church so he can spend a Sunday morning with a woman, he's pretty smart, too."

"I thought I'd come in and pray for a while."

"What'd you pray for?"

"That you'd run away with me to Borneo."

With a laugh, Odette slipped into the chair Declan held out for her. "Aren't you the one."

"Yeah." He looked directly at Lena. "I'm going to be the one."

They settled in with mimosas and the first round from the expansive buffet. While a jazz quartet played Dixieland, Declan told them about the progress on the house.

"I'm going to stick with the outside work as long as the weather holds. Tibald's still dealing with the plastering, and I'm trying to line up a painter for the exterior. I don't want to do that myself. The guy I had paint the parlor came in to take a look at the library, but he left sort of abruptly."

Declan's expression was rueful as he sipped his mimosa. "I don't think he's coming back. Tile man, either. He got one bath half done when he packed it in."

"I can do some asking around for you," Odette offered.

"I'd appreciate it. But I think I'm going to have to start looking outside the parish or try my hand at some of this stuff myself. Things are getting a little lively at the Hall."

"Grown men running off because a couple of doors slam." Lena curled her lips into a sneer. "Ought to have more spine."

"It's a little more than that now. Clocks bonging where there aren't any clocks to bong, music playing in empty rooms. When the painter was there, the pocket doors in the library kept opening and closing. Then there was the screaming."

"What screaming?"

"Tile guy." Declan smiled wanly. "Said he heard somebody come in the bedroom door, thought it was me. He's talking away, setting the tiles, listening to what he assumed was me moving around in there. Since I wasn't answering whatever questions he had, he got up, walked in. Nobody there. From what I could get out of him when he was semi-coherent, the bathroom door slammed behind him, the logs caught fire in the fireplace. Then he claims he felt somebody put a hand on his shoulder. I had to peel him off the ceiling when I got up there."

"What do you think about it?" Odette asked.

"A couple of things. Seems to me the more the work progresses on the house, the more overt and volatile the . . . paranormal activity, we'll call it. Especially, well, when I veer off from the original scheme."

Lena scooped up a forkful of grits—a particular southern culinary custom Declan had yet to get his tastebuds around. "What do you mean?"

"For example, the plasterwork. The areas where that is going on, things are pretty settled. I'm restoring them, replicating. But in places where I've made changes—bathroom setup, tiles—things get really interesting. It's like whatever's in the house gets royally ticked that we're not sticking with the original plan."

"Something to think about," Odette commented.

"I have been. I figure Josephine Manet." Even here, with Dixieland bright in the air and champagne fizzing, the name coated his belly with dread. "Mistress of the Hall. You only have to look at her photographs to see that was a woman who didn't like to be crossed. Now, I come along and put my fingerprints all over what's hers."

"You resolved to living with her?" Odette asked, and watched his jaw firm.

"I'm resolved to living in the Hall, and doing it my way. She wants to kick up a fuss about it, that's her problem."

Lena sat back. "What do you figure, Grandmama? Brave or stubborn?"

"Oh, he's some of both. It's a good mix."

"Thanks, but I don't know how brave it is. It's my house now, and that's that. Still, I think you can't blame a man who doesn't have any more than his time and labor invested for taking a hike. Anyway, Miss Odette, what do you think? Am I tangling with Josephine?"

"I think you've got two opposing forces in that house. The one that brought you there, the one that wants you to go away. It's going to come down to who's strongest."

She opened her Sunday purse, took out a small muslin bag. "I made this up for you."

"What is it?"

"Oh, a little kitchen magic. You just keep that in your pocket. May not help, but it can't hurt." She picked up her glass again, smiled at it. "Imagine, drinking champagne for breakfast."

"Come with me to Borneo, you can bathe in it."

"*Cher*, I drink enough of this, I may take you up on it."

"I'll get us another round."

He was so sweet with her, Lena thought. Flirting with her grandmother until there was a flush of pleasure on Odette's cheeks throughout the long, lazy meal. He troubled himself for people, she mused. Took the time, made the effort to find out what they might enjoy, then saw to it.

He was attentive, clever, sexy, rich, tough-minded and kind.

And he said he was in love with her.

She believed she understood him well enough to be sure he wouldn't have said it unless he meant it. That's what unnerved her.

For added to those other qualities was a wide streak of honesty. And sheer stubborn grit.

He could make her fall in love with him. She was already halfway there and sliding fast. Every time she tried to dig her heels in, she lost her balance again. The tumble was as worrisome as it was thrilling.

But what would happen when she hit? Once she dropped all the way, there'd be no climbing back out. That was something she understood about herself. Relationships were easy when they didn't matter, or mattered only for the moment.

When they mattered forever, they changed everything.

Things had changed already, she admitted. It had started with that yearning for him inside her. And now with the comfort and challenge she felt when she was with him. With being able to imagine feeling it day after day, year after year.

He'd want promises she was afraid to give.

Not afraid, she corrected, irritated with herself. Reluctant to give. Unwilling to give.

Then she watched him lean over and kiss her grandmother's cheek and was afraid—there was no point in pretending otherwise—that she'd end up giving him anything he asked for.

He courted her. It seemed a particularly appealing southern word to Declan, bringing images of moonlight and porch swings, tart lemonade and country dances.

Throughout March, two things occupied his mind, his time and his plans. Lena and the house.

He celebrated the clear results of his neurological tests by taking the day off to antique. Spring had jump-started the flowers and had pedestrians strolling in shirtsleeves. The carriage horses the tourists loved prancing with bright clip-clops of hooves on pavement.

Summer would drop her heavy hand soon enough, and turn the air to molasses. The thought of it reminded him he had to have the air-conditioning upgraded, and maybe reconsider installing paddle fans in some of the rooms.

He bought with his usual surrender to impulse, brightening the day of several shopkeepers before he stopped in a place called, simply, Yesterday.

It was a hodgepodge of statuary, lamps, vintage accessories and jewelry, with three curtained booths on the side where patrons could buy a tarot card reading.

It was the ring that caught his eye first. The blood-red ruby and ice-white diamond formed two halves of an interlocking heart on a platinum band.

The minute he held it in his hand, he knew he wanted it for Lena. Maybe it was foolish to buy an engagement ring at this point in their relationship. And it was reckless to snatch at something before he'd looked at other options.

But this was the one he wanted to put on her finger. And he decided if a man could buy a house on a whim, he could sure as hell buy a ring.

"I'll take it."

"It's beautiful," said the shopkeeper. "She's a lucky woman."

"I'm working on convincing her of that."

"I have some lovely earrings that would complement this. Is ruby her birthstone?" the clerk asked as she showed him a pair of earrings with a dangle of ruby hearts and diamonds.

"I don't know." But he'd gotten her birthday from Odette to make sure he didn't miss it. "July?"

"Then it is. Lucky guess."

"No kidding." It gave him a little tingle as he looked back at the ring. Some things were meant, he told himself. He lifted one of the earrings. He could already see them on her—just as he imagined the clerk could see *Impulse Buyer* stamped on his forehead.

He leaned on the counter and began to pit Yankee bargaining skills against southern horse-trading.

He figured they'd come to fair terms when her smile was still in place but much less brilliant.

"Will that be all for you today?"

"Yeah, I've got to get going. I'm already—" He broke off when he glanced at his watch and saw it had stopped at twelve again. "You know, I could use a watch—a pocket watch. Mine's been acting up, and I'm doing a lot of carpentry right now. Probably smashed this one a few times on the job."

"I've got some wonderful old pocket watches and chains. They're so much more imaginative than the new ones."

She led him over to another display cabinet, pulled out a drawer and set it on the counter.

"Watches like this tell more than time," she began. "They tell a story. This one—"

"No." The edges of his vision dimmed like smoke. The chatter of voices from other customers faded into a hum. Part of him remained aware enough to know he was sliding away from himself. Even as he tried to stop it, to pull back, he watched his own hand reach out, pick up a gold watch and its loop of chain.

The voice of the shopkeeper hovered around the rim of his consciousness. It was another voice that stabbed through, clear as a bell. Female, young, excited.

*For my husband, for his birthday. He broke his. I want to give him something special. This one is so handsome. Can you engrave it?*

And he already knew what he would find, exactly what he would find, before he turned the watch over to read the back.

To Lucian from his Abby.
To mark our time together.
April 4, 1899

"Mr. Fitzgerald? Mr. Fitzgerald, are you all right? Would you like some water? You're awfully pale."

"What?"

"Can I get you some water? Would you like to sit down?"

"No." He closed his hand tightly over the watch, but the sensation was already fading. "No, thanks. I'm okay. I'll take this, too."

More than a little shaken, he headed to Remy's office. He thought some time in the sensible business district, in the rational atmosphere of law, might help settle him down.

More, he wanted a few minutes with a friend who might think he was crazy, but would love him anyway.

"If you'd told me you were coming by," Remy began as he closed his office door, "I'd've scooted some stuff around so we could maybe have lunch."

"I didn't expect to head over this way today."

"Been shopping again." Remy nodded at the bag Declan carried. "Boy, aren't you having anything sent down from Boston?"

"As a matter of fact, I've got some stuff coming down next week. Books mostly," Declan said as he wandered the office. His gaze skimmed over the law books, the fat files, the memos. All of it, the debris of the lawyer, seemed very distant to him now.

"A few pieces I had in my study up there that should work in the library."

He picked up a brass paperweight, set it down. Slipped a hand into his pocket, jiggled change.

"You going to tell me what's on your mind, or just pace until you dig a trench in my carpet?" With his suit jacket draped over the back of his chair, his tie loosened, his sleeves rolled up, Remy kicked back in his chair and began to swish a bright green Slinky from palm to palm. "You're wearing me out."

"I've told you some of the things that've been happening."

"Got a firsthand account of them myself when I dropped in on Saturday. I'd still feel better if you told me that piano music we heard was from some radio you forgot to turn off."

"I guess I'll have to get a piano for the ladies' parlor, since that seems to be the spot. I like to play anyway, when I remember to sit down at one."

Remy shifted the Slinky to vertical, let the colorful spiral drip into itself. "So, you came by to tell me you're in the market for a piano?"

"I bought a watch today."

"And you want to show it off? Want me to call in my assistant, some of the law clerks?"

"It was Lucian Manet's watch."

"No shit?" The Slinky, sloshed into a whole, was tossed aside. "How do you know? Where'd you get ahold of it?"

"Little shop in the Quarter." He drew out the box, set it on Remy's desk. "Take a look at it."

Obliging, Remy took off the lid. "Elegant, if you want something you're going to have to dig out whenever you want to know what time it is. Heavy," he added when he picked it up.

"You don't . . . feel anything from it?"

"Feel anything?"

"Look on the back, Remy."

"Names and dates are right," Remy concluded. "Hell of a stroke of luck, you stumbling on this."

"Luck? I don't think so. I go into a shop, buy Lena a ring, then—"

"Whoa, whoa, whoa, just back up there a minute. A ring?"

"I told you I was going to marry her." Declan shrugged. "I found the ring. It doesn't hurt to have it ahead of schedule. But that's not the point."

"Pretty damn big point, if you ask me. She know you're up to this?"

"I told her how I felt, what I wanted. I'm letting her stew on it awhile. Can we get back to the watch?"

"*Et là!* You always were mule-headed. Go ahead."

"I walk into that shop, decide I need a watch because mine's acting up. I decide I need a pocket watch even though I've never used one, never thought about using one. Then, I see that one, and I know. I know it was his, I know she bought it for him for his birthday. I know what it says on the back before I read it. Exactly what it says. Because I heard it in my head."

"I don't know what to think about that." Remy raked his fingers through his hair. "Isn't there something about how some people touch an object and get images from it? Its history or whatever?"

"It's called psychometry. I've been doing a lot of reading up on paranormal science in my spare time," Declan explained when Remy frowned at him. "But I've never had anything like that happen before. Lena's got a theory. That this is a reincarnation deal."

Remy pursed his lips, set the watch back in its box. "I guess I'd be more inclined to put some stock in that rather than the psycho whatever."

"If it is, then the house, now this watch, are triggering past-life memories. Pretty weird."

"The whole thing's been weird since the get-go, *cher*."

"Here's the kicker. If I accept that I was Lucian, then I know Lena was Abigail. What I don't know is if I'm supposed to bring her into the house, to make things right from before. Or if I'm supposed to keep her away from it, and resolve the cycle that way."

In the Vieux Carre, where Lena prepared to leave her apartment for the bar and the afternoon shift, she opened the door and stepped into another cycle. An old one.

"Baby!" Lilibeth Simone threw open her arms.

Sluggish with shock, Lena was unable to move back before they wrapped around her like chains. Trapped, she was assaulted with impressions. Too much perfume that didn't quite cover the smell of stale smoke, the bony form honed down by years of hard living. Sticky layers of hairspray over curls dyed black as pitch.

And through it all seeped her own dark dread.

"I went downstairs first, and that handsome young man behind the bar said you were still up here. Why, I'm so glad to catch you!" The voice was a bright bubble that bounced and jerked in the air. "Let me just *look* at you! I swear, I *swear* you just get prettier every time I see you. Sweetie pie, I just have to sit down a minute and catch my breath. I'm just so excited to see you, I can hardly *stand* it."

She talked too fast, Lena noted, walked too fast on the spiked backless heels she'd paired with hot-pink and skin-tight capris. Those were warnings that she'd taken a hit of her current drug of choice very recently.

"Look what you've done with this place!" Lilibeth dropped into a chair and dumped a floral suitcase beside her. She clapped her hands like a child so the plastic bracelets on her bony wrists banged together. "Why, I just love it. Suits you, baby. It sure does suit you."

*She'd been pretty once,* Lena thought as she studied her mother. She'd seen pictures. But all that prettiness had been carved down, diamond-hard, to canny.

At forty-four, Lilibeth's face showed all the wear from too much liquor, too many pills and far too many men.

Deliberately, Lena left the door open and remained standing just inside it. The sound of traffic, the scent of the bakery across the street, kept her grounded. "What do you want?"

"Why, to see you, of course." Lilibeth let out a trill of laughter that scraped over Lena's brain like nails on a blackboard. "What a thing to ask. I got such a yen to see you, baby. I said to myself, My Lena's busy, but we've just got to have a little time together. So I got myself on a bus, and here I am. You just have to sit on down here, honey, and tell me everything you've been up to."

Disgust rolled through her, and Lena clung to it. Better disgust than the despair that crept along just under it. "I have work."

"Oh now, you can take a little while for your own mama. After all, you own the place. I'm just so proud of my baby, all grown up and running your own business.

"Doing so well for yourself, too," she continued as she looked around the room.

Lena caught the look, and the cunning in it. It tightened her chest, and stiffened her spine. "I told you the last time it was the last time. You won't get any money from me again."

"Why do you want to hurt my feelings like that?" Lilibeth widened her eyes as they filled with tears. "I just want to spend a few days with my little girl."

"I'm not a little girl," Lena said dully. "Yours in particular."

"Don't be mean, honey, after I've come all this way just to see you again. I know I haven't been a good mama to you, darling, but I'm going to make it up."

She jumped up, pressing a hand to her heart. The nail on the pinkie of her right hand was very long, slightly curved.

Coke nail, Lena realized without shock or regret. Now she knew Lilibeth's current drug of choice.

"I made some mistakes, I know I did, honey." Lilibeth's voice rang with apology, with regret. "You gotta understand, I was just so young when you came along."

"You've used that one up."

Lilibeth dug into her shiny red purse, pulled out a tattered tissue. "Why you wanna be so hard on your mama, baby girl? Why you wanna hurt my heart?"

"You don't have a heart. And you're not my mama."

"Carried you inside me for nine months, didn't I?" Sorrow became temper as if a switch had been flicked. Lilibeth's voice rose, shrilled. "Nine months of being sick and fat and stuck back that damn bayou. Lay there in pain for hours giving birth to you."

"And left me within a week. An alley cat spends more time with its litter than you did with me."

"I was sixteen."

It was that, the sad fact of it, that had caused Lena to make room, time and time again, in her heart. Until her heart had simply calcified from the blows. "You haven't been sixteen in quite a while. Neither have I. I'm not going to waste time arguing about it. I have to work, and you have to go."

"But, baby." Panicked, Lilibeth shifted, back to the teary, choked voice. "You've got to give me a chance to make things right. I'm going to get me a job. I can work for you awhile, won't that be fun? I'll just stay here with you for a couple weeks till I find a place of my own. We'll have such a fine time. Just like girlfriends."

"No, you won't work for me, and no, you can't stay here. I made that mistake four years ago, and when I caught you turning tricks up here, you stole from me and took off again. I don't repeat myself."

"I was sick back then. I'm clean now, honey, I swear I am. You can't just turn me out." She held out her hands, palms up, in a gesture of pleading. "I'm flat broke. Billy, he took almost everything I had and ran off."

Lena could only assume Billy was the latest in the string of users, losers and abusers Lilibeth gravitated to. "You're high right now. Do you think I'm blind or just stupid?"

"I'm not! I just took a little something because I was so nervous about seeing you. I knew you'd be mad at me." Tears spilled out, tracking bits of mascara down her cheeks. "You just have to give me a chance to make it up to you, Lena honey. I've changed."

"You've used that one up, too." Resigned, Lena walked to her purse, counted out fifty dollars. "Here." She stuffed it into Lilibeth's hand. "Take this, get on a bus and ride it as far away as this takes you. Don't come back here again. There's no place for you here."

"You can't be so mean to me, baby. You can't be so cold."

"Yes, I can." She picked up the suitcase, carried it over to the door and set it outside. "It's in the blood. Take the fifty. It's all you're going to get. And get out, or I swear to God, I'll throw you out."

Lilibeth marched to the door. The money had already disappeared into her purse. She stopped, gave Lena one last glittering look. "I never wanted you."

"Then we're even. I never wanted you, either." She shut the door in her mother's face. Then flipped the locks, sat down on the floor. And cried in absolute silence.

She was certain she'd smoothed away the edges by the time she drove out to Manet Hall that evening. She'd nearly canceled the dinner plans she had with Declan, but that would have given her mother too much importance.

That would have acknowledged the grief that had slashed its way into her heart despite the locks.

She needed to put her mind to other things, and would never manage it if she stayed at home, brooding. She'd get through the night, hour by hour, and in the morning Lilibeth would be gone. From her life, and from her mind.

The house looked different, she thought. Little changes that somehow made it seem more real. It was good to look at it, to focus on it, and to contemplate that some things could change for the better. With the right vision.

Over the years, she'd come to think of Manet Hall as a kind of dream place, burrowed in the past. More than that, she decided. *Of* the past.

Now, with new unpainted boards checkerboarded with the old, peeling white, with some windows gleaming and others coated with dust, it was a work in progress.

Declan was bringing it back to life.

Though the front gardens were a bit straggled, a bit lost, there were flowers blooming. And he'd plopped a huge clay pot full of begonias on the gallery.

He'd have planted them himself, she thought as she walked toward the door. He was a man who liked his hands in things. Especially when he considered them his.

She wondered if he thought of her as one of his works in progress. Probably. She couldn't quite decide if the idea amused or irritated her.

She strolled in. She figured that when two people had slept with each other a time or two, formalities were superfluous.

She smelled the lilies first, the good, strong scent bringing the garden indoors. He'd bought a lovely old table, a couple of straight-back chairs and, she saw with a grin, an enormous ceramic cow for the foyer.

Some would call it foolish, others charming, she supposed, but no one would call the entrance to the old hall sterile any longer.

"Declan?" She wandered in and out of the parlor, noting the few new additions. She circled into the library and found herself crossing to the mantel and the heavy candlesticks standing on it.

Why did her fingers tremble? she wondered as she reached out to touch. Why did those old tarnished candlesticks look so strangely familiar?

There was nothing special about them, really. Expensive perhaps, but too ornate for her taste. And yet . . . her fingers brushed down each of them, lightly. And yet they looked right here, so right she could imagine the slim white tapers they were waiting to hold once more; she could smell the melting wax.

Shivering, she stepped back and walked out of the room.

She kept calling his name as she started up the stairs. When she reached the first landing, the hidden door in the wall opened. She and Declan choked back simultaneous screams.

With a gasping laugh, she clutched at her heart and stared at him. He had cobwebs in his hair, dirt smeared on his cheek and hands. The flashlight he carried bobbled.

"Lord, *cher*, next time just shoot me and get it over with."

"Same goes." He blew out a breath, dragged at his hair and the cobwebs lacing it. "You scared five years off me."

"Well, I called out a couple times, then decided I'd just hunt you up." She peered over his shoulder. "What've you got here, secret passages?"

"No, servants' access. There are doors on every level, so I thought I'd take a look. It's kind of cool, but a real mess." He looked down at his filthy hands. "Why don't you go fix yourself a drink or something? I'll clean up."

"I might be persuaded to fix us both a drink. What're you in the mood for?"

"Could use a beer." But he was studying her face now that he'd recovered from the jolt. "What's wrong, Lena?"

"Nothing, other than you frightening the wits out of me."

"You're upset. I can see it."

She tried a suggestive smile. "Maybe I'm sulking 'cause you don't bother to kiss me hello."

"Maybe you don't trust me enough yet, and figure all I'm looking for with you is a good time." He used one knuckle to lift her chin, stared into her eyes until hers began to sting. "You're wrong. I love you." He waited a beat, then nodded when she didn't respond. "I'll be down in a minute."

She started down the steps, then stopped, speaking without looking back. "Declan, I don't think you're looking for a good time, but I don't know as I have what it is you are looking for."

"Angelina. You're what I've looked for all my life."

———

He didn't press. If she needed to pretend she wasn't upset and skittish, he'd give her room. They took a walk through the rear gardens as dusk crept in.

"This place. All these years, people come, people go. Mostly they go. And here you are, doing more in a few months than anyone's done since before I can remember."

She turned to study the house. Oh, it still needed work. Wood and paint. New shutters here and there. But it no longer seemed . . . dead, she realized. It hadn't just been abandoned, it had been dead until he'd come.

"You're bringing it back to life. It's more than the money and the work."

"Could you live here?"

Her eyes, startled, even panicked, whipped back to his. But his gaze stayed calm and level. "I have my own place."

"That's not what I asked. I asked if you could. If you could be comfortable here, or if the idea of sharing the place with . . . ghosts or memories, whatever you'd call it, would bother you."

"If it bothered me I wouldn't have come over tonight so you could feed me. Which reminds me, what are you feeding me, *cher*?"

"I'm going to try my hand at grilling tuna." He pulled his pocket watch out. "In a bit," he said after checking the time.

She was mesmerized by the watch in his hand. Her stomach jittered as it had done when she'd seen the candlesticks. "Where did you get that?"

"I found it at a shop today." Alerted by her tone, fascinated by it, he held the watch out. "Look familiar?"

"You just don't see many men using that type of watch anymore."

"I knew it was mine as soon as I saw it. I think you bought it for me," he said, and her head jerked up. "A long time ago." He turned the watch over so she could read the inscription on the back.

"Lucian's." Because her instinct was to curl her fingers into her palms, she made herself reach out and touch the engraving. "Very strange. Strange indeed, Declan. You think I was Abigail?"

"Yeah, I do."

She shook her head. "Don't you think that's a little too neat and tidy—and self-serving?"

"Murder, despair, suicide, a century of wandering souls?" He shrugged and slipped the watch back in his pocket. "Not very tidy, if you ask me. But I think, Lena, that maybe love is patient enough to wait until its time comes around again."

"God, you are so . . . appealing. And it's irritating that I have to be the sensible one around here. I like being with you, Declan."

She toyed with the key on her neck chain as she spoke. A habit, he thought, she was probably unaware of.

"I like your company, I like your looks. And I like making love with you. That's all I have right now."

He took her into his arms. "I'll take it."

# FOURTEEN

Lena rolled over, slid along one pillow to the other. She heard singing—a deep, male voice in a dreamy refrain. And sighing, she ran her hand over the sheets.

He wasn't beside her in bed, but his warmth was.

Opening her eyes, she blinked against the misty sunlight. She hadn't meant to stay the night. But with Declan, her intentions often twisted around to meet his wishes. More, somehow his wishes circled until they ended up being hers as well.

Clever man, she mused, yawning as she burrowed into the pillow. He rarely seemed to push, never appeared to be unreasonable. And always got his way.

Damned if she didn't admire him for it.

Even now, though she'd have preferred waking in her own bed, she was glad she'd stayed. Her mood had been heavy, and a bit prickly, when she'd arrived. Seeing her mother usually had that effect on her. For a few hours, she'd forgotten about it, and had just enjoyed being with him.

That was enough—and would have to be enough for both of them for as long as it lasted. Seeing Lilibeth was a stark reminder of the promises Lena had made to herself.

To succeed, on her own terms. To live, precisely how she chose to live. And never, never to place her hopes, her needs, her wants in the hands of another.

Declan would move along sooner or later. Everyone did. But she cared more this time, and would make a genuine effort to be and to remain friends.

So, she'd would be very, very careful not to fall in love with him. Very careful not to hurt him while he believed he loved her.

Her brow creased. She *did* hear singing. In the shower, she realized, Declan's voice over the drum of water.

*"Long years have passed, child—I've never wed, true to my lost love, though she is dead."*

An odd tune for a man to belt out in the shower, she thought, and found herself singing the refrain with him in her mind. *After the ball is over, after the break of morn.*

Puzzled—where had those lyrics come from?—she rose and went to the bathroom door. She knew the tune, but more, she knew the words. The sad story of lack of faith, of death, melded to the romantic melody.

And her heart was pounding. She felt the pulse of it jump in her throat.

Dancing in the moonlight with the house a white beacon against the night. A girl in faded muslin, and the young man in elegant black tie. The smell of lilacs. Heavy and sweet.

The air's thick with flowers. So thick it's hard to breathe. So thick it makes you dizzy as you spin around and around through the garden, along the bricks with the music playing.

Dizzy, dizzy from the dance. Dizzy, dizzy from the fall into love.

She swayed, reaching out to brace a hand against the door. But it opened, and steam poured out as she fell forward.

"Whoa!" Declan caught her, scooped her off her feet. Still wet from the shower, his hair dripping onto her face, he carried her back to bed.

"I'm okay. I just . . . lost my balance."

"Baby, you're white as a sheet." He brushed her hair back, rubbed her chilled hand between both of his. "What happened?"

"Nothing." Torn between confusion and embarrassment, she nudged him back to sit up. "I got up too fast, is all. Then I lost my balance when I reached for the door and you opened it. I'm fine, *cher. Ça va.* It's just a little early for me to be up and around."

"I'll get you some water."

"Sweetheart, don't fuss. Simones aren't swooning sorts." She ran a finger over his chin. It was all fading away now, the song, the scent of lilacs, the giddy sense of reeling. "Though that handsome face of yours does take my breath away. You leave any hot water for me?"

"Probably not." He eased down to sit beside her. "I've got to replace that water heater. If you give it a half hour, it should come through for another shower."

"Mmm. Now what could I do with a half hour?" Laughing, she pulled him into bed.

N ow that, Lena decided, was a much better way to start the day. She lingered over her first cup of coffee at the little table Declan had set up on the gallery outside his bedroom. As his breakfast pickings were slim at best, she'd settled on a bowl of Frosted Flakes and had watched him load his down with sugar.

"*Cher,* why don't you just have yourself a big old candy bar for breakfast?"

"Don't have one."

He grinned over at her, and damn it, he *did* take her breath away.

"You've got yourself a nice spot here," she told him. "Good morning-contemplation sort of spot."

"It'll be better when I get some of the boards replaced and it's painted. Needs more stuff, too." He glanced around. "Pots, you know, flowers and things. A glider or a swing."

She spooned up some cereal. "You're just a homebody, aren't you, *cher*?"

"Looks like." And it delighted him. "Who'd've thought?"

"And what does the homebody have planned for today?"

"I want to finish the first section of the exterior stairs. If the weather holds through the weekend, I'll have a good start on the front of the house. I've got guys coming in to start on the other bathrooms. Got some more shopping to do. Want to come with me?"

"I've never seen a man so crazy to shop." It was tempting to give in to the charming image of hunting with him for treasures. And to have some part in selecting pieces for the house.

And wouldn't that go toward forging another link in making them a couple instead of two people just enjoying the moment?

So she shook her head and denied herself the pleasure. "Unless this shopping involves looking at shoes or earrings, you're on your own, sugar."

"I could probably fit that in, between hunting up drawer pulls and hardware. In fact . . . hang on a minute."

He rose and went inside while Lena stretched back and, cupping her mug in both hands, looked out over the gardens to the pond.

She'd distracted him, she thought. Or at least he was pretending to be distracted from what had happened that morning. She'd damn near fainted, and that would've been a first.

Something in the house, she mused, was affecting her, just as it did Declan. One side pulling her in, another pushing her out, but she was determined to stand firm.

Was it possible he was right after all? Could it be so perfectly neat? He had been Lucian in a past life, and she his doomed Abigail?

Had they danced in the moonlight to that old, sad song?

If it were true, what did it mean to them now, in this life?

Her face was clear of worry when he stepped out again. And put a small box on the table beside her bowl.

"*Cher*, you keep picking up presents like this, what're you going to do when my birthday rolls around?"

"I'll think of something."

"Well, I don't think you're going to top my salt and pepper shakers, but . . ." She opened the box, expecting to see some cute and foolish pin or silly earrings. Then just stared down at the pair of ruby and diamond hearts.

"They caught my eye."

"You—you can't give me something like this." For the first time since he'd known her, she stuttered. "You can't just—just give me earrings like these. These are real stones. Do you think I'm too stupid to recognize real diamonds?"

"No." Interesting, he thought, that she'd jump from fluster into temper at the gift of diamonds. "I thought they'd look good on you."

"I don't care how rich you are." She snapped the lid back down on the sparkle of blood and ice. "I don't care how much money you've got stuffed away in your portfolios and your bank accounts. I don't want you buying me expensive jewelry. If I want diamonds and rubies, then *alors*, I'll buy them for myself. I'm not sleeping with you for baubles and profit."

"Well, these were a big hit." He tipped back in his chair to meet her furious eyes, as she'd leaped to her feet as she'd shouted at him. "So, they'd be okay with you if they were glass? Let me get the ground rules clear. If I see something I'd like to get for you, it has to be, what, under a hundred? One-fifty? Give me a ballpark."

"I don't need you to buy me things."

"Lena, if you needed me to buy you things, I'd buy you groceries, for Christ's sake. These were pretty, they made me think of you. And look at this." He picked up the box, ran his free hand around it. "No strings attached."

"Something costs as much as a decent secondhand car's got strings, *cher*."

"Wrong. Money's relative. I have a lot of it, so deal. You don't want them, fine." He shrugged, picked up his coffee. "I'll give them to someone else."

Her eyes went to slits. "Oh, will you?"

"They appear to upset your moral balance, but there's no point in them going to waste."

"You're trying to make me sound like an idiot."

"No, you're acting like an idiot. I'm just playing my part in your little drama. I'd like you to have them, but not if you're going to think they're payment for services rendered. That's just as insulting to me as it is to you, Lena," he said when her mouth dropped open. "Your telling me you don't want payment for sex is telling me I'm willing to buy it from you. They're just goddamn rocks."

"They're beautiful rocks." Damn, damn, damn! Why did the man constantly throw her off balance?

And wasn't it just like him, just exactly like him, to sit there, calmly watching her flash and burn?

She took a deep, steadying breath while he looked at her with both patience and amusement. "I was rude, and I overreacted. I'm not used to men handing me diamonds and rubies over bowls of cereal."

"Okay. Want me to wait and give them to you over a nice steak dinner?"

She gave a weak laugh, dragged her hair back. "You're entirely too good for me."

"What the hell does that mean?" he demanded.

But she shook her head, then picked up the box. She studied the earrings against their bed of velvet for a long moment before taking them out, putting them on.

"How do they look?"

"Perfect."

She leaned down, kissed him. "Thank you. They just scared me a little, but I'm getting over it pretty quick now."

"Good."

"I'm going to have to wear my hair back with them. Show them off. Damn it," she said as she ran for the door. "I have to see." She stopped at the mirror, held her hair back with one hand. "Oh God! They're fabulous. I've never had anything so lovely in my life. You're a sweet man, Declan. A hardheaded, crazy, sweet man."

"When you marry me," he said from the doorway, "I'll give you diamonds for breakfast once a week."

"Stop that."

"Okay, but keep it in mind."

"I've got to get on. I want to stop by and see my grandmama before I head back."

"Give me a ride over? I've got something for her."

Her eyes, when they tracked to his in the glass, were indulgent and just a little frustrated. "You bought her another present."

"Don't start on me," he warned, and stepped back out to gather up the bowls.

"Why do you have to buy things all the time, *cher*?"

She knew him now, and the little ripple movement of his shoulders told her he was annoyed and uncomfortable. So she softened the question by giving him a quick kiss on the cheek.

"I've got money," he said. "And I like stuff. You trade money for stuff, which is more fun and interesting than having a bunch of green paper in your wallet."

"I don't know. Me, I like that green paper just fine. But . . ." She fingered the diamonds at her ears. "I could grow mighty fond of these pretty rocks. Go on, get whatever you've gone and bought for Grandmama. Bound to brighten her day, whatever it is, 'cause it's from you."

"You think?"

"She's sweet on you."

"I like that." He turned, wrapped his arms around Lena's waist. "How about you? You sweet on me?"

A long line of warmth flowed down her spine, nearly made her sigh. "You make it hard not to be."

"Good." He touched his lips to hers, then eased away. "I like that even better."

He carried a little gift bag out to her car. It struck her as odd and charming that he would think of things like that. Not just a present, a token he could so easily afford, but the presentation of it. Pretty bags or bows, ribbons or wrappings most men—or men she'd known— would never bother with.

Any woman she knew would call Declan Fitzgerald one hell of a catch. And he wanted her.

"I'm going to ask you a question," she began as she started the car.

"True or false? Multiple choice?"

"I guess it's more the essay type."

He settled back, stretched out his legs as best he could as she started down the drive. He'd always aced his tests. "Shoot."

"How come with all those fine ladies up in Boston, and all the good-looking women here 'round New Orleans, you zeroed in on me?"

"Not one of them ever made my heart stop, or sprint like a racehorse at the starting gun. But you do. Not one of them ever made me see myself ten years, twenty years down the road, reaching out to take her hand. But you do, Lena. And what I want most in the world is to hold on to you."

She didn't look at him, didn't dare, as everything inside her seemed to fill up so she knew one glance at his face would have it all spilling out. Warm and sweet and conquered.

"That's a good answer," she managed.

"It's a true one." He took one of her tensed hands off the wheel, kissed it. "God's truth."

"I think it is. I don't know what to do about it, Declan. You're the first man who's ever made me worry about what to do. I've got powerful feelings for you. I'd rather I didn't."

"Here's what I think. We should elope to Vegas, then you won't have anything to worry about."

"Oh, I'm sure the Boston Fitzgeralds would just be thrilled hearing you've eloped to Vegas with a Cajun bar owner from the bayou. That'd set them up right and tight."

"It'd give them something to talk about for the next decade or two. My mother would like you," he said, almost to himself. "And she's no easy mark. She'd like that you're your own woman and don't take any crap off anyone. Run your own business, look after your grandmother. She'd respect that, and she'd like that. Then she'd love you because I do. My father would take one look at you and be your slave."

She laughed at that and it loosened some of the tightness in her chest. "Are all the Fitzgerald men so easy?"

"We're not easy. We just have exceptional taste."

She pulled up in front of Odette's house, and finally turned to look at him. "Any of them coming down for Remy and Effie's wedding?"

"My parents are."

"We'll see what we see, won't we?"

She hopped out, headed to the door ahead of him. "Grandmama!" She bumped the door open and strolled in. "I brought you a handsome gentleman caller."

Odette came out of the kitchen, wiping her hands on a red checked cloth. The smells of fresh coffee and baking followed her. She was, as always, decked out in layers of jewelry and sturdy boots. But there was a strain around her eyes and mouth even Declan spotted instantly.

"A gentleman caller's always welcome. *Bébé*," she replied and kissed Lena's cheek.

"What's wrong?"

"Baked me some brown bread this morning," Odette said, evading

Lena's question. "Y'all come back to the kitchen." She wrapped an arm around Lena's waist to nudge her along. "What you got in the pretty bag, *cher*?"

"Just a little something I thought you'd like." In the kitchen, Declan set it on the table. "Smells fabulous in here. Maybe I ought to learn how to bake bread."

Odette smiled as he'd hoped she would, but the tension in the air didn't lessen. "Could be I'll teach you a thing or two. Kneading dough's good therapy. Takes your mind off your troubles, gives you thinking time."

She took the small wrapped box out of the gift bag, turned it in her hand, then tugged the ribbon free. "Lena, you don't nail this boy down, I may just snatch him for myself." When she opened the box, her face softened.

The trinket box fit into the palm of her hand. It was heart-shaped and hand-painted with a couple in old-fashioned formal dress sitting on a garden bench. When she lifted the lid, it played a tune.

"I've been hearing that song in my head for weeks," Declan told her. "So when I saw this, I figured I'd better buy it."

"'After the Ball,'" Odette told him. "It's an old waltz. Sad and sweet." She looked up at him. "Maybe you got a nice widowed uncle you could send my way."

"Well, there's Uncle Dennis, but he's homely as a billy goat."

"He's got half your heart, I'll take him."

"Isn't this a pretty picture?"

At the voice, Lena went stiff as if someone had pressed a gun to her head and cocked the hammer. Declan saw the look pass between her and her grandmother. Apologetic on Odette's part, shocked on Lena's.

Then they turned.

Lilibeth slumped against the doorjamb. She wore a short red robe, loosely belted. Her hair was a tumble around her shoulders, and her face already made up for the day with her eyes darkly lined, her lips slick and red as her robe.

"And who might this be?" She lifted one hand, languidly pushed back her hair as she sent Declan a slow, feline smile.

"What's she doing here?" Lena demanded. "What the hell is she doing in this house?"

"It's my house as much as yours," Lilibeth shot back. "Some of us have more respect for blood kin than others."

"I told you to get on a bus and go."

"I don't take orders from my own daughter." Lilibeth pushed off the jamb, sauntered to the stove. "This here coffee fresh, Mama?"

"How could you?" Lena demanded of Odette. "How could you take her in again?"

"Lena." All Odette could do was take her hand. "She's my child."

"*I'm* your child." The bitter fury poured out and left its horrid taste on her tongue. "You're just going to let her come back, stay until she's sucked you dry again, until she and whatever junkie she hooks up with this time steal you blind? It's cocaine now. Can't you see it on her? And that doesn't come free."

"I told you I'm clean." Lilibeth slapped a mug on the counter.

"You're a liar. You've always been a liar."

Lilibeth surged forward. Even as Lena threw out her chin to take the blow, Declan stepped between them. "Think again." He said it quietly, but the heat in his voice pumped into the kitchen.

"You lay a hand on her, Lilibeth, one hand on her, and I'll put you out." Odette stepped to the stove, poured the coffee herself with hands not quite steady. "I mean that."

"She's got no call to speak to me that way." Lilibeth let her lips quiver. "And in front of a stranger."

"Declan Fitzgerald. I'm a friend of Lena's, and Miss Odette's. I'll get that coffee, Miss Odette. You sit down now."

"This is family business, Declan." Lena kept her furious eyes on her mother's face. She would think of the embarrassment later. Right now it was only a dull pinch through the cushion of anger. "You should go."

"In a minute." He poured coffee, brought a cup to Odette. Crouched so their faces were level. "I'm Irish," he told her. "Both sides. Nobody puts on a family fight like the Irish. You only have to call me if you need me."

He squeezed her hand, then straightened. "Same goes," he said to Lena.

"I'm not staying. I'll drive you back." She had to breathe deeply, to brace for the pain her own words would cause. "Grandmama, I love you with all my heart. But as long as she's in the house, I won't be. I'm sorry this hurts you, but I can't do this again. Let me know when she's gone. And you." She turned to Lilibeth. "You hurt her again, you take one dollar from her or bring any of the scum you like to run with in this house, I'll hunt you down. I swear to God I will, wherever you go. And I'll take it out of your skin this time."

"Lena, baby!" Lilibeth rushed down the narrow hall as Lena strode to the door. "I've changed, honey. I want to make it all up to you. Give me a chance to—"

Outside, Lena whirled. "You've had your last chance with me. Don't you come near me. Don't you come near my place. You're dead to me, you hear?"

She slammed the car door, ground the engine to life, then sped off, spewing up a thin cloud of smoke that obscured her mother and the house where she'd grown up.

"Well, that was fun, wasn't it?" Lena punched the gas. "I bet your family would just love a load of Lilibeth Simone. Whore, junkie, thief and liar."

"You can't blame your grandmother for this, Lena."

"I don't blame her. I don't." The tears were rushing up from her throat. She felt the burn. "But I won't be a part of it. I won't." She slammed the brakes in front of the Hall. "I need to go now." But she lowered her brow to the wheel. "Go on, get out. *Va t'en.*"

"No. I'm not going away." Others had, he realized now. And that's where the hurt came from. "Do you want to talk about this out here, or inside?"

"I'm not going to talk about it anywhere."

"Yes, you are. Pick your spot."

"I told you all you need to know. My mother's a whore and a junkie. If she can't earn enough to feed her various habits on her back, she steals. She'd as soon lie as look at you."

"She doesn't live around here."

"I don't know where she lives. No place for long. She came to my place yesterday. Stoned, and full of lies and her usual talk about new starts and being friends. Thought I'd let her move in with me again. Never again," she said and leaned her head back on the car seat. "I gave her fifty dollars for bus fare. Should've known better. Likely it's already gone up her nose."

"Let's take a walk."

"This isn't something you walk off or kiss better, Declan. I need to get back."

"You're not driving into town when you're still churned up. Let's walk."

To ensure she didn't just drive away when he got out, he took the keys out of the ignition, pocketed them. Then he climbed out, walked around the car. Opening her door, he held out a hand.

She couldn't drum up the energy to argue. But instead of taking his hand, she slid out of the car and dipped hers in her pockets.

They'd walk, she figured. They'd talk. And then, it would be over.

She imagined he thought his gardens—that new blossoming, the tender fragrances—would soothe her. He would want to comfort. He was built that way. More, he'd want to know so he could find solutions.

When it came to Lilibeth, there were no solutions.

"Family can suck, can't it?"

Her gaze whipped to his—dark and fierce, and sheened with damp. "She's *not* my family."

"I get that. But it's a family situation. We're always having situations in my family. Probably because there are so many of us."

"Not having enough canapés at a cocktail party, or having two aunts show up in the same fancy dress isn't a situation."

He debated whether to let the insult pass. She was, after all, raw and prickly. But he couldn't quite swallow it. "You figure having money negates personal problems? Takes the sting out of hurts, buries tragedies? That's pretty shallow, Lena."

"I'm a shallow gal. Comes through the blood."

"That's bullshit, but you're entitled to feel sorry for yourself after almost taking a slap in the face. Money didn't make my cousin Angie feel much better when her husband got her and his mistress pregnant the same month. It didn't help my aunt when her daughter died in a car wreck on her eighteenth birthday. Life can fuck you over, whatever your income bracket."

She stopped, ordered herself to calm down. "I apologize. She tends to put me in a mood that's not fit for company."

"I'm not company." Before she could evade, he cupped her face in his hands. "I love you."

"Stop it, Declan."

"I can't."

"I'm no good for you. No good for anybody, and I don't want to be."

"That's the key, isn't it?"

"Yeah."

He reached down, lifted the key she wore around her neck. "It wasn't a man, but a woman who broke your heart. Now you want to lock it up, close it off so you won't accept love when it's offered. Won't let yourself give it back. Safer that way. If you don't love, it doesn't matter if someone walks away. That makes you a coward."

"So what if it does?" She shoved his hand aside. "It's my life. I live it the way I want, and I get along fine. You're a romantic, *cher*. Under all that Yankee sense, that expensive education, you're a dreamer. I don't put stock in dreams. What is, that's what counts. One of these days you're going to wake up and find yourself in this big, old house in the middle of nowhere, wondering what the hell you were thinking. And you'll hightail it back to Boston, go back to lawyering, marry some classy woman named Alexandra, and have a couple pretty children."

"You forgot the pair of golden retrievers," he said mildly.

"Oh." She threw up her hands. *"Merde!"*

"Couldn't agree more. First, the only woman I know named Alexandra has teeth like a horse. She sort of scares me. Second, and more important, what I'm going to do, Angelina, is live out my life in this big, old house, with you. I'm going to raise a family with you, right here. Golden retrievers are optional."

"You saying it, over and over, isn't going to make it so."

Now he grinned, white and wide. "Bet?"

There was something about him when he was like this, she realized. Something potent and just a little frightening when he wore that sheen of affability over a core of concrete stubbornness.

"I'm going to work. You just stay away from me for a while, you hear? I'm too irritated to deal with you."

He let her walk away. It was enough, for now, that her anger with him had dried up those tears that had glimmered in her eyes.

# FIFTEEN

NEW ORLEANS
1900

Julian was drunk, as he preferred to be. He had a half-naked whore in his lap, and her heavy breast cupped in his hand. The old black man played a jumpy tune on the piano, and the sound mixed nicely in his head with wild female laughter.

Cigar smoke stung the air, giving him a low-level urge for tobacco. But he couldn't quite drum up the gumption for a cigar, or to haul the whore upstairs.

The fact that he was broke—again—didn't worry him overmuch. He patronized this brothel habitually, and always, eventually, scraped together the funds to pay his bill. His credit was good here, for the moment.

He'd selected the prostitute because she was blond and lush of build, vacant of brain. He could tell himself that later, when he rode her, he wouldn't see Abigail's face staring back up at him.

Not this time.

He took another swig of bourbon, then pinched the blond's nipple. She squealed and slapped playfully at his hand. He was grinning when Lucian walked in.

"My sainted brother." Though his words slurred, they were bitter on his tongue. Julian gulped more whiskey as he watched Lucian shake his head at a redhead who sidled up to him.

He looked, Julian thought, pale and gold and perfect through the hazy smoke, against the garish colors, through the raucous noise.

And he wondered if Cain had looked at Abel and felt the same violent disgust as he himself felt now.

He waited, jiggling the blond on his knee, squeezing her breast as Lucian scanned the parlor. When their eyes met—identical eyes—there was a clash. Julian would have sworn he heard it in his head. The sound two swords make when struck in battle.

"What's this?" he said as Lucian approached. "Finally lowering yourself to the rest of us humans? My brother needs a drink, a drink and a woman for *mon frère*!" he called out. "Though I doubt he knows what to do with either."

"You embarrass yourself and your family, Julian. I'm sent to bring you home."

"I'm not embarrassed to pay for a whore." Julian set down his glass and ran his hand up the blond's thigh. "Now if I married one, it would be a different matter. But you beat me to that, brother, as you have so many other things."

Lucian's face whitened. "You will not speak of her in this place."

"My brother married a slut from the swamps," he said conversationally, jerking the blond back when she tried to crawl off his lap. He could feel her heart pounding, pounding under his hand now as the heat between him and Lucian stirred fear.

And her fear excited him as none of the promises she'd whispered in his ear had done.

"Lucian, pride of the Manets, brought his tramp into our home, and now he pines and weeps because she left him for another, and saddled him with her bastard whelp."

He had to believe it. Over the winter he'd drowned in an ocean of bourbon the look of her staring eyes, the sound of her body sliding wetly into the bayou.

He *had* to believe it, or go mad.

*"Allez,"* Lucian ordered the blond. "Go."

"I like her where she is." Julian clamped his hands on her arms as she struggled.

Neither of them noticed as the room fell silent, as the notes of the piano died away and the laughter trailed off. Lucian reached down, dragged the blond off Julian's lap. She bolted away like a rabbit even as Lucian yanked Julian from the chair.

"Gentlemen." The madam of the house swept forward. Behind her was an enormous man in spotless evening dress. "We want no trouble here, Monsieur Julian." Her voice cooed, her hand glided intimately over his cheek. And her eyes were frigid. "Go with your brother now, *mon cher ami*. This isn't the place for family squabbles."

"Of course. My apologies." He took her hand, kissed it. Then turned and leaped on Lucian.

The table and lamp they fell on shattered. While people rushed away and women screamed, they rolled, jabbing with fists, snapping like dogs as the violence of a lifetime sprang out of both of them.

The bouncer waded in, dragged Julian up by the scruff. He quick-marched him to the door, heaved him through. Lucian had barely gained his hands and knees when he was lifted.

Curses and screams followed him out the door. And anger was smothered by mortification. Lucian shook his head clear, gained his feet.

He looked down at his brother, that reflection of self, and felt a different kind of shame. "Have we come to this?" he said wearily. "Brawling in brothels, sprawling in gutters. I want peace between us, Julian. God knows I have peace nowhere else."

He held out a hand, an offering, to help Julian to his feet.

But Julian's shame had a different color. And it was black.

He wouldn't remember drawing the knife out of his boot. Liquor and temper and guilt blinded him. Nor would he remember surging to his feet, striking out.

He felt the blade slice through his brother's flesh with a kind of wild glee. And his lips were peeled back, his eyes mad as he scented first blood.

They struggled, Lucian through the pain and shock, Julian through the black haze, with the hilt of the knife slippery in their hands.

And the bright, bright horror paralyzed him as Julian's eyes widened when the killing point turned on him, into him.

"*Mère de Dieu,*" Julian murmured, and stared down at the blood on his breast. "You've killed me."

MANET HALL
2002

The heat had pumped in from the south. It seemed to Declan that even the air sweat. Mornings and evenings, when it was bearable, he worked outside. Afternoons, he sought the cooler regions of the house.

It wasn't as efficient, dragging his tools in and out, but he was making progress. That was the name of the game.

He didn't call Lena—he figured she needed to simmer and settle. But he thought of her, constantly.

He thought of her as he nailed boards, when he studied paint samples, when he installed paddle fans.

And he thought of her when he woke, in the middle of the night, to find himself curled on the grass by the edge of the pond, Lucian's watch clutched in his fist and his face damp with tears.

He tried to put the sleepwalking out of his mind in the daylight. But he couldn't put her out.

One more day, he ordered himself as he wiped sweat off his face. Then he was going into town, banging on her door. If he had to push her into a corner to force her to talk to him, that's what he'd do.

Remy's wedding was coming up fast. Which meant, not only was he going to watch his best friend get married, but . . . his parents were coming to town.

He was ridiculously grateful they'd declined his offer for them to stay with him. Everyone would be a hell of a lot happier with them tucked into a nice hotel suite.

Regardless, he was determined to finish the galleries, and one of the spare bedrooms. In that way, the house would look impressive when they came down the drive, and he could prove he'd *had* the room he'd offered them.

His mother would look to be sure. That was a given.

He backed down the ladder, grabbed the cooler, and gulped cold water. Then poured the rest over his head. Refreshed, he walked across the lawn, then turned back to look.

Dripping, already starting to steam, he felt the smile spread across his face.

"Not bad," he said aloud. "Not half bad for a Yankee amateur."

He'd finished the dual staircases. The sweep of them curved up opposite sides of the second-floor gallery. The elegance of them negated all the nicks, cuts, scrapes, and the hours of labor.

They would be, he realized, his pride and joy.

Now all he needed was to bribe the painters to work in this heat wave. Or pray for a break in the weather.

Either way, he wasn't going to wait until he'd finished the rear of the house. He wanted the front painted, wanted to stand as he was standing now, and see it gleam in bridal white.

To please himself, he strode back, walked slowly up the right-hand stairs, crossed the gallery, and walked slowly down the left. It gave him such a kick he did it again.

Then he dug through his toolbox for his cell phone and called Lena.

He had to share his excitement with her. What did it matter if he was a day ahead of schedule?

The phone was ringing in her apartment when he glanced over and saw Lilibeth crossing his lawn. He pressed END, got to his feet and put the phone back in his toolbox.

"I swear, this heat's just wilting."

She beamed at him, fluttering her lashes as she waved a hand in front of her face. He noted the bracelets she wore were Odette's.

"And it's barely noon. Look at you," she said in a slow purr.

She sauntered straight to him, trailed a fingertip down his bare chest. "You're all wet."

"Impromptu shower." Instinctively, he took a step back so her finger no longer touched his skin. "What can I do for you, Miss Simone?"

"You can start by calling me Lilibeth. After all, you're a good friend of my mama's—and my little girl's, aren't you?"

She wandered away a bit, let her eyes widen as she scanned the house. "I just can't hardly believe what you've done with this big, old place. You must be awfully clever, Declan." She said flirtatiously, "I can call you Declan, can't I?"

"Sure. You don't have to be so clever," he said. "You just have to have plenty of time."

*And money,* she thought. *Plenty of money.* "Oh now, don't you be modest. It's just a miracle what you're doing here. I hope it wouldn't be putting you out too much to show me some of the inside. And I surely could use something cold. Just walking over here from home's left me parched."

He didn't want her in his house. More than distaste, there was a kind of primitive dread. But whatever else she was, she was Lena's mother, and his own had drummed manners into his bones.

"Of course. I've got some tea."

"Can't think of anything that would be more welcome."

She followed him to the door, was pleased when he opened it for her and stepped back for her to enter ahead of him. She let her body brush his, just the faintest suggestion, then walked into the foyer and let out a gasp.

She didn't have to feign the shock, or her wonder as she gazed around the grand entrance. She'd been inside before. Remy and Declan weren't the first to get liquored up and break into Manet Hall.

She'd never liked it much. The place had given her the creeps with its shadows and dust, its cobwebs and faded glamour.

But now it was full of light and polish. Glossy floors, glossy walls. She didn't think much of the old furniture, not for looks anyway. But she had no doubt the price tags had been heavy.

Old money bought or kept old things. It was a concept that baffled her when there was so much new and glittery in the world.

"My lord, sugar, this is a showplace. Just a showplace," she repeated and wandered into the parlor.

She might've preferred the city, where the action was, but she could see that a woman could live like a queen in such a place. And bring the action in, at her whim.

"Goodness, did I say you were clever? Why, you're just a genius. Everything's so beautiful and fresh." She turned back to him. "You must be awful proud."

"It's coming along. Kitchen's back this way. We can get you that cold drink."

"That would be lovely, but don't you hurry me along now." She slid a proprietary hand onto his arm, clung there as she walked down the hall. "I'm just fascinated by what you've done with this place. Mama said you'd only started on it a few months ago."

"You can get a lot done if you stick to the plan."

And since he seemed to be stuck with her, for the time being, he banked down on the desire to get her out again. Instead, as she turned into the library, made purring noises, he took the opportunity to study her.

He couldn't see Lena in her. There were, he supposed, some physical similarities. But where Lena had that compact, bombshell body, Lilibeth's had been whittled down with time and abuse to nearly gaunt.

Showing it off in tiny red shorts and a tight tank top only made her appear cheap and pathetic—a worn-out Kewpie doll painted up for one last night at the carnival. He felt a stir of sympathy for a woman who sought approval and attention by trying to showcase a sexuality she'd already lost.

She'd used a heavy hand with makeup, and the heat hadn't been kind. Her face seemed sallow and false under all the borrowed color. Her hair had frizzed, and graying roots were streaking through it.

By the time he got her into the kitchen, he found her too pitiful to resent.

"Have a seat," he told her. "I'll get you that drink."

And she mistook the kindness in his voice for attraction.

"A kitchen like this . . ." She slid into a chair. It was cool here, and she tipped back her head to let the air reach her throat—and to watch him. "Don't you go and tell me you cook, too. Why, if that's so, sugar, I'm just going to have to cut Lena out and marry you my own self."

"Sorry." The mention of Lena tightened him up again. But his back was to her, and she didn't see his face. "I don't cook."

"Well, a girl can make allowances." She lapped her tongue over her lips. He had a good, strong build to go along with those deep pockets. And she was starting to itch for a man.

"You wouldn't have anything a little stronger than that tea, would you, honey?"

"Would you rather a beer?"

She'd rather a good glass of whiskey, but she nodded. "That'd be just fine. You gonna join me?"

"I'll stick with tea. I've got work to do yet today."

"Too hot to work." She stretched back, looking at him under her lashes. "Days like this, you just wanna soak in a cool tub, then lie on down in a dim room with a fan blowing over your skin."

She accepted the glass of beer he'd poured her, and sipped. "What do you do to beat the heat, honey?"

"Pour cold water over my head. How's Miss Odette?"

Lilibeth's lips pursed. "Oh, she's fine. House is hot as hell in the morning with her baking. Gotta save her pennies. I've been helping out, best I can, but things are tight. Declan . . ."

She ran her finger down the condensation on the glass, drank some more. "I wanted to apologize for that scene over at the house the other day. Lena and I, well, we just rub each other wrong half the time. I guess I can't deny I didn't do right by her when she was a little thing. But I'm trying to make it up to her."

She widened her eyes until they stung and watered cooperatively. "I've changed. I've come to a point in my life when I realize what's important. And that's family. You know what I mean. You've got family."

"Yes, I've got family."

"And now you're down here, you must miss them, and they miss you. Whatever troubles you might have between you, you'd put them aside and support each other. No matter what, ain't that right?"

"Yes."

She dabbed delicately at her tears. "I need Lena to see that's all I want. She doesn't trust me yet, and I can't blame her. I was hoping maybe you could help convince her to give me a chance."

She slid her hand across the table, skimmed it over the back of his. "I'd sure appreciate it if you did. I feel so alone. Woman in my situation, she needs a friend. A strong man in her corner. If I knew I had you on my side, it would help so much."

"If there have to be sides, I'm on Lena's. Either way, I can't step between family—and if I was stupid enough to try it, she wouldn't listen to me anyway."

"Maybe the two of you aren't as close as I assumed."

"It's always risky to make assumptions," he returned equably.

She took another swallow of beer. "You're sleeping with her, aren't you?"

"I'm not going to discuss that with you."

"Why not?" Lilibeth ran the chilly glass between her breasts, then, laughing, rose. "You shy, honey? Don't you be shy with Lilibeth. We could be friends, you and me." She skirted the table, leaned in behind him. "Very good friends," she added as her arms twined down and her teeth nipped at his ear.

"Miss Simone, you're putting me in the awkward position of asking you to get your hands off me."

"You *are* shy." With a chuckle that blew warm breath and beer over his cheek, she trailed her hands down toward his lap.

He clamped a hand over her wrists, jerked them up again. "You're embarrassing yourself." He twisted so he could lever out of the chair and onto his feet to face her. "That's your business. But you're using me to take a shot at Lena, and that's mine."

Angry color spotted her cheeks. "Maybe you think you're too good for me."

"There's no maybe about it. Get out and we'll forget this happened."

She wanted to scream at him, to strike out. But she still had her wits about her. She hadn't had enough beer to dull them, and the hit of coke she'd had before walking over had been miserly. Playing it out, she sank into a chair, dropped her head on her folded arms and sobbed.

"I don't know what to do. I'm just so alone. I'm just so scared. I need help. I thought—I thought if I let you have me, you'd help me. I just don't know what to *do*!"

She lifted her head, and the two tears she'd managed to squeeze out tracked through her makeup. "I'm in such awful trouble."

He went to the sink, ran the water cold, then got a glass. "What kind of trouble?"

"I owe some money. That's why I left Houston, and I'm afraid they'll find me. Hurt me. Maybe Lena, too. I don't want them to hurt my baby."

He set the water in front of her. "How much money?"

He saw it, the quick glint of satisfaction in her eyes before she lowered them. "Five thousand dollars. It wasn't my fault. Really, it wasn't my fault. I trusted the wrong people. A man," she said wearily. "And he ran off with the money and left me owing. If I don't find a way to pay it back, they're going to track me down and do something to me. Something to Mama and Lena."

He sat back down, looked at her intently. "You're a liar. You want to try to soak me for a quick five K so you can score some drugs and get out of town. You figure me for an easy mark, but you figure wrong. If it wasn't for Lena, I'd give you a couple hundred to send you along. But you see, Lilibeth, there is Lena. She wouldn't like it."

She hurled the water in his face. He barely blinked. "Fuck you."

"I thought we already established that wasn't an option."

"Think you're so smart, don't you? So important because you come from money." She pushed to her feet. "Big, fancy, highfalutin family. I found out all about you, Declan Fitzgerald. Let me ask you just what that big, fancy, highfalutin family's going to think when they hear you're heating the sheets with a Cajun swamp whore?"

The phrase had something clutching in his gut, in the back of his throat, in his head. Her face changed in front of his eyes, became fuller, older. Colder.

Josephine.

"Get out." He wasn't sure, not entirely, if he spoke to the flesh-and-blood woman or to the ghost. His hands shook as he gripped the edge of the table.

"All those fine doctors and lawyers and Indian chiefs up there in Boston, how are they gonna like the idea of their golden boy hooking up with some bastard child from the bayou? No money, no pedigree. Runs a second-rate bar and has a grandmama who sews for other people to earn extra pennies. Gonna cut you right out of the will, sugar. Leave you high and dry with this big white elephant of a house on your hands. Especially when I tell them you slept with her mama, too."

His legs were weak as water, but he stood on them. "Get out of my house before I hurt you."

"Your type doesn't lay hands on a woman. Don't think I don't know the difference." Riding on coke and confidence, she tossed back her hair. "You wanna keep plugging your wick into my girl, and you wanna keep your family out of it, you'll write me a check, *cher*. You'll write it quick, fast and in a hurry. And we're going to make it ten thousand now, because you hurt my feelings."

"Your feelings aren't worth a buck and a half to me, Lilibeth."

"They will be, after I have a little chat with your mama."

"My mother will chew you up and spit you out." He walked to the counter, yanked open a drawer and took out a pad. Scrawled a number on it. "Here, that's her number. Call her. You can use my phone, as long as I can listen in. It'll be a real pleasure to hear her slice you to bloodless pieces."

"I need money!"

"You won't get it here." Out of patience, he grabbed her arm and pulled her to the door. "I can make a lot more trouble for you than you can for me. Believe it," he said, and shut the door in her face.

He had to sit down until he had his legs under him again. He felt ill, physically ill. Something had happened when she'd raged at him over Lena. The face that had become her face was one he'd seen in his dreams.

The face belonged to the house, or to the part of it that slammed doors, that wished him away.

That wished him harm.

No doubt now, he told himself, that Lena's mother now wished him harm as well.

He rose, went to the phone. One positive result of the ugly incident was it had made him appreciate his own mother.

He dialed, and felt cleaner at the familiar sound of her voice.

"Hi, Ma."

"Declan? What are you doing calling in the middle of the day? What's wrong? You had an accident."

"No, I—"

"All those horrible tools. You've cut off a hand."

"I still have two, and all other assigned parts. I just called to tell you I love you."

There was a long, pregnant pause. "You've just learned you have a terminal disease and have six months to live."

Now he laughed. "Got me. I'm a dead man and want to make contact with my family so I get a really cool wake."

"Do you want Uncle Jimmy to sing 'Danny Boy'?"

"I really don't. I'd as soon rest in peace."

"So noted. What is it, really, Declan?"

"I want to tell you about the woman I'm in love with and want to marry."

This pause was even longer. "Is this a joke?"

"No. Got a couple minutes?"

"I think I can rearrange my schedule for this."

"Okay." He walked over, picked up his iced tea. The ice had melted, but he glugged it down anyway. "Her name's Angelina Simone, and she's beautiful, fascinating, frustrating, hardheaded and perfect. She's just perfect, Ma."

"When do I meet her?"

"Remy's wedding. There's this one minor glitch—other than the one where she isn't ready to say yes."

"I'm sure you can overcome that minor detail. What's the glitch?"

He sat down again and told her about Lilibeth.

By the time he got off the phone, he felt lighter. Going with impulse, he went upstairs to clean up and change. He was going to confront Lena a bit ahead of schedule.

# SIXTEEN

Declan detoured by Remy's office on the way to Et Trois. The wedding was approaching quickly, and his duties as best man included coordinating the bachelor party. Though he figured the big picture was clear enough—enough booze to float a battleship, and a strip club—there were some finer details to work out.

When reception buzzed through to Remy's office, he heard his friend's almost frantic "Send him right in."

The minute he opened the office door, he saw why.

Effie, tears streaking down her cheeks, sat in one of the visitor chairs with Remy crouched at her feet. Though Remy kept mopping at the tears, kept trying to comfort, he shot Declan a look of sheer male panic.

In a testament to friendship, Declan resisted the urge to back out and run. Instead he closed the door, crossed over and rubbed Effie's shoulder.

"Sweetheart, I told you I'd tell him you were dumping him for me."

Effie merely looked up, then covered her face with her hands and sobbed.

"Okay, bad joke." Declan scrubbed now-sweaty palms over his jeans. "What's wrong?"

"Problem with the wedding venue," Remy began, and Effie let out a wail.

"There *is* no wedding venue." She snatched Remy's handkerchief, buried her face in it. "They had . . . they had a kitchen fire, and the fire department came, and they . . . they . . . Oh what're we going to do!"

"Smoke and water damage," Remy explained to Declan. "Over and above the fire damage. They're not going to be able to put it back together in time."

"It's my fault."

Mirroring Remy, Declan crouched. "Okay, honey, why'd you start the fire?"

It made her laugh—for a split second. "I wanted to use that old plantation house. It's romantic and so lovely. Remy said it'll all be easier booking a hotel ballroom, but no, I just had to have my way. And now look. We've got less than three weeks, and we're . . . We're just sunk, that's all."

"No, we're not, honey. We'll find another place. *Pleure pas, chère.*" Remy kissed the tip of her nose. "Worse comes to worst, we'll have the wedding, then we'll have our party later. We'll have us a real *fais do-do,* after the honeymoon."

"Where are we going to get married? City Hall?"

"I don't care where we get married." Now he kissed her fingers. "Long as we do."

She sniffled, sighed, leaned into him. "I'm sorry. I'm being silly and selfish. You're right. It doesn't matter where or how."

"Sure it does." Declan's statement had them both staring at him, Effie with tears still swirling, Remy with baffled frustration. "You can't let a little fire screw up your plans. Use my place."

"What do you mean, your place?" Remy demanded.

"The Hall. Sure as hell big enough. Ballroom needs some work, but there's time. I have to strong-arm some painters, but I finished the entrance this morning. Gardens are in really good shape, kitchen's done, parlors, library. Lots of rough spots yet, but people won't care about that. They'll get the house, the grounds, the ghosts. They'll talk about it for years."

"Do you mean it?" Effie snagged Declan's hands before Remy could speak.

"Sure I do. We can pull it off."

"Dec," Remy began, but Effie rolled right over him.

"Oh God. Oh, I *love* you." She threw her arms around Declan's neck. "You're the most wonderful man in the world. An angel," she said and kissed him. "A saint."

"Do you mind?" Declan said to Remy. "We'd like to be alone."

Laughing, Effie spun to her feet. "Oh, I shouldn't let you do this. You'll have all those strangers roaming around your house, trooping all over your lawn. But I'm going to let you because I'm desperate, and it's so perfect. I swear, I swear you won't have to do any of the work. I'll take care of everything. I'm going to owe you till my dying day."

"Giving me your firstborn son will be payment enough."

Remy sat on the edge of the desk and shook his head. "I say I'll marry you anywhere, anytime, all he does is give you a broken-down house and he's the one gets kissed."

"I already got you." But she turned, wrapped her arms around Remy and, with a sigh, rested her head on his shoulder. "I want it to be beautiful, Remy. I want it to be special. It means a lot to me."

"I know it does. So it means a lot to me, too. We'll have us some party, won't we?"

"We will." She gave him one last squeeze, then whirled away. The sad, sobbing woman was replaced by a dervish. "Can I go out now?" she asked Declan. "I need to get my mother and my sister, and we'll go out right now and start figuring it all out."

"Go ahead."

"Thank you." She kissed his cheek. "Thank you." Then the other. "Thank you." Then his mouth with a long, drawn-out smack. "Remy, you come on out soon as you can. Oh, Dec?" She was pulling out her cell phone as she headed for the door. "My bride colors are rose and blue. You don't mind if we have the house painted those colors, do you?"

His mouth dropped open as she shut the door behind her. "She was kidding, right?"

"Probably." Knowing his girl, and the pack she ran with, Remy blew out a breath. "*Cher*, you don't know what you just got yourself into. You made my girl happy, and I'm grateful, but I gotta tell you, you're in for a couple weeks of pure insanity."

"I couldn't stand seeing her crying like that. Besides, it makes sense." Rose and blue, he thought. How much trouble could they get into with nice, harmless colors like rose and blue? "Anyway," he added, rubbing a hand over his sinking heart, "I've been through wedding plans before."

"You haven't met her mother before."

Declan shifted his feet. "Is she scary?"

"Pretty scary."

"Hold me."

G ood deeds put him in a good mood. When he walked into Et Trois, he was ready for a cold one, a self-congratulatory pat on the back. And Lena.

She was behind the bar, pulling a draft and chatting up one of her regulars. He watched her gaze wash over, then land on him. Stay on him as he walked up, flipped up the pass-through.

She had time to slide the foaming mug across the bar to waiting hands, start to turn before he lifted her off her feet and planted his lips on hers.

The scattering of applause and hoots had him grinning as he held her an inch off the floor. "Missed you."

She rubbed her tingling lips together. "Your aim seemed good to me." She patted his cheek, gave him that quick, wicked gleam. "Now down, boy. I'm working here."

"You're going to need someone to cover for you."

"I'm busy, *cher*. Go on and sit down, I'll get you a beer."

He just hitched her up, giving her legs a little swing so he could get his arm under them. He elbowed the door to the bar kitchen. "Lena needs you to cover for her," he called back, then nodded toward the pass-through. "Mind?" he asked the man sipping the draft.

"Sure thing."

"Declan." She didn't struggle, bad for the image. "I'm running a business here."

"And you do a damn good job of it. Thanks," he added when the man flipped up the pass-through. "It ought to run fine without you for a half hour." He nodded as his new friend hustled over and opened the door for him.

He carried her outside. They got a few glances as he walked down the sidewalk and turned into her courtyard.

"I don't like being pushed around, *cher*."

"I'm not pushing you, I'm carrying you. Where's your spare key?" he asked as he climbed the stairs. When she said nothing, he shrugged. "Fine. We're going to get arrested for doing what I plan on doing out here on your gallery, but I'm game."

"Under the pot, second from the left."

"Good."

To her shock, he shifted her, slinging her over his shoulder as he crouched down to retrieve the key. She continually underestimated his strength and, she admitted, her reaction to it.

"You've dropped a couple of pounds," he commented and unlocked her door. "Good."

"I beg your pardon?" she said in her best frigid, southern-belle tone.

"I figure it's because you've been pining for me."

"You're going to want to get a grip, *cher*."

"Got one," he said and reached up to squeeze her butt as he kicked the door closed.

"I can't tell you how flattered I am that you'd take time out of your busy day to come into town for a quickie, but I—"

"Excellent idea. It wasn't my first order of business, but why wait?" He hitched her more securely on his shoulder and headed for the bedroom.

"Declan, you're starting to seriously irritate me now. You'd better just put me down and—"

She lost the rest—and the air in her lungs—when he flipped her onto the bed. He could see her eyes glittering dangerously behind her hair before she shoved it out of her face. And that, he thought, was perfect. He was in the mood for the fast and the physical, the sweaty and the sexy.

"What the *hell's* gotten into you? You come marching into my place like you own it, cart me off like I'm spoils of war. If you think I'm here to scratch your itch whenever it suits you, you're about to find out different."

He merely grinned, yanked off a shoe and tossed it aside.

"Put that back on, or hobble out. Either way, I want you gone."

He pulled off the other shoe, then his shirt. Her response to that was to scramble to her knees and spit out in Cajun so rapid and thick he caught only about every sixth word.

"Sorry," he said in mild tones as he unbuttoned his jeans. "That was a little quick for me. Did you say I was a pig who should fry in hell, or that I should go to hell and eat fried pig?"

He was ready when she leaped, and laughing as she swiped at him. It was time for a fast tumble, fast and violent, and her clawing nails and bared teeth added the perfect punch.

She slapped, cursed, kicked. Then bucked like a wild mare when he crushed her under him on the bed and covered her snarling mouth with his in a hot, hungry kiss.

"Not what you expect from me, is it?" Breathless and randy, he tore at her shirt. "Given you too much of what you expect so far."

"Stop it. Stop it now." Her heart sprinted under his rough hand. No, it wasn't what she expected from him, any more than her electrified response to his dominance was what she expected from herself.

"Look at me." He clamped her hands on either side of her head. "Tell me you don't want me, that you don't want this. Say it and mean it, and I'm gone."

"Let go of my hands." Though her gaze remained steady, her voice shook. "You let go of my hands."

He released one. "Say it." His muscles quivered. "You want, or you don't."

She fisted a hand in his hair and dragged his mouth back to hers. *"J'ai besoin."*

I need.

She used her teeth, gnawing restlessly at his lips. Used her legs, wrapping them around to chain him to her.

"Take me," she demanded. "Fast. Fast and rough."

His hand shot beneath the short, snug skirt, tore away the thin panties beneath. Sweat already slicked his skin and hers as she arched to him.

"Hold on," he warned, and plunged into her.

She cried out as the explosive sensation ripped through her, cried out again as he drove deeper, harder. Filled, invaded, took until needs, frantic, outrageous needs swarmed through her. Her nails scored down his back, pinched into his hips.

*De plus en plus.* More and more, her mind screamed. "More," she managed. "I want more."

So did he. He shoved her knees back, opened her and hammered himself inside her.

It burned. His lungs, his heart, his loins. The ferocious heat, the unspeakable pleasure of going wild with her hazed his vision until the world was drenched with it.

White sun beating through the windows, the brassy blast of a trumpet from the street, the mad squeak of springs as slick skin slapped rhythmically against slick skin.

And her eyes, dark and glossy as onyx, locked on his.

*I love you. Endlessly.*

He didn't know if he spoke, or if the words simply ran a desperate loop in his brain. But he saw her eyes change, watched emotion swirl into them, blind them.

He heard her sob for breath, felt her vise around him as she came. Helpless, half mad, he shattered. And poured into her.

Out of breath, out of his mind, he collapsed onto her. Beneath him she continued to quake, to quiver. And shudder, those aftershocks of eruption. Then she was still.

"Can't move yet," he mumbled. He felt hollowed out, light as a husk that could be happily blown apart by the slightest breeze.

"Don't need to."

Her lips were against the side of his throat, and their movement there brought him an exquisite tenderness. A rainbow after the storm.

"Would you believe I came in to talk to you?"

"No."

"Did. Figured we'd get to this after. Change of plans. I owe you a shirt and some underwear."

"I've got more."

He'd recovered just enough to prop on his elbows and look down at her. Her cheeks were flushed and glowing. Curls of damp hair clung to her temples, spilled over the rumpled spread.

He wanted to lap her up like a cat with cream.

"Pissing you off got me hot," he told her.

"Me too. Seems like. I wasn't going to do this with you again."

"Weren't you?"

"No." She laid a hand on his cheek, amazed by the wave of tenderness. "I'd made up my mind about it. Then you come into my place, all sexy and good-looking, scoop me up that way. You mess with my mind, *cher.* You just go and unmake it for me, time and again."

"You're everything I want."

"And nothing that's good for you. Go on." She gave his shoulder a little push. "Get off me. Two of us are a sweaty mess."

"We'll take a shower, then we'll talk. Talk," he repeated when she raised a brow. "Scout's honor." He held up two fingers.

"I've got to get back to work."

"Angelina."

"All right." She waved him away. It was, she knew, no use arguing with him. God *knew* why she found that mule-headed streak of his so appealing. "Go get yourself cleaned up. I'll call down and make sure everything's covered for the next little while."

She stepped into the shower just as he got out. He imagined she'd timed it that way, to avoid the intimacy. Giving her room, he went to the kitchen, found the expected pitcher of tea, and poured two glasses.

When she came in, wearing that same sexy skirt and a fresh shirt, he offered her a glass.

She took it into the living room.

In the last few days, she'd resigned herself to what needed to be. Throughout, part of her had indeed pined for him. And every time she'd caught herself glancing toward the bar door, looking for him, or waking up in the night reaching for him, she'd cursed herself for being a weak fool.

Then she'd glanced at the door, and there he was. Her own soaring pleasure, depthless relief, had annoyed her even before he'd nipped at her pride by plucking her out of her own bar.

"Declan," she began. "I wasn't fair to you the other day. I wasn't in the mood to be fair."

"If you're going to apologize for it, save it. I wanted to make you mad. I'd rather see you angry than sad. She makes you both."

"I suppose she does. Mostly I hate knowing she's out there with Grandmama, knowing she'll hurt her again. I can't stop it, I can't fix it. That troubles me. But you shouldn't have been brought into it."

"You didn't bring me into it. It happened." He angled his head. "Correct me if I'm wrong. You've got the impression that since I come from where and who I come from, I'm not equipped to handle the darker, the more difficult, the stickier aspects of life. Your life, in particular."

"*Cher*, I'm not saying you're not tough. But this particular aspect of life, my life, is out of your scope. You wouldn't understand someone like her."

"Since I've been so sheltered." He nodded. "She came to see me today."

The healthy flush sex and heat had put in Lena's cheeks drained. "What do you mean?"

"Lilibeth paid me a call around noon. I debated whether to tell you about it or not, and decided that I'm not going to keep secrets from you, or tell lies. Not even to spare your feelings. She came by, invited herself in for a cold one. Then she tried to seduce me."

"I'm sorry." Her lips felt stiff and ice cold as she formed the words. Her throat burned like fire. "It won't happen again; I'll see to it."

"Shut up. Do I look like I need your protection? And save your outrage until I'm done," he told her. "When she reached for my zipper, I told her not to embarrass herself. Her next tack was to fling herself down on the kitchen table and cry."

He eased down on the arm of Lena's sofa. The tone of conversation, he thought in some corner of his brain, didn't lend itself to lounging among all those soft, colorful pillows. "She didn't manage to work up many tears along with the noise, but I give her marks for effort. The story was how bad, mean people were after her. They'd hurt her, you, Miss Odette if she didn't give them five thousand dollars. Where could she turn, what could she do?"

Color rushed back into Lena's face, rode high on her cheekbones. "You gave her money? How could you believe—"

"First a sheltered wimp, now a moron." He gave an exaggerated sigh and sipped his tea. "You're really pumping up the ego here, baby. I didn't give her a dime, and let her know, clearly, I wasn't going to be hosed. That irritated her into threatening to go to my family. Seems she's asked around about me and got the picture. She figured they'd be shocked and shamed by the idea of their fair-haired boy falling under your spell. For good measure, she'd tell them I'd fucked her, too."

"She could do it." It was more than the cold now. The sickness roiled in her belly. "Declan, she's perfectly capable of—"

"Didn't I tell you to wait until I was finished?" His voice didn't whip, didn't sting. It was simply implacable. "The cost doubled to ten thousand for this spot of blackmail. I don't think she was pleased with my response. I kicked her out. That's about it, so you can be outraged now if you want. Don't cry." He spoke roughly when her eyes filled. "She's not worth one tear from you."

"I'm mortified. Can't you understand?"

"Yes. Though we're both smart enough to know this had nothing to do with you, I understand. And I'm sorry for it, sorry to add to it."

"It's not you. It's never been you." She wiped a tear from her lashes before it could fall. "That's what I've been trying to get through your head from the start."

"It's not you, either, Lena. It's never been you. I looked at her. I looked close and hard, and there's nothing there that's part of you. Family's the luck of the draw, Lena. What you make of yourself, because of or despite it, that's where the spine and heart come in."

"I'll never be rid of her, not all the way. No matter what I do."

"No, you won't."

"I'm sorry. No, damn it, I will say it," she snapped when his face tightened. "I'm sorry she came into your home. I'm sorry she touched on your family. I need to ask you not to say anything about this to my grandmama."

"Why would I?"

She nodded, then rising, wandered the room. She loved this place because she'd made it herself. She respected her life for the same reasons. Now, because she cared for, because she respected the man who was so determined to be part of her life, she'd explain.

"She left me before I was two weeks old," she began. "Just went out one morning, got in her mama's car and drove off. Dumped the car in Baton Rouge. I was three before she came back around."

"Your father?"

She shrugged. "Depends on her mood. Once she told me it was a boy she loved and who loved her, but his parents tore them apart and sent him far away. Another time, she told me she was raped on the way home from school. Still another it was a rich, older man who was going to come back for both of us one day and set us up in a fine house."

She turned back so she could face him. "I was about eighteen when I figured she told me the truth. She was high enough, careless enough, mean enough for it to be the truth. How the hell should she know, she said. There were plenty of them. What the hell did she care who planted me in her? One was the same as the other.

"She was whoring when she got pregnant with me. I heard talk when I was old enough to understand what the talk meant. When she got in trouble, she ran back to my grandparents. She was afraid of an abortion— afraid she'd die of it, then go to hell or some such thing. So she had me, and she left me. Those are the only two things in this world I owe her."

She drew a breath, made herself sit again. "Anyway, she came back when I was three, made what would become her usual promises that she'd learned her lesson, she was sorry, she'd changed. She stayed around a few days, then took off again. That's a pattern that's repeated since. Sometimes she'd come back beat up from whatever bastard she'd taken up with most recently. Sometimes she'd come back sick, or just high. But Lilibeth, she always comes back."

She fell silent, brooding over that single, unavoidable fact.

"It hurts when she does," Declan said quietly. "Hurts you, hurts Miss Odette."

"She hurts everyone. It's her only talent. She was high when she showed up on my thirteenth birthday. We were having a *fais do-do* at the house, all the friends and family, and she stoned, with some lowlife. It got ugly pretty quick, and three of my uncles turned them off. I need a smoke," she said, and left the room.

She came back a moment later with a cigarette. "I had a boy I was seeing, crazy about that boy. I was sixteen, and she came back. She got him liquor and drugs and had sex with him. He was hardly older than I was, so it's hard to blame him for being an idiot. She thought it was funny when I stumbled over them out in the bayou. She laughed and laughed. Still, when I got this apartment, and she came back, I took her in. Better me than Grandmama, I thought. And maybe this time . . . Just maybe.

"But she turned tricks in my bed and brought her drugs into my home. She stole from me, and she left me again. From then I've been done with her. I'm done with her. And I'll never be done with her, Declan. Nothing I can do changes her being my mother."

"And nothing she does can change who you are. You're a testament to your own grit, Lena, and a credit to the people who raised you. She hates you for what you are."

She stared at him. "She hates me," she whispered. "I've never been able to say that to anyone before. Why should saying such a thing, such an awful thing, help so much?"

"I won't say she can't hurt you anymore, because she can. But maybe now she won't be able to hurt you as much, or for as long."

Thoughtfully, she tapped out her cigarette. "I keep underestimating you."

"That's okay. That way I can keep surprising you. How's this one? She's connected to Manet Hall."

"What do you mean?"

"I don't know, exactly, and can't explain it. I just know she is. And I think maybe she was meant to come back now, to say what she said to me. One more link in the chain. And I think she's pretty well done around here, this time out. Call your grandmother, Lena. Don't let this woman put a wedge between you."

"I've been thinking of it. I guess I will. Declan." She picked up her glass, set it down again. The useless gesture made him raise his eyebrows. "I was going to end things between us."

"You could've tried."

"I mean it. We'd both be better off if we stepped back a ways, tried to be friends of some sort."

"We can be friends. I want our children to have parents who like each other."

She threw up her hands. "I have to get back to work."

"Okay. But listen, speaking of weddings, slight change of plans in Remy and Effie's. We're having the whole deal at my place."

She rubbed her temple, tried to switch gears and moods as smoothly as he did. "In . . . with half-finished rooms and tools and lumber, and—"

"That's a very negative attitude, and not at all helpful, especially since I was going to ask you for a hand. How are you with a paintbrush?"

She let out a sigh. "Do you save everyone?"

"Just the ones who matter."


Somewhere between Declan's leaving the Hall, and Effie's arrival, Li-libeth paid another call. She was riding on coke and insult. The lousy son of a bitch couldn't spare a few bucks for the mother of the woman he was screwing, she'd just help herself.

She'd cased the first floor when he'd led her back to the kitchen, and going in through the back, she arrowed straight to the library and the big rolltop desk she'd spotted.

People with money kept cash handy, in her experience. Moving quickly, she yanked open drawers, riffled through, then let out a shout when she found a neat pile of fifties. Those she stuffed into her pocket.

She figured the books he'd shelved and the ones yet in boxes were probably worth something. But they'd be heavy, and hard to sell. He'd likely have more cash, a few pieces of jewelry up in his bedroom.

She raced up the main stairs. The fact that he could come back at any time only added to the thrill of stealing.

A door slammed, had her falling straight to her knees. Just a draft, she told herself as she caught her breath, as the pulse in her throat began to pop. Big, drafty old house. In fact, she felt cold air whisk over her as she jumped to her feet again.

She touched a doorknob, yanked her hand away again. The knob was so cold it all but burned.

Didn't matter. What the fuck? His room was down the hall. She wasn't as stupid as people thought she was. Hadn't she watched the house over the last few days? Hadn't she seen him come out on the gallery from the room at the far corner?

Laughing out loud, the sound rolling back over her, she dashed down, streaked through the open door. She yanked open the top drawer of a dresser and hit pay dirt with the old carved box inside.

Gold cuff links—at least she assumed they were real gold. Silver ones, too, with some sort of fancy blue stone. Diamond studs, a gold watch. And in a box inside the box, a woman's ring of . . . ruby maybe, diamond and ruby, fashioned in interlocking hearts.

She set the box on the dresser, hunted through a couple more drawers until she found another wad of cash.

Paid anyway, didn't you, you bastard. Paid just fine.

She tossed the bills into the jewelry box, tucked the box under her arm.

Standing there, her breath whistling out in excitement, cocaine dancing in her blood, she debated the satisfaction of trashing the place. It would be satisfying—more payment. But it wasn't smart. And she was smart.

She needed time to turn the jewelry into cash, time to turn some of the cash into drugs. Time to get the hell out of Dodge. Best to leave things as they were.

She'd go out the other side, just in case her long-nosed mama was looking this way.

But when she stepped back into the hall, she found herself staring at the third-floor stairs.

What was up there? she wondered. Maybe something good. Maybe something she could come back for later. Something that would make her rich.

Her breath wasn't just whistling now, but wheezing. Her skin was ice cold. But she couldn't resist the urge to climb those stairs. She was alone in the house, wasn't she? All alone, and that made it *her* house.

It was her house.

Swallowing continually to wet her dry throat, she started up. Shivering.

Voices? How could she hear voices when there was no one there? But they stopped her, urged her to turn back. *Something wrong here, something bad here. Time to go.*

But it seemed hands pressed to her back, pushed her on until, with trembling fingers, she reached for the door.

She meant to ease it open, slowly—just take a peek. But at the touch of her hand, it swung violently open.

She saw the man and woman on the floor, heard the baby screaming in the crib. Saw the woman's eyes—staring and blind. And dead.

And the man, his hair gold in the dim light, turned to look at her.

Lilibeth tried to scream, but couldn't grab the air. As she opened her mouth, something *pushed* into her. For one horrifying moment it became her. Then it swept through her. Cold, vicious, furious.

Another figure formed in the room. Female, sturdy, in a long night robe.

*Julian.*

And in speechless terror, Lilibeth turned and ran.

# SEVENTEEN

Within twenty-four hours, Declan discovered he had more help on the house than he knew what to do with. Apparently everyone in Louisiana was invited to the wedding, and they were all willing to lend a hand.

He had painters, plumbers, carpenters and gofers. And though it occurred to him in the middle of the melee that if half that amount had pitched in to repair the original venue, the job would have been done in about twenty minutes, he decided to keep the thought to himself.

It seemed rude to voice it.

And he appreciated the labor, sincerely. Reminded himself of it whenever he felt certain pieces of the house slipping away from him into someone else's charge.

He'd been looking forward to screening in the lower rear gallery himself, but comforted himself that one good hurricane would demand rescreening.

He'd intended to sand and varnish the ballroom floors, but bucked up when he thought of all the other floors waiting for him throughout the house.

And he sure as hell didn't mind turning over the exterior painting to others. It was a hot, exacting and laborious job, and crossing it off his list left him free to tackle the downstairs powder room, and to hang the blown-glass chandelier he'd bought for the foyer, and to finish plans for the mud room. And . . .

Well, there was plenty to go around, he reflected.

Then there was the pure pleasure of watching Effie zip in and out on her lunch hour or after work. Even when she brought her mother in tow. Mrs. Renault was a spit-and-polished older version of her daughter with an eye like an eagle and a voice like a drill sergeant.

Remy was right, she was pretty scary. Declan hid from her, whenever possible and without shame.

On the second day of the full-out campaign, Declan strode toward the rear gallery to check progress. He was feeling pretty peppy from the tile he'd just set, was covered with ceramic dust from cutting it.

The noise level was amazing. Voices, radios, power tools. As much as he enjoyed people, he'd have given a thousand dollars for five minutes alone in his house.

"Jim Ready? I want those windows sparkling, you hear? How's it going to look in the wedding pictures if those windows are dull? Put your back into it, boy!"

The sound of Mrs. Renault's voice had Declan turning sharply on his heel and changing direction. He all but bowled over Odette.

"Hey, sorry. You all right? I didn't see you. I was running away."

"You got a houseful."

"You're right about that. If this place isn't fixed up enough to suit General Renault by D Day, we're all going to be shot." He took her arm as he spoke and, thinking only of self-preservation, hustled her into the library. Shut the doors.

"Can I come live at your house?"

She smiled—a curve of lips that didn't reach her eyes. "You're such a good boy, Declan, doing all this for your friend."

"I'm not doing much more right now than staying the hell out of the way."

"And you'd rather all these people go back where they came from, and leave you be so you can play with your house."

"Yeah, well." He shrugged, pushed his dusty hand through his dusty hair. "There'll still be plenty to do once they go. We're not touching the third floor or the servants' area, and only doing one other room on the second. Tell me what's wrong, Miss Odette."

"I gotta work up to it." She set down the shopping bag she carried, then walked over to look at some of his books. There were still boxes of them to be shelved, but she saw what it would be. Towers of words, some old and worn, some fresh and new. Small treasures, deep colors.

"You got vision," she said at length. "You picture what you want, then you make it happen. That's a fine skill, *cher.*"

"Some people call it single-minded."

"You're anything but. You've got a lot of channels in that head of yours. Working on one at a time till it's done shows character to me. I'm awful fond of you, Declan."

"I'm awful fond of you, too. I wish you'd sit down, Miss Odette. You look tired." And troubled. "Why don't I get us a cold drink?"

"No, don't you trouble and risk getting shanghaied by Sarah Jane Renault. Now that's a single-minded individual, and I don't fault her for it."

"She told me to get a haircut by the end of the week so I don't look shaggy or freshly shorn for the wedding." Sulking over it a little, Declan ran a testing hand through his hair. "And that she'll be putting fancy soaps, towels and so on in all the bathrooms the day before the wedding. I'm not to use them under penalty of death. And I'm to get more green plants inside the house. A house can't breathe without green plants."

"She's just nervous, honey. Effie's her baby. Her youngest daughter."

Odette pressed her lips together. "Declan, I'm shamed to say what I have to say to you, and I won't blame you if, after I'm done, you ask me not to come back in your home again."

The words alarmed him, nearly as much as the pain in her eyes. "There's nothing you can say that would make you unwelcome in my home, Miss Odette. Who hurt you?"

"Oh, *mon Dieu*, if this spoils what I see between you and my Lena, I'll never forgive myself. My daughter stole from you," she blurted out. "She came in your house and took what was yours."

With a heavy heart she reached into her bag, took out his carved box. "This was in her room. I knew it was yours even before I looked in and saw a set of cuff links with your initials. I don't know if it's all here, but that's all there was. If anything's missing—"

"Let's just see. I want you to sit down now. I mean it."

She nodded, sank into a chair.

He chained down his rage as he set the box on a table, opened it. He saw the ring box first, opened it, and felt the worst of the anger fade when the stones glittered up at him.

"Okay." He breathed out. "The most important thing's still here." As was, as far as he could see, everything else but the couple thousand in twenties he kept secured with the money clip that had been his great-grandfather's.

"It's all here."

"You're not telling me the truth," Odette said dully.

"A little cash, that's all."

"I need to know how much so I can pay it back."

"Do you think I'd take money from you?" Some of the anger lashed out, made her wince. "Look at my face. Do you think I'd take money from you for this, for anything?"

Her lips wanted to quiver, so she pressed them into a firm line. "She's my responsibility."

"The hell she is. Don't insult me again by talking about restitution."

Despite her promise not to shed one in front of him, a tear spilled over. "I know what she is. And I know she'll never be what I hoped for, worked for, wished for from the moment I knew she was inside me. But she gave me Lena."

She dug out a tissue, patted her cheeks. There would be no more tears. "I expected she'd steal from me before she took off again, but I didn't think she'd take from you. I never thought of it, and I'm sorry for that."

"You want to look at my face again and see if I blame you?"

"No, you don't blame me. Oh, I want you for my Lena. I'm sitting here knowing my child stole from you, and all I can think is I want you for my baby."

"Good thing, because I want me for her, too." He picked up the ring box, crossed over to her chair. "I bought this for her. Maybe you could put in a good word for me so when I give it to her, she takes it."

Odette looked at the ring and sighed. "Suits her. Sure does suit her. She's got a good heart, Declan, but it's got scars on it. She's so strong. Sometimes I worry she's too strong, and she'll forget how to give. I'll have to tell her about this."

"Yes."

"And you'll have to figure out how to keep her from pulling away from you when she knows. That's what she'll want to do."

"Don't worry. Where's Lilibeth?"

"Gone. I found this in her room this morning. She's barely come out of there since the day before. When I went in and found it, I put it away where she wouldn't find it. Then we had words about it. She packed up and left. She'll come back," she said in the same hollow tone he'd heard from Lena. "In a year or two. And we'll go through it once more."

"We'll deal with it when it happens." He leaned down, kissed her cheek. "I love you." When her eyes filled again, he took her hand. "Whether Lena's ready for it or not, we're family now. Family sticks."

"When I meet your mama," Odette managed, "I'm gonna give her one big, rib-cracking hug."

"That'll set her up. Why don't we take a look at what's happening around here, and you can protect me from General Renault."

H e didn't expect it to take long, and wasn't disappointed. About the time most of his free labor was packing up for the day, and Effie and her mother had him out in the back garden, Lena strode around the side of the house.

Since he was in the middle of the series of uh-huhs, you-bets and no-problems that had become his litany of responses to the Renault women's wedding agenda, he decided the confrontation in Lena's eyes would be a relief.

"The railings and baluster will be wrapped in tulle and lace."

"Uh-huh."

"And we'll have baskets—white baskets—of flowers set out on the gallery there."

"You bet."

"The florist will need to start early on the day of the wedding, so you just scoot out of the way and make sure they have access to all the areas of the house I've got marked off on my chart here."

"No problem. Lena." He reached out and clutched her hand. A drowning man grabbing a rope. "We're just talking about flower arrangements."

"Flowers are the landscape of a wedding," Mrs. Renault declared, and made more notations on the clipboard she carried everywhere. "How are you, Lena?"

"I'm just fine, Miss Sarah Jane. Isn't this exciting? Counting right down to the big day. Effie, you must be half mad with the details."

"I've passed half, working toward pure insanity."

"It'll all be beautiful." She kept her smile bright, her voice light even as the dark heat coursed through her. "Those rhododendrons are going to be spectacular on your day."

"The gardens are going to be a sight," Mrs. Renault agreed, and ran down her checklist again. "Pity, though, there wasn't time to put up an arbor, train some sweet peas up." She looked over the tops of her reading glasses at Declan with a faintly accusatory gleam.

"Maybe the Franks can rig something. Ah, can you excuse me a minute? There's something I need to show Lena."

He escaped, pulling her toward the steps to the second-floor gallery. There were still some of General Renault's militia on the lower level. "They're like ants," he babbled. "Crawling out of the woodwork when you're not looking."

"What're you talking about?"

"People. Everywhere. Watch that bucket. I think the ballroom's safe."

"Feeling a little pressed, are you, *cher*?"

"I'm thinking of a nice vacation in Maui until this is over. I've got to say, I admire women."

"Really." She glanced down at the ladders, the tarps, the debris of construction—and the two women picking their way through it with visions of tulle and lace in their heads. "Why is that?"

"You can be spitting mad, and still carry on a polite conversation about rhododendrons." He peeked through the ballroom doors, sighed. "All clear. Anyway, when most guys work up a head of steam, it spews. Well . . ." He stepped inside. "What do you think?"

The walls were a pale rose, the floor gold and gleaming.

"It's big."

"It'll need to be for this little do. The General says we've got two-fifty coming. Otherwise, you can use the pocket doors to turn it into a couple of parlors."

He crossed the floor, drew one of the big doors out of its slot. "Isn't this amazing?" He trailed his fingers over the carved wood reverently. "The craftsmanship in these. More than a hundred years ago. I hate hiding them. See how the pattern matches the ceiling medallions? Tibald did a hell of a job restoring those."

She had worked up a head of steam since her conversation with her grandmother, but found it dispersing now as she watched his undiluted pleasure and pride.

"It's true love, isn't it? You and this house. Most men don't look at a woman the way you look at those doors."

"I look at you that way."

She had to turn away. "You make it damn hard to hold on to a mad. Tell me why you're not mad, Declan. Why aren't you mad she stole from you?"

"I am. And if I have occasion to see her again, she'll know it."

"You should go to the police."

"I thought about it. I might get some of the money back, but it would embarrass Miss Odette."

"She's already embarrassed."

"I know. Why add to it? I got back the things that mattered."

The bitterness gushed through her anew. "She came in your house, she went through your things. She *took* from you."

He lifted a brow at the tone of her voice. "Working up that steam again?"

"Goddamn it. Goddamn it, Declan, she violated your home. It's not like taking from me or Grandmama. How much did she take?"

"Couple thousand."

The muscles in Lena's jaw tightened. "I'll have you a check tomorrow."

"You know I'll tear it up. Put it away, Lena. I figure it was a cheap lesson. If you're going to live in the country, have a houseful of valuables and spare cash, you don't walk off and leave it unlocked and unattended."

"She'd have broken a window."

"Yeah. That's why I'm getting a couple of dogs. Always wanted a pack of dogs. I thought I'd go to the shelter after the wedding. Want to come with me?"

She just shook her head. "You lose two thousand dollars—and I bet it was more—to a thieving junkie, and your response is to buy some dogs."

"Figured I'd get some fun out of it. How about it? They'll be your dogs, too."

"Stop it, Declan."

"Uh-uh." With a satisfied smirk on his face, he walked toward her. "Let's get us a couple mongrel puppies, Lena. They'll be good practice before the kids come along."

"You get your own puppies." But he'd teased a smile out of her. "And run around after them when they pee on your rugs and chew on your shoes."

"Maybe Rufus will teach them their manners. You're wearing my earrings," he said as he slipped his arms around her and glided into a dance.

"They're my earrings now."

"You think of me when you put them on."

"Maybe. Then I think how nice they look on me, and I forget all about you."

"Well, then I'll have to find other ways to remind you."

"A necklace." She skimmed her fingers up the nape of his neck, into his hair. "Couple of nice glittery bracelets."

"I was thinking of a toe ring."

She laughed, eased in closer so that she could rest her cheek on his. They were waltzing, and a tune was playing in her head. One she'd heard him hum or whistle countless times. She could smell his workday on him—the sweat, the dust—and under it the faint, faint drift of soap from his morning shower. His cheek was a little rough against hers as he'd neglected to shave.

If life were a fairy tale, she thought, they could stay just like this. Waltzing around and around on the satiny floor, while the sun slid down, the flowers rioted, and the lights from hundreds of tiny crystal prisms showered over them.

"I've got such feelings for you. More than I ever had for anyone, or wanted to. I don't know what to do with them."

"Give them to me," he pleaded, turning his lips into her hair. "I'll take good care of them."

She hadn't realized she'd spoken aloud. Hadn't meant to. Now, when she would have drawn back, he pulled her closer. So close, so tight, she couldn't get her breath.

Her head spun, and the music inside it soared. The strong scent of lilies rose up and almost smothered her.

"Do you hear it?" His hands trembled as he gripped her arms. "Violins."

"I can't . . ." His voice sounded far off, and as she fought to focus on his face, another seemed to float over it. "I'm dizzy."

"Let's sit down." He kept his hands on her arms, lowered them both to the floor. "You heard it, too. The music. You felt it, too."

"Just hold on a minute." She had to regain her bearings. The room was empty but for the two of them. There was no music, no crystal light, no pots heaped with fragrant white lilies. Yet she had heard, seen, smelled. "I didn't know hallucinations were catching."

"It's not hallucination. It's memory. Somehow, it's memory. They'd have danced here, Lucian and Abigail, like we were. Loved each other, like we do." When she shook her head, he swore. "All right, damn it, he loved her, the way I love you. And there's something still alive between them. Maybe something that needs to be finished, or just acknowledged. We're here, Lena."

"Yes, we're here. And I'm not living someone else's life."

"It's not like that."

"It *felt* like that. And living someone else's life might just mean dying someone else's death. He drowned himself in that pond outside there, and she—"

"She died in this house."

Lena took a calming breath. "Depending on whose story you believe."

"I know she did. Upstairs, in the nursery. Something happened to her up there. And he never knew. He grieved himself to death not knowing. I need to find out for him. And for myself. I need you to help me."

"What can I do?"

"Come to the nursery with me. We're closer now. Maybe you'll remember this time."

"Declan." She took his face in her hands. "There's nothing for me to remember."

"You hang witch bottles out in my tree, but sit here denying any possibility of reincarnation, which you brought into the mix in the first place."

"That's not what I'm doing. There's nothing for me to remember because I'm not Abigail. You are."

She might as well have slipped on a pair of brass knuckles and plowed her fist into his stomach. The shock of her words had him reeling.

"Get out. That's not possible."

"Why not?"

"Because . . ." Flustered, oddly embarrassed, he pushed to his feet. "You're trying to say I was a *girl*?"

"I don't know why that's such a shock to your system. A lot of us get along just fine female."

"I don't. I'm not. I wasn't."

"It makes the most sense, if any of this makes sense."

"No sense. None. No way."

"You're the one who keeps hearing the baby cry." She'd never seen him quite so flustered. "Mothers do, before anyone else. And you're drawn to that room upstairs, the way a mother would be to her baby. Even though the room scares you, you're pulled back. You said how you wandered through the servants' wing, how easy it was to find your way. She'd have known it, but why would Lucian?"

"It was his house." But he remembered how he'd imagined looking out the window, imagined seeing the two men riding toward the house. Why would he imagine seeing Lucian riding home if he'd *been* Lucian?

"A couple other things," Lena continued. "One telling one. That day when I came along and saw you walking toward the pond. Trancelike. You walked oddly. I couldn't figure out what it was about the way you walked that struck me. But now I know. You were walking the way a very pregnant woman walks. Waddling a bit," she said as he turned and gaped at her with something like horror. "A hand pressed to the small of your back. Small, careful steps."

"Now you're saying I wasn't just a girl, but a pregnant girl?"

"Oh for heaven's sake, *cher*, some people believe you can come back as a poodle. What's so bad about a pregnant woman?"

"Because pregnant women go into labor at a certain point, then have to push several pounds of baby out of a very limited space."

The horror on his face was comical, and enough to have her relaxing into the theory. "I don't think you'll have to repeat that performance in this life. Have you considered that if you look at this puzzle from this new angle, you might find the answers you want?"

He found himself wanting to rub at his crotch just to make sure everything was where it should be. Maybe work up a good, manly belch. "I like it better the other way."

"Keep an open mind, *cher*. I've got to get to work."

"Wait a minute, wait a minute." He dashed after her. "You're just going to drop this bombshell on me, then leave?"

"I've got to work for a living."

"Come back after closing. Stay."

"I need to stay at Grandmama's for a night or two, till she's feeling steadier."

"Okay. Okay." He let out a breath when they reached the main floor. "Let me try this." He spun her around, crushed his mouth to hers. Then took the kiss deep and dreamy.

"You didn't get any lesbian-type vibe from that, did you?" he asked when he drew back.

"Hmm." She touched her tongue to her top lip, pretended to consider. "No. I can attest that you're all man this time around. Now, shoo. You've got plenty to do the next few days to keep your mind occupied. This whole thing's waited a hundred years, it can wait till after Remy's wedding."

"Come back and stay when Miss Odette's feeling better."

"All right."

"I love you, Lena."

"I'm afraid you do," she whispered, and walked away.

L ena left the bar as early as she could manage, but it was still after one in the morning when she pulled up to the bayou house. The porch light was burning, and the moths seduced to death by it. She sat for a moment, listening to the music of the frogs and night birds, and the teasing whisper of a faint breeze.

This was the place of her girlhood. Perhaps the place of her heart. Though she'd made her life in the city, it was here she came when she was most happy, or most troubled. Here she came to think her deepest thoughts or dream her most secret dreams.

She'd let herself dream once—those innate female dreams of romance and a handsome man to love her, of home and children and Sunday mornings.

When had she stopped?

That sticky summer afternoon, she admitted. That hot, hazy day when she'd seen the boy she'd loved with all her wild heart and foolish youth coupling like an animal with her mother on a ragged blanket in the marsh.

The marsh that was hers, the boy that was hers. The mother that was hers.

It had sliced her life in two, she thought now. The time before, when there was still hope and innocent dreams and faith. And the time after, where there was only ambition, determination and a steely vow never, never to believe again.

The boy didn't matter now, she knew. She could barely see his face in her mind. Her mother didn't matter, not at the core of it. But the *moment* mattered.

Without it, who knew what direction her life would have taken? Oh, she and the boy would have parted ways soon enough. But it might've been with some sweetness, it might have left her with some soft memory of first loves.

But that stark vision of sex and betrayal had forged her. She'd understood then what it might have taken her years to learn otherwise. That a woman was smarter, safer, to drive the train herself. Men came, men went, and enjoying them was fine.

Loving them was suicide.

Suicide? she shook her head as she climbed out of the car. That was overly dramatic, wasn't it? Heartbreak wasn't death.

*He'd died from it.*

She all but heard the voice in her head. It hadn't been the knife wound, it hadn't been the pond that had killed Lucian Manet.

It had been a broken heart.

She let herself into the house and immediately saw the spill of light from Odette's room. Even as she approached, Lena heard the quick thump-thump of Rufus's tail on the floor.

She stepped to the doorway, cocked her head. Odette was sitting up in bed, a book open on her lap, the faithful dog curled on the floor.

"What are you doing up so late?"

"Waiting for my baby. I didn't think you'd be back for another hour or more."

"Business was light enough to spare me."

Odette patted the side of the bed in invitation. "You took off early because you were worried about me. You shouldn't."

"You used to tell me worrying was your job." Lena lay down on top of the sheets, her head in the curve of her grandmother's arm. "Now it's mine, too. I'm sorry she hurt you."

"Oh, baby, I think that must be her job. God knows she's good at it." Odette stroked Lena's hair. "I got you, though. I got my Lena."

"I was thinking what it was like for you and Grandpapa to raise a baby after you'd already raised your own."

"You were nothing but pure pleasure to both of us."

"It made me think about how the Manets brought your grandmama back here when she was a baby. You remember her pretty well, don't you?"

"I remember her very well. You've the look of her. You've seen the old pictures, so you know that."

"Did she ever say how the Hall should've been hers?"

"Never heard her say anything like. She was a happy woman, Lena. Maybe happier here than she would've been in the Hall, had things been different. She had a fine hand with baking, and that she passed to me. She told good stories, too. Sometimes when I'd come spend time with her, she'd make them up just like they were real. I think she could've been a writer if she'd wanted that for herself."

"She must've thought of her parents, and the Manets. No matter how happy she was here, she must've thought of them."

"I expect so. She used to take flowers to her papa's grave. Took them every year on her birthday."

"Did she? You never told me that."

"Said she owed him life—hers, her children, her grandchildren. She even laid flowers on the graves of Josephine and Henri Manet. Though she never stopped there to say a prayer. And she did one more thing on her birthday, every year until she died. She took flowers and tossed them into the river. And there she said a prayer."

"For her mother, you think?"

"She never said, but that's what I think."

"And do you think that's where Abigail is? In the river?"

"Some say."

Lena raised her head. "I'm not asking some. I'm asking you."

"I know sometimes I walk along the bank, and I feel an awful sadness. And I think, sometimes, old souls search for new life. And keep searching until it comes out right. What're you searching for?"

Lena laid her head down again, closed her eyes. "I thought I'd found it. Now I'm not so sure. He loves me, Grandmama."

"I know he does."

"If I love him back, everything changes."

Odette smiled, leaned over to shut off the light. "It surely does," she murmured and continued to stroke Lena's hair. "It surely does."

# EIGHTEEN

A s host of Remy's bachelor party, Declan felt socially obligated to stay till the bitter end. The bitter end was some dingy, back-street dive in the Quarter where the liquor burned holes in what was left of a man's stomach lining and the strippers were woefully past their prime.

Nobody seemed to care.

In the spirit of good fellowship, Declan tucked a final dollar in the frayed garter on a flabby white thigh, then hauled a glassy-eyed Remy to his feet.

"Let's go, pal of mine."

"Huh? What? Is it morning?"

"Close enough."

As they stumbled out, arm in arm as much for necessity as friend-ship, Remy looked around. His head bopped like a puppet's on a jerked string. "Wherez everybody?"

"Passed out, in jail, dead in an alley."

"Oh. Wimps." Remy grinned his rubber grin. "You 'n me, Dec, we still got it."

"I'm starting a course of antibiotics in the morning to get rid of it." He tripped and had to wrap both arms around Remy to keep from falling on his face. "Too much gravity. There's entirely too much gravity out here."

"Let's go find us another naked woman."

"I think we found all of them already. Time to go home, old buddy, old pal."

"I'm getting married in three days." Remy held up four fingers to demonstrate. "No more carousing for Remy." He looked around. The streets were nearly deserted and oily with the light drizzle. "Do we have to bail anybody out?"

"Screw 'em."

"Damn right. Where's my girl? Effie!" He shouted it, and the name echoed back, making Declan snort drunkenly.

"Stella!" Cracked up by his own wit, he sat down hard in a puddle. "Fuck it, Remy. Let's just sleep here."

"Gotta go find my girl, gonna make sweet, sweet love to my Effie."

"You couldn't get it up right now with a hydraulic pump."

"Bet?" Remy fumbled for his zipper, and Declan had just enough brain cells left to stagger up and stop him.

"Put that thing away before you hurt yourself. Get us arrested for decent exposure."

"'S okay. We're lawyers."

"Speak for yourself. Find cabs. We must find cabs."

"Cab to Effie. Where's my blushin' bride?"

"Home in bed, like every other good woman is at . . ." He lifted Remy's wrist, tried to focus on the watch. "Whatever o'clock in the morning. Lena, she's in bed. She thinks I'm a woman."

"You must not be fucking her right then."

"No, you ass. And remind me to punch you for that later. She thinks I'm Abigail."

"You haven't been trying on her underwear or anything weird like that, have you, son?"

"I like the little black lace panties with the roses best. They slim down my hips."

"Pretty sure you're joking. Wait." He stopped, leaned over the curb, hands braced on his knees. Then slowly straightened again. "False alarm. Not gonna puke."

"There's good news. Cab!" Declan waved desperately when he saw one cruising. "In the name of God. You first," he said and all but shoved Remy inside before diving in after.

"Where do I live?" Remy demanded. "I used to know, but I forgot. Can I call Effie and ask her?"

Fortunately Declan remembered, and as Remy snoozed on his shoulder, he concentrated on remaining conscious until he fulfilled the last of his duties and got his friend home alive.

At the curb, he elbowed Remy and brought him up like an arrow from a bow. "What? Where? Sum bitch, I'm home. How 'bout that?"

"Can you make it from here?" Declan asked him.

"I can hold my liquor. All six gallons of it." Shifting, Remy caught Declan's face in his hand and kissed him hard on the mouth. "I love you, *cher*. But if you'd been Abigail, I'd've slipped you some tongue."

"Ugh," was the best Declan could manage as Remy climbed out.

"You're the goddamnedest best friend I ever had, and that was the goddamnedest best bachelor's party in the history of bachelor's parties. I'm gonna go up, puke and pass out now."

"You do that. Wait till he gets in the door," Declan told the driver, and watched Remy waver, split in two. Both of them stumbled inside the building.

"Okay, the rest is his business. You know where the old Manet Hall is?"

The driver eyed him in the rearview mirror. "I guess I do."

"I live there. Take me home, okay?"

"That's a long way out." The driver shifted, turned, eyed Declan up and down. "You got enough for the fare?"

"I got money. I got lotsa money." Declan pawed through his pockets, came up with bills, littered the cab with them. "I'm loaded."

"You're telling me." With a shake of his head, the driver pulled away from the curb. "Must've been some party, buddy."

"Tell me," Declan muttered, then slid face first on the backseat.

The next thing he knew, clearly, a Dixieland band was blasting in his head. He was still facedown, but the beach of Waikiki had ended up in his mouth and his tongue had grown a fine fur coat.

Some sadist was hammering spikes into his shoulder.

"Holy Mary, Mother of God, pray for us sinners."

"No point falling back on that now. Just roll over nice and slow, *cher*. Don't open your eyes yet."

"I'm dying here. Call a priest."

"Here now, Lena's got you." Gently and with great amusement, she eased him over, supported his head. "Just swallow this."

He glugged, choked, felt something vile wash over the fur, through the sand and down his throat. In defense, he tried to push the glass away from his lips, and opened his eyes.

He'd go to his grave denying the sound that had come out of his mouth had in any way resembled a girlish scream.

Lena clucked her tongue. "I told you not to open your eyes."

"What eyes? What eyes? They've been burned to cinders."

"Drink the rest."

"Go away, go very far away, and take your poison with you."

"That's no way to talk to someone who's come to tend you on your deathbed."

He slid back down, dragged a pillow over his face. "How'd you know I was dying?"

"Effie called."

"When's Remy's funeral?"

"Fortunately, he's marrying a woman with a great deal of tolerance, understanding and humor. How many titty bars did y'all hit last night?"

"All of them. All the titty bars in all the land."

"I suppose that explains why you have a pasty on your cheek."

"I do not." But when he groped under the pillow, he felt the tassel. "Oh God. Have some mercy and just kill me."

"Well, all right, honey." She applied just enough pressure to the pillow to have him flapping his hands and shoving up.

His face was flushed, his bloodshot eyes just a little wild. "That wasn't funny."

"You had to see it from this side." And she laughed. He still wore his clothes, the wrinkled, liquor-spotted shirt half in, half out of his jeans. Another pasty peeked out of the shirt pocket. This one was pink and silver. His eyes were narrowed to a pained squint.

"You're going to feel better in a bit—not good but better. You get a shower and some food, on top of that potion I poured into you, you'll get the feeling back in your extremities in two, maybe three hours."

Someone had shaved the fur off his tongue, he discovered. He wasn't sure it was an improvement. "What was in that stuff you gave me?"

"You don't want to know, but I laced it with four aspirin, so don't take any more for a while. I'm going to fix you a nice light omelette and some toast."

"Why?"

"Because you look so pitiful." She started to kiss him, then jerked back, waving a hand between them. "Christ Jesus, do something about that breath, *cher*, before you kill someone with it."

"Who asked you?"

"And make that a long shower. You smell like the barroom floor." She pushed to her feet. "How come nobody's around here today?"

"In anticipation of a hangover, I let it be known that anyone who came around this house before three in the afternoon would be executed without trial."

She checked her watch. "Looks like you got a few hours yet."

"If I have to get out of this bed, I'm getting a gun. I'll feel bad about killing you, but I'll do it."

"I'll be in the kitchen." She cocked a brow. "Bring your gun, *cher*, and we'll see if you remember how to use it."

"Is that a euphemism?" he called after her, then immediately regretted raising his voice. Holding his head to keep it in place, he eased creakily out of bed.

She chuckled all the way downstairs. Laughed harder when she heard a door slam. Bet he's sorry he did that, she thought, then stopped, looked back when she heard another two slams.

Ah well . . . she supposed he couldn't threaten ghosts with a gun.

"Make all the racket you want," she said as she headed back toward the kitchen. "You don't worry me any."

The library doors shook as she passed them. She ignored them. If a surly, smelly man didn't chase her off, a mean-tempered ghost wouldn't.

He'd looked so damn cute, she thought as she hunted up the coffee beans. All pale and male and cross. And with that silly pasty plastered on his cheek.

Men just lost half their IQ when they had a look at a naked woman. Put a pack of them together with women willing to strip to music, and they had the common sense of a clump of broccoli.

She ground the beans, set coffee to brew. She was mixing eggs in a bowl when it occurred to her that it was the first time in her life she'd made breakfast for a man she hadn't slept with the night before.

Wasn't that an odd thing?

Odder still that she was humming in the kitchen of an annoyed, smelly, hungover man who'd snapped at her. *Out of character, Lena. Just what's going on here?*

She'd been so intrigued by Effie's cheerful amusement over Remy's condition. And here she was, feeling the same thing over Declan's.

She peered out the window at the garden that had been wild and abandoned only months before. It bloomed now, beautifully, with new sprigs, fresh green spearing out.

She'd gone and done it after all. Gone and let him sneak into her, right through the locks and bolts.

She was in love with him. And oh God, she didn't want to be—as much for his sake as for her own.

He'd blown the dust off those young dreams she'd so rigidly put away. The ones colored with love and hope and trust. They were so shiny now that they were staring her in the face. So shiny they blinded her.

And terrified her.

Marriage. The man wanted marriage, and she didn't believe in making promises unless you'd shed blood to keep them.

Would she? Could she?

"I think I'd want to," she said quietly. "I think I'd want to, for him."

As she spoke, a cupboard door flew open. A thick blue mug shot out and smashed at her feet.

She leaped back, heart hammering as shards rained over her ankles. Grimly, she stared down at the blood seeping out of tiny nicks.

"Seems I already have. You don't want that, do you?" Bowl still clutched in her hand, she spun a circle. "You want anything but our being together. We'll see who wins in the end, won't we? We'll just see."

Deliberately she reached down for one of the shards, then ran it over her thumb. As the blood welled, she held her hand up, let it drip. "I'm not weak, as he was. If I take love, if I promise love, I'll keep it."

The sound of chimes had her bolting straight up. It was Declan's tune. The first ringing notes of it. Fear and wonder closed her throat, had her bobbling the bowl.

"Goddamn it, answer the door, will you?" His voice blasted downstairs, full of bitter annoyance. "Then murder whoever rang that idiot doorbell."

Doorbell? She pushed her free hand through her hair. He'd installed a doorbell that played "After the Ball." Wasn't that just like him?

"You keep shouting at me," she called as she marched down the hall, "you're going to have worse than a hangover to deal with."

"If you'd go away and let me die in peace, I wouldn't have to shout."

"In about two shakes, I'm coming up there and wringing your neck. And after I wring your neck, I'm going to kick your ass."

She wrenched open the door on the final threat, and found herself glaring at a very handsome couple. It took only one blink to clear the temper for her to see Declan's eyes looking curiously back at her out of the woman's face.

"I'm Colleen Fitzgerald." The woman, tidy, blond and lovely, held out an elegant hand. "And who are you? If that's my son's ass you're intending to kick, I'd like to know your name."

"Mom?" Dripping from the shower, wearing nothing but ripped sweatpants, Declan rushed to the top of the stairs. "Hey! Mom, Dad." Despite the ravages of the hangover, he bolted down, threw one arm around each of them and squeezed. "I thought you were flying down tomorrow."

"Change of plans. Are you just getting up?" Colleen demanded. "It's after one in the afternoon."

"Bachelor party last night. Hard liquor, loose women."

"Really?" Colleen said and eyed Lena.

"Oh, not this one. She came over to play Florence Nightingale. Colleen and Patrick Fitzgerald, Angelina Simone."

"Good to meet you." Patrick, long, lanky, with his dark hair gorgeously silvered at the temples, sent Lena a generous smile. His blue eyes were bright and bold as he held out a hand.

Then they narrowed in concern as he saw her thumb. "You've hurt yourself."

"It's nothing."

"What'd you do? You're bleeding. Jesus, Lena." Panicked, Declan grabbed her wrist, all but plucked her off her feet and rushed her toward the kitchen.

"It's just a scratch. Stop it, Declan. Your parents. You're embarrassing me," she hissed.

"Shut up. Let me see how deep it is."

Still in the doorway, Patrick turned to his wife. "She's the one?"

"He certainly thinks so." Colleen pursed her lips, stepped into the house. "Let's just see about all this."

"Hell of a looker."

"I've got eyes, Patrick." And she used them to take in the house as they followed Declan's hurried path.

It was more, a great deal more than she'd expected. Not that she doubted her son's taste. But she'd been led to believe the house was in serious, perhaps fatal, disrepair. And what she saw now were gracious rooms, charming details, glinting glass and wood.

And in the kitchen she saw her son, hovering over the hand of a very annoyed, very beautiful woman who looked perfectly capable of carrying out her earlier threat.

"I beg your pardon." Lena elbowed Declan aside and smiled coolly at his parents. "I dropped a cup, that's all. It's nice to meet both of you."

Declan turned to root through cupboards. "You need some antiseptic and a bandage."

"Oh, stop fussing. You'd think I cut my hand off. And if you don't watch yourself you'll step on the shards and be worse off than I am. I'm sorry your welcome's so disrupted," she said to his parents. "I'm just going to sweep up this mess, then I'll be on my way."

"Where are you going?" Declan demanded. "You promised food."

She wondered if he could hear her teeth grinding together. "Pour what's in that bowl into a skillet, turn on the burner and you'll have food." She yanked open the broom closet. "Why aren't you getting your parents coffee or a cold drink after their long trip? They raised you better than that."

"We certainly did," Colleen agreed.

"Sorry. Seeing the woman I love bleeding all over the floor distracted me."

"Declan." Though her voice was low, Lena's warning was loud and clear.

"Coffee sounds great," Patrick said cheerfully. "We came here straight from the airport. Wanted to see this place—and you, too, Dec," he added with a wink.

"Where's your luggage?"

"Had it sent to the hotel. Son, this place is enormous. A lot of space for one man."

"Lena and I want four kids."

She heaved the broken shards into the trash and rounded on him.

"Okay, three," he amended without a hitch in his stride. "But that's my final offer."

"I've had enough of this." She shoved the broom and dustpan into his hands. "You clean up your own messes. I hope you enjoy your stay," she said stiffly to Colleen and Patrick. "I'm late for work."

She strode out the back because it was closer, and fought off the towering urge to slam the door until the windows cracked.

"Isn't she beautiful?" Declan said with a huge grin. "Isn't she perfect?"

"You annoyed and embarrassed her," Colleen told him.

"Good. I tend to make more progress that way. Let me get the coffee, then I'll show you around."

An hour later, Declan sat with his mother on the rear gallery while Patrick—who'd lost the debate—made sandwiches.

The worst of the hangover had receded. Declan imagined he had whatever mysterious potion Lena had given him to thank for it—and the pleasure of seeing her in the same room as his parents.

Jeez, he'd missed them, he thought. He'd had no idea how much he'd missed them until he'd seen them.

"So," he said at length, "are you going to tell me what you think?"

"Yes." But she continued to sit and look out over his gardens. "Warm, isn't it? Early in the year to be so warm, I'd think."

"Actually, it's cooler today. You should've been here a couple days ago. You could've poached eggs out here."

She heard the way he said it, with a kind of pride. "You were never a big fan of the cold. Even when we went skiing, you'd prefer rattling around the lodge to charging down the slopes."

"Skiing's something people invented so they can pretend snow's fun."

"See if we invite you to Vermont this season." But her hand moved over, touched his. "The house is beautiful, Declan. Even what you haven't gotten to yet is beautiful, in its way. I liked to think your fiddling with tools and wood and so on was a nice little hobby. I preferred to think that. As long as you were a lawyer, it was probable you'd stay in Boston. You'd stay close. I dreaded seeing you go, so I made it hard on you. I'm not sorry. You're my baby," she said, and touched him in the deepest chamber of his heart.

"I don't have to be in Boston to be close."

She shook her head. "You won't come swinging in the house unexpectedly. We won't run into you in restaurants or at parties or the theater. That's a wrench in me, one you'll understand when you have those three or four children."

"I don't want you to be sad."

"Well, of course I'm sad. Don't be a boob. I love you, don't I?"

"You keep saying so," he said playfully.

She looked at him, gray eyes steady on gray eyes. "Lucky for both of us, I love you enough to know when to let go. You found your place here. I won't deny I hoped you wouldn't, but since you have, I'm glad for you. Damn it."

"Thanks." He leaned over, kissed her.

"Now, as for this woman . . ."

"Lena."

"I know her name, Declan," Colleen said dryly. "As a potential mother-in-law, I'm entitled to refer to her as 'this woman' until I get to know her a little better. As for this woman, she's nothing like what I'd imagined for you. Not when I imagined you climbing up the ranks in the law firm, buying a house close by and within easy access to the country club. Jessica would have suited my requirements as daughter-in-law quite well in that scenario. A good, challenging tennis partner who plays a decent hand of bridge and has the skill to chair the right committees."

"Maybe you should adopt Jessica."

"Be quiet, Declan." Colleen's voice was mild—and steel. Lena would have recognized the tone instantly. "I'm not finished. Jessica, however well suited for me, was very obviously not suited for you. You weren't happy, and I'd begun to see, and to worry about that just before you broke it off. I tried to convince myself it was just pre-wedding jitters, but I knew better."

"It wouldn't have hurt for you to clue me in on that one."

"Maybe not, but I was annoyed with you."

"Tell me."

"Don't sass, young man, especially when I'm about to be sentimental. You were always a happy child. Bright, clever, a smart tongue, but I respect that. You had, I'd call it, a bounce in your heart. And you lost it. I see you've gotten that back today. I saw it in your eyes again when you looked at Lena."

He took Colleen's hand, rubbed it against his cheek. "You called her Lena."

"Temporarily. I haven't made up my mind about her. And believe me, boy, she hasn't made hers up about your father and me, either. So, I'd advise you to stay out of it and let us get on with the job of doing so."

She stretched out her legs. "Patrick? Did you have to hunt down the pig for those ham sandwiches?"

Declan grinned, gave the hand he held a big, noisy kiss. "I love you guys."

"We love you, too." She squeezed his fingers, hard, then let them go. "God knows why."

H e dreamed of storms and pain. Of fear and joys.

Rain and wind lashed the windows, and the pain that whipped through him erupted in a sobbing scream.

Sweat and tears poured down his face—her face. Her face, her body. His pain.

The room was gold with gaslight and the snap and simmer of the fire in the grate. And as that storm raged outside, another spun through her. Through him.

Agony vised her belly with the next contraction. She was blind with it. Her cry against it was primal, and burned his throat with its passion.

*Push, Abby! You have to push! You're almost there.*

Tired, she was so tired, so weak. How could she live through such pain? But she grit her teeth. Almost mad. Everything she was, every-thing she had, focused on this one task, this one miracle.

Her child. Her child, Lucian's child, was fighting to come into the world. She bore down with all the strength she had left. Life depended on it.

*There's the head! Et là! Such hair! One more, Abby. One more,* chère.

She was laughing now. Better than screaming, even if the laugh was tinged with hysteria. She braced herself on her elbows, threw her head back as fresh, unspeakable pain rolled through her.

This one moment, this one act, was the greatest gift a woman could give. This gift, this child, would be held safe, would be cherished. Would be loved for all of her days.

And on the pain, with lightning flashing, on the roar of thunder, she pushed, pushed, pushed wailing life into the world.

*A girl! You have a beautiful girl.*

Pain was forgotten. The hours of sweat and blood and agony were nothing now in the brilliant flash of joy. Weeping from it, she held out her arms for the small wriggling baby who cried out in what sounded like triumph.

*My rose. My beautiful Marie Rose. Tell Lucian. Oh, please bring Lucian to see our daughter.*

They cleaned both mother and baby first, smiling at the mother's impatience and the child's irritable cries.

There were tears in Lucian's eyes when he came into the room. When he clasped her hand, his fingers trembled. When he looked at the child they'd created, his face filled with wonder.

She told him what she had vowed on the instant Marie Rose had been placed in her arms.

*We'll keep her safe, Lucian. No matter what, we'll keep her safe and happy. She's ours. Promise me you'll love and care for her, always.*

*Of course. She's so beautiful, Abby. My beautiful girls. I love you.*

*Say the words. I need to hear you say the words.*

Still holding Abigail's hand, Lucian laid a tender finger on his daughter's cheek. *I'll love and I'll care for her, always. I swear it.*

# NINETEEN

Patrick Fitzgerald took his wife's hand as they strolled through the Quarter. He knew their destination was Et Trois and their mission another look at Angelina Simone.

"You know, Colleen, this is very close to interference, and spying."

"And your point is?"

He had to laugh. After nearly forty years of marriage, the woman could always make him laugh. He considered that, above all, a sign of a successful partnership.

"You realize she might not be there. Owning a bar doesn't mean you're in it all day, every day."

"So, we'll get a look at her place of business, and have a drink. It's perfectly up front and respectable."

"Yes, dear."

He used that phrase, that tone, only when he was making fun of her. Colleen debated between giving him a good elbow shot in the ribs and laughing. Then did both.

The crowds, the noise, the *heat* and the somehow florid and decaying elegance of the city weren't things that appealed to her for more than a brief visit. She preferred the Old-World charm, and yes, the dignity, of Boston.

Certainly Boston had its seamier sides, but it wasn't so overt, so celebratory about it. Sex was meant to be fun and interesting—she wasn't a prude, for God's sake. But it was also meant to be private.

And still, the tragic wail of a tenor sax weeping on the air touched some chord in her.

If her son was determined to make his home here, she'd accept that. Maybe, with a bit more study and debate, she'd accept the woman.

"You'll have time and opportunity to grill her at the wedding tomorrow," Patrick pointed out.

Colleen only sighed at the minds of men. God bless them, they were simple creatures. Guileless, really. The first step, obviously, was to observe the girl in her own milieu.

She considered the neighborhood, the positioning of the bar, the level of traffic. She decided Lena had chosen wisely, and had taste and sense enough to let the exterior of the bar blend smoothly into the other establishments.

She liked the gallery over it, the pots of flowers—bright colors against the soft creams. It demonstrated taste and style, an appreciation for atmosphere.

She'd pried the information out of Declan that Lena lived above the bar, and wondered now if she should wheedle a visit upstairs to check out the living quarters.

She stepped inside Et Trois, made a good, objective study.

It was clean, which met with her approval. It was crowded but not jammed, which met with her business sense. Too early for the rowdy night crowd, Colleen judged, too late for the lunch shift.

The music coming out of the speakers was Cajun, she supposed, and she approved of that as well. It was lively, but not so loud as to make simple conversation a chore.

A black man in a bright red shirt worked behind the bar. A good face, she decided, smooth hands. A young waitress—blond, perky, wearing jeans perhaps just a tad too tight—served one of the tables.

Colleen spotted what she decided were a number of tourists from their camera and shopping bags. Others she assumed were locals.

Whatever food had been or was being served put a hot, spicy scent over the air.

Lena stepped out of the kitchen. Their eyes met immediately and with instant acknowledgment. Colleen let her lips curve in a small, polite smile and walked to the bar with Patrick following.

"Afternoon, Mrs. Fitzgerald, Mr. Fitzgerald." An equally small, equally polite smile curved Lena's lips. "You've been taking in the Quarter?" she asked with a glance at the shopping bags Patrick carried.

"Colleen rarely passes a store without seeing something that needs to be bought."

"That must be where Declan gets it. Can I show you a menu?"

"We've had lunch, thanks." Colleen slid onto a stool. "I'd love a martini, Stoli, very cold, dead dry, straight up, shaken. Three olives."

"And for you, Mr. Fitzgerald?"

"Make it the same, and make it Patrick." He took the stool beside his wife. "You've got a nice place here. Live music?" he asked with a nod toward the stage area.

"Every night, nine o'clock." As she began to mix the martinis, she sent him a genuine smile. "You like to dance, you should come back. We'll get your feet moving. You enjoying your visit?"

"We're looking forward to the wedding," Colleen commented. "Remy's like family. And we're pleased to see Declan making such progress on the house."

"He's happy there."

"Yes."

Lena took out the two martini glasses she'd chilled during the mixing. "Be nicer for you if he'd be happy in Boston—and with the one he almost married."

"Yes, it would, wouldn't it? But we can't choose other people's lives. Even our children's. And you certainly can't select the person they'll love. Are you in love with my son, Lena?"

Hands rock steady, Lena strained the martinis into the cold glasses. "That's something I'll talk to him about, when I'm ready. These are on the house," she added, sliding the olives in. "I hope they suit your tastes."

"Thank you." Colleen picked up her glass, sipped. Raised an eyebrow. "It's excellent. I've always felt mixing the perfect martini is a kind of art, and have been surprised and disappointed that often those who own a bar or club or restaurant make or serve imperfect martinis."

"Why do anything if you don't set out to do it right?"

"Exactly. It's a matter of pride, isn't it? In self, in one's work, one's life. Flaws are acceptable, even necessary to make us human and humble. But to serve a guest or customer less than the best one is capable of, strikes me as arrogant or sloppy. Often both."

"I don't see the point in doing anything halfway," Lena said, and filled a bowl with fresh snack mix. "If I can't make a martini, fine, then I step back until I learn how it's done. Otherwise I'd disappoint myself and the person who was counting on me."

"A good policy." Colleen sampled an olive. "Without high standards, we tend to settle for less than what makes us happy and productive, and can shortchange the people who matter to us."

"When someone matters to me—and I'm careful about who does—I want the best for them. They may settle for less. But I won't."

When Patrick leaned over, peered closely at Colleen's martini, she frowned at him. "What are you doing?"

"Trying to see what's in yours that isn't in mine."

It made Lena laugh, had her shoulders relaxing. "He's an awful lot like you, isn't he? Got his mama's eyes though. Sees right through you. Even when you don't want him to. He loves you both like crazy, and that says something to me. So I'm going to say something to you."

She leaned a little closer. "I come from plain stock. Strong, but plain.

My mother, she's a dead loss, and more of an embarrassment to me than I care to speak of. But my grandfather was a fine and decent man. My grandmama's as good as anybody, and better than most. I run this bar because I'm good at it—and I like it—and I don't waste my time on things I don't like."

She swept her hair behind her ear, kept her gaze level on Colleen's. "I'm selfish and I'm stubborn, and I don't see a damn thing wrong with that. I don't care about his money, or yours, so let's just set that aside. He's the best man I ever met in my life, and I'm not good enough for him. I say that knowing I'm good enough for damn near anybody, but he's different. Turns out under that affable exterior that man's even more stubborn than I am, and I haven't figured out what to do about that quite yet. When I do, he'll be the first to know. I expect he'll fill you in on that particular outcome.

"Now." Unconsciously, Lena toyed with the key she wore around her neck. "Would you like another drink?"

"We'll just nurse these for a while," Colleen told her.

"Excuse me a minute. I see I have an order to fill." She moved down the bar to where her waitress waited with an empty tray.

"Well?" Patrick asked. "I believe she set you neatly in your place."

"Yes." Well satisfied, Colleen took another sip of her martini. "She'll do."

I'm not nervous." Pale, jittery, Remy stood in the library while Declan attached the boutonniere of lily of the valley to his friend's tuxedo lapel.

"Maybe if you say that *another* dozen times, you'll believe it. Hold still, damn, Remy."

"I'm holding still."

"Sure, except for the mild seizure you seem to be having, you're steady as a rock."

"I want to marry Effie. Want to live my life with her. This is the day we've both been looking forward to for months."

"That's right. Today," Declan said in sober tones, "is the first day of the rest of your life."

"I feel a little sick."

"It's too late to puke," Declan said cheerfully. "You're down to the final fifteen. Want me to call your dad back in?"

"No. No, he'll have his hands full with Mama. How many people did you say were out there?"

"Couple hundred last I looked, and more coming."

"Jesus. Jesus. Why didn't we elope? How's a man supposed to stand up in front of hundreds of people and change his life forever?"

"I think the tradition started so the groom couldn't run away. They'd go after him like a lynch mob."

"That sure does settle me down, *cher*. How about you find me a couple fingers of bourbon?"

Declan merely strolled over to a painted cabinet and took out a bottle. "I figured you'd need a hit." He pulled out a tin of Altoids as well. "And these. Don't want to be breathing whiskey on the bride. She might be the one who runs."

Declan started to pour, but when the door opened after a cursory knock and his mother marched in, he whipped bottle and glass behind his back.

"Don't you both look handsome! Declan, don't give him more than one shot of that whiskey you've got behind you, and make sure he chases it with mouthwash."

"I got Altoids."

"Fine." Smiling, she walked over and fussed with Remy's tie. "You're nervous because this is the most important day of your life. There'd be something wrong with you if you didn't have some shakes. I promise, they'll go away the minute you see Effie. She looks beautiful."

Colleen framed Remy's face in her hands. "I'm very proud of you."

"How about me?" Declan demanded. "I thought of the Altoids."

"I'll get to you later. You're marrying the woman you love," Colleen went on. "You're surrounded by friends and family who love you both. It's a beautiful day, and your brother—the one of your heart—has seen to it that you have a beautiful setting. Now you take a shot of that bourbon, then take a deep breath. Then get your butt out there and get married."

"Yes, ma'am. I purely love you, Miss Colleen."

"I know it. I love you, too, but I'm not going to kiss you and smear my lipstick. One drink, Declan. This boy goes out there tipsy, I'm holding you responsible."

Later, Declan would think his mother was right, as usual. When he stood beside Remy, and Effie, frothy in white, stepped out on the gallery, Declan felt the nerves drain out of his friend—his brother. He saw the wide, wide grin stretch over Remy's face, heard his soft: "That's my girl."

He found his own gaze traveling through the rows of people, meeting Lena's. *And you're mine,* he thought. *This time around we're going to make it work.*

So he stood in the spring garden, with the old white house rising over the green lawn, and watched his friends marry.

When they kissed, when they turned to be announced as husband and wife, cheers rang out, so much more liberating and celebratory than the applause Declan was more accustomed to.

He felt his own grin stretch, nearly as wide as Remy's.

The music started up almost immediately. Fiddles, washboards, accordions. When the photographer whittled down to just the bride and groom, Declan broke free and wove his way through the sea of people to Lena.

She wore red. Bright, poppy red that left her back bare but for an intriguing web of thin straps. Just above her heart, she'd pinned the enamel watch and gold wings Lucian had once given Abigail.

"I wondered if you'd ever wear it."

"It's special," she said, "so I save it for special. It was a beautiful wedding, Declan. You did a fine job getting this place ready for it. You're a good friend."

"I have lots of good qualities, which makes you a very lucky woman. I've missed you the last couple days."

"We've both been busy."

"Stay tonight." He caught her hand, seeing denial and excuses in her eyes. "Angelina, stay tonight."

"Maybe. You've got a lot of people you should be talking to."

"They're all talking to each other. Where's Miss Odette?"

Lena scowled. "Your mother swept her off somewhere."

"You want me to find them, cut Miss Odette loose?"

Pride stiffened her spine, her voice. "My grandmama can hold her own against your mama any day of the week."

"Oh yeah?" Amused, Declan narrowed his eyes in challenge. "If they get physical, my money's on Colleen. She's got a wicked left. Why don't we get some champagne and go find them? See what round they're in."

"If she hurts my grandmama's feelings—"

"She would never do that." No longer amused, Declan gave her shoulders a little shake. "What do you take her for, Lena? If she went off with Miss Odette, it's because she'd like to get to know her."

"I suppose that's why she dragged your daddy into my place. So she could get to know me better."

"They were in your place?"

"My bar, yeah." Annoyed with herself for *being* annoyed, Lena reached out to take a flute from a waiter passing champagne. "She came in to check the place out, and me with it. So, she got her an eyeful, and a damn good martini. And I set her straight."

He experienced jittery male panic at the image of the two most important females in his life squaring off. "What the hell does that mean?"

"I said what I had to say, that's all. We understand each other fine now."

"Why don't you bring me up to date so I can understand you fine, too?"

"This isn't the time or the place."

"We're going to find the time and the place."

Because she heard the temper in his voice, she shrugged. Then smiled and traced a finger down his cheek. "Now don't get all riled up, *cher.* We got us a party here. You and me, we can fight anytime."

"Okay, we'll schedule it in for a little later." He caught her chin in his hand. "I can't figure out who you're selling short, Lena. Me, my family or yourself. Let me know when you've got the answer."

He bent, brushed his lips over hers. "See you later."

The reception moved into the ballroom, and still managed to spill onto the galleries, onto the lawn. For the first time in decades, the house filled with music and laughter. Racing children, crying babies, flirting couples and gossiping friends filled the great room, relaxed in the shade of white umbrellas at tables around the gardens or plopped down on the gallery.

Declan liked to imagine the house absorbing all that positive energy, even into the dark corners of the rooms he'd kept locked.

"Declan." Effie laid a hand on his arm. "May I have this dance?"

"Did somebody kill Remy?" He led her out on the floor. "I figure that's the only way he'd let you more than a foot away from him." He kissed her hand before taking her into his arms. "Can't blame him. When you've got the most beautiful woman in the room, you keep her close."

"Oh, Declan." She laid her cheek on his. "If I wasn't madly in love with my husband, I'd make such a play for you."

"If you ever get tired of him, let me know."

"I want to thank you for everything you did to give me this perfect day. I know my mama, my sister and I drove you a little crazy the last couple weeks."

"Has it only been a couple weeks?" He laughed. "It was worth every hour I hid in closets so none of you could find me."

"I'm so happy. I'm so happy, and I love you. I love everybody today," she said with a laugh. "Everyone in the world, but today, next to Remy, I love you best of all so I want you to be happy."

"I am."

"Not enough." She turned her lips to his ear. "Declan, there's something in this house that's just not finished. I didn't think I believed in that sort of thing, but . . . I feel it. Whenever I'm here, I feel it. I feel it even today."

He could feel the tremor move through her, rubbed his hand over her back to soothe it away. "You shouldn't think about it today. You shouldn't worry today."

"I'm worried for you. Something . . . it isn't finished. Part of it, somehow part of it's my fault."

"Yours?" He eased her back now so he could see her face, then circled her toward one of the corners. "What do you mean?"

"I wish I knew what I meant. I only know what I feel. Something I did, or didn't do for you. It doesn't make a bit of sense, but it's such a strong feeling. The feeling that I wasn't there for you when you needed me most. I guess I'm a little afraid something bad's going to happen again if it's not all made right. So, well, as silly as this sounds, I just want to tell you I'm sorry, so awfully sorry for letting you down however I did."

"It's all right." He touched his lips to her forehead. "You couldn't know. Whatever it was, if it was, you couldn't know. And, sweetheart, this isn't a day for looking back. It's all about tomorrow now."

"You're right. Just . . . just be careful," she said as Remy walked up and gave Declan a mock punch.

"That's my wife you're holding, *cher*. You go get your own girl."

"Good idea."

He hunted up Lena, found her in a clutch of people. The red of her dress was like a sleek tongue of flame over her dusky skin. He imagined his reaction to it, to her, transmitted clearly enough as he saw that knowing and essentially female look come into her eyes as he stepped toward her.

He turned slightly and held out a hand to her grandmother. "Miss Odette, would you dance with me?"

"Day hasn't come when I'll turn down a dance with a handsome man."

"You look wonderful," he told her when they took the floor.

"Weddings make me feel young. I had a nice talk with your mama."

"Did you?"

"You're wondering," she said with a chuckle. "I'll tell you we got on just fine. And she seemed pleased when I told her I saw how you'd been raised up right the first time I met you. She paid me back the compliment by saying the same about my Lena. Then we chatted about things women often chat about at weddings, which would likely bore you—except to say we agreed what a handsome young man you are. And handsome young men should find more reasons to wear tuxedos."

"I could become a maître d'. But they get better tips when they have a snooty accent, and I'm not sure I could pull that part off."

"Then I'll just have to wait until your own wedding to see you all slicked up again."

"Yeah." He looked over her head, but Lena had moved on. "This one's working out pretty well anyway. I was a little panicked that the storm last night would screw things up."

"Storm? *Cher*, we didn't have a storm last night."

"Sure we did. A mean one. Don't tell me you slept through it."

"I was up till midnight." She watched his face now. "Finishing the hem on this dress. Then I was up again 'round four when Rufus decided he needed to go outside. I saw lights on over here then. Wondered what you were doing up at that hour. Night was clear as a bell, Declan."

"I . . . I must've dreamed about a storm. Pre-wedding stress." But he hadn't been up at four. Hadn't been up at all, as far as he knew, after midnight—when he'd walked through the house to turn off all the lights before going to bed.

Dreams, he thought. Wind and rain, the flash of lightning. The yellow flames of the fire in the grate. Pain, sweat, thirst. Blood.

Women's hands, women's voices—Effie's?—giving comfort, giving encouragement.

He remembered it now, clearly, and stopped dead in the middle of the dance.

He'd had a baby. He'd gone through childbirth.

Good God.

"*Cher?* Declan? You come on outside." Gently, Odette guided him off the floor. "You need some air."

"Yeah. Southern ladies are big on swooning, right?"

"What's that?"

"Never mind." He was mortified, he was awed, at what had happened to him inside his own dream. Inside, he supposed, his own memories.

"Go on back in," he told her. "I'm just going to take a walk, clear my head."

"What did you remember?"

"A miracle," he murmured. "Remind me to buy my mother a really great present. I don't know how the hell you women get through it once. She did it four times. Amazing," he mumbled, and headed down the steps. "Fucking amazing."

He walked all the way around the house, then slipped back in for a tall glass of icy water. He used it to wash down three extra-strength aspirin in hopes of cutting back on the vicious headache that had come on the moment he'd remembered the dream.

He could hear the music spilling down the steps from the ballroom. He could feel the vibrations on the ceiling from where dozens of feet danced.

He had to get back up, perform his duties as best man and host. All he wanted to do was fall facedown on the bed, close his eyes and slide into oblivion.

"Declan." Lena came in through the gallery doors, then shut them behind her. "What's the matter?"

"Nothing. Just a headache."

"You've been gone nearly an hour. People are asking about you."

"I'm coming up." But he sat on the side of the bed. "In a minute."

She crossed to him. "Is it bad?"

"I've had worse."

"Why don't you just lie down a few minutes?"

"I'm not crawling into bed on my best friend's wedding day—unless you want to keep me company."

"It's tempting. Seeing a man in a tux always makes me want to peel him out of it."

"Maître d's must just love you."

"There now, you made a stupid joke, so you must be feeling better."

"Considering I gave birth less than twenty-four hours ago, I'd say I'm doing great."

Lena pursed her lips. "*Cher*, just how much have you had to drink this evening?"

"Not nearly as much as I plan on having. You know how you had this theory that I was Abigail Manet? Well, I'm starting to think you're onto something seeing as I dreamed I was in that room down the hall, in the bed I've seen in there—that one that isn't there. I wasn't seeing Abigail on that bed, in the last stages of labor. I experienced it, and let me tell you, it ain't no walk on the beach. Any woman who doesn't go for the serious drugs is a lunatic. It beats anything they dreamed up for that entertaining era known as the Spanish Inquisition."

"You dreamed you were Abigail, and you—"

"It wasn't like a dream, Lena, and I think I must've been in that room when I had the—flash or hallucination, or whatever we call it. I can remember the storm—the sound of it, and how scared I was, how focused I was on bringing that baby out."

He paused, replayed his own words. "Boy, that sounded weird."

"Yes. Yes, it did." She sat beside him.

"I heard the voices. Other women helping me. I can see their faces— especially the young one. The one close to my age—Abigail's age. I can feel the sweat running down my face, and the unbelievable fatigue. Then that sensation, that peak of it all when it was like coming to the point of being ripped open. Bearing down, then the relief, the numbness, the fucking *wonder* of pushing life into the world. Then the flood of pride and love when they put that miracle in my arms."

He looked down at his hands while Lena stared at him. "I can see the baby, Lena, clear as life, I can see her. All red and wrinkled and pissed off. Dark blue eyes, dark hair. A rosebud mouth. Tiny, slender fingers, and I thought: There are ten, and she is perfect. My perfect Rose."

He looked at Lena now. "Marie Rose, your great-great-grandmother. Marie Rose," he repeated, "our daughter."

# TWENTY

T*heir daughter.* She couldn't dismiss it, and something deep inside her grieved. But she couldn't speak of it, wouldn't speak of it, not when her head and heart were so heavy.

Lena threw herself back into the crowds, the music, the laughter. This was *now*, she thought. Now was what counted.

She was alive, with the warm evening air on her skin, under the pure, white moonlight with the fragrance of the flowers and gardens rioting around her.

Roses and verbena, heliotrope, jasmine.

Lilies. Her favorite had been the lily. She kept them, always, in her room. First in the servants' quarters, then in their bedroom. Clipped in secret from the garden or the hothouse.

And for the nursery, there were roses. Tiny pink buds for their precious Marie Rose.

Frightened, she pushed those thoughts, those images, aside. Grabbing a partner, she flirted him into a dance.

She didn't want the past. It was dead and done. She didn't want the future. It was capricious and often cruel. It was the moment that was to be lived, enjoyed. Even controlled.

So when Declan's father took her hand, she smiled at him, brilliantly.

"This one here's a Cajun two-step. Can you handle it?"

"Let's find out."

They swung among the circling couples with quick, stylish moves that had her laughing up at him. "Why, Patrick, you're a natural. You sure you're a Yankee?"

"Blood and bone. Then again, you have to factor in the Irish. My mother was a hell of a step-dancer, and can still pull it off after a couple of pints."

"How old's your mama?"

"Eighty-six." He twirled her out and back. "Fitzgeralds tend to be long-lived and vigorous. Something's upset you."

She kept her cheerful expression in place. "Now what could upset me at such a lovely time and place?"

"That's the puzzle. Why don't we get a glass of champagne, and you can tell me?"

He didn't give her a chance to refuse. Like father, like son, she thought as he kept her hand firmly in his. He drew her to the bar, ordered two flutes, then led her outside.

"A perfect night," she said, and breathed it in. "Look at those gardens. It's hard to believe what they were like just a few months back. Did Declan tell you about the Franks?"

"About the Franks, Tibald. About Effie and Miss Odette. About the ghosts, about you."

"He bit off a lot here." She sipped champagne, wandered to the baluster. Below, people were still dancing on the lawn. A group of women sat at one of the white tables under a white moon, some with babies sleeping on their shoulders, some with children drooping in their laps.

"He was bored in Boston."

Intrigued, Lena looked away from the people, the charm of the fairy lights, and looked at Patrick. "Bored?"

"Unhappy, restless, but in a large part bored. With his work, his fi-ancée, his life. The only thing that put any excitement in his face was the old house he was redoing. I worried he'd go along, end up married to the wrong woman, working in a field he disliked, living a life that only half satisfied him. I shouldn't have worried."

He leaned back on the baluster and looked through the open doors into the ballroom. "His mind, his heart, was never set on the path we—his mother and I—cleared for him. We didn't want to see that, so for a long time, we didn't."

"You only wanted the best for him. People tend to think what's best for them is best for the people they love."

"Yes, and Declan's nature is to do whatever he can to make those he loves happy. He loves you."

When she said nothing, Patrick turned to her. "You said he was stubborn. It's more than that. Once Declan sets his mind on a goal, on a vision, he's got a head like granite. He won't be turned away by obsta-cles or excuses or lukewarm protests. If you don't love him, Lena, if you don't want a life with him, hurt him. Hurt him quick and make it deep. Then walk away."

"I don't want to hurt him. That's the whole point and problem."

"He didn't think he was capable of loving anyone. He told me that after he broke it off with Jessica. He said he didn't have that kind of love inside him. Now he knows he does, and he's better for it. You've already made a difference in his life, an important one. Now you have to love him back, or leave him. To do anything in between would be cruel, and you're not cruel."

She reached up, closed her fingers around the key on its chain, then dropped them—nervous now—to the wings on her breast. "He's not what I planned for. He's not what I was looking for."

He smiled then, kindly, and patted her hand. "Life's full of surprises, isn't it? Some of them are a real kick in the ass." Then he leaned down and kissed her cheek. "I'll see you again," he said, and left her alone.

The party rolled on a good two hours after the bride and groom were seen off in a shower of confetti—which Declan imagined he'd be finding in his lawn, his clothes, perhaps even his food for the next six months.

The music stayed hot, and the guests stayed happy. In the early hours of the morning, some walked to their cars. Others were carried, and not all of them were children.

Declan stood on the curve of his front steps and watched the last of them drive away. The sky in the east was paling, just a gentle lessening of the dark. Even as he stood, he saw a star go out.

Morning was waking.

"You must be tired," Lena said from the gallery above him.

"No." He continued to look at the sky. "I should be, but I'm not."

"It's going to take you a week to clean this place up."

"Nope. The General and her troops are coming over tomorrow to deal with it. I'm ordered to keep out of the way, and that's one command I won't have any trouble obeying. I didn't think you'd stay."

"Neither did I."

He turned now, looked up at her. A kind of Romeo and Juliet pose, he thought, and hoped for a better ending. "Why did you?"

"I'm not sure. I don't know what to do about you, Declan. I swear to God, I just don't know. Men've never been any trouble for me. Maybe I've been trouble for them," she said with a faint smile. "But you're the first who's given me any."

He started up to her. "None of them loved you."

"No, none of them loved me. Wanted me. Desired me, but that's the easy part. You can be careless with wants. And I'll tell you the truth. Sometimes, most times, I enjoyed that carelessness. Not just the sex, but the dance. The game. Whatever you want to call that courtship that's no courtship at all. When the music stops, or the game's over, there might be some bumps and bruises, but nobody's really hurt."

"But this isn't a game between the two of us."

"I've already hurt you."

"Bumps and bruises so far, Lena." He stopped, face-to-face with her. "Bumps and bruises."

"When you look at me, what are you seeing? Someone, something else from before. You can't run the living on the dead."

"I see you clear enough. But I see something else in both of us that shouldn't be ignored or forgotten. Maybe something that needs to be put right before we can move on."

He reached in his pocket, pulled out Lucian's watch. "I gave this to you once before, about a hundred years ago. It's time you had it back."

Her fingers chilled at the idea of holding it. "If this is true, don't you see it all ended in grief and death and tragedy? We can't change what was. Why risk bringing it on again?"

"Because we have to. Because we're stronger this time." He opened her hand, put the watch into her palm, closed her fingers over it. "Because if we don't set it right, it never really ends."

"All right." She slipped the watch into the pocket of the short jacket she'd put on. Then she unpinned the watch on her dress. "I gave this to you once before. Take it back."

When he took it, held it, the clock that had once stood inside the Hall began to bong.

"Midnight," he said with perfect calm. "It'll strike twelve times." And he looked down at the face of the enameled watch he held. "Midnight," he repeated, showing it to her. "Look at yours."

Her fingers weren't so steady when she pulled it out. "Jesus," she breathed when she saw both hands straight up. "Why?"

"We're going to find out. I have to go inside." He looked up, toward the third floor. "I have to go up to the nursery. The baby . . ."

Even as he spoke, they heard the fretful cries.

"Let's just go. Declan, let's just get in the car and drive away from here."

But he was already moving inside. "The baby's crying. She's hungry. She needs me. Lucian's parents are sleeping. I always go upstairs early when he's not home. I hate sitting with them in the parlor after dinner. I can feel the way she dislikes me."

His voice had changed, Lena realized as she followed him. There was a Cajun cadence to it. "Declan."

"Claudine will walk her, or change her, but my pretty Rosie needs her mama. I don't like having her up on the third floor," he said as he hurried down the corridor. "But Madame Josephine always gets her way. Not always," he corrected, and there was a smile in his voice now. "If she always did, I'd be alligator bait 'stead of married to Lucian. He'll be home tomorrow. I miss him so."

As he started up the stairs, his gait slowed, and Lena heard the rapid pace of his breath. "I have to go up." It was his own voice now, with fear at the edges. "I have to go in. I have to see."

Gathering all her courage, Lena took his hand. "We'll go in together."

His hand shook. The cold that permeated the air speared into the bone. Nausea rolled through his belly, rose up his throat. Clamping down against it, he shoved the door open.

He stumbled, and even as Lena tried to catch him, fell to his knees.

"He comes in. He's drunk. I don't want him coming up here, but he won't go away. Everyone says, they say how he looks just like Lucian, but they don't see his eyes. I have to make him go away, away from my baby. I wish Claudine hadn't gone off to meet Jasper. I don't like being alone up here with Julian. He scares me, but I don't want him to see it."

His eyes were glazed, glassy smoke in a face that had gone pale as death. "Declan, oh God, Declan, come back." She squeezed his hand until she felt bone rub against bone.

"When he grabs at me, I get away." His voice was breathless now. He still knelt, a rangy man with sun-streaked hair, wearing a tuxedo with the tie dangling loose. A man with a woman's memories, a woman's terror storming inside him.

"But I can't leave my baby. I get the poker from the fireplace. I'll kill him if I have to. I'll kill him if he touches me or my baby. Oh God, oh God, oh God."

As her knees seemed to melt away, Lena sank to the floor beside him, tried to wrap her arms around him.

"He's stronger than me. I scream and I scream, but nobody comes to help me. He's drunk and he's crazy. He's crazy and he's drunk. He knocks me down, and he rips at my clothes. I can't get away. My baby's crying, but I can't get to her. I can't stop him."

"Oh." Shaking, Lena tried to hold him, rock him. "No. No, no, no."

"He rapes me." Fire burned in the center of him. Pain, the pain, and the fear. Oh God, the fear. "I call for help. I call for you, but you're not here."

His voice tore with tears. "You don't come. I need you."

"Don't, don't, don't." It was all she could say as she clung to him.

"He hurts me, but I fight him. I try to stop him, but he won't stop. I'm so scared, I'm so scared, but even then I know he's not doing this because he wants me. It's because he hates you."

He turned his head, those storm-gray eyes drenched. "He hates you. And because I'm yours, he has to break me. The way he broke your toys when you were children. I beg him to stop, but he won't. He tries to make me stop screaming, but I can't stop. I can't. His hands are around my throat."

It doubled him over, that hideous pressure, that shocking loss of air. "I can't breathe. I can't breathe. My baby's crying for me, and I can't breathe. He kills me. While my baby's crying in her crib. Our baby. While he's still inside me. He breaks me like a toy that belongs to his brother."

He lifted his head, looked at her now. And when he spoke, his voice was so full of grief she wondered they both didn't die of it. "You didn't come. I called, but you didn't come."

"I'm sorry. I'm so sorry."

"She came." Declan got rockily to his feet. "She came, and she saw what he had done to me. She looked down at me like I was a mess that had to be cleaned up before the neighbors came to call."

His eyes were dry now, and narrowed at the slamming of doors on the second floor. "Her house, her sons, and I was the bayou slut who'd trespassed. I watched her look down on me. It was like a dream, that watching. I saw her tell him to carry me out, down to the bedroom, while she cleaned up the blood, and the candle wax, and the broken crockery. He took my body out the gallery, but I watched her, watched her go over to my sweet baby, and I heard her mind wonder if it would be best just to smother the child. She considered it, and I believe if she'd tried, there was enough of me left that I could have struck her down like a lightning bolt."

He walked back to the door. "She thought I was weak, but she was *wrong*. They could kill me, but they couldn't end me."

"Declan, that's enough."

"No, not yet." He walked down the steps, down the hall, opened the door to Abigail's bedroom. "He laid me on the bed in here. And he wept. Not for me, but for himself. What would happen to him? His hand had defiled me, and killed me, but he thought only of himself. And does still. For he's in this house, he and Josephine. Walking and waiting in their little hell."

He crossed over to the wall where the armoire had been, opened the door of it in his mind. "They took some of my clothes. I had the gown in here for the ball. I was so proud of it. I wanted to be beautiful for you. Make you proud of me. She dropped my watch, but didn't notice. She had Julian wrap me up, and they carried me out, with the suitcase full of my things. They got old bricks to weigh me down, and they carried me away.

"It was hard. Even though there was moonlight, even though it was cool, it was a hard walk carting all of that. Julian got sick, but she brooked no nonsense. They would say I ran off with another man. They would let the gossip spread that my baby was a bastard, fawned off on you as your own. She told Julian how it would be as they put the bricks over me, as they tied the cloak around me with rope, as they pushed me into the bayou."

He looked back at her. "You believed them."

"No." Lena was weeping now. For him, for Abigail, for herself, for Lucian. "No."

"Not at first. You feared for me. You searched for me. You wept for me. I tried to reach you, but you wouldn't let me in. You wouldn't let me in because some part of you already believed their lies. I *loved* you. With all my heart, my soul, my body. I died for you."

"I couldn't stop what happened to you. I wasn't here to stop it."

"No, you weren't here that night. And you were never really here again. Not for me, and not for our child. You broke your promise to me, the solemn vow you made to me in that bed the night she was born. More than death, that is what doomed us."

"How did I break my promise?"

"You promised to love our child, to *care* for her always. I was always true to you, Lucian. You have to know."

"I do know." She closed her hand over the watch in her pocket and felt the weight, the grief, the sorrow.

"How could you leave her alone? How could you turn from her? You were all she had. You swore to me."

"I don't know. I was weak. I wasn't as brave or as true as you. Maybe... I think maybe you were the making of me, and when you were gone, I had nothing to hold me straight."

"You had Marie Rose."

"Perhaps I loved you too much, and her not enough. Forgive me. Forgive me for what I did, for what I didn't do. I can't go back and change it." She drew out the watch, held it face up in her palm. "No matter how often time stops, it's too late. If I could, I would never leave you. I'd take you and the baby away. I'd do anything to stop what happened to you."

"I loved you. And my heart *ached* every minute since they took me from you. Ached with grief, then with hope, and then with sorrow. You chose death, Lucian, rather than life. Still you choose loneliness rather than love. How can I forgive, when you can't? Until you do, they've won, and the house that should've been ours still holds them. None of us will ever be free, until you choose."

He turned, opened the gallery doors and walked outside.

The door slamming at her back made her jolt. It was, Lena thought, like a rude laugh aimed at someone else's misery. Ignoring it, she stepped outside, took a deep breath.

"Declan."

He was leaning on the baluster, staring out at the first hints of dawn. "Yeah. I'm trying to figure out if I need an exorcist, a psychiatrist, or if I should cash in and see about starring in a remake of *The Three Faces of Eve.*"

He rolled his shoulders, as if trying to shrug off an irritating weight. "I think I'll settle for a Bloody Mary."

Cautious, she stepped up behind him. "I'll make us both one," she began, and started to lay her hand on his back. He sidestepped, evading her touch, and left her standing there with her hand suspended.

"I don't need to be petted and stroked. Still a little raw here. Comes from getting raped and murdered, I guess." Jamming his hands in his pockets, he strode down the steps.

She waited a moment, struggling for balance, then walked down to join him in the kitchen. "Let me make them. I'm the professional."

"I can make my own goddamn drink."

It stung when he snatched the bottle of vodka out of her hand. Stung like a slap. "All right then, make your own goddamn drink. While you're at it, you oughta think about living your own goddamn life."

She spun away, and when he grabbed her arm, she lashed out with her own slap. When her hand cracked across his cheek, the clock began to strike again, and the doors to slam.

Cold settled gleefully into the bone.

"You ever been raped?"

She yanked her arm free. "No."

"Probably haven't been strangled to death, either?" Forgoing the niceties, he took a long drink straight from the bottle. "Let me give you a clue. It tends to put you in a really foul mood."

Temper drained out of her. "Don't drink like that, *cher*. You'll only get sick."

"I'm already sick. I need a shower."

"Go on and take one. You'll feel better for it. I'm going to make some tea. Just let me do this," she snapped out before he could argue. "Maybe it'll settle us both down some."

"Fine. Whatever." He stomped up the stairs.

She sat for a moment, just sat because her legs were still shaking. Then she took the watch out of her pocket, studied the face. The second hand ticked around and around. But the time never went beyond midnight.

Putting it away again, she rose to brew the tea.

She carried it up, along with the tidy triangles of toast. The sickbed meal her grandmother had made for her in childhood. He was sitting on the side of the bed, wearing a tattered pair of sweatpants. His hair was still wet. His skin was reddened from vicious scrubbing. She set the tray beside him.

"Do you want me to go?"

"No." When she poured a mug of tea, he took it, tried to warm his hands. Despite the blasting heat of the shower, he still felt chilled.

"I didn't just see it, or remember it. I *felt* it. The fear, the pain, the violation. The humiliation. And more—like that isn't bad enough—part of me was still me. That part, the big, tough guy part, was helpless, just helpless watching a terrified woman be raped and strangled. I can't explain it."

"You don't have to. I felt some of it. Not as strong, not as clear as you, but ... When you looked at me, when she was looking at me out of your eyes, I felt such grief, such regret. Such guilt. Drink your tea now, sweetheart."

He lifted the mug obediently. "It's good. Pretty sweet."

"Sweet tea and toast. It's good for you." She crawled onto the bed behind him, knelt and began to knead at his shoulders. "She was stronger than he was. It's not his fault so much. He was raised weak. But he loved her, Declan. I know that without a doubt. Even without knowing the terrible thing that happened to her, he blamed himself. For not being with her, not giving her enough of himself."

"He deserted the child."

There was such finality in his voice. "He did. Yes, he did," Lena replied. "And though it was wrong of him, wrong to take his own life and leave their baby an orphan, she had a better life because of it. She was surrounded by people who loved her, who valued the memory of her mother. She would never have had that life here, in the Hall."

"She was entitled to it. He should have seen to it."

She laid her cheek on the top of his head. "You can't forgive him."

"I can't understand him."

"No, a man like you wouldn't understand a man like him. Maybe I do, maybe I understand a man who'd run off with a woman rather than stand up to his parents. One who'd bring her back into a house full of resentment and shadows instead of making them a home. One who'd fall apart enough to drown himself rather than live with the hurt and raise his own child with the love and compassion that had been denied him. He wanted to be more than he was. With her, he would have been.

"You shouldn't despise him, Declan. You should pity him."

"Maybe. It's hard. I've still got a lot of her despair inside me." Abigail's, he thought, and a good portion of his own.

"Can you rest?"

"I don't think so."

"Why don't you try? I need to go change." She slid off the bed, then lifted the tray and set it aside. "Try to sleep awhile. I won't be long."

He didn't try to stop her. It was probably best to be alone. He lay back, stared at the ceiling as the first birds began to sing.

Abigail had been broken, he thought. Body and heart.

He was feeling pretty much the same himself.

He must have dozed, for when he opened his eyes the sun was up. Still early, he decided, but the General and her troop of whirlwinds would be coming along shortly to storm through his house with mops and brooms and God knew.

Maybe the place needed to be cleaned up, shaken out. It was still his. He wasn't giving it up. Whatever had happened, whatever shared it with him, he wasn't giving it up.

And by Christ, he wasn't giving Lena up, either.

He sat up, scowling, and saw her sitting in the chair across the room. She wore jeans, a plain white T-shirt. There were three small bouquets lying in her lap.

"You up for a little drive?" she asked him.

"I guess."

"Put a shirt on, and some shoes."

"Where are we going?"

"I'll tell you on the way."

She drove, and he kept the flowers in his lap now.

"I want to take flowers to her. To Marie Rose." As her ancestor, Lena thought, as her father. "I thought you might like to visit there, too."

He said nothing.

"Grandmama told me," Lena continued, "how Marie Rose used to go to the cemetery once a year on her birthday. She'd bring him flowers. This morning, when I went over to change my clothes, she told me where we'd find his crypt, and we picked these from the marsh. I want to take flowers to Lucian, too."

He picked one clutch up. "Your symbol of pity?"

"If that's the best we can do."

"And the others?"

"Marie Rose took them to her mother, once a year as well. A part of her must've known. She went to the river, every year on her birthday, and dropped flowers in the water. Grandmama told me where."

She drove smoothly, a little fast, then slowed to turn into the cemetery. "I know you're still angry with him, and with me. If you don't want to do this, you can wait in the car. I won't blame you."

"Why are you doing it?"

"He's part of me. Through blood, and more. If I can find a way to accept who birthed me, if I can live with that, then I can find a way to accept this. To live with it."

She stopped the car, took two of the bouquets. "It's a little walk from here. It shouldn't take me long."

"I'm coming with you."

He got out, but didn't—as she'd grown used to—reach for her hand. They wound their way over the paths between the tombs, the ornate grilles, the marble angels and through shadows thrown by crosses.

She stopped at one of the raised tombs. There were many, simple and unadorned. Her grandfather rested here, and others who were parts and pieces of her. But today she had come only for one.

Her hands gripped tight on the flowers. Marie Rose, she read. Blood of my blood, heart of my heart.

"Grandmama, she told me Marie Rose was a happy woman, she had a good life. She was content with it. That might not be enough to make up for what was done, but if it had been done different . . . Well, I don't see how I'd be standing here with you this morning."

She started to lay the flowers, and Declan closed his hand over hers on the stems. They placed them on the grave—the baby, the girl, the old woman, together.

"He's a ways from here," Lena managed. Her voice was thick, her vision blurry as she turned away.

They walked through the sunlight, through the shadows of the tombs, in silence.

The Manet crypt was a towering square, its porticoes carved, its doors thick and studded. Topping it was a fierce angel, holding a harp as a soldier might a shield.

"Cheerful," Declan commented. "I'd say none of them went gently into that good night." He glanced around, saw the plain concrete box on a raised slab. The plaque read: LUCIAN EDUARD MANET. 1877–1900.

"He's out here?"

"He wasn't to be forgiven," Lena explained. "Not for his marriage, his child, his embarrassing death. They called it accidental drowning, though everyone knew it was suicide. But though Josephine wouldn't have him in the family crypt, she wanted him buried on consecrated ground. Otherwise, there would have been yet another scandal."

Declan looked back at the crypt. "Bitch."

"He had no grandparents, as I did, to love him. To soften the blows. He had a twin brother who loathed him simply because he existed. He had money and position, education and privilege. But no love. Until Abigail. Then they took her from him."

She laid the flowers for him. "He did the best he could. It just wasn't enough."

"You're stronger than he ever was. Smarter, more resilient."

"I hope so. And I hope he rests soon. The flowers won't last long in this sun, but . . . Well, you do what you can."

She walked away without another word. Declan lingered a moment more, staring at the plaque, then the flowers. Then he went with his impulse, took a single flower out of the bouquet, and laid it on top of the tomb.

Lena put her sunglasses on because her eyes were tearing. "That was kind."

"Well, you do what you can." This time, he took her hand.

They didn't speak on the drive back. Nor did Rufus or Odette come out of the house when Lena parked in front of it. He remained silent as she led the way through the marsh. Silent, as he remembered the way in the night, with the chill in the air, the flitting moonlight, the call of an owl. And the panting breaths of a killer and his accomplice.

"Do you want to go back? You're awfully pale."

"No." Sweat ran down his back despite the cold under his skin. "I need to do this."

"It's not much farther."

There were marsh flowers springing up along the edges of the narrow, beaten path. He concentrated on them, on the color, the small beauty. But when she stopped on the bank, he was out of breath and dizzy.

"It was here. Right here."

"I know. Marie Rose came here, to this spot. Her heart knew." This time she handed him the bouquet and drew a single flower out.

Declan let the flowers fall into the river, watched the color, the small beauty, float on the brown water. "Not everybody can put flowers on his own grave."

"I'm sorry." Tears slid down her cheeks. "I'm so sorry." She knelt, tossed the flower where it would drift alone. She groped for Declan's hand. "I'm so sorry I hurt you."

"Don't." He drew her to her feet, into his arms. "It's all right."

"He didn't trust enough. I didn't. Too much grief and not enough faith. Then, now."

"There's been enough grieving. Then, now." He tipped up her face. And said what he'd realized was inside him—inside Abigail—at the moment they'd taken flowers to Marie Rose. "I forgive you."

"You're more forgiving than she was."

"Maybe. Maybe that's why we keep going around. Gives us a chance to fix things we screwed up."

"Or make the same mistakes again. I've got something else to give you. But not here. Back at the Hall. It's the right place to give it to you."

"Okay." He kissed her hand. "We're okay."

"I think we're getting there. I'd like to walk back, get my bearings."

"Good idea."

"There's something I'd like to ask you to do," she said as they took the path again. "I'd like to put up three markers, maybe near the pond.

One for Lucian, one for Abby and one for Marie Rose. I think it's time they were together."

"I think they are together now." Or nearly, he thought. Very nearly, because there was a lightness in his heart he hadn't expected to feel again. "But the markers would be a nice memory. We'll pick out a spot, put them in. Then we'll plant something there, together."

She nodded. "A willow maybe."

"Like the one she liked so much." He nodded. "Sometimes you put things back the way they were, sometimes you change them. We'll do both. Then when our kids come along, we can have picnics near there, and tell them the story." He waited a beat. "You didn't tell me to shut up."

"*Cher*, you just wear me out. Looks like your soldiers are here."

He glanced over, wincing when he saw the cars. "Won't this be fun? Look, let's sneak up the front stairs and lock ourselves in my bedroom. I feel like I could sleep for a week now."

"The bedroom's fine, but I've only got an hour. Then I've got to go in to work."

"I've got an hour in me," he replied, then tapped a finger to his lips and crept up the stairs. "Ever roll around naked in bed with a houseful of women scrubbing floors outside the room?"

"No, and that's not on the schedule for this morning."

"Spoilsport."

"Declan. No, leave the doors open. No, just hold on—"

"That's what I'm doing," he said when he'd locked her in his arms. "Holding on. And God, *God*, it feels good. I've missed you," he murmured, and understood it was Abby as much as himself who held close.

A circle, nearly forged again, he thought. And this time, it wouldn't break.

She's losing, he realized. Josephine. It was all slipping out of her hands.

"I've got things to say to you."

"I'm done with talking." He laid his lips on hers in a soft, sumptuous kiss. "Lie down with me, Lena. Just lie down with me. I've really missed holding you."

"I need to do this standing up." She eased away and stood in the spill of sunlight. "I've done things my way up till now, and that's worked out just fine for me. You've complicated things, confused things, irritated me and turned my life upside down with what was, what is, what might be. I've never cared much for might be's, Declan."

"How about will be's?"

"That's your hard head talking. I love that about you. I love so many things about you, I've lost count. So here I am stuck with some damn rich Yankee."

Everything inside him swelled, then went bright as the sun. "Angelina."

"You just wait till I'm finished." She sighed, paused until she was certain she could speak calmly. "I've got a lot of friends who care about me, maybe even love me the way friends do. I had my grandpapa, who made me the light of his life. I've got Grandmama. But nobody ever loved me just like you do. And the hell of it is, I never loved anybody the way I love you. So."

She lifted her arms, unclasped the chain around her neck. She held it out to him, the little key dangling. "This is yours now, and has been for some time, I guess. You're the key, *cher*. You always were."

He took it, then delighted her by clasping it around his own neck. "I'm going to make you so happy."

"You damn well better. We getting married or what?"

"You better believe it." With a laugh, he scooped her off her feet, spun her around in circles. "Do you feel it?"

"Feel what? My head's spinning."

"The house is ours now. Only ours." He set her on her feet. "No more ghosts. No more lives but ours. And we're just beginning."

She slid her arms around him, lifted her mouth to his. "Welcome home."

Still holding close, she drew out the pocket watch, turned it faceup. They watched time move on.

TURN THE PAGE FOR A LOOK AT

# SANCTUARY

BY NORA ROBERTS. ON SALE NOW!

S he dreamed of Sanctuary. The great house gleamed bride-white in the moonlight, as majestic a force breasting the slope that reigned over eastern dunes and western marsh as a queen upon her throne. The house stood as it had for more than a century, a grand tribute to man's vanity and brilliance, near the dark shadows of the forest of live oaks, where the river flowed in murky silence.

Within the shelter of trees, fireflies blinked gold, and night creatures stirred, braced to hunt or be hunted. Wild things bred there in shadows, in secret.

There were no lights to brighten the tall, narrow windows of Sanctuary. No lights to spread welcome over its graceful porches, its grand doors. Night was deep, and the breath of it moist from the sea. The only sound to disturb it was of wind rustling through the leaves of the great oaks and the dry clicking—like bony fingers—of the palm fronds. The white columns stood like soldiers guarding the wide veranda, but no one opened the enormous front door to greet her.

As she walked closer, she could hear the crunch of sand and shells on the road under her feet. Wind chimes tinkled, little notes of song. The porch swing creaked on its chain, but no one lazed upon it to enjoy the moon and the night.

The smell of jasmine and musk roses played on the air, underscored by the salty scent of the sea. She began to hear that too, the low and steady thunder of water spilling over sand and sucking back into its own heart.

The beat of it, that steady and patient pulse, reminded all who inhabited the island of Lost Desire that the sea could reclaim the land and all on it at its whim.

Still, her mood lifted at the sound of it, the music of home and childhood. Once she had run as free and wild through that forest as a deer, had scouted its marshes, raced along its sandy beaches with the careless privilege of youth.

Now, no longer a child, she was home again.

She walked quickly, hurrying up the steps, across the veranda, closing her hand over the big brass handle that glinted like a lost treasure.

The door was locked.

She twisted it right, then left, shoved against the thick mahogany panel. *Let me in*, she thought as her heart began to thud in her chest. *I've come home. I've come back.*

But the door remained shut and locked. When she pressed her face against the glass of the tall windows flanking it, she could see nothing but darkness within.

And was afraid.

She ran now, around the side of the house, over the terrace, where flowers streamed out of pots and lilies danced in chorus lines of bright color. The music of the wind chimes became harsh and discordant, the fluttering of fronds was a hiss of warning. She struggled with the next door, weeping as she beat her fists against it.

*Please, please, don't shut me out. I want to come home.*

She sobbed as she stumbled down the garden path. She would go to the back, in through the screened porch. It was never locked—Mama said a kitchen should always be open to company.

But she couldn't find it. The trees sprang up, thick and close, the branches and draping moss barred her way.

She was lost, tripping over roots in her confusion, fighting to see through the dark as the canopy of trees closed out the moon. The wind rose up and howled and slapped at her in flat-handed, punishing blows. Spears of saw palms struck out like swords. She turned, but where the path had been was now the river, cutting her off from Sanctuary. The high grass along its slippery banks waved madly.

It was then she saw herself, standing alone and weeping on the other bank.

It was then she knew she was dead.

Jo fought her way out of the dream, all but felt the sharp edges of it scraping her skin as she dragged herself to the surface of the tunnel of sleep. Her lungs burned, and her face was wet with sweat and tears. With a trembling hand, she fumbled for the bedside lamp, knocking both a book and an overfilled ashtray to the floor in her hurry to break out of the dark.

When the light shot on, she drew her knees up close to her chest, wrapped her arms around them, and rocked herself calm.

It was just a dream, she told herself. Just a bad dream.

She was home, in her own bed, in her apartment and miles from the island where Sanctuary stood. A grown woman of twenty-seven had no business being spooked by a silly dream.

But she was still shaking when she reached for a cigarette. It took her three tries to manage to light a match.

Three-fifteen, she noted by the clock on the nightstand. That was becoming typical. There was nothing worse than the three A.M. jitters. She swung her legs over the side of the bed and bent down to pick up the

overturned ashtray. She told herself she'd clean up the mess in the morning. She sat there, her oversized T-shirt bunched over her thighs, and
ordered herself to get a grip.

She didn't know why her dreams were taking her back to the island
of Lost Desire and the home she'd escaped from at eighteen. But Jo figured any first-year psych student could translate the rest of the symbol-
ism. The house was locked because she doubted anyone would welcome
her if she did return home. Just lately, she'd given some thought to it but
had wondered if she'd lost the way back.

And she was nearing the age her mother had been when she had left
the island. Disappeared, abandoning her husband and three children
without a second glance.

Had Annabelle ever dreamed of coming home, Jo wondered, and
dreamed the door was locked to her?

She didn't want to think about that, didn't want to remember the
woman who had broken her heart twenty years before. Jo reminded herself that she should be long over such things by now. She'd lived without
her mother, and without Sanctuary and her family. She had even
thrived—at least professionally.

Tapping her cigarette absently, Jo glanced around the bedroom. She
kept it simple, practical. Though she'd traveled widely, there were few
mementos. Except the photographs. She'd matted and framed the
black-and-white prints, choosing the ones among her work that she
found the most restful to decorate the walls of the room where she slept.

There, an empty park bench, the black wrought iron all fluid curves.
And there, a single willow, its lacy leaves dipping low over a small, glassy
pool. A moonlit garden was a study in shadow and texture and contrasting
shapes. The lonely beach with the sun just breaking the horizon tempted
the viewer to step inside the photo and feel the sand rough underfoot.

She'd hung that seascape only the week before, after returning from
an assignment on the Outer Banks of North Carolina. Perhaps that was
one reason she'd begun to think about home, Jo decided. She'd been

very close. She could have traveled a bit south down to Georgia and fer-
ried from the mainland to the island.

There were no roads to Desire, no bridges spanning its sound.

But she hadn't gone south. She'd completed her assignment and
come back to Charlotte to bury herself in her work.

And her nightmares.

She crushed out the cigarette and stood. There would be no more
sleep, she knew, so she pulled on a pair of sweatpants. She would do some
darkroom work, take her mind off things.

It was probably the book deal that was making her nervous, she decided, as she padded out of the bedroom. It was a huge step in her career.
Though she knew her work was good, the offer from a major publishing
house to create an art book from a collection of her photographs had
been unexpected and thrilling.

*Natural Studies*, by Jo Ellen Hathaway, she thought as she turned
into the small galley kitchen to make coffee. No, that sounded like a
science project. *Glimpses of Life*? Pompous.

She smiled a little, pushing back her smoky red hair and yawning.
She should just take the pictures and leave the title selection to the ex-
perts.

She knew when to step back and when to take a stand, after all.
She'd been doing one or the other most of her life. Maybe she would
send a copy of the book home. What would her family think of it?
Would it end up gracing one of the coffee tables where an overnight
guest could page through it and wonder if Jo Ellen Hathaway was re-
lated to the Hathaways who ran the Inn at Sanctuary?

Would her father even open it at all and see what she had learned to
do? Or would he simply shrug, leave it untouched, and go out to walk
his island? Annabelle's island.

It was doubtful he would take an interest in his oldest daughter now.
And it was foolish for that daughter to care.

Jo shrugged the thought away, took a plain blue mug from a hook.

While she waited for the coffee to brew, she leaned on the counter and looked out her tiny window.

There were some advantages to being up and awake at three in the morning, she decided. The phone wouldn't ring. No one would call or fax or expect anything of her. For a few hours she didn't have to be anyone, or do anything. If her stomach was jittery and her head ached, no one knew the weakness but herself.

Below her kitchen window, the streets were dark and empty, slicked by late-winter rain. A streetlamp spread a small pool of light—lonely light, Jo thought. There was no one to bask in it. Aloneness had such mystery, she mused. Such endless possibilities.

It pulled at her, as such scenes often did, and she found herself leaving the scent of coffee, grabbing her Nikon, and rushing out barefoot into the chilly night to photograph the deserted street.

It soothed her as nothing else could. With a camera in her hand and an image in her mind, she could forget everything else. Her long feet splashed through chilly puddles as she experimented with angles. With absent annoyance she flicked at her hair. It wouldn't be falling in her face if she'd had it trimmed. But she'd had no time, so it swung heavily forward in a tousled wave and made her wish for an elastic band.

She took nearly a dozen shots before she was satisfied. When she turned, her gaze was drawn upward. She'd left the lights on, she mused. She hadn't even been aware she'd turned on so many on the trip from bedroom to kitchen.

Lips pursed, she crossed the street and focused her camera again. Calculating, she crouched, shot at an upward angle, and captured those lighted windows in the dark building. *Den of the Insomniac*, she decided. Then with a half laugh that echoed eerily enough to make her shudder, she lowered the camera again.

God, maybe she was losing her mind. Would a sane woman be out at three in the morning, half dressed and shivering, while she took pictures of her own windows?

She pressed her fingers against her eyes and wished more than anything else for the single thing that had always seemed to elude her. Normality.

You needed sleep to be normal, she thought. She hadn't had a full night's sleep in more than a month. You needed regular meals. She'd lost ten pounds in the last few weeks and had watched her long, rangy frame go bony. You needed peace of mind. She couldn't remember if she had ever laid claim to that. Friends? Certainly she had friends, but no one close enough to call in the middle of the night to console her.

Family. Well, she had family, of sorts. A brother and sister whose lives no longer marched with hers. A father who was almost a stranger. A mother she hadn't seen or heard from in twenty years.

Not my fault, Jo reminded herself as she started back across the street. It was Annabelle's fault. Everything had changed when Annabelle had run from Sanctuary and left her baffled family crushed and heartbroken. The trouble, as Jo saw it, was that the rest of them hadn't gotten over it. She had.

She hadn't stayed on the island guarding every grain of sand like her father did. She hadn't dedicated her life to running and caring for Sanctuary like her brother, Brian. And she hadn't escaped into foolish fantasies or the next thrill the way her sister, Lexy, had.

Instead she had studied, and she had worked, and she had made a life for herself. If she was a little shaky just now, it was only because she'd overextended, was letting the pressure get to her. She was a little run-down, that was all. She'd just add some vitamins to her regimen and get back in shape.

She might even take a vacation, Jo mused as she dug her keys out of her pocket. It had been three years—no, four—since she had last taken a trip without a specific assignment. Maybe Mexico, the West Indies. Someplace where the pace was slow and the sun hot. Slowing down and clearing her mind. That was the way to get past this little blip in her life.

As she stepped back into the apartment, she kicked a small, square manila envelope that lay on the floor. For a moment she simply stood, one hand on the door, the other holding her camera, and stared at it.

Had it been there when she left? Why was it there in the first place? The first one had come a month before, had been waiting in her stack of mail, with only her name carefully printed across it.

Her hands began to shake again as she ordered herself to close the door, to lock it. Her breath hitched, but she leaned over, picked it up. Carefully, she set the camera aside, then unsealed the flap.

When she tapped out the contents, the sound she made was a long, low moan. The photograph was very professionally done, perfectly cropped. Just as the other three had been. A woman's eyes, heavy-lidded, almond-shaped, with thick lashes and delicately arched brows. Jo knew their color would be blue, deep blue, because the eyes were her own. In them was stark terror.

When was it taken? How and why? She pressed a hand to her mouth, staring down at the photo, knowing her eyes mirrored the shot perfectly. Terror swept through her, had her rushing through the apartment into the small second bedroom she'd converted to a darkroom. Frantically she yanked open a drawer, pawed through the contents, and found the envelopes she'd buried there. In each was another black-and-white photo, cropped to two by six inches.

Her heartbeat was thundering in her ears as she lined them up. In the first the eyes were closed, as if she'd been photographed while sleeping. The others followed the waking process. Lashes barely lifted, showing only a hint of iris. In the third the eyes were open but unfocused and clouded with confusion.

They had disturbed her, yes, unsettled her, certainly, when she found them tucked in her mail. But they hadn't frightened her.

Now the last shot, centered on her eyes, fully awake and bright with fear.

Stepping back, shivering, Jo struggled to be calm. Why only the eyes? she asked herself. How had someone gotten close enough to take these pictures without her being aware of it? Now, whoever it was had been as close as the other side of her front door.

Propelled by fresh panic, she ran into the living room, and frantically checked the locks. Her heart was battering against her ribs when she fell back against the door. Then the anger kicked in.

Bastard, she thought. He wanted her to be terrorized. He wanted her to hide inside those rooms, jumping at shadows, afraid to step outside for fear he'd be there watching. She who had always been fearless was playing right into his hands.

She had wandered alone through foreign cities, walked mean streets and empty ones, she'd climbed mountains and hacked through jungles. With the camera as her shield, she'd never given a thought to fear. And now, because of a handful of photos, her legs were jellied with it.

The fear had been building, she admitted now. Growing and spiking over the weeks, level by level. It made her feel helpless, so exposed, so brutally alone.

Jo pushed herself away from the door. She couldn't and wouldn't live this way. She would ignore it, put it aside. Bury it deep. God knew she was an expert at burying traumas, small and large. This was just one more.

She was going to drink her coffee and go to work.


By eight she had come full circle—sliding through fatigue, arcing through nervous energy, creative calm, then back to fatigue.

She couldn't work mechanically, not even on the most basic aspect of darkroom chores. She insisted on giving every step her full attention. To do so, she'd had to calm down, ditch both the anger and the fear. Over her first cup of coffee, she'd convinced herself she had figured out the reasoning behind the photos she'd been receiving. Someone admired her work and was trying to get her attention, engage her influence for their own.

That made sense.

Occasionally she lectured or gave workshops. In addition, she'd had three major shows in the last three years. It wasn't that difficult or that extraordinary for someone to have taken her picture—several pictures, for that matter.

That was certainly reasonable.

Whoever it was had gotten creative, that was all. They'd enlarged the eye area, cropped it, and were sending the photos to her in a kind of series. Though the photos appeared to have been printed recently, there was no telling when or where they'd been taken. The negatives might be a year old. Or two. Or five.

They had certainly gotten her attention, but she'd overreacted, taken it too personally.

Over the last couple of years, she had received samples of work from admirers of hers. Usually there was a letter attached, praising her own photographs before the sender went into a pitch about wanting her advice or her help, or in a few cases, suggesting that they collaborate on a project.

The success she was enjoying professionally was still relatively new. She wasn't yet used to the pressures that went along with commercial success, or the expectations, which could become burdensome.

And, Jo admitted as she ignored her unsteady stomach and sipped coffee that had gone stone cold, she wasn't handling that success as well as she might.

She would handle it better, she thought, rolling her aching head on her aching shoulders, if everyone would just leave her alone to do what she did best.

Completed prints hung drying on the wet side of her darkroom. Her last batch of negatives had been developed and, sitting on a stool at her work counter, she slid a contact sheet onto her light board, then studied it, frame by frame, through her loupe.

For a moment she felt a flash of panic and despair. Every print she looked at was out of focus, blurry. Goddamn it, goddamn it, how could that be? Was it the whole roll? She shifted, blinked, and watched the magnified image of rising dunes and oat grass pop clear.

With a sound somewhere between a grunt and a laugh she sat back, rolled her tensed shoulders. "It's not the prints that are blurry and out of focus, you idiot," she muttered aloud. "It's you."

She set the loupe aside and closed her eyes to rest them. She lacked the energy to get up and make more coffee. She knew she should go eat, get something solid into her system. And she knew she should sleep. Stretch out on the bed, close everything off and crash.

But she was afraid to. In sleep she would lose even this shaky control.

She was beginning to think she should see a doctor, get something for her nerves before they frayed beyond repair. But that idea made her think of psychiatrists. Undoubtedly they would want to poke and pry inside her brain and dig up matters she was determined to forget.

She would handle it. She was good at handling herself. Or, as Brian had always said, she was good at elbowing everyone out of her way so she could handle everything herself.

What choice had she had—had any of them had when they'd been left alone to flounder on that damned spit of land miles from no-where?

The rage that erupted inside her jolted her, it was so sudden, so powerful. She trembled with it, clenched her fists in her lap, and had to bite back the hot words she wanted to spit out at the brother who wasn't even there.

Tired, she told herself. She was just tired, that was all. She needed to put work aside, take one of those over-the-counter sleeping aids she'd bought and had yet to try, turn off the phone and get some sleep. She would be steadier then, stronger.

When a hand fell on her shoulder, she ripped off a scream and sent her coffee mug flying.

"Jesus! Jesus, Jo!" Bobby Banes scrambled back, scattering the mail he carried on the floor.

"What are you doing? What the hell are you doing?" She bolted off the stool and sent it crashing, as he gaped at her.

"I—you said you wanted to get started at eight. I'm only a few minutes late."

Jo fought for breath, gripped the edge of her worktable to keep herself upright. "Eight?"

Her student assistant nodded cautiously. He swallowed hard and kept his distance. To his eye she still looked wild and ready to attack. It was his second semester working with her, and he thought he'd learned how to anticipate her orders, gauge her moods, and avoid her temper. But he didn't have a clue how to handle that hot fear in her eyes.

"Why the hell didn't you knock?" she snapped at him.

"I did. When you didn't answer, I figured you must be in here, so I used the key you gave me when you went on the last assignment."

"Give it back. Now."

"Sure. Okay, Jo." Keeping his eyes on hers, he dug into the front pocket of his fashionably faded jeans. "I didn't mean to spook you."

Jo bit down on control and took the key he held out. There was as much embarrassment now, she realized, as fear. To give herself a moment, she bent down and righted her stool. "Sorry, Bobby. You did spook me. I didn't hear you knock."

"It's okay. Want me to get you another cup of coffee?"

She shook her head and gave in to her knocking knees. As she slid onto the stool, she worked up a smile for him. He was a good student, she thought—a little pompous about his work yet, but he was only twenty-one.

She thought he was going for the artist-as-college-student look, with his dark blond hair in a shoulder-length ponytail, the single gold hoop earring accenting his long, narrow face. His teeth were perfect. His parents had believed in braces, she thought, running her tongue over her own slight overbite.

He had a good eye, she mused. And a great deal of potential. That was why he was here, after all. Jo was always willing to pay back what had been given to her.

Because his big brown eyes were still watching her warily, she put more effort into the smile. "I had a rough night."

"You look like it." He tried a smile of his own when she lifted a brow. "The art is in seeing what's really there, right? And you look whipped. Couldn't sleep, huh?"

Vain was one thing Jo wasn't. She shrugged her shoulders and rubbed her tired eyes. "Not much."

"You ought to try that melatonin. My mother swears by it." He crouched to pick up the broken shards of the mug. "And maybe you could cut back on the coffee."

He glanced up but saw she wasn't listening. She'd gone on a side trip again, Bobby thought. A new habit of hers. He'd just about given up on getting his mentor into a healthier lifestyle. But he decided to give it one more shot.

"You've been living on coffee and cigarettes again."

"Yeah." She was drifting, half asleep where she sat.

"That stuff'll kill you. And you need an exercise program. You've dropped about ten pounds in the last few weeks. With your height you need to carry more weight. And you've got small bones—you're courting osteoporosis. Gotta build up those bones and muscles."

"Uh-huh."

"You ought to see a doctor. You ask me, you're anemic. You got no color, and you could pack half your equipment in the bags under your eyes."

"So nice of you to notice."

He scooped up the biggest shards, dumped them in her waste can. Of course he'd noticed. She had a face that drew attention. It didn't matter that she seemed to work overtime to fade into the background. He'd never seen her wear makeup, and she kept her hair pulled back, but anyone with an eye could see it should be framing that oval face with its delicate bones and exotic eyes and sexy mouth.

Bobby caught himself, felt heat rise to his cheeks. She would laugh at him if she knew he'd had a little crush on her when she first took him on. That, he figured, had been as much professional admiration as physical attraction. And he'd gotten over the attraction part. Mostly.

But there was no doubt that if she would do the minimum to enhance that magnolia skin, dab some color on that top-heavy mouth and smudge up those long-lidded eyes, she'd be a knockout.

"I could fix you breakfast," he began. "If you've got something besides candy bars and moldy bread."

Taking a long breath, Jo tuned in. "No, that's okay. Maybe we'll stop somewhere and grab something. I'm already running behind."

She slid off the stool and crouched to pick up the mail.

"You know, it wouldn't hurt you to take a few days off, focus on yourself. My mom goes to this spa down in Miami."

His words were only a buzzing in her ear now. She picked up the manila envelope with her name printed neatly on it in block letters. She had to wipe a film of sweat from her brow. In the pit of her stomach was a sick ball that went beyond dread into fear.

The envelope was thicker than the others had been, weightier. *Throw it away*, her mind screamed out. *Don't open it. Don't look inside.*

But her fingers were already scraping along the flap. Low whimpering sounds escaped her as she tore at the little metal clasp. This time an avalanche of photos spilled out onto the floor. She snatched one up. It was a well-produced five-by-seven black-and-white.

Not just her eyes this time, but all of her. She recognized the background—a park near her building where she often walked. Another was of her in downtown Charlotte, standing on a curb with her camera bag over her shoulder.

"Hey, that's a pretty good shot of you."

As Bobby leaned down to select one of the prints, she slapped at his hand and snarled at him, "Keep away. Keep back. Don't touch me."

"Jo, I . . ."

"Stay the hell away from me." Panting, she dropped on all fours to paw frantically through the prints. There was picture after picture of her doing ordinary, everyday things. Coming out of the market with a bag of groceries, getting in or out of her car.

He's everywhere, he's watching me. Wherever I go, whatever I do. He's hunting me, she thought, as her teeth began to chatter. He's hunting me and there's nothing I can do. Nothing, until . . .

Then everything inside her clicked off. The photograph in her hand shook as if a brisk breeze had kicked up inside the room. She couldn't scream. There seemed to be no air inside her.

She simply couldn't feel her body any longer.

The photograph was brilliantly produced, the lighting and use of shadows and textures masterful. She was naked, her skin glowing eerily. Her body was arranged in a restful pose, the fragile chin dipped down, the head gently angled. One arm draped across her midriff, the other was flung up over her head in a position of dreaming sleep.

But the eyes were open and staring. A doll's eyes. Dead eyes.

For a moment, she was thrown helplessly back into her nightmare, staring at herself and unable to fight her way out of the dark.

But even through terror she could see the differences. The woman in the photo had a waving mass of hair that fanned out from her face. And the face was softer, the body riper than her own.

"Mama?" she whispered and gripped the picture with both hands. "Mama?"

"What is it, Jo?" Shaken, Bobby listened to his own voice hitch and dip as he stared into Jo's glazed eyes. "What the hell is it?"

"Where are her clothes?" Jo tilted her head, began to rock herself. Her head was full of sounds, rushing, thundering sounds. "Where is she?"

"Take it easy." Bobby took a step forward, started to reach down to take the photo from her.

Her head snapped up. "Stay away." The color flashed back into her cheeks, riding high. Something not quite sane danced in her eyes. "Don't touch me. Don't touch her."

Frightened, baffled, he straightened again, held both hands palms out. "Okay. Okay, Jo."

"I don't want you to touch her." She was cold, so cold. She looked down at the photo again. It was Annabelle. Young, eerily beautiful, and cold as death. "She shouldn't have left us. She shouldn't have gone away. Why did she go?"

"Maybe she had to," Bobby said quietly.

"No, she belonged with us. We needed her, but she didn't want us. She's so pretty." Tears rolled down Jo's cheeks, and the picture trembled in her hand. "She's so beautiful. Like a fairy princess. I used to think she was a princess. She left us. She left us and went away. Now she's dead."

Her vision wavered, her skin went hot. Pressing the photo against her breasts, Jo curled into a ball and wept.

"Come on, Jo." Gently, Bobby reached down. "Come on with me now. We'll get some help."

"I'm so tired," she murmured, letting him pick her up as if she were a child. "I want to go home."

"Okay. Just close your eyes now."

The photo fluttered silently to the floor, facedown atop all the other faces. She saw writing on the back. Large bold letters.

## DEATH OF AN ANGEL

Her last thought, as the dark closed in, was Sanctuary.

Photo © Bruce Wilder

**Nora Roberts** is the #1 *New York Times* bestselling author of more than two hundred novels. She is also the author of the bestselling In Death series written under the pen name J. D. Robb. There are more than five hundred million copies of her books in print.

CONNECT ONLINE

NoraRoberts.com
⬛ NoraRoberts